I0550653

LOW FUEL
"It's not what you think..."

ROZIER PEARSON

Prologue

It's not what you think." he said.

He was an elderly Hopi Indian at a gas station in Middle of No Where, New Mexico and what he said was profound although that fact was lost upon me at the time. His clothes were well worn and he had the appearance of a man who indulged in more than his fair share of whiskey. His speech was slurred and I recall thinking that he must have been drunk. Being inebriated and working in a highly flammable environment is what I like to call a very bad idea. I thought about calling the police but decided that it may not be a good idea considering the events that occurred several hours earlier.

I don't think he knew the significance of his words. He couldn't have because he just continued to sweep trash into his dust pan as I sped off down I-40. I thought him a fool at the time but hindsight is 20/20.

"It's not what you think."....that's so true.

Hell, it's never what you think and most of it isn't even about you. Most of it is about those you find yourself surrounded by after disaster strikes. How else could they even get the chance to speak to you? You, who are too busy with your daily regiment of bullshit to ever get involved in the life of an absolute stranger. The type of absolute stranger who desperately needs to hear you say that which you deem as being so insignificant. You never really know how you influence the people around you.

Even the most "insignificant" person has a tremendous effect on those around them. The power to change minds, the power to give birth to opinions, dreams and prejudice. Disaster is natures why of spreading wisdom, and pain is the price you pay to receive it.

I didn't know this then; but I do now. You know... the older I get the more I realize that this isn't my life, I'm just living it. So what about the old guy? Fuck him! This is my story. Let him write his own book. Every story has a beginning and that wasn't it. This is...

ONE

Culture shock, as defined by The Merriam-Webster Dictionary is "A condition of anxiety and disorientation that can affect someone suddenly exposed to a new culture." Culture shock is what I felt every day I awoke to find myself smack dab in the middle of California's Mojave Desert.

I was stationed at the Marine Corps Air Ground Combat Center in the city of Twenty- nine Palms, California. **MCAGCC (**pronounced mc-cag-see.) for short, was built there back in the 1950's so that the U.S. Military could conduct live fire training without suffering the ignominy of the occasional incident of collateral damage.

The sound of exploding ordnance is a constant, and the resulting hell storm illuminates the night time sky. Nine times out of ten, the tremor you just felt wasn't an earthquake, but the result of several two thousand pound laser guided bombs hitting their target.

All four branches of the U.S. Military as well as the various armed forces of the North Atlantic Treaty Organization come to Twenty-Nine Palms for training, and all of them hate it equally.

The story goes that the Marine Corps established the Combat Center after the U.S. Army abandoned the base. The Army declared the entire region as being inhospitable, and then got the hell out of Dodge. They only return periodically to fire off a few rounds and then head back to civilization. They're the smart ones. The dry desert air gives every newbie intermittent nose bleeds for the first two weeks and the sand storms are a real bitch.

Now, I'm a lot smarter than I look. I know that people live in deserts in the U.S. and all over the world and that's great but I'm from Washington D.C. I'm used to the immensity of the metropolis and the ever increasing menace of urban sprawl. I'm really fond of towns with grass, trees and an entire landscape that doesn't melt whenever it rains. And so it was for four years and I never liked it... not once. Nothing made it better, not getting promoted and not even going on leave. Being promoted meant that I was responsible for even more of that God forsaken place. Going on leave only served to remind me of what the rest of the country was like.

My heart broke each time I returned to the never ending montage of Choya tree, boulder, coyote and tumble weed. Again and again in that order, Choya tree, boulder, coyote and tumble weed. It became monotonous year after year. It was hot as hell in the summer and cold as hell in the winter.

It was damn near impossible for a black man to get a haircut with all the Asian barbers in town who never cut kinky hair before. Marines must have their hair cut at least once a week. I couldn't tell my Platoon Sergeant "Sorry Sergeant but they can't fade black hair at the butcher shop so I decided to skip it this week". We called it the butcher shop because your head had the tendency of looking like it had been in a slaughter house rather than being trimmed by a licensed professional.

While my days consisted of enduring the doldrums of life in the desert, my nights were pretty damn good. If I wasn't in my off base duplex enjoying the bachelor life style, I was in Palm Springs with my girlfriend Danni. We met about five months previously in a bar in Palm Springs.

It had been a long Friday working in the desert sun at the CASP. The Combined Arms Supply Point was a large ammo dump that issued ammunition to every unit on base. Trucks picked up and delivered ammo from sun up to sun down and sometimes beyond. I wanted to stay home and relax that weekend but Sergeant Billy Sims called with the intention of hitting the strip in Palm Springs. It was the closest city with a mall, bars, and more importantly…women.

"Let's see what that new car can do goin' down the hill" Billy said in his Texas accent.
The "new car" was a white 2002 Pontiac Ram Air Trans Am. I bought it from a guy in Apple Valley who needed the money for a divorce attorney.

"Easy come, easy go." He said as he handed over the title. "She's a beast, but my freedom is more important."

I thought of her more as a beauty with a very loud roar. Her freshly waxed body looked more liquid than solid and the engine was tuned up to put out 525 horse power at the rear wheel. It was more power than any young man should be trusted with while unsupervised and it would conquer the "Hill" or any other road in California's high desert.

The "Hill" was a term of endearment given to a long, winding portion of Interstate 62 that cut through a mountain and led down to Palm Springs. Every young man who lived in the desert, Marine or other wise felt as though it was his patriotic duty to speed down the hill on the way to party in Palm Springs, sometimes with disastrous results.

Since the Hill only consisted of two lanes traveling in each direction, it was not uncommon to sit in a traffic jam for an hour or two while the local authorities removed what was left of an automobile from the rugged walls of the mountain road.

We were in luck that night. There were no accidents or Police, just the open road. I did my best to set a land speed record while Billy and company tried to keep up in his blue Chevy Silverado.

We arrived in Palm Springs with a single destination in mind, The Pueblo Pub. It was a small bar right on the strip that featured live music and a more relaxed vibe than the other night clubs in town. A guy could really work a spot like that. I had gotten lucky there a couple of times before so I had the home field advantage, or so I thought. We entered the pub in the finest tradition of the Marine Corps. We were on a mission, and failure was not an option.

We wore smiles on our faces as we joked around, but this was serious business. We had been stuck on base for a whole week, and now it was time for some extra curricular activities. It's common knowledge that "Hard work requires hard play." Such is the natural order of things. Yin and Yang, push and pull, drunk and sober, fuck and fight. "Balance in all things brings harmony." I always say.

We walked passed the stage where a local band played "Outstanding" by the Gap Band. We lined up at the bar and each one of us tried our luck with the very attractive female bartender. The privilege of buying a beer was our only reward.

We immediately conducted a dismounted patrol of the area of operation. It was important to get the lay of the land. After identifying a few targets of opportunity (very attractive women), we found a table that provided the optimal view of the stage and the front door. From there we could see women dancing, women entering and women leaving. From there we could quickly approach a woman, get her name and offer to buy her a drink. It was from there that I saw Danni for the first time.

The pub seemed to fade away as I lost myself in the eyes of this bronze goddess. She looked at me for a moment. There was only me and her in the entire world. I struggled to take a breath but nothing happened. Panic ensued at the thought of being helpless, but she smiled and I quickly regained control of myself.

Danni wore a low cut sundress that complemented her curves and revealed her award winning cleavage. It stopped just high enough to showcase her toned legs, and low enough to conceal the most perfectly proportioned ass that I had ever seen. Her black hair was highlighted and cut short and she had a smile that could stop rush hour traffic on a dime.

Speaking of a dime... she was hot, classy, sexy, beautiful, and every other complementary adjective imaginable. I wanted her, and I'd be God damned if I didn't ask her to dance. Danni stood at the bar with her best friend Maria Medina and some guy.

"Is she with him?" I asked myself out loud. "Hey, Check her out" I said to Billy.

"Sweet Jesus, that bitch is fine". Billy said.

"Yeah, but I can't tell if she's with that guy or not."

Billy's response was to be expected. "Fuck him. She's too good for him and he looks gay anyway."

"Yeah, I think he is gay. You're right, look at the way he walks." I said.

"Go get her dog!" Billy commanded.

Billy was shorter than me but he had a way of getting your attention. He was a scrappy fucker and I didn't want to be called a bitch for waiting any longer than I already had.

Billy was famous for calling someone a bitch whether they were male or female. It was his usual greeting as he entered a room.

"What's up bitch?" Billy would say.

No one dared answer because then they would be the bitch he was talking to.

"He's leaving" Billy said and he was right.

The guy was headed toward the men's rest room. It was then that I knew what I had to do. I had to run and hide because at that very moment Andrea walked into the pub. She had a guy with her but that wouldn't be enough to stop her from causing a scene.

I met Andrea three weeks earlier at another club in Palm Springs. She had a bitchy attitude and an ego to match. Andrea wasn't really my type but she was thicker than a butter milk biscuit, so I decided to find out what she had going on under her clothes. We danced and had a good time, so of course I had to take her back to her place and bang her out.

I call it community service. I'd bang her out, she'd be happy, and the local community would benefit from her new found sunny disposition. It's up to each of us to make these types of sacrifices for our country.

"Think globally, act locally." I always say. This world would be a much better place if more people followed my example.

Well, it turned out that she was a certifiable nut case with an itemized list of issues longer than the Macy's Thanks Giving day parade. She proclaimed that she loved me after a few tongue kisses. Not easily deterred, I continued to grab her ass until she started talking about marriage and how her son would really like me. I barely escaped her that night and there she was only a few yards away.

"Shit! I gotta go." I said.

Billy told me to follow him to the bar in the back of the pub and off we went staying low to avoid detection. We hid there nursing our beers and trying to find a way to salvage the evening. I was sick to my stomach. I couldn't see Danni from there and I prayed to God, something I rarely did begging him to keep her in the pub until I could get to her.

The tap on my shoulder startled me and I considered running off and leaving Andrea to eat my dust. I turned my head but to my surprise it was Danni and Maria.

"We've been looking all over for you guys. We want to dance" Maria said.

Maria was a good girl and I could tell that it was the last two Cosmo's that gave her the courage to approach us. I looked at Billy and we were of one mind.

"Let's go" I said.

It was a perfect set up. Me with Danni, and Billy with Maria. We danced, we spilled our drinks and we laughed.

"Where's your friend? That guy." I asked Danni.

"Oh him, he's a just co-worker. He went upstairs to play pool." Danni said.

God is good! I thought.

Danni and I danced all night long and Andrea stared at us the entire time. Her date was none the wiser. Billy and Maria only saw each other one more time after that night but Danni and I were inseparable.

"Daniella Isabel Padilla Salinas, you are my soul mate." I declared one month later.

The "I love you's." followed not long after that.

"Where have you been my entire life?" Danni would ask.

"Washington D.C." I answered and we laughed at the same old joke as if it were the first time we heard it.

Danni and I had a way of making everyone around us either sick or jealous with our public displays of affection and incessant giggling. We were in love and nothing else mattered to us. The time we spent together was Heaven on Earth. The time we spent away from each other was agony, but such is the case in a weekend love affair. We only had a few arguments the entire time. They were silly trivial spats each of them. Danni yelled at me for brushing against the Christmas tree once. She was afraid that I would break one of the ornaments that her mother gave her when she was a child.

Danni was 37. Eleven years older than I was but it didn't matter. She was so hot and looked as if she were ten years younger. Danni had been married when she was 21 and divorced two years later.

She would get upset if I did something that reminded her of her ex husband. The wrong word could set her off sometimes, but I knew how to make her relax. She described him as a violently abusive asshole. I knew that I could get her beyond it all. Danni just needed to be around me more. I could love the hurt away and we could be happy together.

"We'll get through these small obstacles together. That's what love is all about. "We're a team." I thought.

Each Friday night, I found myself speeding down the Hill in the finest display of gallant patriotism to get to my Danni. Every Monday morning I found myself kissing her lips goodbye and leaving her in bed to make it back to the base in time for physical training at 05:30. I was getting out of the Marine Corps soon and the inevitable question came.

"Baby, are you going back to Washington D.C. when you get out of the Marines? Because I want to go with you if you do." Danni said.

She was serious. I was touched, I was shocked. She was so sweet to me. She really loved me.

"No, I'm not going back to D.C. I intended to stay here in Southern California. I guess I'll settle down wherever I find a job. You know there's not much of a job market in Palm Springs." I said.

Danni agreed and a short time later she told me that she was offered a job in San Diego. Rachel, a former co-worker recommended Danni for a sales position with an office services company in San Diego and she got the job. Danni wanted to relocate but not without me.

"We should go check it out. The city I mean. We could make a weekend of it. I know you'll love it. It's so beautiful there and I want us to have a beautiful life together." Danni said.

It made perfect sense. It was a brand new place to start a brand new life. We were of one mind.

"Let's go." I said.

We drove into San Diego on Interstate 5 and the city was absolutely beautiful. It looked just like an episode of Magnum PI. Tall palm trees lined every street and the sun light danced on the waves of the bay.

"This must be what Heaven is like." I thought.

The more I saw, the more I wanted to see. I subconsciously gave into my lead foot and the skyline passed by even faster. I turned my head to check on Danni and she was smiling from ear to ear.

It made me happy to see her that way. There were times when she was tortured by her past. Danni endured a pain that ran so deep that you couldn't understand it unless you had lived it. Each person's pain is unique. I guess it's like they say, you can't judge a person until you've walked a mile in their moccasins.

My attention was diverted to the low fuel light which lit up the dash board.

I parked the car at pump number two at the service station and stepped out of the car to stretch my legs. We had been on the road for three hours and it felt good to be able to stand up.

I opened the door for Danni and helped her out of the car. It took me forever to get her accustomed to being treated like a lady.

"I've been doing things on my own for so long that it's hard to get used to you being there for me." Danni would say.

I topped off the tank, bought a couple bottles of water and we hit the road again. We found our hotel and checked in. It was an incredible weekend and I was sold on the idea of moving to San Diego.

Low Fuel

A month past and we signed a lease at an apartment complex in San Diego. A couple of Danni's friends and I spent a weekend moving her stuff down there. Danni started her new job and I was excited for her. I was excited for us and I couldn't remember my life before her.

"This is it." We would say to each other. Meaning that out of an entire world of people and countless failed relationships, we managed to find each other. We vowed that we would never let go of our new found purpose in life. Loving each other was our highest priority.

I drove to San Diego each weekend for the next few weeks. I missed my baby and I was worried about her safety. She was all alone in a big, brand new city. Danni would welcome me like a conquering hero when I arrived and to show my appreciation, I conquered her.

Our love making was the type of freaky passion that most people could only dream of.

It was as if we were made for each other. She was only 5'3" and I'm 6'4" but our bodies fit perfectly in any position. Whether boning or spooning, she felt right. Danni loved the way I gave it to her and she would tell me that I was the best. I didn't know if it was true or not but it didn't really matter. I was her King and she was my Queen.

I hadn't been discharged from the Corps yet. I still had a few more weeks until I was out but I did move some of my possessions to San Diego at my earliest convenience. Danni and I took a ride to La Jolla after I put everything away and had a chance to rest. She wanted to take me to an Italian restaurant that her boss told her about.

"I'm so glad you're here Cole" Danni said as she rested her head on my shoulder.

We would always sit together on the same side of the booth at a restaurant. The distance across the table was too much to endure.

"I'm glad to be her too baby. I missed you." I said.

She kissed me and slid her hand between my thighs.

"You did miss me." Danni said.

"This is good." I thought.

I was happy for the first time in my life. I felt as if I was finally starting to live a life worth living. I didn't have the worst time growing up but it wasn't a rose garden either.

When I was a kid, my old man was more concerned with running the streets and making up for the fun he missed out on than he was about his family. He was 19 when he knocked my mother up and felt as if he had done the right thing by getting married. He had a whole other life outside of the family by the time I was six. He had friends and co-workers that we never got to meet. He seemed to be so happy until he got home. Then it seemed as if reality smacked him in the face when he walked through the door. You could see the depression wash over him as he thought "God, is this my life?" I don't approve of his choices but I do understand why he made them.

My mother was a workaholic. It was how she escaped her unhappy marriage. It was how she escaped herself. She was never home except for the weekends and even then she was always at a friend's house to gossip. This left my younger brother Mark and I in the middle.

"Latch key kids" they used to call us. Kids that came home from school alone while both parents were at work. My father eventually found the courage to leave. They got divorced when I was 11. We only saw him a couple times after that. I guess he felt obligated to make things look right until it just didn't matter anymore. He wasn't fooling anyone, not even himself. He was through with us and his new life was calling.

My mother's reaction was to be expected. She worked even harder to compensate for the lack of a husband and to numb the pain. She found a boyfriend, Darrell. He was the first of many low lives that she sought refuge in. She rationalized it all by saying that he would give us what we needed. That he would show us how to be men, that he would show her love.

Maybe it seemed like the right thing to do at the time, but she should've taken sometime to herself rather than grabbing the first guy to give her a compliment. Darrell moved in and the chaos resumed. The arguments, the screaming and the fighting. My brother and I awoke in the middle of the night to the sound of her calling him a punk mother fucker. I learned to swear from my mother, it's one of her many talents. The next sound was the thunder. Well it sounded like thunder to us, but it was actually the sound of Darrell running across the room to hit her, which was then followed by the sound of her falling to the ground scrambling to get away.

It didn't take Darrell long to get around to us. His bad temper was accentuated by his hair trigger. He would apologize after the dust settled but it didn't help. I hated the fucker and I wished that I was big enough to forcibly evict him. He had it coming for what he had done.

He changed us, my brother and me. We were bright kids. We were outgoing, well behaved, friendly kids. He made us quiet, timid, secretive kids. Darrell taught us to be afraid. He taught us to hate. He taught us that anger can fuel you through the rest of your life.

He left out the part about anger isolating you from everyone and everything good in life. Mark and I began to sneak around the house so as not to disturb him. Later we became masters of avoiding detection all together. We were like ghosts. It was as if we didn't exist when Darrell was home. We were only vocal when he was gone. We could live again when the coast was clear.

Darrell wasn't all bad. He did spend some quality time with us. His favorite hobby was choking me until I passed out. It never got old to him and he always got a chuckle out of watching me gasp for air as I regained consciousness. There was also "Duck the shoe". This game was played when you pissed Darrell off from the opposite side of the room. Breathing a little too much or soft laughter was reason enough to initiate this display of his athletic prowess. The rules were simple. Upon being sufficiently angered, Darrell would whip off his shoe as quickly as possible and throw it at us as hard and as fast as possible. It was our job to avoid being struck by the aforementioned shoe. Darrell would earn a point each time he struck one of us and we got to live bruise free for each shoe that was ducked. A foul was given for every lamp or framed picture that was broken. Fouls really didn't lead to a suspension since there were no officials to enforce the regulations of "Duck the shoe."

Mark was a champion since he was five years younger and a much smaller target. Darrell was an All-star. To this day, he is the fastest shoe thrower I have ever seen. The game didn't last long due to the fact that Darrell could only wear two shoes at a time. Both shoes being thrown signaled the end of "Duck the shoe" and the start of "Oh Shit!" The objective of this game was to run slightly faster than the other guy so that he got caught and you didn't. I always won since I was five years older than Mark and much faster.

It wasn't long before the inevitable happened. My mother was severely injured during a championship round of "Oh Shit!" I just remember him chasing her up the stairs and her screaming. I stood there watching this spectacle just as I would watch television. Darrell caught her leg before she reached the top of the stairs and yanked her back to him. The thunder came once again as he repeatedly slammed her head against the steps. Oddly enough, I remember thinking that he wasn't really mad at her. She was just within arms reach. The more she struggled, the more he pounded.

"Better her than me." I thought.

He managed to injure her back in the fray. A slipped disk or something like that the Doctor said. My mother was bed ridden for a while and the pain was very intense. That's when the drugs started. The pain killers were the only thing that mattered to her after a while. She was pleasant when she had them and the Devil without them. Darrell gave a tearful apology. It still didn't help and I still hated the fucker. There was no more love in our home. It was every man for himself.

My mother's addiction became worse and even Darrell couldn't take it anymore. His work there was done anyway. He re-created us in his own image. We began to prey upon one another in his absence. It was a typical power vacuum. Someone had to fill the void of resident asshole and we all jockeyed for position.

My mother beat me and I beat my brother. I felt bad for Mark because he was last in line and had no one to take his frustration out on. That's probably why he's a drug addict to this day. I guess it's like they say, "Hurt people, hurt people."

Darrell left only to be replaced be a series of assholes, each more pathetic than the one before. The only constant was the violence, the drugs and the neglect.

I graduated from High School and got out of there as fast as I could. I never looked back. I figured that I couldn't do any worse on my own. I've been a loner ever since. I had girlfriends but I had never been in love, not until I met Danni that is. She was it and I was going to make it work. I had broken the cycle of abuse. I would never be so cruel. I would never hit a woman and I thanked God that I was able to do so.

We left the restaurant and walked along the beach as we admired the setting sun.

"I love this place baby" I said. "This is the right move to make."
Danni smiled and held my hand even tighter.

"You would be a great father." Danni said.

"Really, you think so?" I asked.

"Of course, even Maria thinks so. You are such a sweet man and we would have a beautiful baby." Danni said.

I had never thought about it like that before. I mean, I wanted kids one day but I didn't want to risk doing them unintentional harm. Given my background I mean.

What frame of reference did I have for raising a child to be anything other than a neurotic mess? I couldn't take that chance. It was the one thing that I was truly afraid of. That I could do the same damage to my child that was done to me. But for Danni and Maria to say that I would be good at it blew my mind.

I could see what she meant. I was a good guy despite everything. I had my faults but doesn't everyone? I worked hard at becoming a man. There was no one around to teach me, so I used to hang out with and imitate guys that I thought were cool. This got me in a little trouble every now and then. I had that habit of trying to emulate bad boys. Outlaw bikers, combat veterans, and the neighborhood tough guy for example. Needless to say I was taught a variety of street skills, and I did waste a lot of time with the wrong crowd. I had more than my fair share of fist fights, and I had a gun put in my face on more than one occasion.

Somehow over the years, I managed to pull it all together and create something that wasn't a total mess. The fact that a woman like Danni thought that I would be a good father was validation that I had gotten some of it right. I looked her up and down from head to toe. Danni had a way of making a sundress look like an evening gown. I mean she was radiant. How could I not start a family with her? How could we not be husband and wife? Who was I to let my own insecurities and fears stand in the way of something as beautiful as that? This was it!

I parked in front of the East Gym for PT (Physical Training) at 05:18 on Monday morning. I was early and I was tired. San Diego was about a four hour drive away from Twenty-Nine Palms. I left late because I couldn't pry myself away from Danni until the absolute last minute. I had a total of four hours of sleep which actually wasn't bad considering the circumstances. I rubbed my eyes and watched the other Marines from my unit pull into the parking lot. There was Billy, Hamilton, Diaz, Barnes and the rest.

"Damn, I'll probably never see these guys again." I thought.

As crazy as it sounded, they had been my family. I stepped out of the car and made my way toward the front of the gymnasium. I heard the usual groans and moans along the way. It was either too hot or too cold. There's never good weather when it comes to running PT at 05:30 on a Monday morning. You could still smell the alcohol vapors emanating from Hamilton and Billy. The two of them were like binge drinking tag team partners. If there was a championship belt for being able to spend a weekend drinking and then running six miles first thing on Monday morning with no problem, they would've won it. They reminded me of PFC. Stewart.

Stewart and I went to ammo school together. This son of a bitch would stay up 'till 2:30 in the morning drinking and then pass out drunk. I'd wake him up and drag him out of the barracks for PT, and an eighth of a mile into the run he would light up a cigarette and haul ass like a scalded dog struck by lightning. It takes all kinds to make a Marine Corps. I swear, we were all a little off in some way. There's no telling what horrible fate would have befallen any of us if it weren't for the Marine Corps channeling all of that crazy dysfunctional energy into something positive.

"Hey yo." I called out.

"What's up playa?" Billy responded.

"Fuck it's cold." was Barnes' only contribution to the conversation.

"Semper Fi man!" I said. "Don't act like you didn't know it was gonna be like this. You saw the Goddamn commercial with mother fuckers jumping over shit, running around with rifles and their faces painted. The Marines Hymn playing in the back ground. I bet you got a hard on watching that shit. I bet you couldn't wait to be hard and here you are bitching about it."

"Whatever! You know your freezing too" Barnes said.

"All I know is that I'm short and this is gonna be a memory pretty soon. But don't worry Barnes. I'll think of you as I'm chillin' on the beach. I said.

"That's fucked up!" Barnes said.

"Who's leading PT" a gruff voice called out.

No one answered.

"Bunch of punks." the voice said under its breath.

I laughed to myself as did Billy and the rest. The voice belonged to one Master Sergeant Richard Strummer. Top, as he and all Master Sergeants of Marines were referred to, was Old Corps in the truest sense of the term.

Top joined the organization back in '71 just in time to catch the ass end of Vietnam. He'd been there and done that. There weren't too many parts of this world that he had seen and that hadn't seen him. You could always count on Top Strummer to tell it like it was and to put boot to ass whenever necessary.

"I've got it Top." I said.

No one was willing to step up until Top made them so I just did it. Besides, it was a bad example to set for the boots...I mean the junior Marines. It wasn't good for them to see us blowing off the privilege of leading them. It's not that we were lazy; it's just that we were all short. Ham, Walker, Delgado, Gonzalez and I were all getting out within the same 45 day period.

Billy was the only one to re-enlist. It's always the one who complains the most about being in the Corps that decides to stay in. You can always spot a lifer by how much they bitch and moan. I guess it's because they know that they've got at least sixteen more years to get through, and the thought of it is totally depressing.

We were short timers so we were all being a little rebellious. Top knew it, but it was tradition for Marines that were short, at least in our unit anyway.

I accepted the clip board from Top and took my place in front of the formation of Marines to take roll. You must maintain accountability of Americas force in readiness. I managed to get through five names when I heard the sound of a car screeching to a halt.

Three familiar faces ran across the parking lot of the gym toward the formation.

"Good to Go!" I said. "Now I have a working party to dig out the drainage ditches".

"But Sergeant Westlake, there was a lot of traffic at the back gate and …" one of the Marines said.

"Devil Dog, I don't make excuses and I'm not in the mood to accept any. You're late and that's the bottom line. Everything else is a bullshit sob story that I'm really not interested in. Take it like a man and do better next time." I said.

I finished the roll call and formed the Marines up for physical training. We usually ran six miles across the dessert. Top loved to do that on a Monday morning. It got everyone's attention and reminded them that they were Marines.

A wild weekend could almost make you forget. Besides, running the hell out of us made Top feel like he still had it. It took us about 55 minutes to run three miles out across rough terrain and three miles back to the gym.

"Be at the CASP by 08:30." Top said.

It was about 06:50 so we had plenty of time to go home, shower and change into the   uniform of the day which was always cammies. My watch read 08:28 as Billy gave the command to fall in. We complied and Billy began to take roll.

You do that a lot in the military, taking roll I mean. You have to get in the habit of knowing where everyone is at all times. You don't want to leave anyone behind or have someone alone and in trouble for any longer than necessary. We all didn't like each other but we all took care of each other. That's what makes the Corps and its Marines such a close knit family. I've met white WWII Marine veterans who really didn't care for colored folks but wanted to adopt me as soon as they found out that I was a Marine. I'm too big to be a lawn Jockey so I know that they were being sincere.

Billy got to the G's and called out "PFC Grey".

There was no response. This happened at least twice a week. PFC Grey was the quintessential soup sandwich. I don't know how he graduated from boot camp but he did, and Parris Island no less. It was disgraceful that something as God awful as Grey was allowed to be a Marine. Gomer God Damned Pile made a better jarhead than this incomplete abortion.

Grey looked like a retarded version of Charlie Brown wearing camouflage utilities and combat boots. On a daily basis his uniform looked as if it was the casualty of a wrinkle bomb attack and his facial expression screamed "Duh".

I imagined that his head was full of scrambled eggs instead of brains every time I looked at him. That was the only explanation. There is no way a twenty one year old man could be so fucked up unless he had a Denver omelet for a Cerebral Cortex. Grey was my problem child and I vacillated between stabbing him to death with a dull, rusty tent pole and trying to get through that boulder skull of his just one more time. I wanted him out of the Marine Corps., but Top told me that this was the new Corps; that I would have to generate a couple more counseling sheets on Grey before he could send them up to the Battalion for review. Top told me to consider it a leadership challenge.

"There are no bad troops, just bad leaders." Top would say.

Grey was brain dead since birth and even Dr. Frankenstein couldn't change that.

"In my day we would've just taken him out to the tree line and beat the piss out of him." Top would say.

"A good ass whippin' will change anyone's mind about being a jerk off."

But this was the new Corps and I was too short to try it. I had to get back to Danni. All of this was a speed bump on the road to happiness. I wasn't going to jeopardize getting out on time for anything in the world. Not even beating the piss out of Grey, no matter how much I would have enjoyed it.

Staff Sergeant Kyle stood beside Billy saying something about issuing or receiving ammo and then Billy yelled the command to "fall out". The Marines began their march up the road to their respective ammunition bunkers. Billy, Ham and I grabbed a seat in the Receiving/Inspection office and took up our favorite past time…talking shit. We were champion shit talkers. There was very little else to do in the desert.

Either talk shit or drink, or both. It was either who could whip whose ass, or who banged the hottest chick the previous weekend, or what new movie was in the theater.

Lcpl. Baker walked in to the office five minutes after we did.

"Easy Leather nuts, this is Sergeants country" Ham said.

Billy followed with "Why weren't you in my formation this morning meat gazer?"

"Well, I had a dental appointment at…"

"Stand by, here comes a truck load of horse shit". I interrupted.

Baker stood there pissed off and trying not to show it. He knew that we wouldn't tolerate any disrespect. He wanted to defend himself and inform us that he was at a dental appointment that morning, but he couldn't figure out how to do it without telling us to fuck off first.

I almost felt sorry for him but this was too much fun to miss out on. Besides it wasn't that long ago that I was getting the same treatment. It was tradition. We wouldn't be able to legally mistreat anyone again for the rest of our lives, so we had to take full advantage of the opportunity. Baker finished explaining where he had been earlier that morning but it wasn't necessary. We already knew about the dental appointment. We were Marine Sergeants, it was our job to know where our troops were, are and will be.

"Here, take these documents up to the magazine and pull today's ammo issue. I'll be up in a little bit." Ham commanded.

Baker took the documents and walked out of the office. We chuckled and the topic of conversation drifted toward the last wrestling pay per view.

"Five Whiskey this is Five Hotel" the radio squawked.

"Go." I said.

It was Hamilton calling me.

"I need a ride." Ham said.

"Oscar Mike." I replied which was fancy Marine talk for "I'm on the move to your position."

I commandeered one of the tactical pick up trucks and rode up the hill to the ammo bunker that Ham and Lance Corporal Baker worked in. I got out of the truck and walked into the bunker. I made my way past the pallets of artillery rounds trying not to choke on all of the dust that Baker's forklift kicked up. Baker placed a pallet of artillery rounds down neatly next to the others. There were six rounds per pallet and at 80 pounds a piece, you could make a pretty big hole in the ground if you weren't careful. He engaged the lift's parking brake and hopped off to face me.

"Hey Sergeant Westlake, I bet you've never seen a magazine this clean and neat before in your life" Baker said.

Baker was a big boy, almost as big as I was. I liked to give him a hard time just so he remembered who was boss.

"Where's Sergeant Hamilton" I asked without acknowledging Baker's question.

"Back here, gimme a second" Ham yelled.

I cut my eyes back on Baker and gave him the type of look that asked "Who in the fuck are you looking at?" Baker was a good Marine and he was nobody's punk so I knew that it was only a matter of time until he tried me.

"Sgt. Westlake you think you're a bad ass but I'll run you out of this magazine." Baker said.

"Son, I'll beat you to death with one hand tied behind my back…twice." I said as I slowly put my left hand behind my back and tucked it into my belt for effect.

Baker slowly moved toward me, never taking his eyes of my right hand. He lunged at me but I stepped to my right side and proceeded to jab his ass into submission, talking shit the entire time.

"You thought you could handle me? You must be high." I said.

"You're just gonna walk into my magazine and take over? I don't think so." Ham said.

Ham was in my face just as soon as Baker went down. I tried jabbing him too but it really wasn't working. Ham was a tough bastard and I would need both hands to deal with him. There are times in life when talking shit can get you into trouble and this was one of them. I got my left hand in front of me just in time to block Ham's right cross.

He tried to sweep my leg but I lifted it in time to avoid the blow. I was off balance and moving back wards. We began to fall and at the last minute, I grabbed Ham's right arm. By the time we rolled over and stood back up, I had Ham's right arm behind his back. I widened my stance and twisted his arm just enough to make him call it quits.

"Ok. Ok. You got it." Ham said.

I let him go and cut my eyes back on Baker who would've jumped in to help if the whole thing hadn't happened before he got up from the ground. Ham told Baker to mind the store. We got into the truck and headed back down the hill laughing about the whole episode.

That's how Marines are, violent and aggressive. It's really not like any other branch of the military. It's more like a tribe of warriors, and you won't get any respect unless you're hard no matter what your rank is. I've received more respect and love from my troops than men who had been in for twenty years because I was hard but fair. Besides, I have an award winning personality and who could resist that?

We turned the corner near a parked tactical five ton vehicle and headed down the road toward the main gate.

"Are you really going to move to San Diego with your girl?" Ham asked.

"Hell yeah! It's beautiful down there." I can't wait.

"I'm not talking about the city I'm talking about the arrangement." Ham said.

"You mean living together right? Look, don't shit on my girl just because that chick you moved into your place turned out to be a psycho. Danni is all good. She wouldn't do me dirty." I said.

"It's different when you live with them. They can hide stuff when you're just dating them but when you live together, well that's when it all comes out, and you find out who you've been fucking the whole time. Just be careful. I'm just saying it because you don't know anyone down there but her and you're from D.C. It'll be rough if it doesn't work out." Ham said.

I had to let what he said sink in. Ham had a valid point but he never met Danni. He had never seen me when I was with her. I was like a new man when I was in her presence.
This was one of those rare moments, two bad asses being vulnerable and honest with each other.

"I've never felt like this about anyone. She actually loves me. Besides, I've been through plenty of shit in my life so I'll be ok if it doesn't work out. I'll just move on." I said.

"Well I can't wait to get back home to Chicago. Home is where your heart is." Ham said.

"No, home is where your shit is, and my shit is going to be in San Diego." I said.

We pulled up to the front gate in time to see Billy racing toward the guard house.

"What in the hell is he doing?" Ham asked.

I searched the area in front of the gate and saw what got Billy so riled up.
PFC Grey finally decided to show up and Billy was on a direct intercept coarse to launch a preemptive verbal assault. I parked the truck and slowly made my way toward the guard house as Ham took a seat on a water cooler that was outside of the Receiving/Inspection office. I would need to compose myself for this one. I had to get back into Marine mode.

Billy was on the other side of the front gate, and Grey had locked his body in the position of attention.

"You must be out of your fucking mind. You just show up three hours late and don't even bother to call the front office. Your high, is that it? Have you been smoking bat shit?" Billy screamed.

I reached the gate at that point and stretched out my right arm toward Billy and yelled

"Tag me in!"

Billy slapped my hand and I jumped over the gate as if it were the top rope in a wrestling ring. I joined Billy and got in Grey's face.

"You better have a damn good explanation for this." I barked.

Grey attempted to speak but was silenced when Billy interrupted.

"Shut up you poor excuse for a human being. What is your major malfunction?"

Grey's voice trembled as he tried to speak once again.

"Don't talk to us. You aren't worthy of speaking to us. Just push." I said.

Grey hit the deck and for a split second Billy and I were shocked. We didn't know that he could move that fast. Grey's cover fell off when he landed in the push-up position. To our horror, we saw why he was so late.

"Recover! Who did that to you?" I said as he returned to the position of attention.

"Sweet Jesus boy you are a fucking mess". Billy said as he laughed hysterically.

Grey's head looked like it had been attacked by a renegade weed whacker. His high and tight was rough and jagged. It looked terrible but it almost suited him. The sight of Grey standing there whisked away all anger and hostility. I was more concerned than angry.

"What happened, who did this to you" I asked thinking that one of the local butcher shops was the culprit.

"I didn't have any money for a haircut so I tried to cut it myself" Grey said.

"You did what?" I asked.

"I thought that it would look ok if I put my cover on and trimmed around the bottom of it, but I kept messing it up and I couldn't fix it." Grey said.

"What happened to your money?" Billy managed to ask in between the laughter and the gasps for air.

"Why didn't you just shave it all off?" I asked.

Grey looked at me as if shaving his head bald was utterly unacceptable and then responded to Billy's question.

"I spent the money my wife gave me on cigarettes. I didn't want to ask her for more because I'm supposed to quit smoking and I didn't want her to know that I hadn't. Grey said.

"But you don't mind her thinking that you dipped your head into a wood chipper?" I asked.

Grey was speechless, and after waiting a full 20 seconds for his response I looked in Billy's direction for help, but he was now sitting on an empty ammunition crate wiping away his tears and laughing uncontrollably.

"Get off my hill" I said.

I was pissed. I could've killed him. I followed Grey toward the main office and Billy stayed in the wire. It was my mess to sort out. I entered the office after Grey did.

"Well I'll be God damned. You finally decided to show up. You must have been promoted to General last night and didn't bother to tell anyone." Top said.

"No sir." Grey responded softly.

"Don't call me Sir God damn it! I'm a Master Sergeant not a sir and don't whisper at me. Are you flirting with me? You're not my type so sound off when I ask you a fucking question. Where in the hell have you been and what in the fuck happened to your head?" Top said

Top's raspy voice carried all of the way to the Gunner's (Chief Warrant Officer) office. The Gunner stepped out of his office to investigate the source of the commotion. The Gunner was the officer in charge of the **CASP** and Top was his right hand man.

"What are you yelling about Top?" the Gunner asked.

"PFC Grey Sir." Top said.

Grey was an absolute waste of flesh and that's exactly what the Gunner said.

"Jesus, Grey. You are a pitiful waste of flesh aren't you?"

Top jumped in before Grey could answer. "Sgt. Westlake. Why is your Marine so fucked up?"

"PFC Grey is so fucked up because current Marine Corps regulations prevent me from beating the shit out of him Master Sergeant." I said.

It was a disrespectful answer but I was shit hot and I could get away with that sort of thing every now and then.

The Gunner returned to his office and told me not to worry. "Top will take care of it."

But that wasn't true. Top wouldn't do anything and neither would I. Top was close to retirement and I was short. Top didn't want any trouble on his way out the door and neither did I. I understood his position; I just didn't like it. Anyone who can stay in the Marines for over twenty years should be made a special class of citizen. Like royalty to be revered and idolized. The amount of bullshit and sacrifice that one has to endure is incomprehensible. The man had earned my respect many times over, so I was ready to follow his orders when they came.

"Put him on Tiger team. He can dig out the drainage ditches by himself." Top said.

I would rather have sent a counseling sheet up to the Battalion but we did need to have the drainage ditches dug out before it rained again. It didn't rain that often in the Mojave Desert but we could have a flash flood on our hands if we didn't have serviceable drainage ditches.

"Aye Top" I said and walked out of the office.

The door closed behind me and I heard Top telling Grey to get out of his sight ten seconds later. I could hear Grey's light foot steps behind me. He was an idiot but he was smart enough to maintain a safe distance. Grey knew that I could kick the shit out of him if he got to close.

That's the Marine Corps for you. From the outside it looks like a disciplined well oiled machine, but on the inside…well, it was different. It was a savage well oiled machine, and only the toughest and most brutal ran things, regardless of rank. I like to think that I walked a thin line between bully and big brother; leader and asshole. Each had their place, but only in the proper dosages.

No matter what I was, the Marines did what I said, and when I said it. I guess that's all that matters at the end of the day. I really wasn't concerned with being liked. I had a job to do. It was a tough job and I was almost ashamed that I was so eager to relinquish it… almost.

5:40PM and we were all in formation. It was the end of a long day. I stood in front of the Marines, this time with Billy standing about fifteen feet to my right. I passed the relevant information about the day's events and what the next day had in store. Staff Sergeant Kyle spoke about inventories and the need to be accurate.

"Hurry up." I thought.

I needed to go to the gym. I needed to vent some frustration. I thoroughly believe that the reason that so many people are so frustrated about the smallest things in life is because they aren't active at all. They sit on their asses at a desk at work, and then go home to sit on their asses to watch television and eat high caloric food the entire time.

All that energy has to go somewhere and it will manifest itself as anger, frustration or disease if you don't burn it off. Some choose basketball, some tennis, some yoga. For me it was the weights. It kept me sane. It kept me safe, safe for others to be around.

Staff Sergeant Kyle wrapped up his monologue and I "Dismissed." the Marines. I was in my car heading toward the west gym a few minutes later. It was about a 3 mile drive back to the main side of the base. They put us that far out in case we had an accident which is a nice way of saying an explosion.

I parked in front of the gym and ran inside. Mike and Leeson were standing by the incline bench press. Mike was my best friend on base. Hell, he was my best friend in the world.

"A yo." I said.

"Cole!" Mike responded.

"This is it huh?" I asked.

"Yeah, we'll be moving this Saturday." Mike said.

Mike had re-enlisted for another four years. His wife Faith and his stepson Dion were moving to Camp Pendleton with him, which was not always the case with military families. Camp Pendleton was about a 40 minute drive north of San Diego so we would still be neighbors... kind of. At least I would have a friend down there. We could catch up on the weekends I imagined. Maybe we could even go to the gym on the base together.

"Gabrielle was asking about you" Mike said.

"What? She won't ever give up." I said.

Gabrielle was a civilian who worked at one of the chow halls on base. I would either run into her there or at the gym. Some how, she got my number and started calling incessantly. I think Mike gave it to her but he always denied it. Gabrielle would call some nights just to say hi, which was code for "Can I come over so you can fuck me?" I always told her no which was code for "NO!"

I never asked her how she got on base, but near as I could tell she was once married to some Navy officer. They had a thirteen year old daughter together. Gabrielle divorced him and was still living on base in the land of the big PX. The Navy diverted a percentage of her ex husbands pay to her account every two weeks for child support. Gabrielle had it made, military benefits and a never ending supply of young men to keep her entertained.

Gabrielle would probably die in Twenty-nine Palms. Why go any where else? It would only mean facing the fact that she was a slightly attractive, single mother in her late 30's with more emotional baggage than a mule team could haul. Reality sucks but it never lies.

"You should just hit that and get it over with. Do your community service." Mike said at the top of his voice.

Mike was loud…too loud…inappropriately loud.

"Fuck that." I said

"Yeah, that's what I mean." Mike said.

"Dude, you know what I'm working with. Danni is a goddess. I wouldn't ruin this for anything in the world. You just want me to bone Gabrielle so that I can tell you all about it. You fuck her if you're so curious." I said.

"Hell no! Faith would kill me." Mike said.

"How would she know? Are you going to tell her?" I asked.

"See, you don't know this but women know everything when you live with them. Faith could probably tell by the way I was walking that I got some strange." Mike said.

"Well, it's up to you Lee" I said.

We all laughed and Leeson turned a bright shade of red.

"Hell yeah, I'd tap that ass." Leeson said.

"Better not, your right hand might get jealous and key your car." Mike said.

Leeson was a virgin, and like all virgins he lied about it. He wasn't fooling anyone. Leeson even had the walk of a virgin. A man's walk changes after he has sex for the first time. He walks with more confidence and even talks a little louder. Leeson still spoke with that "Please fuck me!" voice.

Mike and I asked Leeson to join us on the Squat rack but he was afraid.

"You guys lift too heavy. I just want to look strong." Leeson said.

"That would be an improvement over looking like a virgin." Mike replied.

I savaged the chicken quesadilla that I picked up from Andrea's Cafe as soon as I got home and then showered the desert sand off of my body. The wind blew it into the strangest places. I gave myself the once over as soon as I finished drying off and prepared for the high point of my day. I needed to call Danni.

"Hey sexy."

"Oh baby, come home." Danni pleaded.

"I am home."

"No Cole, our new home in San Diego. Come be with me." Danni
said.

"Right now?"

"Yes, right now. I'm scared being here alone." Danni said.

"I'll be there soon baby and I won't ever leave you."

"Cole I miss you so much." Danni said.

"I miss you too baby."

"I need you Pappi." Danni said.

"Well put the phone between your legs." I said.

I started to hum loudly and Danni laughed hysterically.

"No I want the real thing. I want you." Danni said.

"I'll be there soon."

"LLame manana Papi. ¡Te quiero mucho!" Danni said.

I loved it when she spoke Spanish to me. It was so sexy.

"Igualmente Mama." I responded.

"Beso me Papi." Danni said.

I blew a kiss into the phone and fell asleep dreaming of her.

The next morning started out as each morning had for the past four
years. Billy held formation and then called roll. The Marines were given
the plan of the day and then finally the command to "Fall out." They
began their trek toward their individual magazines and I stood silently
staring at the mountains. I surveyed my surroundings. The desert, the
fork lift shed, the Marines in their Logistic Vehicle Systems waiting to
pick up their ammunition and take it to the field for training.

"Was it the right thing to do? I mean, getting out of the Corps and
living a civilian's life." I wondered.

I loved the Corps like I loved my Momma. I loved my fellow
Marines. Just the site of them was awe inspiring. I loved leading
Marines. It is the ultimate privilege to be entrusted with their safety,
well being and combat effectiveness. On the other hand, I loved Danni
and I couldn't let her go.

I couldn't have both. The Corps demanded 120%, and believe me it
would get it.

Where would that leave Danni, and would that be fair? I mean for me
to be deployed over seas, or to be standing a 24 hour duty shift
guarding some ammunition pile somewhere. I had to face the facts. If I
stayed in the Corps, even for another four years it would mean a severe
commitment, and that wouldn't be fair to her. That's why I promised

myself that I would never get married while I was in the Marines. It's not fair to a family and I wouldn't go for it if the roles were reversed.

No, this was the right time to go. I was a man of my word. I signed a contract and I had fulfilled it. That's what **USMC** stands for: Yo**U** **S**igned a **M**other fuckin' **C**ontract. I gave up four of the best years of my life serving my country. That's good enough in my book. There was no question in my mind. I was going to San Diego with Danni. I felt a sense of inner peace and confidence. The feeling was refreshing. Too bad it was temporary.

"Sgt. Westlake?"

Reality slowly re-established itself and I turned my head to focus on the individual who had broken my moment of clarity. My eyes burned a hole through his, and I hated him but just for a moment.

"Who in the hell do you think you are and how dare you interrupt this epiphany?" I thought.

Epiphanies don't happen that often which is why you should cherish them when they do.

I'm not good at hiding my emotions, I never have been. I know this because he stopped dead in his tracks when his gaze met mine.

"Speak." I commanded.

I could be an absolute asshole sometimes but it was so much fun, and the Marines in the platoon seemed to love it. They probably took notes and spit it back out to their troops when I wasn't around. That's what I did when I was a boot and Top used to yell at me.

Corporal O'Brien was his name and bullshit was his game. O'Brien couldn't speak the truth if he had a pistol jammed against his temple. Trying to sort fact from fiction with him had pissed me off about a year and a half ago which is coincidentally when he checked in to the CASP. I took a don't talk just listen to me when I speak approach with him. I did know best after all.

"It takes all kinds to make a Corps." I always said and O'Brien was living proof.

He was dating some local girl and she was just about to dig her claws into him. O'Brien was about to fall victim to the oldest game in the book, and the sad part was that he would never see it coming. This is the standard operating procedure for local women around military bases throughout the world. It's a case of desperate people making desperate choices which always ends with disastrous results.

O'Brien wasn't about to make any one's most desirable bachelor list but he was a Marine with benefits and base privileges. The PX and base housing were all at his disposal and he instantly went from a 6 to a 10 in her book. She started demanding that they get married and he asked me for my advice.

She was 20 years old and she wanted out of her parent's house by any means necessary. With the exception of the newly built Denny's, the city of Twenty-Nine Palms had zero economy off base. The chances of her getting a job and finding a place of her own were about 10 to 1. O'Brien was her ticket to freedom. A little head and a few sweet words would seal the deal. She could then go back to being a bitch after the wedding ceremony which invariably took place in one of the many Las Vegas drive through chapels, only a three hour drive away.

A friend of mine once said that you get out of a marriage what you put into it. That's why the divorce rate in the U.S. military is even higher than that of the civilian populace. Bullshit in, bullshit out.

I told O'Brien that I had seen this sort of thing happen many times before and always with the same catastrophic results. I told him to break up with her immediately.
"She'll be in your pocket for the next 18 years if you screw this up. Do you want that son? Do you?" I said.

I was only four years older then he was but my stature and tone of voice allowed me to get away with murder. Calling him son with no questions asked, barking orders and being untouchable were all par for the course when ever I stepped on deck.

I was the ultimate authority in these matters because for some reason, I managed to stay immune to the usual trappings that most young Marines fell into. No one was more amazed than I was.

People don't realize how much young service members are preyed upon by used car dealerships, strip clubs, cash advance stores and the local populace. Ripping off young boots who don't know jack is a cottage industry. What does a young kid from Utah know about "Three Card Monty", the art of the "Gold Digger" or a lap dance? Lambs to the slaughter one and all I tell ya.

"Well, did you do it or did you bitch out again?" I asked.
He tried to break up with her two times previously but to no avail. Each time she pulled out the ultimate weapon...tears. They would stop most men dead in their tracks. I've seen three tear drops reduce the most fearsome men into cowards, afraid to go in for the kill.

"I did it!" O'Brien shouted.

He closed the gap between the two of us until we were only two feet apart and speaking in much more subdued tones. We didn't want to offend anyone with our misogynistic dialogue. That was unacceptable in the modern day Marine Corps.

"I told her that she was selfish and that she should appreciate my commitment to defending my country and that she shouldn't make any demands of me. I told her that I couldn't take her nagging anymore and that it would be in the best interest of national security if I stopped seeing her." O'Brien said.

"And then?" I asked.

"Then she started crying just like you said she would."

"And then?" I asked once again.

The tone of my voice demanded that he hurry and get to the good part. I hate it when someone starts telling you a story and then takes forever to get to the end.

"She said that she loved me and that she only wanted to be with me but I stayed strong and walked away." O'Brien said.

"Good job now don't answer her phone calls under any circumstances and sooner or later she'll find some other dumb jarhead to run her scam on." I said.

"Don't worry about that, I feel so much better without her in my life. It's like the weight of the world has been lifted from my shoulders." O'Brien said.

It was true. He looked a lot happier. I almost smiled for a second...almost. I was actually proud of the jackass or maybe I was really proud of myself. Proud that a guy like me could give someone some advice and that they trusted me enough to follow it. I joined the Marines because I couldn't find steady work. I had a lot of different jobs in construction, warehouses, as a janitor and as an electrician's helper. None of them really worked out. I mean none of them allowed me to live up to my full potential. I joined the Corps hoping that it would make me into someone respectable and apparently it had.

"I'm sure going to miss you Sergeant Westlake." O'Brien said. "You give advice and discipline us with out disrespecting us or talking down to us. I always learn something from you. Sergeant Sims and the other Sergeants go out of there way to make us feel stupid."

I thanked O'Brien for the sentiment as he walked away to carry out the plan of the day. I was dumbstruck. For a year and a half I thought of O'Brien as a pain in the ass and then he goes and says something like that. I guess you never really know how you affect the people around you.

Low Fuel

TWO

Ham and I walked out of the base library with our check out sheets in hand. The check out sheet listed every office on base that we needed to check out with in order to process out of the Corps. Initials were placed on a line beside each office to prove that you had been there and that you were cleared to go. Check out sheets were the standard operating procedure when leaving one base for another or for good.

Getting sent to Okinawa, Japan, you need a check out sheet. Going to Mountain Warfare School…checkout sheet. Sergeants Course for training…checkout sheet, getting deployed to the latest hotspot or combat zone…you'd need a checkout sheet.

To the Marine Corps, it was an administrative necessity; to me it was my golden ticket to freedom. Ham called it a big green scavenger hunt, just for shits and giggles. I however loved every minute of it. Every initial on each corresponding line brought me one step closer to Danni and San Diego. I watched countless Marines go through the check out procedure during my time in the desert and now it was my turn.

We went directly to the Naval Dental office that morning instead of going to the CASP. I knew that the young sailor behind the desk was envious. He looked at me with a look that had the words "Lucky Bastard" written all over his face. It wasn't luck, just time.

They can do what they want but they can't stop the clock. They can make you push, deny your leave time, have you field day the barracks each night for a week straight, but they could never stop the clock. Time waits for no man, not even the Commandant of the Marine Corps. It was the only thing that you could really count on, and each day brought you closer to that ultimate decision. Should I stay or should I go?

"I should go." I said.

"Where to?" Ham asked.

"Top told me to go by GMED (Garrison Mobile Equipment Division). Taylor and Wilson's forklift licenses are ready and they need to be picked-up." I said.

We parted company and I drove across base toward the GMED. I slowed down as I passed a platoon of Marines marching toward the base theater on one of the small two lane roads that ran in between the various lots and departments on base.

I didn't want to break the sound barrier as I drove past them. The resulting sonic boom could be dangerous. I saw an MP parked at the next street corner as I passed the platoon. He was leaning out of the window of his cruiser with a radar gun pointed in my direction. He would have gotten me if I hadn't slowed down for that Platoon on the road. It's a good thing that I'm so thoughtful! One more speeding ticket and I would lose my base driving privileges. It would be a real bitch walking across the desert to get from place to place.

MPs are almost as bad as real Police. They even have the nerve to say "I'm a cop or I'm in law enforcement." until you remind them that they're just another jarhead and that they have zero jurisdiction off base. They even wear those cop sunglasses and they like to fuck with people for no reason just like real cops. Harassing innocent hardworking people for no reason at all is sadistic. Sooner or later they'd learn the hard way that getting into trouble is easy, but getting out of it is so very hard.

I slowly drove past the wannabe and looked in his direction with my trade marked shit eating grin plastered all over my face. He was pissed off and it showed. I wished him better luck next time as I made my way through the front gate of GMED.

A field of vehicles parked in rows lay before me. Most were loaner vehicles waiting to be picked up; some were being repaired, and the rest were the victim of various collisions. It looked like a big vehicular grave yard. I entered the front door of the training office and approached the counter.

Corporal Williams was standing there with a smile on her face.

"Good morning Sergeant." She said.

"Corporal" I responded sternly with a nod of my head.

I didn't want to be too friendly. That's how it starts. I'd be friendly and smile and things would take off from there. The next thing you know, we would be in my bed room or any bed room ripping each others clothes off. It would end five or six months later as it always did, with her hating my guts. It never ceases to amaze me how quickly you can go from being the best thing since sliced bread to being an asshole.

Williams was so very cute and she was giving me that look. Yeah, that look. Temptation reared its ugly head once again. She was definitely my type and I would've asked her out if I weren't with Danni. She was a petite 5'5" tall, 135 pound, brown skinned sista with just enough curves to keep things interesting. I would have hooked up with her if I was a rotten bastard and no one would ever know about it. I'd be down in San Diego and what happened in Twenty-nine Palms would stay in Twenty-nine Palms. Needless to say, I remained as professional as humanly possible.

"I'm here to pick up two new forklift licenses for Lance Corporal Wilson and Private First Class Taylor from the CASP."

"Here you go Sergeant" she said as she handed over the two licenses. "Master Sergeant Strummer called and said that you were on your way over."

"Outstanding. Thank you Corporal." I said.

I took the licenses and turned to go but was interrupted in mid stride.

"Sergeant Westlake. Lieutenant Colonel Lassiter would like to speak with you." She said.

"Really?" I asked in disbelief.

This wasn't good. A Lieutenant Colonel in the Marine Corps is a very big deal and they don't bother with Sergeants unless there's a problem.

I walked into Lieutenant Colonel Lassiter's office, locked my body in the position of attention and reported in as all good Marines do. He gave the command "At ease." and I obeyed it.

"Sergeant Westlake, I hear that you're checking out." he said.

"Yes sir."

"Now son, how could a shit hot hard charger like you leave all of this behind?" he asked.

I had to think fast. He was a savvy old bird and he had the ability to whip up an instant re-enlistment ceremony if I wasn't careful. I could be marooned in this place for another four years or worse, I could be issued orders for Okinawa, Japan.

"Well sir, I love the Corps and I appreciate all that it has done for me. It has molded me into the man that I am today. It has taught me the meaning of the words Honor, Courage and Commitment. I believe that I could best serve this nation by living among the civilian population and sharing what I have learned in the Corps. There are many people who could benefit from seeing these core values in action. All are sorely needed in modern day society and I feel that it is up to Marines like me to set the example." I said.

It was a flawless monologue and if you listened carefully you could hear the Marines hymn playing off in the distance. I just hoped that I hadn't layed it on too thick.

"Horse shit." the Colonel replied. "You've got a first class PFT (Physical Fitness Test) score; you received a meritorious promotion to the rank of Private First Class while in MCT (Marine Combat Training), and another to the rank of Corporal through a meritorious promotion board. It took you two and a half years to go from Private to Sergeant. You could be a Staff Sergeant with in the next two years and you could be a Gunnery Sergeant with eight years time in service. Now how could you walk away from all of that? At this pace you'll be a Sergeant Major by the time it's all said and done." he said.

I was rendered speechless. Somebody mark your calendar, it didn't happen often. I stood there a big, dumb, silent, dazed tower of confusion. He caught me flat footed and I was on the ropes. He was right. I was giving it all up. I reflected on what he said.

"It hadn't been all bad, had it? The desert and the past four years?" I thought.

"Look son, I hate to see you throw it all away. All of your hard work, all of the blood sweat and the tears. Not many people can do what you've done. I know it's been tough but it's what we do. It's what you are and this nation needs you. You can't turn it off… no matter how hard you try. You're not the same person you were before Parris Island. You'll be a Marine for the rest of your days and you'll miss the Corps each and every one of them. Now, I wish only the best for you son, but smart money says that you won't last one year out there in the civilian world. You're no longer one of them. It won't be long before you come back home." He said.

"Thanks for the vote of confidence." I thought.

"We'll see you soon." he said with a smirk as I walked out of his office.

I passed by Williams and she mouthed the words "I'm sorry". I stopped and leaned toward her and whispered "It's ok, I forgive you." and that's when it happened.

We looked into each others eyes just a little too long, just a little too deeply, just a little too intensely. At that very second we shared a moment. It looked like a brief exchange to anyone on the outside looking in but the eye contact, the way her upper lip quivered, the way I studied her with my eyes, the way she responded with a look that begged "Take me with you", and for an instant I almost kissed her. At that moment we both realized that we had an undeniable connection and that's when I broke it.

I smiled a smile that said "maybe next life time" and walked out of the office.

"Something isn't right." I thought as I backed my car into a parking space outside the main office of the CASP.

It was about 09:45 and there was no one insight. There should've been Marines on the move, forklifts shuttling pallets of ammo to and from the five ton tactical vehicles in the lot but there was nothing. There was only a lone Military Police cruiser parked in front of the main office.

"That's never good." I thought.

They only came out this far when the intruder detection system was activated.

It happened every so often, usually triggered by the severe desert winds. They would haul ass all the way out to the CASP for the chance to see some action, and they would leave heart broken each and every time after they discovered that it was only a false alarm. One time in particular, Baker was on duty and swore that he saw an intruder lurking around the outside of an ammo bunker at about 01:30. He gave chase but the intruder climbed over the fence and escaped.

Baker said that he couldn't fire his weapon due to several pallets of 155mm artillery rounds that were in the way. He called the Military Police to report the incident but no good deed goes unpunished. The MP's grilled him for five hours straight. They called him a liar and said that he made the whole thing up. They said that there was no way that anyone could climb a seven foot tall fence with razor wire at the top that fast without leaving a blood trail to follow. They loved interrogations. Closing the investigation was almost irrelevant at that point. Making Baker sweat was the true objective. That was important. They fed on his anger and frustration like a school of piranhas.

I would normally check in with Top but under the circumstances, I thought I'd stay out of it. I headed up toward the guard shack and took note of the expression on PFC Taylor's face. His body language and entire demeanor was all wrong. He seemed genuinely concerned about something. Taylor was usually so jovial. He was a self described amateur comedian and nothing ever distracted him from that endeavor.

Taylor could do a ten minute stand up comedy routine at the drop of a hat. He could make you laugh uncontrollably at an incoming sand storm or a broken down Hummer. A "professional jackass" I used to call him and he was the best I'd ever seen.

"What's going on? What's the law doing this far away from main side?" I asked.

"You didn't hear Sergeant? About Sergeant Sims and Lance Corporal Barnes?" Taylor said.

"What...did they get into a fight out in town again?" I asked.

"No, they had an accident late last night and Barnes wrecked his car. They took Sergeant Sims to the hospital. They're saying he can't move his legs." Taylor said.

Taylor should have cracked a smile by that point but he hadn't. He had a propensity for going go too far in the pursuit of a laugh but this time he was dead serious. I turned around without saying a word and slowly walked back toward the main office. My mind was filled with what ifs.

"What if Taylor heard it wrong, what if Billy broke a leg or two. What if they strapped Billy's legs down when they pulled him out of the wreckage and that's what that meant."

I opened the door of the main office and caught sight of Top on the phone and an MP standing by his desk.

"Yes sir, I understand. The Marines are fine, they're just concerned. Roger that sir." Top said as he paced back and forth but only as far as the telephone cord would permit. An eternity seemed to pass by. Top hung up the phone 40 seconds later and continued to stare at it. He took a deep breath, sighed and spoke.

"Barnes rolled his car at 02:30 this morning. He blew a .13 on the breathalyzer. He was fucking drunk and he was fucking driving."

Top took his eyes off of the phone and placed them on me.

"Billy was sleeping in the passenger seat. He never knew what hit him. The docs say he's paralyzed from the waist down. They don't know the severity of the paralysis." Top said.

"The Gunner's at the Naval Hospital." Top continued. "They're gonna helo Billy down to Palm Springs to be seen by a Neurologist.

"What about Barnes?" I asked.

"Scrapes and bruises. He got off easy." Top said. "Get up there and hold things together. You've got to keep the Marines busy. They still have work to do."

There was a subtle tone in Top's voice that gave me the impression that he had given the same order one too many times during the course of his military career. He was entirely too calm about the entire matter. He had seen Marines die before. He had seen them seriously injured and he still accomplished the mission.

"Aye Top!" I said.

"And don't answer too many questions. They need to focus God damn it. One fuck up and we'll have a hole in the ground the size of Laughlin, Nevada. The Gunner will be back later to speak to them. He'll have all of the facts when he arrives." Top said.

Ham pulled up just as I walked out of the main office. He had been at the PX trying to pick up the new girl who was working at the Jewelry counter. The word was that she was some Major's daughter but Ham didn't care. He figured that he would be back in Chicago before anyone found out and once again, what happened in Twenty-nine Palms would stay in Twenty-nine Palms.

I waited for him to get out of his car. I wanted to intercept him before he went to check in with Top. He should hear the news from me, besides Top had told the story enough for one day. I recounted the facts to Ham as we walked up the hill and passed PFC Taylor at the guard shack. Ham asked for more info but I had none.

Everyone was in a state of shock but we kept them busy. We made it a point to talk about anything other than Billy but he was on all of our minds. I pulled up to the small arms magazine and Lance Corporal Kelly Robinson ran out of the bunker to meet me. Her eyes were red and she looked as if she had been crying. Robinson had a crush on Billy and everyone knew it.

"Sergeant Westlake have you heard anything?" she asked.

"No. Hopefully the Gunner will tell us something in this evening's formation. Until then, I need you to pull 15,000 rounds of linked 5.56 SAW rounds. 7th Marines will be picking them up within the next 20 minutes." I said.

The rest of the day followed suit as various Marines asked for any word but there wasn't any. It's human nature to allow your mind to imagine the worst and that's exactly what we did. We stood at attention as the Gunner took over the formation from Sgt. Diaz. He put us at ease and began to speak.

"Now you've all heard that Sergeant Sims and Lance Corporal Barnes were involved in an accident last night. The vehicle they were traveling in rolled several times near Joshua Tree National Park at approximately 02:30. Barnes walked away with some abrasions and bruises but the docs are saying that Sergeant Sims is paralyzed from the waist down." The Gunner said.

A series of gasps and "Oh shits!" came from the formation. It's one thing to imagine a tragedy but confirmation is a bitter pill to swallow.

"He was flown down to Palm Springs this morning after his vitals were stabilized." The Gunner said. "They have a shit hot neurologist down there and they're hoping that they can improve his condition. I've spoken with his parents and they'll be flying in from Texas tomorrow morning. I'll be providing updates as I receive them. Oh yeah and as you have also heard, Barnes was drunk and faces a DUI charge.

Alcohol and cars don't mix well and there's your proof. Now we still have work to do. Those of you who choose to make this a career will find yourself in this type of situation again. Focus on the mission Devil Dogs. That's all that you can do at a time like this." The Gunner said.

The Gunner returned the platoon to Sgt. Diaz and stood by the door of the Receiving/Inspection office. Diaz gave the command to fall out and the Marines saluted the Gunner as they exited through the front gate.

"West, Hamilton, Diaz, come here." The Gunner said.

We approached the Gunner and saluted. He returned our salute.

"Barnes is facing charges for DUI; he is also under suicide watch. He blames himself for what happened to Billy and made some comments to the Navy docs about taking his life." The Gunner said.

"Jesus Christ!" Ham said.

"This is going to get worse in the next few days and I'm counting on the three of you to keep us in business up here, copy?" the Gunner said.

"Yes sir." we responded.

It was a long drive home. I only lived 4 miles down Adobe road from the base but the trip seemed to take forever. I could only think of Billy and how his life had changed in the blink of an eye. I grabbed the phone as soon as I walked through the door. I just needed to hear Danni's voice. What happened to Billy made me realize how fast things can change for the worse. It made me want to be with her even more.

"What's wrong? I can hear it in your voice." Danni said.

"Billy was in an accident last night. The car rolled and he's paralyzed from the waist down baby."

"Oh my God. What was he doing, racing down that hill or something crazy?" Danni said.

"No, He was with Barnes. Barnes was drunk and rolled the car." I said.

"I'm glad that you weren't with him. He's like one of those wild red necks. You can pick better friends than that." Danni said.

"Baby, he was the passenger. He didn't do any thing wrong. It was Barnes not Billy. He was driving drunk." I said in a futile attempt to defend a helpless friend.

"Well he shouldn't have gotten into the car then." Danni said.

"Are you serious?"

"Yes. He put himself in that position." Danni responded.

"God damn it Danni, a friend of mine is paralyzed and I feel sick to my stomach about the whole thing. I called you for some support and this is what I get from you. I can't believe this. Think about Billy and that he could live the rest of his life paralyzed. He's only 22 for Christ sake. I'll talk to you later." I said as I hung up the phone.

Danni called back several times but I was to upset to talk to her. I tossed and turned all night thinking about Billy's and Barnes.

Morning came all too soon and the week passed all to slow. Billy's parents arrived on Wednesday. By Thursday we received the final diagnosis that he was a paraplegic and would spend the rest of his life in a wheel chair. Top and Staff Sergeant Kyle planned on going down to Palm Springs to visit him on Saturday.

Saturday morning started as they usually had. Breakfast, the gym, back home to shower and then lunch. I walked out of my front door and headed toward my car. I could see my next door neighbor Mrs. Davis standing beside her car. I always wondered how she ended up in the middle of nowhere and why she stayed there.

"Maybe she was ridding on a Greyhound bus headed for Vegas when it broke down on the Interstate. Maybe she just said "Fuck it, I'll stay her and die." I thought.

She was staring at her car. It was an old Buick Le Sabre with a long history of breaking down. There was no telling what was wrong with it this time.

"Good morning." I called out. "Is that thing giving you trouble again?"

"I got a flat and I need to head to the grocery store." She said.

She looked as if the entire world just came to an end. It was obvious that she didn't know how to change a tire. It was even more obvious that she didn't have anyone to help her.

"Oh, is that all. I'll change it in no time. I happen to be a tire changing champion. I used to compete in tire changing matches all over the world when I was younger." I said.

She let out a chuckle and told me that I was crazy. I popped open my trunk and grabbed my four way lug wrench and the floor jack.

"Don't believe me? Time me. I'll have this done in seven minutes." I said as I slid the jack under her car.

"The key is that you've got to have the proper tools for the job. Those scissor jacks that the cars come with these days are worthless. It takes entirely too long to use one of those." I said.

The tire was changed within minutes and I examined the flat to see if it was salvageable.

"Here's the culprit." I announced.

There was a nail that sat dead center in the middle of the tread of her tire.

"You are the greatest tire changer that I've ever seen." she said, still laughing. "Thank God for you. I would have been stuck if you hadn't come along."

"You should have come and knocked on my door." I said.

"I thought your lady friend might be visiting again and I didn't want to interrupt." She said.

I laughed uncomfortably. She sounded jealous.

"Was that possible? Would a 54 year old White lady living in the middle of the Mojave Desert be jealous of a 37 year old Mexican woman because she was with a 26 year black man and she wasn't?" I thought.

She was right about one thing, I was crazy. I was crazy to even worry about it. I told her that she could have her tire patched and that it would be cheaper than buying a new one. She thanked me and said that she was on a fixed income and that she needed to save all of the money that she could. Mrs. Davis got into the Buick, started it up and left on her way to the grocery store. I waved goodbye as I walked back to my car.

I wondered why she didn't have any family around. Why didn't she move closer to them if she did have children somewhere? The desert was no place for her to be living alone. There was nothing there but the base and the homeless Crystal Meth addicts.

I drove down the hill but much slower this time. I didn't want to arrive at the hospital while Top and the others were there. I wasn't good at stuff like that. I never knew what to say when someone was grieving or when there had been a death in someone's family.

"Please accept my condolences" or "Everything will be alright".

What in the hell kind of a thing was that to say? I didn't know what to expect when I got there and I didn't want to go through that in front of everyone.

I parked in the visitor parking lot of the hospital and walked in. I already knew his room number and headed that way after speaking to the guy at the information desk. I exited the elevator on the fourth floor and heard a familiar raspy voice as I rounded the corner. It was Top. Staff Sergeant Kyle and Diaz was with him, and they all looked as if they'd seen a ghost.

"Hey Westlake." Top called out.

"How is he?" I asked.

"He's Billy." Top replied.

"Well no shit Top." I thought.

I wanted to ask them what it was like to walk in that room and see him like that but I didn't. I would find out for myself soon enough.

I knocked on the door and I was told to come in by a female's voice. I pushed the door open and to my surprise Lance Corporal Kelly Robinson was sitting on the edge of the bed holding Billy's hand. She looked different in civilian clothes. She was actually very attractive.

"Hey." I said

"What's up brother?" Billy said.

His voice was weak but still retained that Texas accent.

"Hello Sergeant." Robinson said.

I grabbed the chair that was in the corner of the room and pulled it to the bedside and sat down.

"Got you something." I said as I pulled out a tin of Copenhagen from the bag that I brought along with a 20 oz. bottle of Mountain Dew.

"Fuck yeah." Billy said.

Billy spoke softly, I guess that was due to the medication but there was something else. He was different now. He wasn't the same guy. It was as if his spirit was broken.

I handed the bag to Robinson and she gave Billy the dip and sat the soda on the tray on the bed. Billy slowly took it and packed it the way that he always did. He took a pinch and tucked it between his lower lip and gum.

"Thanks man. All I've had to eat is this crap ass hospital food. It's good to have something else." Billy said.

"I figured you could use a dip so I stopped and picked some up. Is that the race?" I asked as I looked at the television and saw that he was watching NASCAR.

"Yeah. Thank God for small favors." Billy said.

He was putting a brave face on things but he wasn't that scrappy, cocky little fuck anymore. He was scared. He was so very disappointed that this was now his life.

"Give us a minute Kelly." Billy said.

Robinson excused herself and walked out of the room.

"I heard that your folks were in town." I said.

"Yeah they went to grab some chow. I asked them to give me and Kelly a minute alone. She's a good kid." Billy said.

"Yeah she's crazy about you too. Did you ever hit that?" I said.

"No, no I never did. I wanted to. But no, I didn't. I started flirting with her and realized that's she was a good girl, too good for me. I didn't think that it would be the right thing to do. I wasn't going to love her you know what I mean." Billy said.

"Yeah I know." I said.

"She told me that she loves me and that she wants to be there for me." Billy said.

"Really?" I asked.

"I told her that I couldn't let her waste her time on me like that." Billy said.

"Come on, what do you mean waste her time? You're a good man, not a waste." I said.

"Cole, I'm paralyzed. I'll never walk again. The Doc told me so." Billy said.

He got a little choked up. I'd never seen him like that before and he never called me by my first name either.

"I'm not going to let her waste her life on me. She's a good girl, a really good girl and she could have a really nice guy to marry. She wants a family you know. I wouldn't take that away from her. You've got to play the cards that you get dealt in this life. If this is my hand then I need to deal with it but I won't let her get caught up in any of this shit. She deserves better than that. She deserves better than me." Billy said.

The silence was deafening and finally he asked about Barnes.

"He's been talking to a shrink. They had him on suicide watch for a while. Now he's in therapy. He blames himself ya know." I said.

"It could've been me." Billy said. "I could've been driving that night. It could've gone either way. I just had too much to drink and passed out. We could both be here or dead. I just remember waking up and the truck was flipping over and over. It was so loud and it wouldn't stop. We just kind of laid there when it was over. I couldn't move and Barnes wouldn't leave me. At least he got that part right. The CHP cop pulled up like ten minutes later. It seemed like we were out there forever. I could see the stars in the sky through the cracked wind shield. I was bleeding but I couldn't feel any pain. I remember thinking that I was going to die. It didn't bother me…being done with life I mean. I was ready. Then I woke up again in the ambulance. Tell him I don't blame him ok. Please tell him. You gotta tell him." Billy said.

A tear slipped from Billy's eye and he quickly wiped it away.

"Ok, yeah I'll tell him." I whispered fighting back tears of my own.

We sat there, quietly for another few moments as if we both ran out of things to say. Finally, I asked him if he needed anything else but he said that he was fine. That was it. I didn't know what to say or do at that point. I just sat there feeling dumb and useless. We were interrupted by a knock at the door and Billy's parents entered the room along with Robinson.

Billy conducted the introductions from his hospital bed and I hurried to compose myself. I made some small talk and then said good bye.

I sat in the car in the hospital parking lot replaying the past couple years in my head. I recounted all the times we partied, argued and chased women. It could have been me in that hospital room with IV's and tubes running out of my body. We were always drunk or so it seemed. There wasn't anything else to do out in the middle of no where.

I remembered when Billy first checked into the CASP. He had come in from Okinawa and we didn't get along at all. Soon we were enemies and we actually had people picking sides, his or mine. I guess it was a case of the two toughest kids on the block maneuvering for the role of the Alpha male. Then one night at a party out in town we buried the hatchet over a couple beers. I guess we finally realized that we were more alike than we were different.

Never in a million years would I imagine that this would happen. Life is crazy! Billy had just re-enlisted one day and he was staring at pushing a wheel chair for the rest of his life the next.

"Where is God in all of this? How does he let something like this happen?" I wondered. Life can change drastically for the worst when you put your trust in the wrong person. You can lose everything in an instant.

Gabrielle called me one more time and I said "No!" one more time. I spoke to Billy on the phone and he was in rehab. He was learning to use his new wheel chair and going to therapy to cope with his new life, his disability and being a paraplegic. He was also waiting to process out of the Corps. He was no longer mission capable so he would be honorably discharged. Billy was injured off base through Barnes' negligence so the Veteran's Administration wouldn't grant him any disability money. He would have to begin the petition process to salvage what ever benefits he could. God only knew how long that would take. Billy would head back home to Texas a few weeks after I left the desert and I would never see him again.

Barnes was in and out of therapy trying to find a way to live with himself. He was an emotional wreck on the inside and he looked the part on the outside. I delivered Billy's message the Monday following my visit to the hospital. I told Barnes that Billy didn't need to forgive him because he never blamed him in the first place. I gave him the whole speech about playing the cards that you're dealt and never looking back. The message was met with a salvo of tears and a low yield nervous break down. I watched him collapse to the ground weeping and I felt bad for him for the first time since the accident.

His pain ran deep and thick. He was engulfed in it. It was like trying to swim for the shore of sanity through a sea of crazy glue. I didn't think that anyone, mental health professional or otherwise could save Barnes from the despair. That was for him to do. He had to find a way to forgive himself and start to move past it all. Barnes had to learn to live again. It was his choice to make and honestly, I didn't think that he had the ability to find his way out of the darkness. Barnes was a broken man and I don't know if he ever recovered from what happened to Billy that night.

When I was 17 I used talk to this homeless guy who panhandled at the McPherson Square Metro stop near my summer job in down town D.C. I wondered how he survived each day. How he stayed dry when it rained? How he managed to endure the cold, the heat and exactly when he went crazy. I remember that he looked to be about 60 years old but looking back, I realize that he was probably only 32. The streets were as cold as ice even during an August heat wave.

"Life is a nightmare and the worst is yet to come." He used to say.

I couldn't understand the sentiment then, but I do now. Barnes was trapped in just such a nightmare. His life was now a never ending blur of "what ifs" and "why did I's?" Barnes entire life was now defined by the events of that night, and they would haunt him to some extent for as long as he lived.

"I wish I could go back." Barnes said over and over again while sobbing. "I wish I could go back and fix this. This is so fucked up. I wish I could go back and stop myself. Why can't it be like that? God please! Oh God!"

If scientists ever manage to create a time machine they'd better prepared for a very long line. With or without permission there are going to be a lot of people who intend to go back to some point in their lives and undo some horrible incident or correct some awful choice that was made. The entire universe would probably implode from all of the "do-overs."

Billy was right. For whatever reason, things happened the way that they did and you had no choice but to play the hand that you were dealt. There's no looking back. Your only recourse is to move forward and hope for the best.

I found an envelope taped to my door when I got home. It looked like the kind that a greeting card usually came in.

"That damned Gabrielle!" was the thought that immediately came to mind. "Won't she ever give up?"

The phone rang as I pushed through the door. I dropped the card on the coffee table and answered it.

"Baby, you'll never believe what happened today." It was Danni and she was very excited about something.

"What? What? What happened? Are you ok?" I asked. My mind was in tragedy mode and Danni's tone gave me reason to be concerned.

"Yes! Oh my God baby! I made a big sale today, a huge sale and my boss Rachel got so excited and we were running around the office celebrating." Danni said. Danni could get so excited sometimes that she couldn't catch her breath.

"Baby that's great! I was scared that something bad happened." I said.

"No, everything is good except that you're not here." Danni said.

I reassured her that I would be with her soon. I ended the call and placed some left over spaghetti in the microwave. I sat on the couch and placed my dinner on the coffee table. I reached for a napkin and that's when I noticed the envelope again.

"I could use a good laugh. Let me see what Gabrielle has to say." I thought.

I opened the envelope and to my surprise it wasn't from Gabrielle.

Dear Sergeant,

Thank you for being a good and kind neighbor. You remind me of my late husband, Master Sergeant Kenneth Davis. He was a good man just as you are. You are a class act and I will miss you. Good luck in all of your future endeavors. The desert won't be the same without you.

Sincerely, Allison Davis

P.S. If I were a much younger woman, I would be sitting beside you in that car as you drove us away into the sunset and trust me, I would make you very happy.

I had no idea that she felt that way. I would never have guessed that she would say something like that. Now I understood how she came to be in Twenty-Nine Palms. Her husband probably retired there and passed away leaving her all alone. I wanted to go knock on her door and thank her for the sweet words. I wanted to hug her and tell her that everything would be alright but decided against it. She may have wanted some community service.

I awoke at 5:30 am on Saturday morning to the sound of a ringing telephone. Danni wouldn't do that. She was not a morning person at all. Gabrielle was probably still underneath whatever guy she left the night club with three hours earlier.

A phone call at that time of day only means one thing to a Marine… trouble. I took comfort in the fact that I had less than a week left. I would turn in my check out sheet on Thursday morning and leave the desert that Friday. Then I would be a free man and I would have the luxury of turning the ringer off.

"What?" I said.

"Cole, its Diaz."

"What's wrong? What's going on?" I said.

"I need you to come in and stand duty for me today. McMahon got arrested in Arizona and Top ordered me to get a vehicle from GMED and go pick him up. I have to be on the road by 07:00. I'm taking O'Brien with me. I'm hoping that we can be back sometime tonight." Diaz said.

Lance Corporal McMahon was a new Marine and had only been with the unit for about 10 months. He was married and had two kids back home in Arizona. Mac joined the Corps and kind of started a new life. He separated from his wife and started a new relationship with Lance Corporal Celia Blake at the same time. They came to depend on each other to cope with the rigors of life in both the desert and the Marine Corps.

Things were going well for them with the exception of his still being married. They found a place out in town and moved in together. They were almost happy until Mac began to ask Blake for help paying his bills. His wife demanded more and more money each pay day or she would call his command and inform them that he had abandoned his family and that his children were going hungry. Something like that would ruin your military career and his had just begun.

"What did he do, beat up his wife or something?" I asked.

I knew his love for her had turned sour and such a thing was possible.

"No. He owes her a lot of money so she set him up. She took out a restraining order on him and asked him to come home to visit the kids. She called the Police as soon as he arrived and they arrested him. They'll release him into our custody because they know we'll discipline him and make him pay her each pay day." Diaz said.

"OK. Shit! Who's my Duty Tech?" I asked.

"Lance Corporal Larson." Diaz said.

"Fuck! Larson. Are you shittin' me? I gotta spend 24 hours with Larson." I said.

"It'll be Ok West. You can take him, unless you want to let him win." Diaz said.

"Fuck you! When you see McMahon tell him that I'm gonna kick his ass." I shouted and then hung up the phone.

I drove through the front gate of the base and began to travel the three miles down Adobe road toward the CASP. I kept a watchful eye out for the MP's. The desert was beautiful this time of day without all of the Hummers and Light Armored Vehicles driving across the sand as well as the Super Cobras and Harriers flying overhead. The sound of freedom got to be overwhelming at times.

I met Corporal Johnson at the front gate and she cleared her M-9, 9mm pistol to ensure that it was empty before handing it over to me. Just then Larson was dropped off by Private First Class Williams. Williams drove off and I began to wonder,

"Williams and Larson...hmm?"

"Good morning Sergeant. What happened to Sergeant Diaz?" Larson asked.

"Mac ran into some trouble in Arizona. Sergeant Diaz had to go get him. I'm the Supernut so it's you and me." I said.

Supernut is short for supernumerary. The duty schedule had been created for the month and Top was good enough to leave me off since I was getting out soon. He did however, make me the Supernut and it was my job to come in if anyone was ill or couldn't make it as was the case with Diaz.

Larson and I locked the gate after the off going duty departed and headed up the hill in one of the tactical pick ups. The duty hut was on top of the tallest hill in the CASP. It provided a spectacular view of the surrounding desert. We could see anything in our area during the day and at night with our night vision goggles.

The morning passed as it typically did when standing duty on the weekend. We watched cable TV and took turns patrolling the area. I called Danni at about 11:30 am and told her that I was on duty.

"What, I thought you were done with that." Danni said.

"I'm the supernut and one of the Marines got into some trouble." I said.

"Who?"

"McMahon." I answered.

"Oh, and Blake too?"

"No baby, just him. Diaz went to get him." I said.

"All the way to Arizona?"

"Yep." I said.

Danni was well versed in all things Marine Corps. She loved hearing my stories about the CASP and its Marines. She toyed with the idea of joining the Air Force when she graduated high school but decided that she wasn't cut out for military life and went straight to college instead.

"God baby, I miss you so much." I said.

"You could be here with me right now if Diaz didn't have to go get Mac."

"I'll be there on Friday baby. Hold on till then." I said.

"Ok. It's just that I need you. It's been a while. I need to feel you."

"Really?" I asked.

"Yes. I'm so horny for you."

"I'm horny for you baby. God, you get me so hard when you talk like this." I said.

I looked up and saw Larson sitting there watching the television with a sly grin on his face.

Larson was gay. He didn't walk around saying it but it was a fact. He was professional and competent but he was a little off. He didn't act like a man should act. He acted like he was a gay guy keeping his business to himself. It was the whole "Don't ask, don't tell" thing. Nobody asked because they already knew, and he didn't tell because everybody already knew. It wasn't a problem in the CASP because we worked too many hours in the hot desert sun to be worried about it. He was too hard working and good at his job to gay bash, so the whole issue was moot. But in other units, well he would've had his teeth kicked in repeatedly until he just left or died.

There was this one Marine, Lance Corporal Anderson with 1st Tank battalion. He would always come into draw ammo for the tankers. One day he got caught being a little too friendly with another guy out in town and the word spread back to his unit. By "being a little too friendly" I mean swapping spit in the back of a Ford Explorer. I guess he should've gotten darker tint.

He went UA (Unauthorized Absence) the next day. Anderson ran away, far away. The word was out that he was going to catch a beat down. This news means so much more when it comes from men who are trained to kill people with a dull rusty spoon and can't wait for the chance to actually do it.

Anderson headed all the way back home to Arkansas and stayed there for a month and a half until he was assured that his safety could be guaranteed. This type of thing happened every now and then.

Larson was fortunate. He would be OK as long as he was at the CASP. After that, God only knew. I often wondered why he joined the Corps. He had to be aware of the risk. Larson was older than I was so I was sure that this was his way out just like it was mine.

"I'll be there soon baby. Let me get off the phone. I love you Mama." I said.

"¡Te Quiero tambien Papi Chulo!" Danni said.

I hung up the phone and sat there deep in thought. There was no doubt in my mind that I would be with her soon but it seemed so very far away.

"It must be hard having to stand duty when you are so close to getting out." Larson said.

"What? Fucking eaves dropper!" was my initial reaction and I'm sure my facial expression conveyed that very thought.

On further examination I came to realize that he was a genius. It was the perfect way to break the ice after I damn near had phone sex with Danni right there in front of him. I didn't even consider that I had created an awkward situation for him to be involved in. This was the Marine Corps and another Sergeant could have looked up to see him sitting there and put him to work mopping floors to mask their embarrassment. As for me.....well, I was much more egalitarian in my leadership style. I knew why he said what he said and I appreciated it.

Not only was it a perfect segue out of my session with Danni, but it was a smooth transition into the rest of our duty shift together.

"Well, Saturday duty is a lot easier than duty during the work week and it is my last time. Besides, it is for a good cause with Mac being in Arizona and all." I said.

"Yeah, I guess so. I heard you were moving to San Diego. That's going to be awesome for you." Larson said.

He was attempting to manipulate me. Trying to get me to open up and spill my guts. He was a genius. Now I was on guard and attempting to get him to reveal a chink in his armor.

"You're right. It is beautiful down there. My girl and I found a spot in the city. We're going to start a new life down there." I said.

I played dumb as if I was answering his questions but I was now engaged in a launching a full scale offensive.

"Sergeant Sims said that she was hot." Larson probed further.

"Yeah, she's a goddess. Sometimes I think that I don't deserve her but neither does anyone else, so I guess I'll stay with her." I said.

It was an answer that conveyed humility and also convinced him that he was achieving his goal. I hadn't told him anything of substance but he felt that he was making progress. Larson laughed at my response and we watched Rocky IV on TNT. It was the eighth time that I'd seen the movie but it never got old to me. I loved watching that Russian tell Stallone "I must break you." He almost seemed apologetic for having to beat him to death. He was a man who was a warrior by nature but remorseful about what he had to do. It's very tragic when you think about it.

"Do you have any advice?" Larson asked just as Stallone entered the Soviet arena. I shot him a look that begged for further explanation.

"I mean you picked up rank really quickly and you seem to have a good situation here. You know how people treat you and how you do things. You seem to be able to come and go as you please. You're like the only person I've ever seen push shit up and down hill." Larson said.

"You mean I appear to be above the bullshit?" I said.

"Yes, that's exactly what I mean." Larson said.

"OK, take notes. This gets said once and only once." I said.

I didn't do this sort of thing often, revealing tricks of the trade I mean. But I would hate to leave this place without leaving a legacy behind me and Larson, for better or worse would be just that, my legacy.

"You have to play by the rules and master them before you can attempt to break them. You have to know what you're doing and what you're talking about if you expect anyone to promote you and if you expect anyone to faithfully follow your orders. They have to believe in you even if they don't like you." I said.

"I always thought people liked you." Larson said.

"Maybe now but there was a time when I was the only black man in this unit and things began to get out of hand. There were some racial comments that were made and Sergeant Sims even hung up a confederate flag in his room in the barracks. Maybe they didn't mean any harm but I could tell where it was leading. It was only a matter of time until they crossed the line and I would have to do something about it or take it in the ass." I said without realizing that Larson may have been offended by the statement.

"It was at that time that I decided to go on the Meritorious Corporals board. I won, got promoted and things changed. It was at that moment that I had a say on how things went, which brings me to my next point. The more rank you have, the fewer people there are who can fuck with you. Study your Guide Book for Marines, score high on your physical fitness tests, shoot well on the rifle range and become an expert on all things Marine Corps. Things will be better for you from then on. Studs run the Marine Corps, regardless of their rank." I said.

Larson knew exactly what I meant. I didn't have to come out and say, "Larson, I know that you are a homosexual so if you get promoted the chances of you being called a faggot or getting kicked in the face are going to be greatly reduced with each rank you attain."

Now, I hate it when gay rights activists try to equate being gay with being black. Gay people can always try to act more heterosexual but a black man is a nigger until the day he leaves this world and maybe even after that. I'm sure that Willie Lynch went straight to hell and I feel for any brother that has to suffer "Jim Crow" Satan style. Can you imagine burning for an eternity in the "Colored" fire pit?

There's no way to hide your blackness no matter how many degrees you earn or how well you speak. You'll always be a suspect, you'll always have trouble catching a cab in New York city , and white women will always panic whenever the elevator door opens and they see you standing there waiting to go to the 6th floor. That being said, Larson was white and I was black but we had a similar problem. Being a minority can either work for you or work against you. Nine times outta ten, it worked against you unless you were a black man in the Philippines, Australia or Germany, then you were in Heaven.

Any where else and you would have to be the black guy who was different from the others. The black guy who could speak English instead of Ebonics, the black guy who could be twice as good as his white counterparts in order to achieve half as much as they did.

We spoke for an hour and a half or so. Larson asked me questions about how to handle insubordinate troops and how to win a meritorious promotion board, and I didn't mind providing the answers. He asked detailed questions and listened closely to each one of them. You have to respect a man that knows enough to listen. So many people ask a question and then cut you off in mid-sentence just to disagree with you. This incidentally, is the mark of a true fool.

I wished Larson well and hoped that it all worked out for him. Larson wasn't anything like Corporal Miles. Miles was also gay but always made comments about how fine or pretty a woman was. I guess he felt pressured to fit in but it was a waste of time. There's a saying that goes "It takes a woman to know a woman." Well, men can tell when another man just ain't right also. There's nothing funnier than a gay man trying to tell you why a woman is hot except for a woman trying to tell you why she isn't. The gay guy isn't fooling anyone and the woman is just being insecure.

Miles found a twenty something, single mother with a five year old daughter out in town and began to date her. She said that he was such a sweet man. She had no idea just how sweet he really was but odds are that she would find out sooner or later.

If catching a man cheating breaks a woman's heart, than catching a man cheating with another man has got to put her in therapy for the rest of her life. It's such a terribly selfish thing to do. A person's heart is all they really have. You can break them along with it if you're not careful.

Billy said that he was going to tell her the truth before the wedding but he never got around to it. I guess he had too much beer to drink. It wouldn't have done any good anyway.

That's how love is. It makes you defend the one you love even when they're dead wrong and the source of your misery. Miles married her as soon as he could and got orders to Camp LeJuene, North Carolina a few months later.

Miles needed to create a fantasy in order to escape reality. It was easier to lie to her and pretend to be straight than to be honest and just be gay. Maybe he was hoping that she was woman enough to make him straight. I guess it's like they say "The road to hell is paved with good intentions." I often wondered how she would kill him when she found out the truth.

I cleared my weapon and handed it over to the oncoming Duty Sergeant at 08:00 Sunday morning. I dropped Larson off at the barracks and headed home. I finished my laundry, ironed my uniforms, and took a nap to catch up on the sleep that I missed while patrolling the CASP looking for intruders. I spoke to Danni that evening and we finished the phone sex that was interrupted the day before.

I didn't get the chance to speak to Diaz until Monday morning. He and O'Brien picked Mac up and brought him back to MCAGCC. Mac was in deep trouble. His wife had indeed set him up. She even told the command that Mac was living out in town with Blake. Odds were that Mac would be forced to move back into the barracks and be restricted there, unable to leave until his time was served. His entire paycheck would be directed to his wife's account until she received the money that she was due. Hell hath no fury like a woman scorned.

Adultery in the Marine Corps happened all of the time but you could cancel Christmas if your command found out about it. They'd take your rank and your pay and you could forget about getting promoted again. That's what Mac faced. Blake wasn't in the clear either. She wouldn't be subjected to the uniform code of military justice, but she had earned the reputation of being an adulteress and that isn't good for a career either.

I had an open door policy with my Marines just as my senior Marines had with me when I was a PFC. Managers and Supervisors in both the military and civilian world alike always say that they have an open door policy, but that alone is not enough. You have to be approachable and your people have to trust you enough to confide in you. They have to believe that you're competent enough to resolve the situation and that you have the integrity to keep it confidential. Meaning that you have to have your shit together before anyone will ask you for help or advice.

In the past, Blake often came to me for career advice and it wasn't long before she started asking me about her relationship with Mac. Blake said that she loved him so much and that she would do anything for him. They were happy to be living together and she said that she didn't mind waiting for his divorce to be final. She didn't even mind Mac's wife calling to argue with him about the money or his sons missing him or asking for a second chance to work things out and then ultimately screaming "Fuck you!" into the phone.

It's funny how all relationships pass through the "Fuck you!" zone sooner or later. The problem was that Mac was leaning heavily on Blake for financial help. They were the same rank with the same time in grade and time in service. All this means that they were getting paid the same amount of money twice a month. Their relationship was moving along entirely too fast and it wasn't by coincidence. Mac needed Blake to love him, and he did everything necessary to make that happen. Romance, flowers, and the sweetest of words spoken in rapid succession. Mac needed Blake just as much as a leach needs a healthy thigh to suck on. He needed her unconditional devotion and dedication. He needed her affection. He needed a woman to argue with. He was codependent and he couldn't survive this world alone.

I had seen this before. He was Darrell without the violence and without the shoe throwing. Mac was trying to keep his wife at bay by giving her just enough money necessary to keep her from calling his command. She used this ploy in a desperate attempt to wake him up and bring him back to his family but she only succeeded in pissing him off. Men think that women hate them when they resort to tactics like these. It's really a last ditch attempt at getting their attention and saving the relationship before they walk away for good.

Mac's wife was done with him and had declared war. It was now Blake's job to pay the rent, light bill, auto insurance and all the rest. Needless to say they survived on a steady diet of microwave noodles and fierce verbal arguments. Blake never addressed the issue of finances with Mac specifically, but she would argue with him about every other topic. He used the old "it's just temporary and it shouldn't be a problem if you really loved me." line and that normally shut her up. Mac was four years older than Blake and that was enough life experience to send her into the downward spiral of a guilt trip. Life was easier in a strange new place with her as a crutch then being on his own.

I listened carefully to what Blake had to say, analyzing every word before taking a deep breath and giving her my sage advice.

"Leave him." I said.

Dead silence was her response as well as a look that read "What?"

I in turn gave her a look of my own that read "Did I fucking stutter?"

This of course, wasn't at all what she expected. Blake sat there in my office confused and disappointed. I guess she thought I would give her some secret to make him see the error of his ways which would motivate him to find a part time job and carry his weight. Yes, people in the military often have part time jobs, food stamps too.

"But Sergeant, I love him." Blake cried out. "We're…we're in love. I don't want to leave him. He makes me happy."

She was on the verge of tears and I really hate that shit. Seeing a woman cry reminded me of my mother and ate at me deep inside.

I interrupted her to wrap things up and to spare myself the arduous task of handing her a box of tissues.

"Look Devil Dog." I said. "This is the United States Marine Corps not the 13th grade, and I'm your Platoon Sergeant not your guidance counselor. I don't have anything against Mac. He works hard and does what he's told but he is using you."

Blake's eyes widened in disbelief. She was shocked that I would actually say such a thing. I think that was the exact moment that she began to hate me.

Out went the admiration, in came the contempt. The truth hurt just a little too much.

"A man's job is to provide for a woman not to find a woman to provide for him." I said. "You guys are the same rank, making the same money. You should be paying the bills fifty-fifty but he's got you paying everything. There are too many guys living off of women these days and if you don't think that you deserve better than who will? The man is married with two boys that need their father. Mac hasn't been sending his wife any money and now he's leaving her for you. No, scratch that. Now he's leaving his family for you. Now what makes you think that he won't do the same thing to you in few years when you're married with kids if you even get that far? Odds are he'll use you to get through this drama and then move onto the next victim.

Now don't get upset with me for saying all of this. Be grateful that someone has the courage to tell you the truth. Now you know what to do. Leave him before this shit gets any worse because it's only a matter of time before it does. LEAVE HIM!" I shouted with enough drama and conviction sufficient to win an Academy award.

Blake assured me that she would take my advice but I knew better. She returned to talk to me on several occasions but it only resulted in me telling her the same thing. I guess she thought that I would say something different sooner or later but I'm consistent to a fault. Slowly but surely she began to turn against me. Slowly but surely Blake began to despise me. The very sight of me reminded her that it was all a pack of lies. Mac lied to her, she lied to herself and I refused to play along. I was the only one with the nerve to kick her little fantasy squarely in the nuts. How dare I tell her that the love of her life was playing her like a harp? After all that I had done for her she began to speak badly about me. It's a small Corps and word got back to me as it always did. I didn't worry about it though. I was short and I had bigger fish to fry.

Blake betrayed me, and while I wasn't too broken up about it I did learn a valuable lesson. I realized not to carry dead weight. I'll help anyone who is trying to help themselves, but I won't waste time on anyone who asks for help and then stabs me in the back because the solution requires more effort than they bargained for.

Sergeant Hamilton and I finished checking out earlier than expected and spent our time just kind of hanging out. I had been replaced by a new Staff Sergeant named Woods who had just checked in to the CASP. While I didn't officially have a job anymore, I was expected to continue to support the mission. I maintained a low profile and watched TV in the Receipt/Inspection office with Ham instead.

Sometimes we would drive around the area in one of the Tactical Pick-up trucks, and sometimes we would sneak away to the PX so that Ham could get one more crack at the girl in the jewelry department. We only had three days left and there had been no word of a going away party. Perhaps no one was in the mood with all of the drama. Billy's paralysis, Barnes' mental health issues, Mac's arrest and Blake's temper tantrum.

"Can you believe this shit?" I asked Ham.

"What shit?"

"We've been here for four years and they aren't even gonna throw us a going away party." I said.

"Fuck it dude. I just wanna go home. Fuck this place." Ham said.

"Yeah, I got all that but come on, they threw one for Jimenez and he was an asshole. Nobody even liked him. Sandoval got one. She was a fucking deadbeat. Even Perry got one and he was a God damned racist. It's tradition. Why stop with us?" I asked.

We turned right at the fork in the road and drove past the grenade magazine. I caught a glimpse of Blake on a forklift moving a pallet of fragmentation grenades. Her eyes caught mine and she gave me a look that could freeze Lake Havasu at 300 yards.

"What's her problem? Did you fuck her and forget to call and say thanks?" Ham asked.

"No, she's just pissed off because I told her that this shit with Mac would happen months ago, and now she's caught up in his mess. I guess it's my fault that he left his family for her." I said.

"Dude, fuck it." was Ham's response.

That seemed to be his response to everything but he was right. I was loosing sight of the true goal. San Diego was only a few days away. Danni and my future life were right around the corner. If these people didn't want to say good bye to us then fuck 'em. They could kiss my ass as I drove off base.

The next couple of days passed without a single surprise. Grey was late to formation and still incompetent. Blake still hated me and held on to a rapidly decaying fantasy. Mac was still fucked and I was getting more accustomed to the idea of not being responsible for thirty two

Marines anymore. Don't get me wrong. There is no greater privilege than leading U.S. Marines but a wise man once said it best. "Being in Management is great, except for the people." The Navy shrinks cleared Barnes and he returned to work. He still wasn't himself yet. How could he be?

Wednesday's afternoon formation was the last one I had to endure. Sergeant Diaz held the formation and The Gunner came up with Top to present us with plaques thanking us for our service. We received them with the usual right hand over left as we shook his hand. The Gunner asked us to make a speech. Ham was first. He thanked everyone for everything and I noticed a total lack of interest as he spoke. The Gunner asked me but I declined. I wasn't going to waste my time. The command "Dismissed" was given and everyone left. A few Marines stopped to shake our hands and wish us well including Lance Corporal Wilson.

"Hey Sergeant, I just wanted to say thank you for everything." Wilson said

"You're welcome." I said.

We shook hands and I remembered the first day that he checked into the unit. We were always so happy to get new Marines because we had so much work to do. The more the merrier.

"Do me a favor." I said

"Sure, anything." Wilson said.

"Get promoted. Become a Corporal as soon as possible." I said.

"Aw Sergeant, you know I..." Wilson said.

"Aw Sergeant my ass! Do it for me if you won't do it for yourself." I said. "I want to leave here knowing that you and the others will be ok. It's important. You'll see."

Wilson promised me that he would and then walked me to my car. We shook hands once again and I thanked him for his kind words.

"The whole thing just goes on with or without you." I thought as I drove down Adobe road on my way home. "I drive off of the base and it's like I was never there. Well, it's like I always said. "The only thing better than being in the Marines is being a former Marine." All of the respect and none of the responsibility. Semper Fi!

I awoke at 6:00 AM on Friday morning and placed my remaining possessions into my car. A crew form the Travel Management Office removed my furniture and house wares the day before and would deliver them to a public storage unit in San Diego that I rented a couple weeks earlier.

My landlord came through at 9:30 AM to inspect the duplex. I had been up all night cleaning the place. It's amazing how much junk you acquire that you don't really need. I ended up throwing much of it away. The Meth addicts would catch hell trying to pawn the broken vacuum cleaner that I tossed in the dumpster.

The place was spotless and in better condition than it was when I moved in with the exception of the gapping hole in the bed room's closet door. My ex-girlfriend Nikki thought it would look better that way.

I allowed her to convince me that we should see each other one more time after our break up. Somehow she thought that our having sex meant that we were a couple again. Nikki threw her curling iron at me after I informed her that her assumption was incorrect. I was agile enough to duck the curling iron. The closet door wasn't. The sight of a curling iron sticking out of the closet door was enough for me to finally call it quits. I met Danni three months later and she taught me that curling irons were used to style hair and not as weapons.

My landlord asked me to explain the hole in his closet door so I told him the entire story.

He responded with a roaring belly laugh and said "Boys will be boys". He gave me an A for effort and I handed over the keys. He wrote out a check for the security deposit minus the cost of a new closet door. He told me to get the rest from Nikki but I decided to pass. She might decide to throw a bullet at me the next time, and I wasn't sure if I was up to the task of dodging it.

I bid him fair well and thanked him for the memories. I fired up the Trans Am and pulled out of the sandy field that could only qualify as a parking lot in the desert. Adobe road streaked by at 55 miles per hour as I memorized each and every detail of the town. I felt that I should remember it all since I vowed that I would never return. I passed the butcher shop and I could see the barbers inside committing crimes of fashion against their unsuspecting victims. I chuckled to myself. Some things never changed.

I made a right turn near the Denny's on to Rte 62 and floored it. The engine roared that familiar sound that always put a smile on my face and I was slammed back into the driver's seat a split second later. I passed the city limits after a short time and there was only the desert, for the next 40 miles at least.

Choya tree, boulder, coyote, tumble weed, again and again in that order. The never ending vastness of the desert put me into sort of a trance. You know, the type that enables you do something and then not remember doing it 10 minutes later. It's amazing that you can drive twenty miles and not really recall any of it. You know that you did it but you don't remember how.

"Well, it's finally over." I thought.

It didn't end the way I thought it would. I had been waiting for this moment for what seemed like an eternity. Strangely, I wasn't elated about my new found freedom. I felt the same way about leaving Twenty-nine Palms that I did when I left to go to boot camp. Nervous about the unknown, yet excited about all the possibilities and options that a new life brings.

It was hard to admit it but the desert had become my comfort zone and I was leaving it behind at over a mile a minute. It hadn't been as bad as I made it out to be. It was just different but it had been my home. My mind was busy reflecting on matters existential when I realized that I was already half way down the Hill.

I didn't even remember doing it but I must have. I decided that it wasn't the place to daydream and I began to scan the road ahead. I never noticed that there were Choya trees growing on the almost sheer face of the mountain walls before. Mother Nature had adapted to the highway's incursion through the desert and continued to thrive.

I'm sure that the construction crew's dynamiting their way through the mountain seemed like the end of the world to the plants and animals that lived there but they managed to deal with it all. You would think that the blasting and digging would ruin everything but life is too resilient to quit. This world will be here no matter what we do to it. Why worry? A man has to be like a Choya tree. He must adapt to thrive in the face of great change or perish.

I reached the bottom of the hill, rounded the final curve and headed past the massive windmills that littered the surrounding landscape. That trip down the Hill had been my slowest ever. I was thinking too much. Billy would have called me a bitch if he were there. I turned up the stereo and decided to get down to business. The needle on the speedometer climbed up and settled on 85 mph. I may have been out of the Marine Corps but I still had on one last mission to complete.

THREE

I swung my legs over the side of the bed and sat there for a minute trying to get my bearings. I had that "Where in the hell am I?" feeling that you get when you wake up in a strange bed. That is, if you're lucky enough to wake up in a strange bed. I looked down at me feet and stretched out my toes and then repeatedly made them into fists grasping at the carpet each time. My vision was a bit blurry but I could still make out the time on the alarm clock that sat on the night stand. It was 6:13 pm.

I looked over my shoulder and caught a glimpse of Danni. She had a face like an angel when she slept and she slept like a log whenever I banged her into a coma. She lay there partially exposed and I could trace the contours of her body under the sheet. I watched over her admiring my handy work.

"Mission accomplished." I thought.

It had been quite a home coming. Danni jumped into my arms as soon as I came through the door. We hugged, kissed and hugged again. We pulled at each others clothes leaving a trail from the front door to the bedroom. We looked into each others eyes for a moment as if to reassure each other that this moment was real. She started to cry and I kissed away each one of her tears as they fell.

I placed my mouth on every part of her body. Danni held on tightly and locked her legs around me. I drove deeper with every stroke as she thrust back toward me until we climaxed simultaneously. We knew each others bodies so well that we were in sync. We had pushed sex beyond the physical realm into the ethereal.

I found the strength to stand upright and headed into the living room. I parted the blinds with my finger tips until they were just wide enough for me to peek through the sliding glass door. I couldn't see the sunset directly but its dark golden rays bathed everything within view. I've loved sunsets ever since I was a kid. They give the entire world a different appearance just as cloudy days do. Even the slightest change of lighting allows you to see textures and facets of everyday life that were hidden from view by the intensity of the naked Sun.

"Baby." Danni called out softly. "Cole where are you?" Danni repeated but this time louder and slightly agitated.

"I'm out here Mama." I said.

Danni stumbled out of the bedroom while rubbing her eyes. She had this way of stomping when she walked sometimes that was comical. It seemed as if she might actually stumble and fall but she never did.

Danni hugged me tight as if the Titanic just sank and I was the last life preserver left. There we stood in a nude embrace. We watched the Sun make its descent below the urban horizon that was the roof of the shopping center across the street. Nothing was said, not a word. It wasn't necessary. We were in a zone that transcended words.

"You really love me don't you?" Danni asked as she looked into my eyes.

She needed frequent reassurances that I really loved her and that I actually wanted to be with someone like her, whatever that meant. As if moving to San Diego wasn't enough to prove to her that I did in fact love her. As if the past eight months weren't enough. I thought that she was a little insecure but a lot of women are. Having my intentions toward her questioned repeatedly was irritating but I got used to it. Chock it up to one of the many sacrifices you make when in a relationship.

"Yeah baby. I love you." I said.

That was all it took. Those three words and she was happy, either that or satisfied. Danni seemed to melt in my arms upon receiving the news that I wasn't going to leave her. I could now reset the "Do you really love me?" clock to go off in another 48 hours. That's when she would ask me the same question all over again; I would give her the same answer all over again, and I could get on with the rest of my life all over again.

My stomach began to rumble as if to remind me that I couldn't spend four hours on the road and then have sex three times in a row without eventually eating. Food I mean. Danni rubbed my stomach and told me that she had something for me. I had been too busy pulling off clothing and getting an erection to notice that she prepared a homecoming feast. Never let it be said that I don't have my priorities in order.

Baked chicken, mashed potatoes, string beans and homemade biscuits were all set out on the table before me and I availed myself of the opportunity to feed and refuel for round four. Danni was an incredible cook. She could have been the Executive Chef in a restaurant if she wanted to.

"Is it good baby?" Danni asked just after I took the fifth bite.

"Hell yeah it's good." I answered after I finished chewing.

"Really?" Danni asked in feigned disbelief.

Danni knew that she was a great cook and I could never understand why she did that. I constantly complimented her. Did she really need more?

"They say the way to a man's heart is through his stomach and you get the job done every time." I said.

"Really? You love me Papi?" Danni asked.

Foul! She wasn't scheduled to ask me that for another 48 hours. Now she had to be penalized.

"Of course I love you? Hell, I'd love a monkey if it could cook like you do." I said.

A balled up napkin hurled at my forehead was the punishment for such insolence.

Danni and I finished dinner, tossed the dishes into the sink and headed back to the bedroom.

"If going to sleep on a full stomach is so bad for you then why does it feel so good?" I wondered.

We drifted off to sleep as she took up her favorite place in the world, lying on my chest. The thing I love most about San Diego is the view of the bay. You can see it from many different locations throughout the city and each offers a picture perfect vantage point. It snakes through the city, past the jetty and out to the Pacific Ocean. A mixture of Navy warships, international commercial tankers and privately owned boats slice through the water making their way for parts unknown.

The U.S. Navy's S-3 Vikings and F/A-18 Hornets roared through the sky on their way to and from the Naval Air Station on Coronado Island. There were families having picnics on the coast and lovers out for a romantic stroll. It was absolutely beautiful and I found it hard to focus on the road as I headed north on Interstate-5.

I had a job interview that morning with Ready Temp, a local temporary agency. I figured that it wouldn't hurt to earn a couple bucks until I found the job that I really wanted.

Finding a job before I got out of the Corps proved to be difficult and I was never very good at that sort of thing.

The unit doesn't want to give you the time to go on interviews because they still needed you. No employer wants to wait two months for you to get out because they need to fill the position as soon as possible. Some people were able to secure employment prior to being discharged but I had to wait to start an effective job search. The one saving grace was that I was still on terminal leave, meaning that I was using my remaining leave time and still had four paychecks coming in. That and my savings account kept poverty at bay.

There are many differences between life on the East coast and life on the West coast and they never cease to amaze me. One of them is that people on the west coast are much more laid back than their east coast counterparts. They have a much more relaxed approach to life even in the most severe circumstances. They have been fortunate to have escaped that on the go, rush, rush mentality that they have back east. I imagined that the weather had a lot to do with it. It's hard to stop and smell the roses in the middle of a hurricane or blizzard.

I entered the door of the Ready Temp office and introduced myself to the receptionist. She handed me a clip board and I took a seat in the waiting area. I filled out my name and social security number before I looked up and took note of the other young men with clip boards who were filling out applications. They were all dressed in khakis and polo shirts. One of them even wore a t-shirt and jeans. I, on the other hand was wearing a black, three button, single breasted suit. My dress shoes were spit shined and could have been mistaken for black mirrors.

The receptionist called my name and led me toward a room in the back of the office. There I met Dina who invited me to sit down and tell her a little about myself. Dina was the staffing specialist who would conduct the interview and hopefully find an assignment for me.

"Wow, that's a really nice suit." Dina said.

It really wasn't but I thanked her anyway. I got the impression that she had never in her life seen anyone go to a job interview in a suit before. Well, maybe on TV but never in real life. I was way over dressed for this cavalcade of Polo shirts. It was then that I first took note of a crisis that had taken hold of the country. That crisis is ESS. Empty Scrotum Syndrome.

That's right. I said it, a complete lack of balls. It seemed that regardless of race, creed, color or religion, there were men in this country who suffered from a complete lack of manhood. They were males but they didn't carry themselves as men should.

They were men who didn't inspire you with confidence or fear when you saw them. Men who didn't say what they meant or mean what they said. Men who couldn't change a flat tire and just sat there in a car waiting for Road Side Assistance to show up and change it for them. Men who went shopping just as much as women did. There was a whole generation of sissy's out there who didn't know the first thing about being a swinging dick. I guess I had been sheltered from this phenomenon while in the Corps.

"Had the country changed that much in four years or had I?" I asked myself.

Dina and I spoke about my past work history and then about the Marine Corps. She thought my experience at the CASP would be a great fit for an electronics warehouse near La Jolla that needed someone to fill a Shipping and Receiving Clerk position. They needed someone to start as soon as possible and I agreed to start the next day.

I had shipped and received more bullets, missiles, grenades and explosives than I could remember. Shipping and receiving was in my blood. I could do it in my sleep and kicking a couple boxes of circuit boards to bum-fuck Kentucky would be a cake walk.

Dina thanked me for coming in and called me "A very interesting person". She had no idea.

I left the office with the usual bundle of paper work, time sheets and the ubiquitous employee code of conduct that you always get at a temp agency. It seemed like such a waste of effort. Someone actually created all of those policies and committed them to paper. It would only end up in the trash as it always did.

Code of Conduct….I was a temp. The code of conduct is that they would call me when they needed me and they wouldn't when they didn't. I'd work when I needed to and I'd leave the job site whenever I wanted to. I was just an account to them and they were just a paycheck to me. That's it, short and sweet. How they got an entire thirty page packet out of that was a mystery to me. Either they were full of shit or I was. I guess it was a little of both or maybe someone got paid by the page. The Temp game cuts both ways. There's no loyalty in the work place anymore. These days, it's every man for himself.

It was Danni's idea to meet at Shelter Island for lunch that day. She picked up a couple of Burgers from Mimi's and was already seated at one of the picnic tables that lined the area near the water. Danni was happy to see me but I could tell that she was upset about something. Have sex with anyone enough times and you'll get to know them pretty well.

"What's wrong Mama?" I asked.

"Nothing Papi." Danni said which actually meant that it was something and that she wanted me to ask her again so that she could tell me without feeling as though she were complaining. It took me a while but I had gotten use to the process. Chock it up to one of the many sacrifices you make when in a relationship.

"I can tell that it's something. What happened? Do I need to rough somebody up? You know I'm not afraid. I'd go to jail for you." I said. That was enough to get a chuckle out of her.

"It's my boss Rachel." Danni said. "She's been acting shady ever since they hired Amber, the new sales rep. They're both isolating me from the decision making process. We're supposed to be a team but they're keeping the good sales calls for themselves. I'm getting the leftovers. They have me going all the way out to Temecula and Escondido while they go to La Jolla and Mira Mesa and have lunch together. I walked into Rachel's office to drop off an expense report yesterday and they both stopped talking and acted shocked like I had caught them talking about me or something. I didn't think Rachel was like that." Danni said.

"Like what?" I asked.

"Rachel's like a racist or something. She was so nice at first but now they hire Amber who's white also and they both treat me like the hired help. Like they would rather I was cleaning the toilets and doing their laundry." Danni said.

"Maybe she's not a racist. I think that they're just upset because you're so hot. You know how women are." I said.

I try my best to give people the benefit of the doubt. I also try to call it like I see it. Well, like I hear it in this case. Minorities are quick to scream racism but it's not always the case. This seemed like two women who were mad at Danni for being so gorgeous. Mad at Danni for being on the job for two months and becoming one of the top sellers in the company. She was a natural. Her charisma, beauty and work ethic made her a triple threat. Danni had become a victim of her own success. She had out performed her own boss and now she had enemies.

"It sounds like they're jealous to me." I said.

I hugged Danni and kissed her on the cheek. I told her that we would make it through this together.

"Don't worry. I've got you." I said.

"You got me baby." Danni asked searching for security and protection in my response. The wrong answer could have broken her.

"Yeah, I got you Sweetness." I said as I grabbed her ass. She hollered and we laughed until we were both in tears.

Danni headed back to work but only after I gave her one of my famous pep talks.

I stopped off at a local florist on the way home and bought a dozen roses. I placed them on the dinning room table as I walked through the door of the apartment. They would be a nice surprise for her when she came home.

I changed into my gym clothes and rushed back out the door. Miramar Marine Corps Air Station was a short drive up Interstate-15. I still had my Military ID card and I could get on base whenever I needed to. I drove through the front gate, presented my ID to the gate guard and made a few wrong turns until I found the gym.

It was an indescribable feeling. To be a Marine and not have to take orders anymore. It was the best of both worlds. It was as if nothing had changed. That's what it is to be a Marine. You're in for life no matter how old you are, no matter how long it's been. I made some new friends after a couple sets of bench press.

I hated to leave but I had to go home and check on Danni. I told the guys that I would be back the following day but I knew that this would be a temporary relationship. My ID card would expire in two months time and then I would be just like everyone else and the base would be off limits. Besides, Danni wanted to find a gym closer to home for us to work out in, and that would be my new home away from home.

I pushed through the front door of the apartment and was greeted by Danni standing there in a sexy negligee. It was sheer in all the right places and she left it open so that it barely covered her breast. Her torso was visible all the way down to the matching thong she wore. In her right hand was one of the roses that I left for her. She held it by the stem and gently feathered it up and down her cleavage.

"You are too good to me." Danni said as she walked toward me. She took me by the hand and led me into the bedroom. I pushed her onto the bed and climbed on top of her. I took her negligee off, pulled her thong to the side and made love to her.

"How did the rest of your day go baby?" I asked as I licked the sweat from her navel.

"Just like the beginning." Danni responded, breast still heaving up and down from the heavy breathing. "I haven't gotten any new accounts in two weeks. Rachel is acting funny and the money isn't what she said it would be. I haven't made close to what she said I would. I can't believe she had me move all the way down here for this. I quit my job, left my friends so this bitch could screw me over." Danni said.

"I'm sorry that this is happening baby but we can make it through this. We can find another job for you." I said.

A single tear formed in the corner of her eye and began to roll down her cheek. I moved forward to kiss it away but she pushed me off of her and then sat up right.

"I don't want another job. I moved here for this job." she snapped. "What's everyone going to say when I quit? It would be like I failed. It would be like I couldn't make it down here."

"Baby it's not like…" I said as she jumped out of bed and headed around the corner into the kitchen.

I could no longer see her but I could hear the familiar sound of wine being poured into a glass, Chardonnay to be precise. Her tone of voice and body language had gone from "I love you" to "Don't fucking touch me." in about 5 seconds flat. It would have been impressive if it wasn't so startling. I had never seen her that way. She was isolating herself from me. She had never pushed me away before. She was treating me like I didn't matter. I realized that what little self esteem she had was connected to the success of her new job, and that the idea of it not working out was earth shattering.

Danni finished self medicating and returned to the bedroom. She was in no mood to speak and she didn't want anything to do with me. I decided that it would be in the best interest of world peace for me to keep my hands and words to myself. Sleeping next to a woman who doesn't want you to touch her is harder than it seems. I was so accustomed to reaching out for her in my sleep and holding her close to me. Fighting my desire for her kept me up all night.

Danni's mood hadn't improved by the morning. She dreaded the idea of going to work. She stomped around and made a cup of coffee. She mumbled under her breath about trying to find an outfit to wear and my attempt to hug her and tell her that I loved her was met with a one way kiss.

My work day on the temp job went well and as I imagined, it was no sweat. I over heard one of my co workers talking about a restaurant down town in the Gas Lamp Quarter and I decided that a night out on the town would lift Danni's spirits. We had been so busy getting moved in that we hadn't ventured out to explore the city. Danni just needed to get out and enjoy herself. She needed the chance to go out and be beautiful with me by her side just like old times. A change of pace would do her good.

I raced home after work. It took some coaxing to get Danni to go out that night. She seemed more concerned with going to bed.

"No Danni, we're going out to dinner. I want the entire city to see how beautiful my baby is." I said.

"OK, OK." Danni said as she climbed out of bed.

She used to love going out with me. We used to have so much fun together. I just had to be there for her to lean on until she got over the disappointment of the job.

The Gas Lamp Quarter has so much character and you would never know that it was there. The stores, bars and restaurants were the attraction. There were teenagers, families, couples on dates as well as Marines and Sailors enjoying a little liberty. It reminded me a little of Georgetown in Washington D.C.

We found the restaurant and were soon seated. Our waitress introduced herself and complimented me on the shirt that I wore.

"Thanks." I said.

Danni gave me a look that was part panic, part fury.

"She was cute." Danni said sarcastically.

I never understood why women did that, and I never knew what I was supposed to say when they did.

"I didn't notice." I said.

"Yeah right"

"Danni, I love you. I didn't come all the way down here for the waitress." I said.

"You love me baby?" Danni asked.

"I love you madly." I said as I reset the "Do You Love Me?" clock.

I managed to get Danni to smile and she leaned over the table to kiss me. It had been a whole day since the last time I saw her smile. My confidence shot through the roof and I was able to keep her laughing until dinner was over.

The side walks were crowded for a Tuesday night. The parking lot where we left my car was only two blocks away. I held Danni's hand and guided her to walk behind me so that I could cut through the foot traffic. There were people coming, people going, people bumping into me, and one asshole in particular who was drunk and felt the need to prove his manhood to the nearest unsuspecting passerby. That would be me.

He was a small guy with a big walk and he was full of liquid courage. The fact that he was with two friends only fueled his macho fire. His shoulder bumped into me and he spun around. These types of things often happened when in a busy city and I hadn't paid it too much attention until I heard him say "Hey, what the fuck man."
I took another two steps while simultaneously moving Danni in front of me as I looked over my shoulder.

"Sorry." I said as I looked him up and down.

It was important to evaluate him in order to gauge his threat potential. Did he have any weapons or a bottle? Did he look tough? Were his feet positioned as a trained fighter would position his feet? More importantly, where were his hands and had he balled them up into fists yet?

After a quick and careful analysis, I surmised that he was a big wet pussy and that it wouldn't have taken me long to cut through him like a hot hatchet through butter. He was also drunk and there wasn't much sport in that. Besides, I had Danni with me and my first priority was ensuring her safety.

"You just gonna fucking walk into me? That's bullshit." He said. He was serious. So was I.

"I apologized. But that's all you get. How about you go your way and I go mine? Does that work for you?" I said in a tone of voice that seemed to instantly sober him up and inform him that he was way out of his league.

His two friends looked on nervously. One in particular looked pissed off as if to indicate that this happened more than once while in his company. The drunk's friends grabbed him by the shoulders and ushered him away.

"Drunken asshole!" Danni said as we walked away. "I can't believe him. He's lucky you let him go. You would have totally beat his ass."

"Watch your mouth." I said hoping that I could one day break her from the habit of swearing.

"I wouldn't beat him baby. He was drunk and he got a little ahead of himself. I'm not a bully and I don't commit to violence unless I have to. Besides everybody deserves a second chance and he just got his." I said.

"Well, he needs to be taught a lesson" Danni said.

"Don't you worry baby. Vengeance is mine sayeth the Lord. He'll get his and we won't have to lift a finger." I said.

"Listen to you. You haven't been to church in years and now you're talking like a preacher or something. How can you be so sure?" Danni said.

"Karma's a bitch and in that way life is fair. No one gets away with doing wrong. Everybody pays sooner or later." I said.

"You're such a wise man baby." Danni said as she held my arm and snuggled closer to me as we walked. "You make me feel so safe."

We reached my car and I opened the door for Danni and closed it as she put on her seat belt. We eased out of the parking lot and drove home. Our night out on the town was just what the doctor ordered. Danni was herself again, smiling and riding shotgun with her man.

5:30 am came a lot faster than either one of us wanted it to. I turned off the alarm clock and Danni took refuge from the sound by pulling the covers over her head and holding me even tighter.

"Time to go baby." I said as I kissed her forehead.

"No baby. Stay with me." Danni said.

She didn't have to leave until 9:30am to make a sales call in Balboa.

"I have to be to work at 7:30, remember?"

"It's just a stupid temp job. You could go late if you really wanted to. Who cares what they say Cole." Danni said.

"I care Danni. I said I'd be there at 7:30 and that's when I'll be there. I'm a man of my word remember. That's supposed to be one of the things you love about me."

"Yeah, you're so perfect." Danni said.

It was border line disrespectful. The very thought of going to work upset her and brought out her dark side.

"Danni, don't mistreat me because your job isn't going the way you want it to. I wouldn't do that to you." I said.

I was doing my best to be understanding but she was beginning to grate on me.

"I know. I'm sorry baby." she said. "I just hate going to work anymore. Every morning I wake up I wonder what Rachel will do next. How she will criticize me? What nasty comment she'll make next? She's making me miserable."

"She's making me miserable too." I thought.

A few months passed by and each morning went the same way. Danni and I joined the local Bally Total Fitness in Mira Mesa and I hoped that the exercise would help her manage her stress but it didn't. The government security clearance that I was given in the Marine Corps enabled me to get a job working as a Logistics Specialist for Tacwar systems. Tacwar was a defense contractor that developed advanced sensor suites for the U.S. Navy's next generation surface fleet.

Danni was still working for Rachel and each day took its toll on both of us. The only time that she wasn't sad was on the weekends but she suffered a mild panic attack each Sunday evening, dreading what the following Monday would bring. I encouraged her to let me help her find another job but she still wouldn't let go. She was waiting to get a quarterly bonus and she was also trying to transfer to another group within the company to work for Chip Price.

Chip was a very successful Team Leader who had a great track record. He took notice of Danni's ability to close the deal on a consistent basis as well as her ass. He made mention that he would like to have Danni on his team on more than one occasion, but Rachel was doing her best to prevent Danni's continued success. She knew that Danni would be the next big thing if Chip took her under his wing and mentored her. On the other hand, my new position with Tacwar was going extremely well.

Tacwar's headquarters building was located right on the edge of the San Diego bay near Point Loma. My boss Dave was an easy going guy who seemed more concerned with getting off work early to go surfing than with my performance. My new coworker Jessi had been promoted and was training me to take her old position. She was 41 years old and hot!!! She had a twenty year old son and a four year old grand daughter named Maribel. Maribel's mother was in rehab so Jessi and her son raised her together.

Jessi and I always found something to laugh about which made the day go by faster. I was excited about going to work each day but found myself the victim of Danni's sarcasm any time I mentioned Jessi or how well we got along.

I made several friends on the job, one of them being James. James was a carpenter who was there working to reconfigure an existing office space. One day James asked me if I wanted to go to the Gas Lamp Quarter and grab a drink and I accepted. It had been a while since I'd gone out and had a drink. I realized how much of my life I had dedicated to Danni and her troubles.

Danni called that morning as she always did and had a minor meltdown when I told about my plans for the evening.

"Why do you have to go out tonight? I wanted to see you." Danni said.

"You'll see me when I get home baby. I'm just going to have a drink and some guy talk and then I'll be home."

"So now you're hanging out in bars. What are you guys going to do, meet up with some girls that he knows?" Danni said.

"Danni, I'm at work and I can't get into this here. You are really over reacting."

"Am I really? You go ahead and have your drink. I knew this would happen." Danni said.

"What? You knew what would happen? What are you talking about? It's just a beer." I whispered. "I can't do this now. I'll talk to you when I get home."

"FINE!" Danni said and punctuated her statement with the dial tone.

"Trouble in paradise?" Jessi asked.

"She's acting crazy. She was never been like this before. I'm just going to grab a beer with James after work and she's acting as if I'm going to hook up with some chick. Then she says that she knew this would happen. What in the hell does that even mean?" I said.

"It's ok." Jessi said as she rubbed my shoulders. "She sounds like she's under a lot of pressure with the new job and moving. You're a nice guy. She'll come around soon. There is also the age difference Cole. I'm sure that the stress from the new job is just adding to her feeling insecure about a few things, especially you." Jessi said.

"But I've never cheated on her or anything." I said.

"I didn't say that she had a point. I just said that she was feeling insecure. Look, you're a good looking guy and there are a lot of women in this city." Jessi said.

"Yeah, I noticed." I said.

"It's just that you're eleven years younger than she is and my guess is that she's worried about you eventually leaving her for a younger woman. It may not sound like much to you but it's a big deal to her. That's why I never date younger men. My boy friend is four years older than I am and I like it that way." Jessi said.

"She's driving me crazy Jessi. You're a smart woman. Tell me what I should do to make things like they used to be." I said.

"Well" Jessi began and then paused for a second as she gathered her thoughts. It was the kind of pause that made me think that she didn't know what she was about to say next.

"Well, try to be a little more patient with her. Take her out with you and your new friends so she can meet them and see that they aren't the type that will invite you to an orgy at the Play Boy mansion. But just realize that you can't make things they way they were. That was the desert, this is San Diego. Things are going to be different, and the two of you will have to adjust or go your separate ways. There's nothing wrong with that you know." Jessi said.

"What do you mean?"

"I mean that if you guys have to part as friends, then that's better than hating each other and parting as enemies. It's not a good idea to make enemies out of people who know you that well." Jessi said.

I told James that something came up and that I wouldn't be able to hang out with him. He gave me a look that loosely translated into "You're a Pussy!" and he was right. I wanted to speak to Danni about all of this as soon as possible. We couldn't go on that way. I thought about everything Jessi said as I drove home from work. Jessi was like the big sister that I never had but always wanted. I hated being the oldest child. I used to wish that I had an older sister to ask for advice, to nurture me the way my mother should have and to beat at a round of "Duck the Shoe".

I came home but there was no sign of Danni. I immediately headed to the refrigerator and grabbed a beer. I popped the top of the bottle and was in mid chug when the phone rang.

"What" I snapped.

"Hey Cole. It's Maria."

Her voice was a welcomed relief. It was familiar and comforting, and reminded me of that night at the Pueblo Pub and how happy we all were. Maria and Danni spoke on the phone all of the time but not even Maria cheered her up any more.

"Maria...how are you?" I asked.

"I'm good. Where's Danni?" Maria asked.

"She's not here. I just got in from work. I was looking for her myself."

"How is she doing? She sounds so miserable each time I talk to her. I've been asking her what's wrong but she won't tell me." Maria said.

"Don't tell her I told you this but her job hasn't been working out and it's killing her."

"What is that bitch doing to her?" Maria asked.

"What... you know about Rachel?"

"Yes! I met her at an office Christmas party that Danni invited me to once. I hated her from the start. Danni never admitted it, but she thinks hanging out with her will make her legitimate or something. It's like Danni is ashamed of being a Latina and she wants to be white. She's always been like that" Maria said.

"I know exactly what you mean. Maria, I'm at the end of my rope with her. I used to be able to cheer her up but nothing I do helps anymore. You've known her longer than I have. Do you have any ideas?" I said.

"You know what, I think I do. I'll call her later tonight and tell her that I want to come down to visit. Maybe I can break her out of this, Latina to Latina." Maria said.

I thanked Maria and finished my beer and the next two as well.

Danni came home two hours later and told me that she went out to happy hour with her co-workers when I asked her where she had been. I chugged beer number four and went to straight to bed.

Maria left work early and arrived that Friday evening. Danni and I took her out to dinner and it felt just like old times. Danni actually smiled. I proposed a toast. "To good times and better friends."

We laughed and told old stories and stumbled out of the restaurant looking for a bar with a live band.

Danni and Maria went to La Jolla to go shopping the next day. I went to the gym and came straight home when I was done working out. I called my friend Wayne who lived back east. He was nine years older than I was and like a brother to me. He never missed an opportunity to act the part and I credit him with putting me on the right path in life.

Wayne had served in the Marine Corps as well and I listened intently to his stories of boot camp, Panama and bar room brawls.

We met when I was nineteen. I brought my car into the garage that he worked in with a broken tie rod and we had been friends ever since. Oddly enough, Wayne didn't approve of me joining the Marine Corps.

"You don't know what you're in for!" he warned but I was determined.

His tune changed when I came home from boot camp in my new uniform. We hadn't spoken in a while and had a lot of catching up to do. Wayne had opened his own garage a year and a half earlier. His son had just turned three and was as smart as a whip. He and his wife were having trouble but he said that they could work it out. Wayne asked about Danni and when I was bringing her back east to meet him. I told him about our latest troubles to which he responded "Women, you can't live with 'em and you can't fuck without 'em."

Danni and Maria returned from their shopping excursion with bags from every boutique in La Jolla. We ordered a pizza and watched a movie that evening. It was a forgettable film about the love affair between a wealthy real estate mogul and a waitress. Women pick the worst movies. I think they do it on purpose to cleverly torture the men in their lives. Either that or they actually believe in all of that fairy tale bullshit. Danni self medicated a little too much that evening and went to bed early. Maria and I stayed up talking and laughing until 2:30 am.

Maria mentioned that Danni and I seemed very distant. It was as if we weren't the same couple that she once knew. I agreed and grabbed another beer from the refrigerator.

"Danni's already drunk Cole. She doesn't need any more to drink." Maria said.

Maria was so funny and her sense of humor was just like mine. Maria was taller than Danni was and six years younger too. She wore her hair longer and I always liked the way she looked when she pulled it into a pony tail. Maria wasn't dating anyone at the moment and was always so complimentary toward me. I began to think that I had it all wrong that night I met them and I wondered if I picked the wrong one.

The three of us had brunch together on Coronado Island at the Hotel Del Coronado the next morning. The pelicans flew overhead in an ominous formation and there were children at play in the sand. The ocean breeze blew Maria's hair into her face and she gently brushed it back into place. She was captivating and I wondered how it was that I never really noticed before. Maria caught me staring at her and smiled. It wasn't just a smile, it was more.

My eyes darted back to Danni. She was busy waving at the passengers on a passing ocean liner. Mimosas always put her in a good mood. We finished our meal and watched the waves pound the beach. It was a beautiful sight and I hoped that it would have a lasting effect on us. Maria left a few hours later. Danni hugged her and looked as if she may cry. We waved good bye as Maria drove off and that's when all hell broke loose.

"I bet you'll miss her more than I will." Danni said as soon as we walked back into the apartment.

"What?"

"I heard you two last night. Laughing and whispering. It sounded like you were having a real good time. You didn't even come to check on me." Danni said.

"Are you serious?" I asked.

"You know what Cole, you shouldn't be so obvious. If you want her then go be with her or anyone else you want." Danni said.

"You know what, you have been impossible to live with for the past four months. I'm damn good to you and I don't deserve this shit." I yelled.

"Don't curse at me. I won't stand for it." Danni said.

"Quit the job Danni. It's killing the both of us." I said.

"You don't tell me what to do Cole. I'm not one of your Marines." Danni said.

"Quit the job Danni." I repeated but this time much louder.

"No!" Danni yelled.

"Quit the job Danni. The job is the problem, not me." I said getting more furious with each passing second.

"No!" Danni yelled even louder as she headed into the bed room and slammed the door shut.

"Quit...the ...fucking ...job....Danni!" I said, over annunciating each word to drive the point home.

Danni yanked the bedroom door open and threw a full water bottle hitting me in the chest.

"Fuck you Cole!" Danni screamed as she slammed the door shut again.

She had never been violent before. I couldn't believe it. Flashbacks of growing up and watching Darrell pummel my mother flooded my mind. I left the apartment and didn't really know where I was going until I parked at Shelter Island.

"Ham was right. God damn it, he was right. It is different when you live with them." I thought.

I called Mike. I hadn't talked to him in a couple of weeks.

"Damn, she did that to you?" Mike said. "Faith just hits me but she never throws anything. That's crazy! She could have really hurt you."

"Yeah I know." I said.

"How long do you plan on sitting in the car watching the world go by?" Mike asked.

"I hadn't really thought about it."

"I'm cooking on the grill. Why don't you come up and hang out for a while before you go home?" Mike said.

I accepted his offer and made the drive to Camp Pendleton. I found Mike in the back yard grilling a couple of steaks. His son Dion was playing football with a couple of neighborhood kids. Faith brought Mike some hot dogs and burgers to cook and asked me how I was. I lied and told her that I was fine. Mike tossed me a beer and then a second after I chugged the first.

"So she threw a whole bottle of water at you?" Mike asked.

"Yeah, and the worst part is that it hit me." I said.

"And that's when you walked out?" Mike asked.

"Yeah."

"Well it's good that you left because you would've killed her if you threw it back." Mike said.

"That's true but I would never do that. I would leave before I did something like that." I said.

"I remember the first time I met Danni. I was jealous. I thought she was a perfect angel but now...shit! Welcome to the club." Mike said.

"Yeah, I know exactly what you mean."

"What's the problem? Is her job really that bad?" Mike asked.

Low Fuel

"She's changed. She's not the same person anymore. I'm trying to make a new life for us down here and she's falling apart and blaming me for everything. If her boss screws her over, it's my fault. It rained yesterday and she blamed it on me. I told her to quit the job but she won't. It's like her self esteem is tied up in the position and the title. She's acting like she's nothing without it. She used to think I was the best thing since seedless grapes and now she's throwing shit at me. I can't take it anymore Mike. This is beneath my dignity. I'm going to leave if this keeps up. I'm all out of patience." I said.

"Damn dude. Well just know that I support you if you feel as though you have to go. But you know you wouldn't be having this problem if you would have just given Gabrielle some community service. She would never throw anything at you. She'd be too busy trying to fuck you to death." Mike said.

I left Mike's place at about 11:00 PM that night. I took my time getting home and spent the night on the couch. I left for work before Danni woke up. I just didn't feel like arguing with her or worse...listening to her tearful apology. I hate it when they cry.

Danni called me at work that morning and apologized. She ranted non-stop about her job and about being emotional and that it wouldn't happen again.

Jessi walked by and asked me for the latest inventory report.

"Anything for you." I said in jest as I handed it to her.

"Who is that?" Danni asked.

"That's Jessi."

"Oh, so you flirt with her on the job in front of everybody." Danni said.

"Baby, I'm not flirting, I'm working. What are you talking about?" I whispered.

"Do what you want Cole!" Danni said before hanging up the phone.

At that moment something funny happened. I was relieved. I should have been upset that Danni hung up the phone but I wasn't. I was glad that it was over. I grabbed a chicken club sub sandwich from Gus's sub shop after work and headed for my home away from home, Shelter Island.

It was becoming a habit but I was happier there than I was at home. It was beautiful and going home was a pain in the ass. It wouldn't be safe to return home until at least 8:00 pm any way. Then I could take a shower and listen to Danni's bitching and moaning as I drifted off to dream land. I watched a cruise ship sail out of the bay and I wondered how many people on board were in my same predicament. I wondered how many passengers on board that ship would rather be going off to sea than going home to their so called "loved one".

It's a damned shame when you can't go home for fear of drama.

I left Shelter Island after the sunset and drove over to the mall in Fashion Valley. I figured that I would just do a little window shopping. That's what people do when they are troubled.

It's either shopping or drugs. I preferred shopping.

I walked in to Miller's Outpost. It was one of those trendy, hip stores that sold those obnoxious t-shirts to teenagers. You know the ones that say "Boy's suck!" or "I lie!" or my personal favorite, "Juicy". I found a pair of boxer shorts that I liked and stood in line to buy them. They were black and made of a polyester-spandex blend and featured a button fly and a condom pocket.

"Wow, a condom pocket, what will they think of next?" I thought.

I took them to the register and was greeted by a very friendly blonde with breast implants.

"Wow, man made tits, what will they think of next?" I thought.

"Hi." She said.

"Wow, man made tits and she can speak too. Isn't 21st century technology amazing?" I thought.

"Hey, what's up?" I said as I handed her the boxers.

"Oooh, these look so comfortable." She said as she held the boxer shorts up at waste level and imagined me in them. "And they even have a condom pocket!" she said as she arched an eyebrow and smiled.

"What will they think of next?" I asked as I handed her the cash.

The thought of asking her out so that I could bang the silicone out of her crossed my mind, but I decided that going home to argue with Danni would be much more fun.

Women should never, under any circumstances accuse a faithful man of cheating. He may ignore it the first time but he will eventually begin to feel as if he has suffered the punishment without actually enjoying the crime. All of the pain, none of the pleasure. He will then either cheat or wish that he had, and neither one is good for a relationship.

I found myself thinking of the "Bionic Blonde" a little more than I should have and I actually considered going back to Miller's Outpost that weekend to buy some more boxers.

I turned the key, opened the front door of the apartment, and proceeded to walk right passed Danni as she asked me where I had been and if I had was out with Jessi. I sat down on the edge of the bed and took off my shoes. I was in my own world and I couldn't hear anything she was saying.

"DO YOU HEAR ME?" Danni asked as she grabbed my arm. "WHERE WERE YOU? DO YOU HEAR ME?" Danni demanded.

Every man has his limit. Some men you can push, some men you can't. Some men let you get away with it because they love you and hope that you'll come to your senses before it's too late. Some men just remain calm and do what needs to be done.

"I can't take this anymore. I'm moving out." I said. "DO YOU HEAR ME? I'M MOVING OUT."

FOUR

"Too crowded." I thought as I read the ad for the apartment for rent in Little Italy.

"Too far." I thought as I read the ad for the apartment for rent in El Cajon.

I had four leads to check up on that week and they all looked promising. They were all close to work and the rent wasn't too much. They each had a washer and dryer as well. I hated going to the Laundromat ever since Twenty-nine Palms. The wait for a washer was unbearable and it took two washes to purge the sand from your clothing.

Danni was in a state of shock. She begged me to stay but the topic wasn't up for discussion. I told her that it was for the best but she refused to accept the truth. I hated to leave her that way because it made me feel like a failure. We were supposed to start a new life together not new drama.

There was however, a part of me that was delighted to see her hurting. Danni should have known better than to mistreat me. I loved her and would've done anything to make her happy. Anything except being mistreated. Danni said that I felt distant and that she was afraid that she would lose me. I told her that I still loved her and that we would still be together. It was just that we couldn't live together anymore.

Danni asked me to make love to her and I was more than happy to oblige. It had been a while since we had sex but it was different this time. Pleasing her was the last thing on my mind. I was indifferent about it all. I usually took pride in the pleasure that I could deliver to her but no longer. It was time for me to be concerned with myself. Being Mr. Nice Guy had gotten me absolutely no where. Being Mr. Nice Guy gets everyone absolutely no where.

We lay there when we were done and it almost felt like it had before. That was until she began to cry.

"Please don't leave me Cole. I don't want to lose you. Please give me another chance. Please Papi." Danni said.

I couldn't take the sight of her crying. It tore at me. I thought I was immune to the "Ultimate Weapon" but it was different with her. I felt as if I may even cry myself. I was vulnerable to her despite all of my anger and for a moment, my resolve wavered…just a bit.

"Danni, I love you but you've changed so much since we got down here. You treat me like I don't even matter."

"You do matter to me Cole. I'm sorry." Danni said.

"This job is killing us both Danni. I know we came here for it but is it really more important to you than I am? Why can't you find something else? I'll help you."

Danni looked distressed. Her tears dropped even faster for a moment and then stopped abruptly. She closed her eyes tightly and then opened them after a few seconds.

"I'll get another job." Danni said softly.
So softly that I could tell that it hurt her to say it. In fact, it almost killed her to say it. The sacrifice did not go unnoticed.

"I get my bonus next month. I've worked too hard to leave without it. I'll find something else after that. I promise." Danni said.

"OK baby. I understand." I said.

I held Danni close and tried to reinvest my faith in her.

Danni and I faced the next few weeks with a renewed sense of optimism. It was almost like old times… almost. Christmas passed and so did New Years day. We exchanged gifts, made our resolutions and hoped for the best.

We sat on the couch one night and watched a comedy about a love affair that would have been doomed from the start in the real world, but seemed to work out by the end of the film. I shifted my attention toward her during the second act of the movie. Danni was laughing uncontrollable and she would have looked happy to anyone else. Anyone other than some one who truly knew her. Something was bothering her and I began to wonder if she would keep her promise after she received the bonus.

Jessi and I left work that Friday and walked to the parking lot together as we always did.

"So, today's the big day?" Jessi asked.

"Yeah, she should have gotten it already." I said.

"What do you mean she should have? Haven't you spoken to her? Danni always calls you each morning, doesn't she?" Jessi asked.

"Yeah, she normally does but not today. I tried to call her but I didn't get an answer." I said.

"What do you think is going on?" Jessi asked.

"I'm afraid to tell you."

I said goodbye to Jessi and left the parking lot on a collision course with chaos. I had that feeling again, that feeling that something was very wrong. That felling that you get all though you don't have a shred of evidence to support it. That feeling that you should have learned to appreciate by now but haven't.

Danni was a motor mouth and the only time that she didn't call me was when she was depressed or upset.

"What if she got the bonus and decided that it was too much money to give up? What if she changed her mind about quitting her job? What if…..what if…. what if?" I wondered.

A shiver of trepidation ran down my spine as I neared the door of the apartment. I mustered the courage to turn the key and push. Danni was sitting in the living room floor with an empty bottle of wine at her side.

"Baby, what's going on?" I yelled as I ran over to her.

Danni didn't acknowledge me, not even when I kneeled down beside her and took her by the hand. She was in her own little world and judging by the looks of her, it was coming to an end.

"Baby, what is it?" I asked.

It was almost as if I were trying to assist a stranger who had taken a stumble. I gently turned her head so that she was facing me.

"Baby…?" I tried again.

"Rachel…dumb bitch." Danni said incoherently. "They gave me $600.00 not the $6,000. Rachel screwed me."

Danni's speech was slurred and her eyes were vacant.

"What?" I asked.

"The bonus was only $600. Rachel gave me a bad evaluation and that's what they gave me. The bitch screwed me. I'm sorry Cole. I failed you. I can't do anything right. I wanted to make you proud of me." Danni said.

"No, no baby. I'm very proud of you. I love you. We'll get through this together. We'll find you another job baby. Come here. I'll take care of you." I said.

I picked her up, carried her into the bedroom, undressed her and placed her under the covers. I watched over her that night and even held her hair out of the way when she puked. Now that's love.

"Coffee, black. That's good for a hangover right?" I thought.

I struggled to remember the ingredients of a hangover cure that I was given years earlier but I was too drunk at the time to recall what was in it. I heard something about Tabasco sauce but I couldn't remember what.

"Were you supposed to put it in the coffee or drink a shot of it? Black coffee's bad enough, what could it hurt if I added a shot of Tabasco." I thought.

I handed the mug of coffee to Danni as she stepped out of the shower.

"Thanks." She whispered and then took a sip.

"Oh God! What did you put in here? It tastes sour." Danni said.

"Oh, that's my grandfather's old hang over cure. It really works. He did a lot of drinking and perfected the recipe over a lot of hangovers. You'll feel better soon. You'll see." I said.

"Do I look as bad as I feel?" Danni asked.

"You're my beautiful angel." I answered as I kissed her lips.

"You didn't really answer my question but thank you." Danni said.

She looked a little queasy but she was still gorgeous. I looked at her doing my best to locate a trace of the women I met that night at the Pueblo Pub, but we were a long way from the desert.

"Had she actually changed that much or was it that I never really knew her at all?" I asked myself.

Danni sat on the edge of the bed and rubbed lotion on her legs.

"¡Aye Dios mio!" Danni said and then sighed. "Why God, why?"

"There's a happy ending coming baby. Just hold on 'till it gets here." I said as I sat down beside her. Danni leaned against me and put her head on my shoulder. I wrapped my arm around her and she promised me that she would get in touch with a few contacts about finding another job.

We went to the gym together that night. I figured that it would be good to work out together just like we used to. Hopefully it would help her burn off some of her anger and frustration. Danni headed to the elliptical trainer for some cardio vascular exercise and I made my way toward the squat rack. I finished squatting 405 lbs. when I noticed a woman who was looking for a couple of 45 pound plates to place on the leg press machine.

She was tall and she had a very hot body. Her face on the other hand looked like an old car wreck.

"Here you go." I said as I removed two 45 pound plates from the bar that I was using and placed one on each side of the leg press machine for her.

"Thank you. Those things are heavy and I have a problem with my lower back. You're a life saver." she said.

I told her that it was no problem and walked away toward the pull up bar.

"You've never done that for me."

I turned around and saw Danni standing there with her hands on her hips and wearing a pissed off expression.

"Do you want her?" Danni asked.

"What...what are you talking about? I asked.

"You have never put the weights on a machine for me but you did it for her. Are you after her? Is it because she's black? Is that it?" Danni asked.

"Danni lower your voice for Christ sake." I pleaded.

I was embarrassed as well as frustrated.

"Do you want to be with a black woman again? Is that what it is Cole?" Danni asked.

I stared at her for a moment attempting to figure out what crime against humanity I committed to deserve such punishment and then walked away.

"You need therapy." I said as I headed for the front door.

I was through with her and her bullshit. I just needed some air. I just needed a break before I caused a scene.

I walked through the parking lot and sat in my car. I turned the radio on and let the seat all the way back. I lay there for twenty four minutes exactly until Danni opened the passenger side door and sat down beside me. It actually took her that long to realize that I left the gym. I started the car up as she put on her seat belt. We drove out of the parking lot and down the road. I took the on ramp to the I-15 freeway when she told me that she was sorry.

I remained silent and changed lanes to get around the dump truck that was going much too slow for the fast lane. I kept my hands on the wheel and a stoic expression on my face. I didn't say a word but I was thinking of plenty of them.

"That's it. I have to go. This is ridiculous. She's not going to change." I thought.

We got home and I took a shower. I grabbed a bite to eat and lay on the bed to watch television.

Danni came in to the bedroom and lay down beside me. I didn't speak to her. I didn't have the energy to dedicate toward her anymore. Arguing consumes so much energy, mentally, physically and emotionally.

"I'm sorry Cole, ok." Danni said.

"You're always sorry. You're apologies are losing their significance." I said.

"I just get jealous sometimes." Danni said.

"Jealous of what? I moved down here for us, so that we could be together. This has been such a waste of time. I have to go Danni but you should get a therapist or something. I'm not the one you're angry with. I'm just the one you're taking your anger out on." I said.

It was business as usual for the next two weeks. We both went to work and tip toed around each other when we were home. I found myself parked at Shelter Island watching the sunset more and more. Danni made the attempt to smooth things out but I didn't care. I was preoccupied with looking for another apartment to move into. Besides, I was sick and tired of dealing with her.

Danni hadn't found another job but she did find a therapist. Her name was Heather and they met one Tuesday at 5:30 pm. It went well according to Danni and she would be returning each Tuesday at that same time.

I finally won a game of phone tag when Mike answered the phone. We made plans to grab a beer that Saturday afternoon. I hung up the phone and saw that Danni was almost in tears.

"What?"

"You hate me." Danni said.

"No. I don't hate you." I said.

"Then why won't you even look at me anymore?" Danni asked.

"It'll be better once I move out. This didn't work out too well and we need to do what is best for both of us." I said.

Danni and I awoke on Saturday morning and had breakfast. She had a sales call to make in Mira Mesa and I planned on going to the gym. I kissed her goodbye and sat down on the couch to watch television. I began to feel sick to my stomach a short while later. It was alarming because I never got sick. I had a cast iron stomach and an immune system that would make a billy goat jealous. My right eye began to twitch uncontrollably.

I poured a glass of milk hoping that it would coat my stomach and it did. I lay on the couch for about an hour until I felt well enough to get up. My eye slowly stopped twitching. I didn't feel well but I didn't care. Being with Danni was stressing me out and I needed to hit the weights before I hit her.

I came home from the gym and ran into Danni as I came out of the shower wrapped in a towel.

"Hey, how was work?" I asked.

"It was ok. How was your work out?" Danni asked.

"It was ok". I said as I watched her take off her blouse.

It's amazing how being pissed off at a woman can cause you to ignore that fact that they are absolutely gorgeous. It's even more amazing that you can forget how pissed off you are at a woman when you watch them getting undressed.

Danni noticed me checking her out and asked if I saw something I liked.

"Maybe." I said as she unzipped her skirt and let it fall to the ground revealing her thong.

"How about now?"

"Possibly." I said.

Danni began to walk toward me and removed her bra.

"And now?" Danni asked as she stood there nude from the waist up.

"Took you long enough." I said as I dropped my towel.

"It's called foreplay, junior." Danni said as she lay down on the bed with her legs spread.

"You coming?" Danni asked.

"Yeah, but not for a while." I said.

I got up at about 3:30pm and took a shower. I grabbed a towel from the linen closet, dried off and got dressed. I would be meeting Mike downtown at 5:00PM.

"Cole, what are you doing?" Danni asked.

"I gotta meet Mike downtown. I'll be back in a few hours."

"You're just going to leave me here like this?" Danni said.

"What do you mean? You knew that I was going to meet Mike today." I said.

"So I guess I'm the victim of a hit and run? You're just going to fuck me and then go to some bar and then what?" Danni said.

"Danni, we've been down here for 9 months and I don't have any friends. You get upset anytime I want to go anywhere. You're so selfish. I knew Mike before I even met you and if I want to have a beer with him than I will." I said.

"Well, I don't want you to go." Danni said.

"Why Danni? What's the problem?" I asked.

"Because Cole, like there won't be girls there." Danni said.

"Well there is an entire city out there and they do let women go to bars if they want to. Are you serious?" I said.

"I feel neglected." Danni said.

"You're so full of shit. You thought that you could just throw that ass on me and I would forget about meeting up with Mike. Is that what you thought?" I said.

"Don't talk to me like that." Danni said.

"Like what? Like the truth?" I asked.

"No, like I don't matter, like I'm some chick standing on the corner waiting for a trick." Danni. said.

I left the bedroom for the front door as I buttoned the last few buttons on my shirt.

"Gotta go." I said.

"So you just walk out on me Cole? Is that it?" Danni asked.

"Danni, you're crazy but don't worry. We'll argue....I mean talk later." I said.

"You're an assho…" Danni said as I slammed the door closed.

"Why me?" I thought as I drove out of the parking garage that was under the apartment building.

I parked the car in one of the many public parking lots that occupy the Gas Lamp Quarter. A short walk later and I found Gatsby's. It was one of the many bar and grills that populated downtown San Diego. It was full of character, history and booze. Just what the doctor ordered… the booze I mean.

I walked inside and traded the busy streets of downtown San Diego for the dimly lit bar and the partially inebriated patrons inside. Maintaining a buzz is a tricky thing. It's just like the "Goldie Locks Zone". That's the place the Earth occupies in the solar system.

Too close and you'll be a scorched skid mark like Mercury. Too far away and you'll either be a giant ball of gas like Jupiter or an ice cold waste of time like Pluto. A good bar patron must learn to understand their tolerance and nurture their buzz. You must achieve the "Goldie Locks Zone" and orbit there until an hour before you leave the bar. Any more than that and you would be a certifiable asshole, or the recipient of the "Black Eye" award which was proudly presented by the nearest bouncer.

Bouncers love to present awards. Chief among them are, the fist across the chin award, the knee to the nuts award and the coveted "Throwing your ass down the mother fucking stairs award" but more on this later.

The digital juke box was playing "Free Bird" by Lynard Skynard and I wondered if I should've taken the advice and left town. There were a couple of dart boards and a pool table in the far corner of the bar with several young men creating a ruckus as they played. I greeted the hostess and walked past her looking for Mike. I couldn't find him until I heard him yell "Cole!" and turned my head to see him standing by the bar.

Mike was loud, inappropriately loud. I walked past the many bar patrons whose attention was now focused on me thanks to Mike's mouth.

"Hey brotha." I said as we shook hands and hugged.

"What's up?" Mike asked as we sat at the bar.

"More of the same." I said.

"That bad?" Mike asked.

"Man, I just argued my way out of the door on the way over here. We had sex and I thought she wanted to be with me. It turns out that she thought that I would fall asleep and forget about coming out tonight if she gave me some." I said.

"Yeah, they do that sometimes. It's just part of being in a relationship." Mike said.

"Danni actually told me that she didn't want me meeting you here tonight because there would be girls here. Can you believe that dumb shit?"

"Did she catch you screwing around? Did you get busted with Gabrielle?" Mike asked as he busted into uncontrollable laughter.

Once again every head in the bar turned to see the source of the commotion.

"Do you know that you're inappropriately loud?" I asked.

"Shit, I gotta be me. I don't know no other way. Besides, these people love me. Thank you, thank you." Mike said as he stood up to take a bow to his adoring fans?

He received several boo's for his trouble and promptly took his seat.

"What you gotta be is a fool, and that's every chance you get. Now let's stay on topic. I can't live like this. I haven't done anything wrong but I've been treated like property and not like a boyfriend. I've never cheated on her and I've never wanted to. I have however had many opportunities, but I have chosen to remain faithful each and every time. I'm the greatest boyfriend in the history of the world." I said.

"No. You're miserable, just like the rest of us." Mike said.

"It doesn't have to be this way" I said.

"No it doesn't, but it is. You've got a choice to make Cole. Be lonely and lead a simple life, or be in a relationship and every day will bring new drama that doesn't make any sense." Mike said.

"Can't live with 'em, can't fuck with out 'em?" I asked.

"Bingo! Now you're learning." Mike said.

I sat there, staring at my beer pondering Mike's last statement.

"Don't look so sad. It's just the way things are. What is it that you always say about reality?

It sucks?" Mike said.

"No, no. It goes. "Reality sucks but it will never lie to you. That's how it goes." I said.

"Yeah, that's what I'm saying. Reality dude, it sucks but that's the way it is." Mike said.

We were interrupted by a loud "Whooo!" that emanated from the direction of the pool table. I looked up to see 7 young college aged guys whooping it up in the hopes of getting the attention of the 5 college aged girls who were seated nearby.

"You see that dumb shit?" I asked.

"You mean the guy who just missed the combination shot?" Mike asked.

"No! I mean those guys over there trying to get the attention of those girls by yelling and making all that noise." I said.

"Oh, that. Yeah I saw that. They must be too chicken shit to talk to them." Mike said.

"Exactly, when did that start?" I asked.

"It must be new for a man not to ask a woman for her phone number in a bar. I thought that's why they made bars, so that you could meet women. I would ask them if they wanted to play pool and leave with the prettiest one after that. That is if I weren't happily married." Mike said.

"Ya' know those young boys don't know what they're in for." I said.

"What do you mean?" Mike asked.

"I met Danni in a spot like this and now look at us. What if one of those boys finds the courage to speak to one of those girls? Odds are that he'll be miserable too in a short while." I said.

"Only if they move in together." Mike said and then let out a loud roar of laughter.

"So much for true love." I said.

"Oh, there's true love, truly a mess. Just look on the bright side, at least you don't have any kids together, then things would really be a mess." Mike said.

"You know, if I had it to do all over again, I wouldn't be in a relationship until I was 27 years old. I'd be a millionaire by now." I said.

"Yeah but you'd be so naive that the first woman you slept with would marry you and take all your money." Mike said.

"I guess you're right." I said.

"You'll be alright, you're a Marine." Mike said.

"Semper Fi".

Danni asked me to go to her therapy session that Tuesday. Heather thought that it would be a good idea to hear my take on the relationship. We parked in front of the building and held hands as we entered the office. I wasn't too sure about the whole thing. I had a bad headache and I wasn't in the best mood since my eye continued to twitch.

"Hello Danni." Heather said as she walked into the lobby. "Is this Cole?"

I introduced myself and Heather walked us back to her office.

Danni and I took a seat on the couch while Heather sat on the opposite side of the room in her chair. Heather pulled out a pad of paper and started the session.

"Well first I want to thank you for coming in today Cole. I thought it would be productive to hear some of your concerns about the challenges your relationship faces." Heather said.

"Productive... Challenges, who talks like that?" I thought.

I could see Danni out of the corner of my eye. She was looking at the floor and her body language had changed. Danni was nervous about me being there. I guessed that Heather talked her into it but maybe it wasn't time for this just yet.

I told Heather everything from Danni's insecurity, to the arguments and my wanting to move out. Danni cried several times during my monologue.

"Can you see Danni's side in all of this?" Heather asked.

"Yes but I can see mine as well, and I've made a lot of sacrifices for us to be together also, but that seems to go unnoticed." I said.

"Danni, do you understand what Cole is saying?" Heather asked.

"I do. Cole I love you and I really appreciate your support during all of this. I know that I have been difficult and hard to get along with, but I'm working on changing and I need you." Danni said.

"Cole, how do you feel about that?" Heather asked.

"I know that you love me and I love you too but your issues are bigger than I am. You don't want my help and you've isolated me away from everyone, and now you are pushing me away. I feel as though we need some time apart for a while." I said.

Danni started to cry again and Heather handed her a box of tissues.

"So you are ready to walk away from her?" Heather asked.

"I didn't say that, but I need some time away while we are still in love or soon we won't be. I just think that would be for the best." I said.

"That's kind of harsh. Danni's under a lot of pressure with her job and she needs your continued support." Heather said.

I was pissed off by that point. Heather was saying whatever she thought Danni wanted to hear. Maybe because she was paying her. Maybe I could get some reciprocity if I cut her a bigger check. I was done talking and it was more than obvious.

"How are you med's?" Heather asked.

"What medication?" I asked.

Danni was quiet.

"I recommended the anti-depressant Somaxa for Danni. She has been displaying classic symptoms of someone battling Clinical Depression. You didn't tell him Danni?" Heather said.

"I didn't know how to bring it up. I was waiting for a good time." Danni said.

"How do you feel?" Heather asked.

"I feel better. My mood is more stable and I don't feel devastated by every little thing that happens especially with work." Danni said.

"That's good. Be sure to update me with any changes you experience. It would also be a good idea to document your progress with a journal." Heather said.

I zoned out for the rest of the session. I knew how the rest of it would go. Besides, it was two against one and I needed to wait until I had the tactical advantage.

I opened the passenger door of Danni's car and sat down.

"When were you going to tell me about the pills?" I asked.

"I don't know. I was going to… at the right time."

"Like twenty minutes ago?" I asked.

Danni was silent and focused on the road.

"Danni, you don't need drugs, you need a new job. This is drastic. Did you get a second opinion?" I said.

"Heather came highly recommended and I trust her judgment." Danni said.

"Heather's a quack and she's only concerned with getting paid. She's a parasite and she's preying on you in a moment of weakness. There's nothing wrong with you. You don't need medication." I said.

"It makes me feel better about myself Cole. Things don't feel so impossible all the time. I don't feel so overwhelmed."

"So what am I here for?" I asked.

"I thought you were leaving." Danni said.

Checkmate! My eye began to twitch again and my head was still aching.

"You win Danni." I said.

Danni refused to listen to me. I didn't want the love of my life to be the latest lab rat in one of the greatest travesties in the history of medical science.

The cold, stark fact of life is that there is no such thing as "Clinical Depression" and that the root of Danni's problem was her job. No pill was going to change that. There isn't even a test that can detect the existence of "Clinical Depression" in a person. There is not one shred of empirical evidence that suggests such a condition even exists and that a person is depressed for no reason at all. It's ironic that none of these diseases; Clinical Depression, Attention Deficit Disorder, or Attention Deficit Hyper Activity Disorder existed prior to the major pharmaceutical company's lobbyists being able to entice congress. They cleverly enticed congress into passing legislation to legalize the sale of these "medications" which are basically schedule three narcotics. It's even more ironic that these same pharmaceutical companies claim to have conducted research and testing to develop medications to treat diseases that they can't even prove you have in the first place. Furthermore, these diseases only exist in Western countries and are unheard of in Asia, Africa, South America and the Middle East.

Is it an advancement in medicine or in profiteering? And they call leaching and blood letting savage. Playing with the brain's chemistry is a dangerous game. To prescribe pills to a person who is depressed makes about as much sense as prescribing painkillers to a person with a stab wound but not stopping the bleeding. You won't last too long that way. Physical pain is the body's way of telling you that there is a problem. Whether you're bleeding or you forgot that the stove was hot and put your hand on one of the burners. Your body will let you know through pain that you should stop whatever is causing the pain. Depression works the same way. Being depressed is an indicator that something in your life is not working for you. Whether it's an abusive boy friend, a financial crisis, disobedient children, a bad marriage, or a job that drives you crazy.

The solution is to correct the situation not to take pills. You could take pills until your untimely demise and the only good you would do would be to enhance the coffers of the various pharmaceutical companies. The bottom line is that this entire country has been socially engineered into believing in diseases that don't exist anywhere else in the world, and that taking the latest pill is the only salvation. It sounds like the plot of a bad novel to me.

I finally located a nice one bedroom apartment in Mira Mesa. It would mean a longer commute of twenty minutes but I liked the place.

I could see myself being happy there. It was centrally located. Close to the city but not too close. I filled out the lease agreement and paid the security deposit. I would be close to Danni but far enough away to start over again in case things didn't workout between us. Danni and I hardly spoke unless we had to. She was doped up in my opinion and I was ready to go.

I agreed to return to Heather's office for the next therapy session. I wasn't excited about being there. Actually, I couldn't tell you why I went at all. Maybe I was just trying to keep the peace until I left. I loved Danni but it was a waste of time. I expected Heather to say whatever kept Danni coming back even if it meant demonizing me.

The hardest thing about being a man is being told that your feelings don't matter, and then being called cold and hard because you've learned to act as if your feelings don't matter. Danni seemed especially nervous. I was so close to her that I could feel it before I actually saw it.

"Well..." Heather began. "During the last session I mentioned that honesty is very important for a relationship. In order for this relationship to work, Danni needs to tell you a few things so that she can be free of them and move forward."

Danni was staring at the ground again and I knew that this would be heavy. There had never been a time when Danni couldn't look me in the eye. I braced myself in order to prepare for what was coming next.

"Please Danni, begin. I'm here with you." Heather said.

"Cole..." Danni said very softly. "I told you that I was married when I was younger but I didn't tell you everything...Not the whole truth." Her voice quivered and buckled under the strain of speaking of a burden that had been so hard to bear these past 14 years.

"My ex-husband was very abusive. He used to hit me and call me a dumb bitch and things like that. I couldn't take it anymore after about a year and I cheated on him with a man named Alex who I met at work. I ran away to move in with Alex and I got pregnant. Alex didn't want the baby and put me out. I was on my own and I put the baby up for adoption. I didn't have anyone or anything and it was the best thing for the baby." Danni said.

She began to cry and paused to compose herself. "I think about my baby everyday and I feel so guilty. I just want my baby back and I don't even know where she is. I want her back." Danni said. Danni wept and wept so heavy and so hard that it killed me inside.

I held her close to me as Heather looked on attempting to conceal her joy. It was as if she fed on Danni's pain. She was akin to a vampire. She didn't care about anything other than herself and her hunger.

Danni and I didn't speak on the way home. Danni just laid there in the passenger seat looking out the window. We arrived home and she went straight to bed. My head was killing me and my eye was imitating a strobe light. I grabbed a beer from the fridge and headed for the couch. I sat there staring off into space wondering how things could get any worse. About twenty minutes passed when Danni called for me.

"Cole...Cole."

"Yeah." I said in an exasperated tone of voice.

"Don't leave me, please." Danni said as she sat down on the love seat that was perpendicular to the couch. My synapses were blown by the therapy session and the revelation about Danni's child. Once again my mind reached maximum capacity with what ifs.

"I have to go. We can't live together anymore." I said.

"I need you. What can I do to change your mind?" Danni said.

"How could you keep that from me? That you had a child out there some where. How do you not tell me that? And then you have the nerve to accuse me of being dishonest and cheating and all of it is because you were cheating on your ex-husband 15 years ago when I was 13 fucking years old." I said. "I'm out. I won't do this anymore. How dare you have me come all the way down here based on a lie? I dedicate my life to you for this bullshit. I'm leaving and I'm not looking back."

"You can't Cole... I'm pregnant." Danni said.

My eyes grew as wide as saucers as I heard the words that every single man fears. I looked at her silently for a moment as I waited for the hidden camera crew to step from behind the potted plant that was in the corner of the living room. For them to tell me that this was all a joke. That it would air on CBS in three months as a segment on the new television program "Ha ha, dumb ass!"

"What?" I asked.

"I'm pregnant." Danni said as she transitioned her gaze from me to the carpeted floor.

"You're on the pill. How do you get pregnant on the pill?" I asked.

"I stopped taking it. I didn't want you to go. I wanted a part of you to stay if you did." Danni said.

"Are you crazy? I asked as I jumped up from the couch.

The horror of what Danni said began to sink in. I was at her mercy, if she had any.

"Don't leave me Cole. I can't do this alone, not again." Danni said.

Unfortunately, this is a plight that many men find themselves in. If I left her, I would've been a dead beat dad. If I stayed, she would win and I would be miserable. I trusted her and she screwed me. It's no surprise that I said what I said.

"Ok, I'll stay. I won't let you do this alone. I'll be here for you until the baby is born but I'm leaving after that. We'll have to work something out with custody and everything." I said.

"We can be a family. We can do this." Danni said.

"How are we going to make it when your job is making us both miserable and you won't quit." I asked.

I stood there watching her as she continued to watch the floor.

"No good can come from this." I thought.

I went to work the next day looking as if my dog just died. Jessi greeted me with a big smile as she always did.

"What's wrong with you? You don't own a dog. Who died?" Jessi asked.

"Danni set me up. She stopped taking her pill and now she's pregnant. She's trying to manipulate me into staying with her." I whispered.

"Oh my God!" Jessi screamed. "Are you serious? She actually did that? Oh my God."

"Yeah, she got me. I can't stand her anymore. I don't know how I'm gonna raise a child with her. I don't know what to do." I said.

"There's not much that you can do. Damn Cole! What if she's lying to get you to stay?" Jessi asked.

"She's not lying. She doesn't lie, she just omits the truth." I said.

"Like how?" Jessi asked.

I told Jessi about the therapy session and about Danni cheating on her ex and putting the baby up for adoption.

"She's a psycho." Jessi said and then apologized. "I'm sorry. That wasn't nice to say but that is crazy. She's been hiding that all of this time. Oh my God Cole! I'm sorry."

"Me too Jessi." I said.

Jessi was right. Danni deliberately deceived me. I should have listened to Ham. He tried to warn me but I wouldn't listen. I had no one to blame but myself.

"You can't stay with her Cole. This isn't going to work out. You can't trust her. She could do anything." Jessi said.

"I don't know anymore. She's got my child. I can't just run out on my child. I promised myself that I would never do that."

"Danni lied to you Cole whether you think so or not. She tricked you into getting her pregnant. You need to get as far away from her as possible. You have to protect yourself. You could still be there for her and the baby but maybe she wouldn't have it if you left. She said that she couldn't do it alone." Jessi said.

"I don't know if that's the right thing to do. God, I just need a minute to figure this all out." I said.

"Cole, you're a good guy. This woman is dangerous. I don't want to see something bad happen to you." Jessi said.

I made it through the rest of the day and wound up watching the world go by at Shelter Island yet again. My head began to ache again and I decided to go home and to get some sleep.

Danni was cooking dinner when I arrived home. She seemed a little jittery.

"Hey, what's for dinner?" I asked.

"Pot roast. I'm eating for two now." Danni said proudly.

"Yeah, how could I forget?" I asked as I sat at the dinning room table.

Danni wiped her hands off on a dish towel and approached me.

"Cole, we can do this. Things are going to work out for the best. You'll see." Danni said.

"Danni, how could you do this?" I asked.

"Because you're just giving up on us. We came here to start a new life together Cole, and we will. The three of us." Danni said.

I stood up and walked away disgusted.

"What?" Danni asked.

"I need to lie down. My head is killing me." I said as I walked into the bedroom. I felt sick to my stomach and I couldn't tell if it was the result of the headache or Danni's words.

"Don't worry baby, I'll take care of you." Danni said.

Her behavior was strange and manic. She wasn't herself.

"What's going on with you?" I asked.

"Nothing, I'm just cooking YOU dinner."

"Are you still taking that medication?" I asked.

"No, I'm pregnant. I can't take that stuff."

"You just quit taking it?" I asked.

"I want the baby to be healthy. I'm not taking any chances."

"Can you do that? Can you just quit taking that stuff? What did Heather say?" I asked.

"This is my baby Cole, not hers. I don't have to ask her permission to ensure the health of my child."

"I thought you trusted her judgment. What if you can't just quit the Somaxa?" I said.

"Cole relax, you're going to make your head ache worse."

I looked into her eyes and they were the eyes of a stranger.

"Here." Danni said as she brought in a plate of food for me to eat. "You need to keep your strength up. We're counting on you Cole."

I could only groan as the room began to oscillate from side to side.

"I have a doctor's appointment tomorrow at 2:30pm. Can you go with me?" Danni asked.

"I can't leave work early tomorrow. Why didn't you tell me sooner? How long ago did you make the appointment?" I asked.

"The other day. Don't worry about it. I'll do it by myself." Danni snapped and then walked out of the room.

My head continued to throb as I finished eating my dinner and placed the plate on the night stand. Jessi was right. I had to get out of there. Danni was capable of doing anything. I was scheduled to move into the apartment in Mira Mesa in two weeks but I didn't tell Danni the exact date.

"I'll get out of this mess somehow." I thought as I drifted off to sleep.

Carrying the weight of the world on your shoulders makes doing even the simplest things so very difficult. It was impossible to focus on even the smallest task the next day at work. Jessie checked on me and I told her of my decision to move out.

"Don't tell her anything. Just go. Let it be a surprise." Jessi said.

I came straight home and changed out of my work clothes and into a short sleeved t-shirt and jeans. Danni arrived home a short time later.

"So how did it go?" I asked.

"Fine, the doctor wants me to take it easy because of my age. I'm a high risk pregnancy." Danni said with a smile on her face.

"Really?" I asked.

She was so attractive that I forgot that she was 11 years older than I was.

"Yeah and we need to go shopping."

"Shopping for what?" I asked.

"Baby stuff. I don't want to wait till the last minute. I'm going to do it right this time."

"Isn't that what baby showers are for?" I asked.

"Who am I going to invite, Rachel?" Danni asked.

"Well we could invite our friends if you would let us have any." I said.

Danni gave me a dirty look and I headed back to the bed room.

"You might want to start acting like a father. You do have a child on the way."

"You say that like I had a choice." I said as I lay down on the bed.

"Like I raped you." Danni said sarcastically.

"Like you deceived me." I said with equal sarcasm.

"You need to take responsibility for the consequences of your actions Cole." Danni said as she pointed her finger at me.

It was one thing to deceive me, but it was another to act as if I were wrong to be upset about it. I had been on my best behavior but I couldn't take it anymore. Every man has his breaking point, and that was mine.

"I need to take responsibility for my actions? Is that right? You got a lot of nerve. You're a liar and you're selfish. Now you want me to pay for your mistakes and the fact that your ex-husband was a woman beater. I won't. Why don't you take responsibility for your actions and go find your daughter and leave me out of it!" I said.

Danni became enraged and I was about to learn a very valuable lesson.

"Fuck you!" she screamed as she jumped on top of me.

Danni landed straddling me and began to throw punches at my face and pounded my chest. I did my best to block her blows without hurting her.

"Danni stop." I said calmly but to no avail.

She continued to strike at me in a whirlwind of hair, curses, fists and tears.

"Fuck you!! I hate you! I fucking hate you!" Danni said.

One of Danni's blows caught my left eye. Being no stranger to fisticuffs, I was more upset than hurt physically.

"Stop God Dammit!" I said as I used my left arm to hook between her left arm and torso. I rolled her off of me and on to the carpeted floor. The vision in my left eye was a bit blurry but I could still make out the image of Danni springing to her feet.

"Fuck you. Don't you ever put your hands on me again. I won't take this shit anymore. You'll never see this baby. I'll move away and you'll never find us." she said as she ran out of the bedroom.

Danni grabbed the cordless phone from its cradle in the kitchen and dialed 911.

"You have got to be kidding me." I thought.

"Hello, hello! Yes. I want to report an assault." Danni said. "Yes. It's my boyfriend. Yes. He just assaulted me. He's black. Listen…he's a black man and he's 6'4." Danni said.

My mind was blown. I had completely forgotten that we had an interracial relationship. My being black was never an issue before, neither was her being Mexican. I never thought in those terms. I just loved her and wanted to be with her. She only told the cops that a big black man was beating her in order to get a quicker response. I put on my shoes and walked past her and out of the front door. I closed the door behind me and had a seat on the ground outside of the apartment. I thought about leaving but I didn't want to create a replay of OJ Simpson's white Bronco chase. Besides, the police would arrive and see that she was lying. I'd leave that night and move into my apartment in two weeks.

I waited outside for a few minutes until I saw the silhouette of a man in uniform headed my way. He was a police officer, slim, about 6' 1" tall with a shaved head. The name tag on his uniform read "Parker."

"Hey buddy. What's going on? Are you Cole?" Parker asked.

"Yeah, my girlfriend has lost her mind. She started hitting me and called you guys when I pushed her off of me."

"Ok." Parker said as he looked me up and down. There was something familiar about me to him and like wise.

"Were you in the Corps?" Parker asked.

"Yeah."

"Who were you with?" Parker asked.

"29 Palms MCAGCC, Combat Service Support Group 1, attached to the CASP, Lieutenant Colonel Lassiter commanding." I said as smoothly as a first phase recruit.

"Semper Fi! I got out of Pendelton three years ago." Parker said.

This was a very good thing. Marines take care of Marines. I would need all of the help that I could get being a black man in a white neighborhood that just happened to be the subject of a call to 911. A second police officer showed up and greeted Officer Parker. "Hey Smitty. The perp is cooperative. He's cool, he's a Marine." Parker said.

This was really a very good thing.

"Two Marines, I'll be out of here in no time." I thought.

"Don't worry." I'll talk to her and then I'll just need you to stay somewhere else tonight." Parker said.

"Thanks."

"Watch him for me Smitty?" Parker said.

Officer Parker knocked on the door. Danni opened it a crack to see who it was, closed the door to undo the security chain and then opened it to let Officer Parker in. A third officer arrived minutes later. He was a Police Sergeant named Burke. He was older and a lot more serious than the first two officers. Burke spoke to Smitty and gave me a look as he passed by and entered the apartment.

I realized that the officers had been gone much too long about twenty minutes later. I would have given anything to have known what was happening on the other side of the door. Parker exited the apartment and was visibly upset. Something had just gone horribly wrong.

"How're we doing?" I asked.

"I'll let you know in a minute." Parker said.

Smitty gave him a look and they took a couple steps away to have a brief conversation. I don't know what Parker said but I could read Smitty's lips as he said "Fuck, not again."

Police Sergeant Burke walked back out of the apartment and pulled Parker a few paces away. They were having a heated conversation under their breaths. Parker was busy protesting whatever Burke said when Burke pointed to his collar and reminded parker of his superior rank. Burke went back in to finish speaking to Danni and Parker came back in my direction. He gave Smitty a look that even I could translate.

"Oh shit! Here we go." I thought.

"Sorry." Parker said. "Go ahead and stand up for me and turn around. Interlace your fingers behind your head and spread you feet apart."

I did as he instructed and found myself cuffed behind my back and my pockets being searched.

"Do you have anything I need to know about? Parker asked.

"I'm clean." I said.

You don't have anything that's going to stick me do you?" Parker asked as he began to check my back pockets and waist band.

"Do I look like a hype?" I asked.

"She said that you have a drug problem and that some of her jewelry is missing. Do you know anything about that?" Parker asked.

"I know it's a truck load of horse shit." I said.

"I know you're upset but I'm doing what I need to do to protect the both of us." Parker said as he finished his search and walked me down the steps toward his police cruiser that just happened to be parked right in front of the leasing office.

"You've got to be fucking kidding me." I said.

Parker opened the back door of the police cruiser and told me to have a seat.

"Watch your head. I'm sorry there's not much room back there." He said as he shut the door.

I found that sitting side ways with my legs on the seat was the only way to fit. The metal cage that separated the back seat from the front dug in to my left shoulder.

Parker returned to the apartment and left Smitty to stand guard. Parker was gone for about 32 minutes and in that time my shoulders and legs went numb. I had to piss like a race horse and it seemed as if each one of my neighbor walked past the cruiser to take a peak at the caged animal inside. I could read their minds from the expressions on their faces.

"Yeah, I knew he was trouble." They thought.

Forget that fact that I was a U.S. Marine or a tax paying citizen or that I had never been arrested before in my life. I was the nigger they thought I was and nothing I could say or do would change that. I was too angry to feel anything. That was Danni's gift to me. She gave me the rage she felt. She gave me the rage someone else gave her. She gave me a scapegoat to blame all of my problems on. She gave me justification to do whatever I wanted to anyone else. Hurt people, hurt people.

The cycle was complete. It was just like a vampire movie. I was bitten and filled with spite. I had been infected with the victim virus. I was just like her. The only question left was would I lie to myself about it like she did, or would I be honest about being fucked up inside.

Parker returned and started up the cruiser. We exited the apartment complex and I breathed a sigh of relief. The crowd of spectators seemed disappointed that the mobile zoo was making its departure for parts unknown.

"I'm going to jail. I can't believe that I'm going to jail." I said to myself over and over again.

Parker drove the cruiser through the streets of down town San Diego and tried to engage me in a conversation about the traffic and the short cuts he took to get through town. I ignored him. I wasn't in the mood to talk. We pulled into the parking garage of a police station and I asked about making a phone call.

"Soon." Parker said.

Parker opened the door and I was allowed to use the rest room. It was a relief. I thought my bladder would burst all over the inside of the cruiser. Being a caged animal is a lot harder than it looks. Parker sat me down at a table in the garage and began filling out some paper work.

"Do you want to make a statement?" Parker asked.

"I told you what happened and look where it got me. Why would I say anything else?" I said.

"It would put your side of the story on record. It would be an official documentation of the events that transpired today and it would be admissible in court." Parker said.

"So this could help me get the truth out... that I didn't attack her?" I asked.

"Yeah. The prosecution and the judge would have to take it in to consideration." Parker said.

I thought about it for a while and decided to make the second major mistake of the day.

"Ok, I'll do it." I said.

I told Parker what happened. That Danni had a doctor's appointment that day, that I came home and had a killer head ache. I told how Danni came home making demands to go shopping, and that she jumped on me after a verbal argument. That I pushed her off of me after repeatedly telling her to stop.

Parker took down my statement and finished his paper work. He then placed me back in to the cruiser. Another officer asked Parker if he could transport a prisoner for him so that he could make it to his son's soccer game. Parker agreed and took custody of the prisoner.

He was a young man, about 20 years old, average height and very slim. He looked like a heroin addict that I saw once. He was emaciated and I could trace his circulatory system through his skin. I did my best to make room for him as he climbed into the back seat of the cruiser. The strain of being jammed in so tightly became unbearable after a few minutes.

"I don't mean any disrespect but I'm going to put my legs on you." I said.

"It's cool." he said.

We traveled further downtown by Horton shopping plaza and pulled up to a tall garage door. It slowly opened and we drove inside. Parker removed the second prisoner and then came back for me. He instructed me to exit the vehicle and I climbed out without the use of my cuffed hands. Parker escorted me to a plain looking metal door and pressed a button on a wall mounted intercom. A buzzer sounded and the door's lock could be heard disengaging. Parker opened the door, removed my cuffs and told me to walk through it.

"Good luck" he said as the door slammed shut behind me.

My wrists were bruised and welted. My shoulders were stiff and sore from having my hands cuffed behind my back for two hours.

"What do I do now?" I thought.

"Move forward." A voice said over a loud speaker.

I could see a glass window up ahead with two Sheriffs Deputies behind it. They opened a sliding glass door and told me to empty my pockets. I gave them my keys, wallet and Chap Stick.

"Move through the door." The voice said again.

I walked through a second door at the end of the corridor and found several deputies waiting for me. They put me into a line with four other men and started taking our mug shots and fingerprints. A deputy named Jefferson told me to step in front of the camera and took my picture from the front and then from the side.

"Great, now my mug shot and prints are in the system. I am now an official black man." I thought.

"What happened Westlake? Did your girlfriend set you up?" Jefferson asked.

"Yeah."

Jefferson shook his head and then placed me into a holding tank with five other men in it. It was a small room with what looked to be a pay phone in it. There was a young black guy on the phone in the middle of a conversation. His hair was braided and his pants hung off of his ass. His shirt looked to be two sizes too large and he needed a shave…on his chin at least.

He spoke softly but his conversation was still audible.

"I need you to get the money out from under the mattress. Yeah, yeah I need you to bail me out Janeice. Come on girl. Damn!"

I took a seat on the metal bench that ran parallel to the painted brick wall. It was cold and harsh with bits of graffiti that had been carved into the chipped paint on its surface. I began to ask myself how often this sort of thing happened if the deputy knew that I had been set-up.

"Hey buddy, do you know how long we'll be in here?" a voice asked.

I turned to see a middle aged white man looking in my direction. There were four other guys in the tank and I was curious as to why he asked me the question. It was as if he assumed that I had a habit of getting arrested just because I was black. Maybe I was being too sensitive but the question pissed me off none the less.

"I don't know." I said.

"We'll be here until tomorrow morning if we're lucky." Another voice called out.

The voice belonged to a Mexican man, about 5'9" and in his mid thirties. He was dressed in shorts with grass stains on them and a white t-shirt. He had several tattoos including one on his neck that said "Quick."

"What do you mean if we're lucky?' the white man asked.

"They should get us to see the judge and out processed by tomorrow morning. This is jail homes, they do what they want. Ain't no guarantees. Get comfortable. Make yourself at home. You're among friends." The Mexican said with a chuckle.

"I can't stay here. I don't belong here." The white man said.

"None of us belong here fucker. Who in the hell belongs in a cage because he had an argument with his old lady? You're one of us now. You better start acting like it. It's us against them. You better recognize fool." The Mexican said and then chuckled again but louder.

He was having entirely too much fun in such a dire circumstance.

"Is that what they got you for?" I asked.

"That's what they keep getting me for homes. Ain't nothing worse than going to jail three times over the same woman." The Mexican said.

"Why do you stay with her?" I asked.

"She's got my niños homes. Besides, I love that crazy bitch. I tried leaving her but I can't. We'll work it out one day. I just hope I'm not in here for life when it happens." The Mexican said and then laughed at himself.

"I need to make a phone call." The white man said as he stepped up to the young black guy who was still on the phone.

"Hey, you've been talking for a while. When are you going to be done?" The white man asked.

The black guy turned his back toward the white man and ignored him.

"What do they call you?" The Mexican asked me.

"Cole."

"That's it? I'm gonna call you Big loco." The Mexican said.

"It's Cole." I insisted.

"Are you a banger?" the Mexican asked. "You got some cool tats."

"No, I was in the Marines."

"Oh, yeah ok. My cousin Ernie is at Pendleton homes. I got you. My name is Hilario but everyone calls me Quick." The Mexican said.

"Quick?"

"Yeah, I was a banger when I was younger. 5-0 could never catch me, so the homies called me Quick."

We both laughed but were interrupted by the white man pleading for the phone again.

"Look buddy, I need to make a call too. You need to hurry up."

"Oh, shit homes. Check it out. It's about to go down. This mayate is gonna knock his ass out. Mira homes." Quick said.

"Watch your mother fuckin' mouth nigga. You don't know me fool." The black guy said.

The white man stood there in a state of shock. I completely understood. I had the same reaction the first time I was called a nigger.

"I'll bet you five bucks he goes down with the first punch." Quick said.

"They took our money remember. I don't have five bucks."

"I'll get it from you when we get out." Quick said.

I wasn't a betting man but I needed a diversion to take my mind off of my troubles.

"You got it. I say he lasts at least three punches and he'll tag the brotha once before he goes down." I said.

Quick was overjoyed. We shook hands to seal the deal and turned our attention back to the two competitors.

The white man composed himself rather quickly after his first brush with racism.

"Hey!" he said raising his voice with an air of authority that belied his current status as a prisoner. Perhaps he had been watching too much national geographic. They always suggest speaking loudly to scare off wild animals.

"This isn't fair. Now you need to get off of the phone right now. I won't be that long. You can finish your call when I'm done." The white man said.

The black guy told his girlfriend to hold on for a second and proceeded to slap the white man in the head with the phone. The white man recoiled backward in horror and pain. The black guy went after him but had to leave the phone behind since the cord wasn't long enough to reach the other side of the tank.

"I told your bitch ass to go ahead nigga." He shouted at the white man and then threw a flurry of punches.

"Hey, he's pretty good." I told Quick.

"Fuck him homes. He just lost me five bucks." Quick said.

The white man grabbed the black guy by the waist and twisted him to the ground. He was bigger and used his weight to his advantage. He began to hit the black guy back and was called a dumb bitch for doing so.

Quick and I were on our feet and following the action which had now spread to the far corner of the holding tank.

"Hey watch out, get back. Here come the deps." Quick said.

Quick took me by the arm and motioned me back just as five Sheriffs deputies came running in to break up the fight.

"He started it. He hit me first." The white man said as they hustled them both out of the tank.

"Fuck all you bitches." The black guy said as he flailed about while being dragged out by both legs.

The two subdued pugilists were rushed past us and out of the holding tank. The heavy steel door closed and locked behind them. From there they would be placed into solitary confinement where they could do no harm to one another.

"Hey that was pretty good." Quick said. "I'll get that fiver to you on the outside."

"No, we bet that he would go down with the first punch not after getting hit with the phone. Who saw that coming?" I said.

"Yeah, that shit was funny. You're ok homes." Quick said. "What'd they get you for?"

"My girl set me up. I was going to leave her and then she tricked me into getting her pregnant. We got into an argument and she lied and told the cops that I beat her down but I didn't do shit." I said.

"That's how it is in California homes. You know, after the first time I got locked up it was like there was a big magnet out there that could pull me back in here at any time. It's kind of fucked up homes." Quick said.

I sat there pondering what he said. The depth of it hadn't hit me yet but it soon would.

"Hey fool. You better make a phone call before they put us in the modules." Quick said.

"What?"

"The phone fucker. Call your mama or your hermano or who ever ese." Quick said.

"Oh, yeah, I forgot all about it."

The phone was still dangling at the end of the cord and swinging from left to right. I grabbed it and held it up to my ear.

I didn't have any family to call but I did call my boss Dave. It was 9:30pm and I would almost certainly miss work the next day. I left him a voice mail message explaining that I had a family emergency and that

I may not be to work the next day. Then I called Jessi and told her the truth about what had happened. I promised her that I would call her as soon as I could and I asked her to cover for me.

I was off of the phone by the time the deps opened the door of the tank and escorted us upstairs.

We entered a large concrete room and were told to undress.

"Neatly stack your clothes in front of you." one of the Deps said.

We got undressed and stood there completely naked.

"Lift up your arms. Now turn around. Bend over and spread your buttocks." The Deputy said.

We followed his orders much to our embarrassment.

"Spread your ass cheeks so that I can look up your asshole for contraband." The Deputy said to one of the prisoners in our group.

Another deputy entered the room with enough blue San Diego county jail uniforms, white cotton briefs, white tube socks, and orange sandals in various sizes for all of us. A second deputy entered carrying old, used, green wool Army blankets, pillows and thin foam pads. They threw them on the floor in front of us.

"Get dressed. Hurry up!"

We were all getting dressed when I noticed that my pants were too big.

"Damn, like I don't have enough problems." I thought.

"Out of the room. Follow me." Sheriffs Deputy Jefferson said as he led the four of us out and into a hallway. From there we were taken to see the nurses. They interviewed each of us, asking if we were intravenous drug users or had Hepatitis or HIV. Next on the agenda was the documentation of any tattoos. Cops used these to identify which gang you belonged to. "Have a seat." the dep said.

"Do you have any tattoos?" the nurse asked. She didn't even look at me. The answer was obvious. All good Marines have tattoos. It's a fact of life.

She had been there too long. It was more than apparent that she was just going through the motions until quitting time.

"Stand up!" Jefferson said.

He escorted me away from the nurse and down the hall with the other three prisoners. I carried the pillow, blanket and foam pad in one hand, and held up my pants with the other. We rounded a bend of concrete and steel and found ourselves standing in front of two glass doors with steel frames. This was Module C, our new home for as long as we were guests of the county.

There was a control center that was two floors above us. The deps used it to monitor their prisoners on closed circuit television and to open and close the cell doors. It looked like miniature version of an air traffic control tower from the outside, and was clearly visible form the inside of the module.

"Ayala. Tier one, cell 3." Jefferson called out.

The heavy door slide open with a clank and Ayala head for cell 3. Jefferson continued to call names and the prisoners entered the module one by one. I was last in line. A deputy named Carson stepped toward me.

"Westlake." He whispered. "Keep your hands tucked into the front of your pants whenever you leave the module or are approached by a deputy. They're already talking about what they're going to do to you if you do anything. The word is out that you're a Marine and they're afraid of you. Keep your hands in your pants. Got it?"

"I got it." I responded.

"Westlake!" Jefferson called out. "Tier two, cell 5. Go!"

I walked into the empty module, passed the wall mounted television and the stainless steel tables and benches. There were two levels of cells in front of me and all of them were closed and occupied with the exception of cell number 5 on the second tier. I walked up the stairs and entered my assigned cell. There were two stainless steel shelves, one over the other just like bunk beds. The opposite corner had a stainless steel sink and toilet that were joined. The cell was absolutely immaculate. There wasn't a speck of dirt or grime to be found anywhere. There was a drain in the center of the floor and I imagined that they just hosed the place down when ever someone bled to death or pissed all over the walls.

I stepped toward the bottom shelf and tried to imagine how to make it as comfortable as possible. I was interrupted by the loud clank of the metal door as it closed behind me. I placed the pad on the shelf and the blanket on top of that. I sat down on the edge of the shelf and stared at the toilet and sink combination. The cell was cold and spartan. I could only hope that Quick was right and that I would be out by the next morning. There was however, a silver lining to this dark cloud. My headache was gone and my eye was no longer twitching.

FIVE

The only benefit to being put in jail is that it taught me a very important lesson. That lesson is that in 21st century America, you are not free. Although it contradicts everything you were taught since you were a child, the truth is that in the good ole US of A, you are a subject of the state. It doesn't matter what George Washington, Thomas Jefferson, Benjamin Franklin or the Constitution of the United States says. Those days are long gone as are justice, democracy and common decency.

At any moment, for any spurious reason, you can be slammed into a cage until the powers that be say other wise. Until they can no longer dangle liberty over your head and extort money from you, or until they find bigger fish to fry.

It happens to law abiding citizens in America everyday and more often than you think. They'll handcuff you and take you out of your home in front of your daughter as her eyes fill up with tears. For what? For no more than a dollar. Placing people in cages for fraudulent reasons has become very lucrative. Just check the Dow Jones stock exchange.

Police have gone from serving and protecting the public to extorting and bullying them. Just take a look at the uniform of the modern day police officer. Gone are the neat creased uniforms with the neck tie and shiny badge. They have been replaced by the Taser, submachine gun, over the shirt body armor, six pocket military style trousers, combat boots and a t-shirt that says "Police" on it.

This Para-military make over is designed to intimidate and inspire fear. They've been transformed into revenue clerks for the city, county or state. Their primary concern is charging you with a bogus speeding or reckless driving charge. New laws and new violations are created every couple of months with the sole intention of taking your money and in so doing, your freedom.

When is the last time you saw a police officer stop to help someone who was broken down on the side of the road? When is the last time you saw a cop take down an accident report and document the position of two cars involved in a fender bender? They won't do it unless they can write a ticket for a busted tail light or an unfastened seat belt.

Their hypocrisy is only matched by their creativity. They'll stop at nothing to find new ways into your pocket. Red light cameras, speeding cameras, and the national mandatory seatbelt law which are all unconstitutional to name but a few. It's not always racism when they pull over minorities for no reason. It's worse. It's a racket in the finest tradition of organized crime and trust me, they are very organized. They know that odds are a minority doesn't have the money or education to tell them to fuck off and actually make it happen.

That's why none of these offenses carry any points. They want you to remain free so that you can continue to violate the laws and feed the corrupt machine. They'll put you in jail if you can't pay up and make money of off you that way. Making license plates and getting paid pennies to do so sure sounds like a get rich quick scheme to me.

The average American citizen is only two honest mistakes away from being put in jail regardless of race, religion, color, creed or class. I was living proof of that. Many a dollar has been made and many a life destroyed in the pursuit of an unregulated profit margin. My bail was set at twenty thousand dollars.

"I didn't kill anyone. I didn't rob a bank. How could my bail be twenty grand?" I thought.

A bail bondsman would cover it if I could come up with ten percent. But that would only be the beginning of my contribution to the criminal justice system.

It was damn near impossible to make myself comfortable in my cell. They never cut the lights off in the Module C. They never cut the lights off in any of the modules. It wouldn't be safe if they did. Imagine the beat downs and murders that would occur if they did. This gang against that gang, this beef against that beef, and this race against that race. I'll say this much for the deps and this is all that I'll say, they ran a tight ship. No more, no less.

It was cold in the cell and the brick walls and stainless steel didn't help either. The shirt that they gave me had short sleeves and the thin green blanket did very little to provide insulation from the chill in the air. The metal shelf I laid on constituted a mild form of torture. It was like trying to sleep on a block of ice. I tossed and turned all night. I finally managed to fall asleep but that didn't last long.

The sound of someone yelling at the top of their lungs brought me back from the edge of slumber. The bare walls of the cell were an unpleasant surprise. I was dreaming about being at Shelter Island. I was happiest at Shelter Island. The sunset, the ships, and most importantly, the peace of mind. There's a lot to be said for peace of mind.

I rubbed my eyes and started to shiver again. I pulled the blanket up to my chin but it was too short. Tugging on it only left my feet uncovered. Nothing I did helped. I resigned myself to shivering for the rest of the night. There was no clock in the cell and the sensory deprivation took its toll. My stomach roared with hunger.

"No midnight snack tonight." I thought.

There was a slim translucent window in the corner of the room. It was much too small to escape through and was reinforced with wire. I could see that it was dark on the other side and could only surmise that it was between midnight and 6am. My stomach began to rumble again and I decided that some water would quell the uprising.

I walked toward the steel sink and gave it the once over.

"Well, at least it's clean." I thought.

The faucet was short and barley extended two inches from the top of the sink. There was just one button to press and there was no stopper in the drain. I leaned over the sink, pressed the button and prepared to catch a stream of cool, refreshing water in my mouth. I stood there, bent over, mouth wide open, waiting and waiting and waiting. I could hear the sound of running water and quickly deduced that there was a problem. I decided to close my mouth, open my eyes and investigate.

There was water but only a trickle. It slowly seeped from the faucet, down the basin and into the drain.

"Oh well, it probably tastes as bad as this place looks." I thought.

The prisoner began yelling again. It was the sound of desperation and utter frustration. The next sound I heard was the door of the module sliding open. The dep's foot steps echoed throughout the module as they rushed up the steps.

He stopped yelling soon after that. I sat back down on my shelf hungry, angry, lonely and tired. I thought about whether the call I made to my boss would hold up until I could get out of there. I hoped that they didn't call home to speak to me.

"What would happen if Danni answered the phone? Would she be crazy enough to say something that would cost me my job?" I asked myself.

I wondered what Danni was doing. I wondered if she missed me and if she was sorry. I even wondered if she was coming to bail me out.

"I would have never done this to her. She was dead wrong. How could she do this to me? She must not know what this place is like. She's been watching too much TV, where they just cut you loose after a few hours or let you off with a stern warning. I wish they had let me off with a warning." I thought.

I lay there shivering, staring at the shelf above me, wondering what the morning would bring when I finally drifted off to sleep again. I was awoken by the sound of the door of my cell unlocking and sliding open with a loud clank.

I sat up right and then stood up. I cautiously approached the door and looked down into the common area of the module. There were inmates exiting their cells and sitting at the stainless steel tables below. They were reading two day old news papers and watching the TV that was mounted on the wall. They were strangely quiet. Only the sound of yawns and folding newspapers permeated the air.

I walked out of my cell and headed down the stairs. I took a seat at one of the tables closest to the stairs and focused my attention toward the TV. It was tuned into a local news broadcast. It was good to see the time and what was going on in the world. 5:30 AM and the world was still in one piece.

The main door of the module slid open with its usual clank and two inmates pushed in a couple of carts as the Sheriffs deputies stood watch outside. They were trusties, inmates that displayed a level of trust worthiness. They were allowed the privilege of working and handing out meals. It helped the time go by faster.

Everyone slowly stood up and formed a line to receive breakfast. They moved without a sense of urgency or even the motivation of hunger. They were either veterans of the criminal justice system or had the shit beat out of them once or twice by the deputies. "When in Rome do as the prisoners do." I always say.

While I was happy to receive breakfast I had a new reason to be troubled. The inmates were programmed. They had been through the drill before. I wondered how long they had been in the module and more importantly, how much longer I would be with them.

I joined my fellow inmates standing in line and received the hot mess they called breakfast. It came in a prepackaged foil tray that contained powdered eggs, a thin slice of ham, a piece of stale white bread, and a greasy heap that slightly resembled hash browns but only slightly. They gave each of us a carton of fruit punch to wash it all down with.

The portions were meager and I wondered if they would even put a dent in my hunger.
I sat back down in my original spot and ate breakfast.

I scarfed it all down as bad as it tasted and looked for more. The only thing worse than eating it was being hungry after eating it. I noticed my neighbor seated to my left. It was the black guy who got into the fight in the holding tank. He had yet to take a bite of his breakfast and I wanted it just as much as he hated it.

"First order of business is to keep my strength up. I may be in a fight or have to break out of here if it gets any colder." I joked with myself.

"Hey brotha, are you going to eat that?" I asked.

He slowly turned his head in my direction to see who had the nerve to ask him for a God damned thing. He had his toughest expression on his face which quickly disappeared when he saw my toughest expression. The fact that I out weighed him by 70 pounds didn't hurt either.

"Naw big dog. I don't want none. Taste like shit to me. Here, you got it." he said as he brought the tray over to me.

"Thanks. I'm starving." I said as I shoveled the rubbery eggs into my mouth.

I made it a point to swallow them whole so that I wouldn't have to endure the trauma of tasting them.

"What did they get you for? Did you kill somebody or something?" he asked.

"No, I ain't a fucking murderer. No, they got me on a bogus domestic violence charge. My chick lied on me. What about you?" I asked.

"Man, shit, I was tryin' to move a couple 8 balls when they pulled me over. Now I'm lookin' at a second strike." He said.

"Damn! That sucks. You need to move out of the state before you get caught again. I'm Cole." I said.

"They call me T-bone." he said.

"Now, I know there's a story behind that." I said.

"Man, shit, I boosted this car one time when I was fifteen and was tryin' to get away from 5-0. I took this turn too fast and ran into the side of a parked car. My boys was like damn you dumb. You T-boned a parked car. That's been my name ever since." He said with a look of pride on his face.

"Well look at the bright side, they could have started calling you Fender Bender." I said.

We began laughing but stopped when the deps and trusties came back in to collect the trays and plastic ware. The deps counted everything before it came in and would count it all on the way out. The numbers had better match up or they would search the entire module just to find a single missing plastic fork.

A basically trained inmate could turn the simplest of house hold items into a deadly weapon to be used on deputy or fellow prisoner alike. Necessity is the mother of invention after all.

T-Bone and I turned in our plastic ware and trays. I did however, hold on to my empty carton of fruit punch. I would use it as a make shift cup to catch water from my cell's faucet as it trickled out. The clock on the TV read 5:45 am before the deps turned it off from their control center. We were ushered back into our cells and I told T-Bone that I would see him later. I entered my cell and the door clanked shut behind me. I finally got a drink of water and it did taste as bad as the place looked.

I had too much on my mind to get back to sleep. Danni, my job, the baby, the future.

"I'm going to be a father." I thought.

This wasn't the way that I thought it would happen.

"Should I try to make it work with Danni for the baby? How could I ever trust her again?

How could I trust anyone who could put me in jail based on a lie? How could I trust her when she kept the affair and adoption from me?" I thought.

I lay there staring at the metal shelf above me for exactly two hours and fifteen minutes before the door slid open again.

I joined my fellow inmates in a line at the door of the module and for a brief second, I wondered how many of them had been framed as I was.

T-Bone fell in behind me.

"Where are we headed?" I asked.

"Shit, man, we going to see the judge, big dog." T-Bone whispered back.

"Good. Maybe I'll get out of here today." I said.

I didn't have a place to live but there was a chance that I could salvage my job. We were each hand cuffed behind our backs at the door and escorted out of Module C in a single file line. The flanking Deputies kept a watchful eye for the slightest movement. We outnumbered them and they were the most vulnerable while we were in transit. They led us down the hall and we arrived at Holding Tank 13 after a few twists and turns.

"More of the same." I thought.

There were steel reinforced glass panels along two walls of the room. The rear wall was all brick and the front was the door. There was a steel bench that was attached to the three walls of the tank. It was much too thin to sleep on all though a few inmates tried to balance on them.

"Hey fucker." A familiar voice called out.

"Quick!" I shouted.

It was good to see a familiar face.

"Where did they put you?" I asked.

"Module A homes. That's my second home. They save me a cell just in case I get arrested. They love me here." Quick said.

Part of me wanted to believe him although I knew that he was full of shit. Sinner and saint alike loved Quick whether they wanted to or not and I was no different.

I introduced him to T-bone.

"Hey fucker, I liked the thing with the phone." Quick said as we made ourselves comfortable on the steel benches.

"So we get to see the judge now?" I asked.

"Yeah, unless there's a riot." T-bone said.

We sat there telling stories and passing the time. I now know what fish in an aquarium feel like. Being surrounded by glass with no way out and strange people on the outside looking in as you live what's left of your life is a strange experience.

I learned more about Quick's sexual history than I ever wanted to over the course of the next two hours. T-Bone suddenly turned his head toward the front door just before it slid open again.

"What's up?" I asked just as seven of the toughest looking bastards you've ever seen in your life entered the tank at the behest of the deps. Two black, three Mexican and one white. The white one was different from the rest but not because of his race. He wasn't a hard core criminal at all.

He had a fair complexion and sandy colored hair. He was of average stature, and had that white collar corporate look to him if you over looked the jail attire. He seemed to be in a world of his own. He paid no attention to anyone. He just took a seat on the floor near the door and looked at the wall while slowly rocking back and forth.

We were officially over populated and the new occupants were clearly the real deal. They began to assert their dominance and the men were quickly separated from the boys. Seating was at a premium and only the strong would prevail in cooling their heels.

"Move your trick ass!" one of the new prisoners said to a prisoner who was sitting on the bench.

He was one of those burly fat guys that tried to act as if he had some significant muscle mass somewhere underneath all of the flab. Gang tattoos covered his hands and arms including two tear drops under his right eye.

The "Trick ass" in question was much smaller and decided to do the sane thing and give up his seat.

"That's what the fuck I thought." The new prisoner said as he sat down.

The rest of the new prisoners filed in and those seated on the bench slid closer together to make room for them. I examined each of them one by one. It was important to evaluate them in order to gauge the threat potential of each. Who looked tough or crazy or both. After careful analysis, I surmised that it was only a matter of time until someone in the holding tank got their ass kicked.

"Damn nigga! Who you looking at?" The burly prisoner asked me.

"What's your name?" I asked him as calmly as possible.

My heart began to beat faster but I wouldn't let him know it. Quick and T-bone looked on in anticipation of what would follow next.

"What nigga? I'm D- Real."

"I'm looking at you D-Real." I responded.

The entire tank was quiet as the two of us locked eyes on one another.

"Digame cholo. How'd they pick you guys up?" Quick asked one of the Mexican prisoners.

His name was Rudy Reyes and damn near every cop in the city had run into him at one time or another. Rudy was a dark skinned Chicano, about 5'10" and had a muscular build.

"County cops are doing a sweep for all outstanding felony warrants fool. They're calling it Operation Clean Sweep. They hit the hotels, the parks and the beaches and all the hang outs. They're even at the mall." Rudy said.

"Yeah but how'd they get you ese?" Quick asked.

"I'm driving down fucking Rosecrans Street right. I'm at the light when the cops pull up behind me. So I'm like chillin'. I don't get scared 'cause they look for that shit you know. But I'm driving a Monte Carlo. It's like a fucking cholo mobile ese. All that was missing was a neon sign saying "Please arrest me!" So the fuckers run my tags and lit me up. I get pulled over and they cuffed me and sat me on the curb near these bushes, right. OK, so they're both going through my car when I slipped the cuffs and slid through the bushes. They didn't notice until it was way too late. I was running down the street and shit, ducking through allies, jumping over trash cans." Rudy said.

"Shit man. How'd you get outta them cuffs?" T-bone asked.

"The game is to be sold not told." Rudy said.

"That's some ole bullshit nigga. You can't just slip out no cuffs. Who the fuck is you? Danny Copperfield or some shit?" D-Real said.

"It's David Copperfield puta and I always keep a cuff key on me." Rudy said.

Rudy was pissed off and it was written all over his face. The others were quietly making bets as to who would fight D-Real first, me or Rudy.

"Were you keep it at then?" D-Real asked.

"Up your mama's ass!" Rudy snapped back.

The rest of the tank erupted in laughter.

"Shut your bitch ass mouth before I fuck you up!" D-Real said as he jumped to his feet.

Rudy met D-Real in the middle of the tank. He balled up his fist and stared into D-Real's eyes.

"I'll bust your ass nigga." D-Real said.

"You'll die trying." Rudy responded as he stood face to chest with D-Real.

The tank became silent as everyone waited for the first blow to find its mark.

"You're done! Sit down!" a Sheriff's Deputy's muffled voice said through the reinforced glass.

"Got lucky mother fucker." D-Real said as he sat back down.

A shit eating grin came over Rudy's face.

"Then what happened fool?" Quick asked.

Rudy took his eyes off of D-Real and finished telling his story.

"So then I called my home boy Paco and he picked me up and took me to his place in San Ysidro. I called my girl Anna and told her what happened. I already got two strikes so they're trying to put me away for life this time. She was crying and told me that she loved me and that she couldn't live without me. Anna was gonna quit her job at the bank and meet me in Tijuana so that we could make the trip down to Ensenada together.

I got family down there and we were gonna go there to start a new life. So I had to sell some shit to make some quick money and Anna was going to pack our stuff and cross the border later.

So, I called this buster Manito for a ride to the deal but he tells the cops were I am for the reward money. They raided Paco's place, kicked the door down and shit. Next thing you know I'm in here with you fuckers." Rudy said.

"Damn dude. You're a fucking Aztec warrior. They should put you in a TV show." Quick said.

"They did homes. It's called the news." Rudy said.

I thought of how Anna was willing to give up everything and live a life on the run to be with the man she loved. Rudy was a criminal but Anna loved him for who he was. Meanwhile Danni put me in jail because she was mad at the world. I treated her like a queen and she treated me like shit.

"Damn!" Quick said.

"What is it?" I asked.

"This shit ain't good." Quick said.

"What, What?" I asked.

"All these fools coming in here with felony warrants means that they gotta see the judge first." Quick said.

"Why? We were here first." I asked.

"Well we're here now nigga." D-Real said.

"That's strike two." I said.

"Shit, man, it don't work that way. You and Quick got misdemeanor charges. Ya'll gotta wait for us to go first 'cause our charges are more serious than yours." T-Bone said.

"I can't stay in here for days. I'll loose my job." I whispered to Quick.

"Don't worry. They can't keep you longer than three days. They gotta cut us loose if we don't get to see the judge with in seventy two hours." Quick said.

"You're not paying attention. I won't have a job if I stay in here for three days." I said.

"Don't worry ese. My brother owns a detail shop. I can get you on with him. Wax on, wax off fucker. Stick with me dude. You'll be ok." Quick said with a chuckle.

Rudy was busy telling another story about running from the police when the door to the tank clanked open again. A trusty set down a bunch of brown bag lunches and the door shut behind him when he left.

"Lunch is here big dog. I'll get you one." T-Bone said.

T-Bone walked to the front of the tank and waited in the line. He took two bag lunches and made his way back toward me when D-Real stepped in.

"Your narrow ass don't need no two damn lunches nigga." He said as he snatched one of the bags from T-Bone.

T-Bone reached for the bag but was shoved backwards in the process. I had already sprung to my feet and caught T-Bone as he toppled backward.

"Strike three mother fucker!" I said as I pushed T-Bone to the side.

D-Real hadn't disrespected T-Bone with that stunt. His intention was to disrespect me. I couldn't let that challenge go un-answered, not in jail. I threw a right cross and stuck D-real in his face and dodged his jab simultaneously. I followed up with a left and caught the top of his head as he lunged forward and wrapped his arms around my waist. He was faster than I thought his fat ass would be. He drove me to the back of the tank and on top of Quick who was still seated on the bench.

"Oh shit! You're crushing me ese! Help!" Quick groaned as D-real threw body punches and elbows to my fore head.

Everyone was on their feet cheering and yelling.

"Work that fat fucker!" Rudy yelled.

"Fuck him up Cole." T-Bone said.

"You owe me twenty bucks." One prisoner said to another.

"Help me!" Quick begged.

"Fat bitch." I yelled as I struggled to get free of the clinch.

D-Real was heavy and I needed to think of something fast to get him off of me. I hooked him in the side of the head a couple times as Quick continued to scream for help. My eyebrow was split open form the elbows to the face and a trickle of blood began to flow down my face. I decided that bleeding wasn't the best way to win a fight and found his weak spot. I took my right thumb and drove it between his ribs and hip bone again and again until his grip loosened enough to allow me to finish the job.

I slid out from beneath him and hit the floor in a rapid crawl. He was almost on top of me when I got into a crouch and punched his left thigh as hard as I could. He let out a yelp and began to fall down when I caught him in the chin with a left upper cut. He was out like a light and fell backward to the floor. Top Strummer taught me that move and it never failed.

I proceeded to stomp and kick his chest again and again while holding up my oversized pants.

"Deps! The deps are coming!" One of the prisoners said.

I grabbed D-Real's unconscious body and pulled him on top of me. I lay there on the floor, flailing about and screaming for help like a scared school girl.

"I didn't do anything. Help! Stop!" I yelled.

The deputies opened the door and began to beat D-real with their batons. It took them a while to get him off of me since he was so heavy. They cuffed him and three Deputies dragged him away.

"You Ok?" One of the deputies asked.

"He's crazy. He took my bag lunch and then started hitting me. I didn't do anything. Oh my God is that blood? I'm bleeding. Oh my God." I said.

"Ok, you're ok. Just relax." The deputy said.

T-Bone stood to the right of the deputy watching over me. Rudy and Quick were laughing so hard that they were in tears.

"It's not funny. You act like animals and then wonder why we treat you like animals." The deputy said as he cuffed me and escorted me out of the tank.

I was taken to the infirmary were the nurse stitched up my eye brow and cleaned up my scrapes and bruises. They returned me to my cell with a bag lunch and told me that it was for my safety. I was never so happy to see that metal shelf in all my life. I slowly lied down on it and fell asleep. No dreams this time. I was too exhausted to be concerned with my life before this place.

I woke up an hour later. My body was sore from the fight and I had to take a dump. I took a seat on the steel toilet and felt at peace. A wise man once said "There is nothing as over rated as bad sex or as under rated as taking a good shit."

The door to the cell slid open and a deputy walked in.

"Can't a guy take a shit in peace around here?" I asked.

"Westlake. You got a visitor." The deputy said.

I cleaned myself up, washed my hands in the trickle of water from the sink and stepped to the door.

"Got a towel?" I asked.

"Use your shirt." The deputy said as he cuffed me and led me down the stairs of the module and out the door.

"No one knows that I'm here. It must be Danni. She's coming to get me out of here." I thought.

The deputy took me to a visiting room. It was a small room that was decorated in the same motif as the rest of the place. There was a thick glass window in the middle of the room that separated both halves. There was a metal vent in the center that allowed you to communicate with the person on the other side. The deputy left me cuffed and closed the door behind me. I was angry and sad at the same time. I loved Danni and couldn't wait to see her. I couldn't wait for her to see me like that. In jail clothes with a split open eyebrow. She'd be sorry when she saw me. She'd apologize. She'd beg me to forgive her and take her back.

I stood there holding up my over sized pants and trying to look cool at the same time when the door on the opposite side of the glass opened.

My heart sank as another deputy walked in holding a piece of paper in his hand.

"Westlake. I have a 3126 form here. This is an official request from a Danni Salinas. She would like her keys back." The Deputy said.

"No pockets... no keys." I said.

"We took keys from you when you entered the facility. She says that you have keys to her car and keys to her apartment and she wants them back. You don't have to if you don't want to." The deputy said.

"I'd rather not." I said.

The deputy exited the room and took his 3126 with him. I was taken back to Module C and un-cuffed. I walked into my cell and discovered that the top shelve was now occupied. The prisoner laid there in the fetal position. He almost resembled a child. He rolled over and looked at me as the door clanked shut behind me. It was the white guy who sat on the floor in Holding Tank 13 rocking back and forth. I stared at him for a moment not sure if I was happy to have company or if I'd rather have my privacy.

"Time will tell." I thought.

"The toilet doesn't work. It won't flush." He said in a soft voice.

I was still pissed off about Danni and the 3126 form and I'm sure that I looked like I wanted to kill the next person I ran into.

"It only flushes once every 15 minutes. That's how they save money on the water bill around here. The faucet only lets out a trickle of water so save the fruit punch carton they give you tonight at dinner and use it for a cup." I said as I lay down on the bottom shelf.

"Oh, ok thank you. Um...my name is Robert Harris. I'm a dentist....." He said and then stopped himself when he realized how stupid he sounded.

"Well Bobby, this is jail not a job interview and I got a news flash for you. You're not a dentist anymore, you're a prisoner. You may get to be a dentist again but only if God loves you. My name is Cole, and allow me to apologize in advance for snoring." I said.

"Yeah, I know." Robert said.

I wasn't in the best mood and I got off of the shelf and stood up to face him.

"How do you know that I snore?" I asked.

"I don't. I mean, I didn't. I was in the tank when you fought the big guy and I heard them call you Cole. That's all." Robert said.

Robert looked scared and I couldn't blame him. I was too angry to be afraid but who knew what tomorrow would bring.

"You strike me as the type of guy who doesn't keep company with too many colored folks. Am I right?" I said.

"Well, I mean…well, yes your right." Robert said.

"Look, you need to relax. I've already been in one fight today and I'm running out of eyebrows to have split open. You're safe. Besides, all black men aren't violent criminals and thieves and…." and then I realized that I was in a jail cell talking to another prisoner while trying to hold up the size XXXXL pants of my jail uniform.

"God damn it, I'm not even supposed to be here. I didn't do anything." I said.

"Oh." Robert said.

"What'd they get you for any way, insider trading?" I asked.

"I'm not supposed to talk about it." Robert said.

"Bobby, I'm in a locked jail cell, with you. Who am I going to tell?" I said.

"This guy assaulted my wife." Robert said timidly. "He was her co-worker and he was leaving her notes. I found them in her purse one day. He was writing sick stuff like he wanted to fuck her and suck her tongue. I asked her about the notes and she said that she was going to show them to her boss but she was scared. I told her that I would go to speak to her boss with her but she said no. Then she came home late one night and I asked her what happened. She told me that he waited for her in the parking garage and assaulted her." Robert said.

"He beat your wife up?" I asked.

"No, he pulled her behind one of the columns and groped her and kissed her." Robert said as a single tear rolled down his cheek. "She said that she was too ashamed to come home."

"So you kicked his ass right?" I asked in an attempt to rush to the point of his sob story before I lost interest.

"No. He was a lot bigger than me. I don't fight, I mean I haven't been in a fight since the 6th grade and I lost that one." Robert said.

"So what in the fuck did you do? Come on man. Tell the God damned story." I said.

"I waited for him at the parking garage the next day and when he got out of the car I did it." Robert said.

Robert started to tremble and the beads of his sweat were falling slightly faster than his tears.

"Did what Bobby?" I demanded. "I need to know what type of man my new celly is. I have to sleep in here and I wanted to know if I should do it with both eyes closed or only one."

"He got out of the car and I drove into him as fast as I could. I pinned him between his car and mine. Then I backed up and hit him again." Robert said.

Robert was crying uncontrollably by this point.

"My car wouldn't drive anymore and I just got out and started walking down the street. The police picked me up and told me that he was dead. They brought me in here." Robert said.

"Did you see the judge today?" I asked.

"Yes." Robert said.

"What'd he give you?" I asked.

"He said I was a flight risk and that I would stay in custody until my trial." Robert said.

"So, your wife kept the notes?" I asked.

"Yes." Robert said.

"And she came home late after the assault and didn't call the police?" I asked.

"Yes." Robert said.

"Well Bobby, I'm not the brightest bastard walking God's green Earth but did you ever think that she was fucking the guy the whole time and lied to you about it when you found the notes?" I asked.

Robert's face went ashen. He looked as if he would faint.

"No. No. she wouldn't do that. She wouldn't lie to me. We have children and a dog and investments. NO! NO! She wouldn't do that!" Robert said as he rolled over on the top shelf and began to sob uncontrollably.

"Well, if I were President you would get a full pardon and a medal. He should have known better than to fuck your wife. That shit is in the bible. Don't take it personal Bobby. It happens to the best of us. You know, if I had it to do all over again I wouldn't be in a relationship until I was 27. I'd be a millionaire by now." I said as I lay back down on the bottom shelf.

Maybe jail was getting to me but it felt good to know that someone else had it worse than I did. Robert's sobbing was soft and rhythmical, just like the falling rain. I fell asleep and decided that I was indeed happy to have a little company.

The cell door opened for dinner. Robert wasn't in the mood to eat but I was. I met T-Bone at the table and told him about my new celly.

"And he believed her and killed the guy?" T-Bone asked.

"Shush! It's a secret and yeah, the dumb ass believed his wife and killed the guy. I guess things are different in Mayberry."

"The guy had it coming anyway. He fucked his wife. He should've known better." T-bone said.

"Either that or he shouldn't have gotten caught. It's a sad story. I'm hoping that Bobby can get off on temporary insanity or something. He seems like a decent guy. Just a little gullible." I said.

"What's that mean?" T-Bone asked.

"Gullible, it means he's a sucker."

"Oh. Man, shit. You're smart as hell." T-Bone said.

"No I'm not. I wouldn't be in here with you if I were smart. I just make it a point to read the occasional book every now and then. How old are you T-Bone?" I said.

"Man, shit. I just turned 21." T-Bone said.

"What's your plan when you get out of here? You can't keep hustling. They'll put you in jail for life." I said.

"Man, shit. I don't know." T-Bone said.

"Do you have any children?"

"Yeah, I have a 4 year old son." T-Bone said.

"You know, nine times out of ten, a kid follows in their parent's foot steps. Do you want your boy in a place like this?"

"Man, shit. My son ain't never gonna be in no mother fuckin' jail. My son's gonna be a doctor or something." T-Bone said.

"How is he going to do that when his father is a triple striker doing a life time bid in Pelican Bay?"

"I take care of my son." T-Bone said.

"From prison? What are you gonna do, put him through medical school one carton of cigarettes at a time?" I asked.

T-Bone sat there looking at his reflection in the stainless steel table top.

"There comes a time in every man's life when he either decides to make a change or to continue full speed ahead in the wrong damn direction. What's your real name?" I asked.

"Dante." He said.

"Dante, both of us are here because our fathers didn't keep us out of here. You haven't even said it but I know that your father didn't do shit for you. We are basically the same guy. I'm just older than you are. Dante, I'll make you this promise, your son will be in a place just like this unless you get your shit together." I said.

"I don't know how." Dante said as the tears began to flow down both of his cheeks. "I can't do nothing but hustle."

"If you can hustle then you can sell. If you can sell then you could be a sales man and sell cars or stocks or services. All it would take is a little determination and a hair cut. You owe it to your son. You owe it to yourself." I said.

Dante thought for a minute and then gathered himself.

"I can do it. I can do that shit." Dante said.

"I know you can. You have the intelligence and tenacity to do it." I said.

"Really?" Dante asked.

"Fuckin' A! You just need to do one thing first." I said.

"What's that?" Dante asked.

His enthusiasm was apparent and I couldn't make him wait a second longer.

"You need to stop saying "Man, shit" at the start of each sentence. It's annoying and it's unprofessional." I said.

"Thanks man." Dante said.

"Don't thank me. God wanted me to tell you that. I told you that I wasn't that smart."

"I mean for everything. I mean for beating that big mother fucker's ass in the tank today." Dante said.

"Hey, he took my lunch, what was I supposed to do?" I asked.

"Whoop his monkey ass!" Dante said.

We laughed until the dep's turned the television off. We returned to our cells without even being told to do so.

"I'll see you tomorrow Dante." I said.

"Alright Cole." Dante said.

"Get out of the shelf." I said as I walked into the cell.

Robert popped his head up thinking one of the deputies was in the cell.

"I brought you some food and a fruit punch."

"Thank you but I'm not hungry." Robert said.

"It doesn't matter if you're hungry or not and stop whispering to me. There's no lace on my drawers and you're not my type. Listen Bobby, you have to survive this shit. You have kids and a dog and investments."

Robert started to laugh a little and climbed out of the top shelf.

"They take the trays and plastic ware back but I made you a ham sandwich. Here's a fruit punch. Remember, you have to save the carton." I said.

"Thank you." Robert said as he ate the sandwich.

"You don't have the right to quit Bobby. You have kids counting on you. You can get past this. Remember that. You can get past this." I said.

Dante and I ate breakfast the next morning and were herded back to holding tank 13. Robert had already seen the judge and was still asleep when I left our cell.

"Hey, it's the heavy weight champion of the San Diego County Jail." Quick said as I entered the tank.

"Where's my buddy?" I asked as I took a seat.

"You mean D-Real? He's probably in the infirmary. You fucked him pretty bad homes. You were stomping on him and shit. You're fucking crazy homes. You don't have to worry about him or anyone else." Quick said.

"That shit was funny. Especially when you started screaming about bleeding." Rudy said.

"Hey, the dep's bought it. That's all that matters." I said.

"Quicky told me your woman set you up. I know a guy that can take care of her." Rudy said.

"You mean beat her ass?" I asked.

"What ever you want fucker." Rudy said.

"I can't do that. I can't harm her." I said.

"Why not? Look what she did to you. You probably don't have a job anymore. You don't have any family or friends out there. You gotta start all over again. She's got it coming for fucking you over homes. Don't worry, it won't cost that much." Rudy said.

"No man! You don't understand. She's pregnant…with my child. I can't let anything happen to her." I said.

"My dude could take care of that too. Do you really think she's gonna do anything but take the baby from you and drag your ass through the system. Child support is a bitch homes. She already told you that she would move with the baby. She won't let you see it but she will take you to court for the money. She's just started fucking with you. You'll be her puppet for the next 18 years." Rudy said.

"The child is innocent Rudy. I can't do that. Look I just want to get beyond this and move on with my life. This shit is just a speed bump." I said.

Quick stepped in to set me straight.

"You haven't been through the system yet fucker. You don't understand what this is. Remember what I told you about the big magnet that can drag you back in here at any moment? It's true homes.

This is my third time in here over the same bitch. She's the mother of my children and I love her but it's too easy for her to call the cops and put me in here when she gets mad at me for not doing what she wants. Your woman did the same thing to you. The cops love to lock us up. Blacks or Latinos, it don't matter. It makes them happier than a truck load of donuts. Your woman knows that now. She'll put you back in here the first chance she gets. Next time you don't pick up the baby when she wants, next time you don't give her extra money because she's behind on her bills 'cause she bought her new boyfriend a DVD player, next time she asks you to give her a second chance and you say no. She'll dial those three magic digits and presto, your black ass is behind bars again. Either that or the Family Court judge will hit you with enough child support to raise five kids. She'll take her new boyfriend to Acapulco and give him a blowjob while the sun sets and you'll be paying for the trip. " Quick said.

"Look, this is survival. She's not playing fair. Why are you?" Rudy asked.

"I hear you. I mean you got a point but I can't do that. Not to my child. This will all work out. I don't know how but this will all work out." I said.

"Sometimes in life you have to be a little selfish and do what's necessary to save yourself because no one else will do it for you. You'll see." Rudy said.

I sat there on the bench reflecting on everything they said. Quick and Rudy started to exchange stories again when Dante asked me what I was going to do.

"I won't hurt her and I won't hurt my child. That's not an option." I said.

"So what if she moves and takes the baby and drags you through court?" Dante asked.

"Listen, my life was fucked the day she called the police but I can't do that. I wouldn't change anything and it would only make things worse for me. Then I would be guilty of a crime. I'm innocent now. That's not much but it's all I have." I said.

"I guess you're right." Dante said.

"Have you thought anymore about what we talked about yesterday?" I said.

"What?" Dante asked.

"About your son, about a real job, about using your talents to make an honest living. Remember that little conversation? Have you thought about that or do you plan to spend the rest of your life in places like this?"

"Yeah, I guess I can sell stuff. I mean I could." Dante said.

"If you don't believe in yourself then who in the hell will? You can do this Dante. Don't forget that. You can turn this all around. The rest of your life doesn't have to be like this. You can be happy. You can walk down the street without having to look over your shoulder. You can make your son and family proud. It can all be different." I said.

The deputies returned and took Rudy and Dante out of the tank to see the judge. We wished them luck and went back to the very important business of passing the time. The deputies returned several hours later although I couldn't be sure of how many.

"Damn! Back to the module." Quick sighed as the deputies opened the door and began to cuff us one by one.

"Later." I said to Quick as his group stopped at Module A and mine continued down the corridor. We arrived at Module C and the deps systematically removed the cuffs and admitted the prisoners one by one until they got to me.

"Hold up." Deputy Carson said as he approached me.

He leaned in closely to ensure that no one could hear him.

"Listen, I'm not supposed to tell you this but keeping this a secret goes against my religion. Your cell mate committed suicide in your cell five hours ago." Carson said.

My eyes darted toward his.

"How could that be? I gave him one of my award winning pep talks…and a ham sandwich." I thought.

"He swallowed a bunch of wet toilet paper until he choked himself to death. They just wrapped up the investigation and hosed down the cell. He was looking at some serious time so he took the easy way out. I'm sorry about this but you have to go back in that cell now. I'll get you to the judge tomorrow, I promise. Just maintain until then. Ok?" Carson said.

"Yeah. Ok"

Carson removed the cuffs and I stepped into the Module, up the stairs and to the door of my cell. I peered in searching for some proof of Robert's suicide. My shelf was dry but the floor was still a bit damp. I walked in slowly and stared at the top shelf.

"Unreal. Fucking unreal." I said as I lay down on my shelf.

The hair on the back of my neck stood up. It was still cold and now damp but there was an intangible residue that lingered in the air. It was heavy and sad. I could feel the regret and tragedy of Robert's last moments in this life.

He changed his mind. Robert changed his mind as he gagged to death. I could feel it. I would have known that something happened in the cell even if Carson kept it to himself.

I thought about Robert's kids and his dog and his investments. I wondered if his wife would even care or would this be the perfect way to get to the life she truly wanted. I wondered if he saved her the trouble of paying someone to kill him for her.

I was taught that suicide is a sin but the guy was looking at a lot of time. I didn't approve but I understood. I couldn't judge him for what he did. All I could do was promise myself that I wouldn't do that to my child no matter how bad things got. No matter how crazy Danni was, no matter what the judge decided to do.

It was even more difficult to sleep with Bobby's suicide on my mind. I imagined him thrashing about on the floor as he choked to death every time I closed my eyes. His face contorted and panic stricken as he realized that he had made a terrible mistake. I was eager to head back to the holding tank by the time morning came. I would be able to get some sleep there if Quick would shut up long enough.

No such luck. Quick was like a machine gun with a never ending supply of stories and bad jokes. He talked to me incessantly and undeterred by the fact that I continued to nod off in between punch lines.

"Hey fucker, you're missing the joke. Wake up." Quick said.

The deps came for me and Quick a few hours later. We were transported through an under ground tunnel which crossed the street to the court house in the adjacent building. Once there, we were un-cuffed and placed in a cell that actually had bars. It looked to be a lot older than the modules of the County facility. Countless men passed through those cells to learn their fate and so would we.

I couldn't afford an attorney so one was appointed to me. He entered the cell as the deputies stood watch just at the threshold of the cell door. He was a tall, slim gentleman in his late thirties. He wore the tired expression of a man who had seen too much and had come to the realization that idealism was a luxury of the young. I almost felt sorry for him.

"Cole? Hi, I'm Spencer Nichols. I'll be your public defender. I think I can get you off easy if you take the plea bargain agreement the D.A has offered." He said.

"Plead guilty. Just like that, just that easy?" I said.

"Well, you have an assault charge against you on a woman half your size. The judge can hammer you with serious jail time if she wants too or you can take the plea." He said.

"And just what does the plea entail?" I asked.

"I can get you off with a little community service, a year of anger management classes, a year of narcotics anonymous classes, a donation to the victim's restitution fund and a year's probation in which time you'll have to be on your best behavior. One speeding ticket or God forbid, another assault charge and you'll be in jail for a year at least." He said.

Quick nudged me with his elbow. We had been in the same holding tank long enough for me to know what that meant.

"And what if I plead innocent?" I asked.

"I can't guarantee anything if you plead innocent. The District Attorney will set a trail date and launch a full investigation to look into every aspect of your life. The fact that you're a Marine won't help any." He said.

"What in the hell is that supposed to mean?" I asked.

"I just meant that being a Marine is a violent occupation. The judge will think that you have a greater predisposition toward violence than a civilian." He said.

"You mean the same civilians who commit home invasions, armed robberies and drive by shootings?" I asked.

"Look, I don't' mean any offense but the statement you gave the arresting officer says that you assaulted Ms. Salinas by pushing her to the ground after she attempted to speak to you about her pregnancy. That's going to be hard to refute in the court room." He said.

"What? That's not true. That's' not what I said." I shouted.

Even officer Parker was too concerned with getting off work than with getting the facts straight.

"It's your choice to make. I just want to offer the best legal advice that I can. I'll most certainly represent you to the best of my abilities no matter what you decide to do. I've got to meet with another defendant. I'll see you in the court room." He said as he walked out of the cell.

Some how I felt as though that wasn't the way either of us wanted it to go.

"Fuck him. That's why they call them Public Pretenders. He don't care about you. He looked at your black ass and decided that you were guilty just like that. They just want your money. You have to pay to do the community service and the year of anger management classes cost $30.00 per class, one class a week. It's the same thing for the Narcotics

Anonymous classes. That's over three thousand dollars. He didn't even give you the option to plead innocent. You're just another case to him." Quick said.

"So what do I do? I mean he makes it sound like pleading guilty is the only way to go." I said.

Quick looked me in the eyes and asked me if I did what I was accused of.

"No! I didn't hit her. I didn't do anything but push her off after she hit me." I said.

"Then you plead innocent and trust God to do what's best for you." Quick said.

"Just like that, just that easy?" I asked.

"Ese, there comes a time in a man's life when he's shit outta luck and the only one in his corner is God. I'd help you but we're in the same cell if you hadn't noticed. This ain't the end of the line. This is just the hard part. Do what you gotta do to get through it. Do what you gotta do to get to the rest of your life. That's the difference between you and Robert. Now man up fucker!" Quick said.

The deputies opened the door of the cell and called me and Quick forward. They placed a thick leather belt around each of our waists. They cuffed our hands to the belts and then chained the belts together and the locked shackles around each of our ankles. We shuffled our feet as they escorted us down the hallway. Walking while connected to another man at the waist is just as difficult as it sounds.

I could now see the light of day through the windows in the court house corridor. It was 9:47 AM according to the clock on the wall. The deputy guided us past various people in the hallway as we stepped no farther than the shackles allowed. I looked each of them in the eye as they watched us.

We encountered two female deputies escorting two female prisoners in the opposite direction. One of them looked at the ground. The embarrassment of being in jail was written all over her face. The other made it a point to look at everyone. I locked eyes with her as we passed and I think it turned her on. She had a tattoo on her neck that said "Beto". She looked like the type that was guilty of committing a crime but I couldn't help but wondered if she really was.

Quick and I were taken into a Court room and ushered to a section reserved for prisoners. The deputies sat us in steel chairs that were bolted to the floor. They detached our cuffs from the leather belts and attached them to the steel loops that were in the arm rest of the chairs. The deputies backed off and I took notice of the additional armed deputies in each corner of the court room. Everyone gawked at us and I could read their minds. They wondered how many people we had killed or how much money we scored in the latest heist.

That was far more sensational than the truth. That we were the latest pawns in a revenue producing scheme and that they were next. It was so much easier to think of us as dangerous monsters than to see us as the guy next door.

"I looked at Quick, searching for a clue on what was to come next.

"The judge is gonna come in next and then…." Quick said before he was told to shut up by the deputy standing guard.

The door to the Judges chambers opened and the bailiff spoke.

"All rise, the Honorable Judge Judith McKenzie presiding. Please be seated."

We remained seated since we were chained to the floor. I gave Quick a look and he shook his head. We were in deep trouble. A black guy with a domestic violence charge and a Mexican guy in for violating a restraining order in a white female judge's court room. We could expect no mercy.

We sat through about five cases including two prisoners from our holding tank until the judge finally got to my case.

"Your Honor, next on the docket is the matter of the people of San Diego County versus Cole Westlake." The clerk of the court announced.

"Mr. Westlake you stand charged in the assault on one Danni Salinas. How do you plead?" the Judge asked.

My heart began to race and my eye twitched but I remained cool as ice on the outside.

"Not guilty your Honor." I said.

"Mr. Westlake has entered a plea of not guilty. When is the next available trail date." The Judge asked the clerk.

"February 23rd your honor with a discovery hearing on February 12th." The clerk responded.

"Noted. Mr. Westlake, you were very cooperative according to the arresting officer's report. The court will take that into account and release you on your own recognizance. You have been determined a non- flight risk but you are prohibited from leaving the state. A warrant will be issued for your arrest if you fail to appear in court for your discovery hearing. Ms. Salinas has taken out a restraining order on you and the county of San Diego has issued a stay away order. I would encourage you to stay as far away from Ms. Salinas as possible or you will be arrested and placed in jail to serve no less than one year. Do you have any questions?" the judge asked.

"No your honor."

I gave Quick a look and he responded with a smile. I would be released that day as would he. He pled guilty and the judge sentenced him to 100 hours of community service as well as anger management courses. It was what he expected.

We were taken back to our individual modules. Hours passed until Deputy Carson came for me.

"Grab your blanket, pillow and mattress and step to the door." Carson said.

I was cuffed and taken out of Module C to "out process."

"Congratulations. Just stay away from her and you may have a chance." Deputy Carson said.

"Don't worry." I said.

"You say that now but you'd be surprised to learn how many guys come back here three and four times for the same reason. Mess this up and we'll be seeing each other again." Carson said.

Carson placed me in another holding tank along with twenty prisoners and I thanked him for looking out for me. Quick arrived with another group a short time later.

"Hey, do you know what time it is?" I asked.

"No homes but I'll tell you when they give me my watch back." Quick said.

Each man was called up to the window to sign for his possessions thirty minutes later. Quick grabbed the brown paper bag with his clothes in it from the clerk on the other side of the impact resistant glass and got dressed right there in the middle of the tank. He scratched his phone number on part of the paper bag that his clothes were in.

"Call me when you get out. This shit has just started for you." Quick said.

The deputy called his name and he walked out of the door on the far end of the room. It was my turn about fifteen minutes later. I got dressed in my short sleeve t-shirt, jeans and shoes. The deputy called me to the door and I walked through it to find myself in a long dimly lit corridor with a flickering fluorescent light on the far end. There was a yellow arrow painted on the wall that pointed down the corridor. I took the hint and found myself passing through another door with a stairwell on the other side of it.

I walked down the steps and through the final door and ended up on the streets of down town San Diego. The wind cut through me and I realized that I was poorly dressed for the weather. I stood there on the side walk and caught sight of a Wendy's only a block away. I had fifteen dollars in cash on me and I was starving. I hurried down the side walk outrunning both my hunger and the cold. I walked through the door and took refuge in the warmth of the heat lamps and deep fryer. I waited in line until I could order a Spicy Chicken filet sandwich and medium French fries. It had to be the best meal that I ever had in my entire life. I was elated to be out of jail and I promised myself that I would rise again just as the South will.

I needed to get my car but I had both a Stay Away order and a Restraining order to contend with. The nearest Trolley stop was only two blocks away and I ran the entire distance. It felt as if the temperature was dropping with each passing minute. My teeth began to chatter as the wind blew even harder.

I bought a ticket and took a seat in the third trolley car. The clock at the station read 9:32 PM. It had taken hours to get out processed from jail. I got off of the trolley at the Fashion Valley stop and walked toward the apartment. I found a pay phone that was 500 feet away from the complex and called the police. I told them that I had just been released from jail and that I didn't want any more trouble. I just needed my car and my cell phone. I wouldn't get too far without them.

It took the police about 35 minutes to get there since it wasn't an emergency. I saw a police cruiser parked outside of the complex and approached it cautiously.

"Hey, I'm the guy who called you." I said.

"Ok, yeah. We were looking for you. You're just getting your car right?" The officer asked.

"Yeah and my cell phone." I said.

The officer walked me down into the parking garage that was below the apartment building. I could see five Police officers in various positions in the garage as we walked down the ramp.

"Damn, am I really that dangerous or just really that black? What did she tell them about me?" I thought.

I approached my car and placed the key in the door.

"Ms. Salinas says you have her keys." The officer said.

"Yeah and she has one of mine and my cell phone. Want to trade?" I said.

"I'll ask her about them." The officer said as he opened has hand.

I was too tired to fight anymore. I was too tired to demand anything. I just wanted to sleep in a room with the lights off and on a mattress that didn't resemble an exercise mat. I needed to pick my battles and I didn't want to waste my time or energy on this one.

I gave him the key and waited as he walked over to another officer. He returned a short while later and stated that Danni didn't have my car keys or my cell phone. I just stared at him.

"We can't stand out here all night. You can file a compliant about the keys and the phone later but it would be best if you left now before you get angry and something happens." The officer said.

"Before I get angry, before something happens? You haven't been paying attention have you?" I asked.

"Mr. Westlake it's time you left." The officer said.

I searched the parking garage looking for a glimpse of Danni but there was none. I got into the car and started the engine. I pulled out of the garage and headed to the one place where I knew I could find peace and quiet.

I parked a few spaces away form one of the public rest rooms that were placed through out the coast line of Shelter Island. I sat there for a moment trying to decide what to do next.

"Mike! I'll call Mike!" I said.

I grabbed a couple quarters that I always kept in the center console and jumped out of the car. I walked over to the pay phone that was on the brick wall of the rest room and dialed Mike's number.

It was 11:19 PM. The phone rang several times and I knew that he may be asleep but what could I do.

"Hello." Faith said as she answered the phone.
Her voice was raspy and I could tell that I woke her up.

"Faith, this is Cole. I'm sorry to call so late. Can I speak to Mike?"

"He's on duty tonight. He'll get off at 8:30 tomorrow morning." Faith said.

"Ok. I'm sorry for waking you up."

"You don't sound so good. Is everything all right?" Faith asked.

"Danni put me in jail three days ago. I just got out and wanted to talk to Mike."

"Oh my God. Why? Why would she do that? What happened?" Faith asked.

"I don't even no where to start. She stopped taking her pill without telling me and now she's pregnant. She was in therapy and she was on anti-depressants and then quit taking them. She jumped on me and I

Low Fuel

pushed her off and then she called the police and told them I was black and they locked me up." I said in a manic flurry.

"Are you going to be ok?" Faith asked.

"Yeah, I'm fine. I just needed to vent to Mike. I'm sorry for waking you up. I'll call him tomorrow." I said and then hung up the phone.

I lied to Faith because I didn't want to stress her out. I wasn't fine and I was scared.

I walked back to the car and drove over to the Motel 6 off of Rosecrans Street and got a room. I went back to my car to get my gym bag out of the trunk. There were a clean pair of socks, a sweat shirt and sweat pants inside of it. Getting sick wouldn't help matters at all and I would need to stay as warm as possible until I could get my clothes from the apartment.

I popped the trunk open and discovered that the gym bag was gone as was the blanket that I kept there. Upon further investigation I found that my jack and spare tire were missing as well.

"What in the Hell? That bitch." I screamed as I stood in the parking lot.

A couple turned in my direction as they walked by.

"What? Who in the fuck are you looking at?" I yelled.

They walked away as fast as they could and I turned my attention back to the empty trunk.

"What is she trying to accomplish? She's taken everything from me, even my spare tire.

"What good would that do her?" I thought.

SIX

I awoke with that "Where in the hell am I?" feeling again but this time I was alone in a room at the Motel 6.

"Thank God!" I said to myself.

I had been dreaming about being in jail. Robert's body twitched in a macabre jig on the floor while D-Real ran through Module C screaming my name and looking for revenge.

Breakfast at the Denny's around the corner from the Motel 6 was twenty times better than what I had become accustomed to in jail. I poured the maple syrup in swirls on top of the stack of pancakes and carefully cut into them. I raised the fork in anxious expectation of the first bite and saw an elderly couple eating breakfast out of the corner of my eye. They were happy together. Happy after all of those years. I hadn't eaten at a restaurant alone since I met Danni and it felt awkward.

I walked back into the hotel room and lay down on the bed. I turned on the TV and the time in the lower left corner of the news broadcast read 6:48 AM. I would have to call my boss at 8:00 AM to see if I still had a job. My stomach was full of butterflies.

"I'm sorry Cole but you lied to me. You told me that you had a family emergency but that wasn't the truth. Your girlfriend called and told me that you had been arrested for beating her. She said that you have a drug problem and that you hit her when she begged you to stop. I didn't believe her until I called the police department and they said that you were in custody. The only thing I hate more than a drug addict is a woman beater and you're both. You missed three days and lied to me. I had to let you go. I had to. You put yourself in this position. You'll probably lose your clearance over this. The best I can do is pay you for your outstanding leave." Dave said.

"Well, I got it over with. Now I know." I thought.

I dialed the number to Jessi's desk but got no answer. I needed to talk to her. She always gave the best advice. I lay back down on the bed and closed my eyes. So much had happened over the past few days. Slumber was a welcomed escape although it was short lived.

I woke up in time to make the 11:00 AM check out time. It was necessary to take stock of my situation and devise a master plan to save my life. I had $1,153.47 in my savings account but that would go fast. I needed a job. I needed a home. I needed help.

I called Jessi again but the phone was answered by our co-worker Norma.

"Hey Norma, it's Cole. Is Jessi there? I really need to talk to her."

"Cole? Where have you been? Where are you?" Norma asked.

"I was fired. Where's Jessi? I really need to speak with her."

"You didn't hear?" Norma said.

"Hear what? What's going on? Is she ok?" I asked.

"No! No she isn't. Her son was killed two days ago." Norma said.

"What?"

"The police were looking for one of his friends that had a warrant for something. They found the two of them with some girls at the park and things got out of hand. All I know is that they shot him and now Jessi is on leave taking care of her grand daughter." Norma said. Operation Clean Sweep claimed yet another victim. I called Jessi's voice mail later that day, telling her what had happened to me and that I was sorry to hear about the loss of her son. I wanted to tell her to call me if she needed anything but what could I do? It was as if the whole world was coming to an end. My heart ached for Jessi. She was such a good person. She didn't deserve any of this. Neither one of us did.

I sat at Shelter Island until about 4:45PM before calling Mike again.

"She locked you up? She actually did that shit?" Mike asked.

"Yeah and she stole everything from my car. Then she called my job and told them that I was on drugs and that I beat her. They fired me Mike. I've never been fired from a job before in my life. I've got a trial date. I've got a restraining order. I'm homeless, all because she told a lie. This shit is crazy!"

"Where'd you stay last night?" Mike asked.

"I got a room at the Motel 6."

"Stay here tonight." Mike said.

I drove to Camp Pendleton and Mike met me at the door with a beer.

"Damn! You look bad." Mike said.

"Thanks. You're so considerate. That's one of the things I admire most about you." I said.

"I'm handsome too." Mike added.

"Can you cut the stand up comedy routine? I'm a little stressed out."

"Don't worry. You can stay here. We'll work something out." Mike said.

Faith was in the middle of cooking dinner and took a minute to ask me how I was.

"I'm fine." I said.

"Is she crazy? Faith asked.

"I guess. I mean she just exploded and...well yeah, she must be crazy." I said.

"I thought Danni was a little strange. She's been calling here asking to talk to Mike about how to make you want to be with her. I told her to stop. I mean she's older than I am. She should know better than to call here and ask to speak to my husband." Faith said.

"She did what? She was calling here, for how long?" I asked.

"The past couple of weeks." Faith said.

"I wish you had told me. She's totally out of control." I said.

Mike and I sat down in the living room after dinner to watch a movie. Faith and Dion washed the dishes until the phone rang.

"Hello. Danni. Are you Ok?" Faith said as she looked in my direction.

I mouthed the words "I'm not here!" I wasn't supposed to have any contact with her and I didn't want to argue with her on the phone in Mike's living room.

"Danni what's going on? Cole called here last night and said that you had him arrested.
Yeah, um hum, ok." Faith said as she took a seat in the kitchen.

"You Ok?" Mike asked.

"No! She had me locked up, slandered my name, cost me my job. This is a nightmare. I didn't do anything to her." I said.

"Then why is she trying to screw you over?" Mike asked.

"I keep asking myself the same question. I don't know." I said.

"I don't believe that. Cole isn't a drug addict." Faith said.

Faith and Mike took turns trying calm Danni down for an hour and a half but nothing helped other than ending the conversation. I sat on the couch feeling stupid. I thought I was the luckiest man in the world the night that I met Danni. Now I felt like a fool. I should have stayed home and watched the Sci-Fi Channel that night.

"Damn! Danni's crazy. I mean she sounds crazy. She doesn't sound like herself." Mike said.

"Danni said that you do cocaine and that you told her to abort the baby or you would kick it out of her." Faith said in an accusatory tone.

"I never said that. I would never say that." I said.

"She said that she has been begging you to stop getting high and that you've been pawning everything including some of her jewelry so that you could get more coke." Faith said.

"I'm not a coke head. I don't get high. I was in the Marines for Christ sake! They gave us random drug tests." I said.

"Yeah, but you got out 9 months ago." Faith said as she searched for a tell tale sign that I was lying.

"I don't get high." I said softly.

"She said that it wasn't the first time you hit her" Faith said.

"I never hit her. She hit me." I said.

"She also said that you grew up in an abusive home and that you watched your mother get beat up. You know, most abused kids grow up to… well you know." Faith said.

It was no use. I was big, black and a Marine. I was a prime candidate for the women beater of the year award as far as Faith was concerned.

It was two on one and I wasn't doing a very good job of defending myself.

Faith grew weary of the cross examination and went upstairs to get Dion ready for bed. Mike and I talked for a while until 9:45 PM. He had PT the next morning and had to get up early.

"I'm going to hit the rack. I'll see you in the morning." Mike said.

"Mike… thanks man. Thanks for letting me stay here tonight. I didn't want to be a burden but I didn't have any where else to go." I said.

"Don't worry about it. It's all good. Besides, I owe you one." Mike said.

It wasn't all good. I knew Mike pretty well and I knew when something was wrong.

I remember when Mike and Faith first started living together. They would argue all of the time and he would come to stay the night at my place. It was the only time he stopped smiling and laughing. He was one of those guys who couldn't hide his emotions no matter how hard he tried. I kept a six pack in the fridge just for him and he had carte blanche at my place. He could walk right in the front door and open the fridge and have a cold one to take him off the edge. Mike spent the night on my couch so many times that I almost gave it to him as a wedding gift.

Now it was my turn to sleep on his couch. I closed my eyes and left reality behind. That was until I was awoken by the sound of thunder. It was the sound of feet stomping and moving into position which was quickly followed by the sound of Mike's voice. They were trying to quietly carry out a heated argument but the two don't go hand in hand. Besides, I was an expert in detecting the late night scuffle.

"I don't care what Danni said. That's my friend and he'll stay here if I say so. I'm the man of this house. I wear the pants up in here." Mike said.

"I don't want a violent drug addict around my son Mike. He told her to abort their baby. If he'll kill his own baby than he'll do anything." Faith said.

"He didn't kill their baby Faith. God Damn it! Mike said.

"What if he does something while he's here?" Faith asked.

"What's he going to do?" Mike said.

"I don't know and I don't want to know. I don't want him in here Mike! You need to be a man and do what's best for your family not what's best for your drinking buddy." Faith said.

"You don't tell me what the fuck I'm gonna do." Mike shouted.

I was ashamed of myself for making Mike's home unhappier than it had been five minutes before I walked through the front door. I should have just gotten another hotel room. Better yet, I should have been a man and slept in my car. That way I could have saved money and not brought my troubles into Mike's life.

Mike woke me up early the next morning.

"Hey, I made breakfast. Come on and get some." Mike said.

"Thanks. Where's Faith? Doesn't she have to be to work in a little while?" I asked.

"Oh, she doesn't really eat breakfast." Mike said.

He wasn't smiling.

"I hope you don't mind but I called a friend of mine last night and he said that I could stay with him. He's single and has the space. I figure that would be better and I don't want to be in your way. You've got a family and all." I said.

"OK, I mean if you think that's best but you're still welcomed to a home cooked meal when ever you need one." Mike said.

I could see the relief on his face. We finished breakfast and said our goodbyes. Mike headed out the door to PT at 5:15 AM. I gathered my things and walked out of the door and closed it tightly behind me, tugging on it to ensure that it was locked. I didn't bother to say good bye to Faith. She would be happy to see me go. She never really liked me anyway. It might have had something to do with me telling Mike that marrying her would be a big mistake.

"The two of you fight too much. How is that going to make for a successful relationship?" I asked.

Mike never really had a good answer. He just married her. Mike probably told Faith everything I said. She had him wide open and he couldn't resist her. Danni's ranting was just the excuse Faith was looking for to push me out of the picture.

I parked at Shelter Island near the same public rest room as the night before. I laid the driver's seat back and went back to sleep.

I awoke at 9:19 AM to the sound of a container ship sounding its horn. That usually happened when a sail boat got a little too close. I reached for the note pad that I kept in the glove compartment and began to make a plan of action. I would need a new cell phone. That way I could take calls from my public defender and potential employers. I needed to arrange another police escort to retrieve my possessions from the apartment. But most importantly, I needed to find a job.

I drove over to the Fashion Valley mall and bought a phone and the all important car charger. I didn't know how long my car would be my base of operations but I did know that I would need the ability to keep the phone charged. I fished out the scrap of paper with Quick's phone number on it from my pocket and gave him a call.

"Shit fucker! It's 11:30." Quick said.

"Wake your ass up. It's Cole, from Jail."

"Hey Ese. ¿Que Pasa?" Quick said.

"I lost my job. They fired me."

"Damn! Don't worry. I got the perfect job for you. My cousin is the head of security at the Bay Breeze night club. I'll get your big ass a job as a bouncer. You can beat the hell outta fuckers for money." Quick said with his trade marked chuckle.

"I'm a professional not some jack ass bouncer in a night club looking for a fight." I said.

"No ese. You're a homeless, jobless, black guy about to go on trial for assault. It's like I said. You're one of us now. You better start acting like it. You think anyone is gonna give a woman beater a job. Being a bouncer is the best you can do right now." Quick said.

I sighed and considered his words.

"Where are you staying?" Quick asked.

"I stayed at a friend's house last night but I heard him and his wife arguing about me. I guess I'll stay in my car until I find a job and a place of my own." I said.

"Damn, that's fucked up! I would let you stay here but my Tia don't like black people. One of you guys snatched her purse thirty years ago and she's been holding a grudge ever since. Sorry!" Quick said.

"Don't worry about it. I'm getting used to being on everyone's shit list. When can I meet your cousin?" I said.

"Let me give him a call. I'll tell him all about you and D-Real." Quick said.

"Thanks but can you leave out the part about jail. It's been my experience that potential employer's don't like to hear that you've been in jail." I said.

"Relax fool, my cousin's one of us too." Quick said.

I called the office of Spencer Nichols in order to touch base with him regarding my case.

"This is Nichols."

"Hello Mr. Nichols, This is Cole Westlake. I just wanted to contact you regarding my case and trial date." I said.

"Westlake, Westlake let me see here…" he said.

I could hear him shuffling through papers as he repeated my name over and over so as not to lose his train of thought. This continued for about thirty seconds too long and I could tell that I was a priority.

"Westlake… Can you jog my memory?" He said.

"Sure…I'm the black guy who was in jail." I said heavy on the sarcasm.

"Oh, well I've got a couple of those. Can you be more specific?" he said.

"Sure, anything for a professional. Danni Salinas filed an assault charge against me on January 21st. I was arrested and released from the county jail on January 23rd." I said,

"Hmmm…" and then more shuffling.

"Would it help if I called you back? That way you could buy a couple of file cabinets and put them to use?" I said.

"Got it!" he said more surprised than relieved. "Ok, I think I can get the judge to accept your plea bargain and you can walk away with a little community service, anger management and Narcotics anonymous courses and a donation to the victim's restitution fund. You would be on probation for a year but that's just the nature of the beast. What do you think?" he asked.

"I think you have a very bad memory. I think you need your secretary to help you clean up your office and most of all I think that I'd rot in hell before I plead guilty to a crime I didn't commit." I said.

"Now there's no need to be surly." He said.

"I also think that you're a little slow. Let me ask you a question. Why is it that you refuse to offer me legal counsel regarding my pleading innocent?" I asked.

"Well, I just don't think your chances are that good." He said.

"Why?" I asked.

"Well, I mean... because I have experience in these matters and I know how the judge is likely to rule." He said.

"I think you'd be happier with me being found guilty and paying into the system than you would be with me free and innocent. I think you don't care too much about putting in the work and effort to help me beat this. I think you're lazy and that there are probably a lot of innocent people in jail because of you." I said.

He was silent for a moment before he thought of an appropriate response.

"I'm sorry you feel that way." He said.

"That makes two of us. Get me a new public defender or I'm going to be more trouble than this phone call." I said.

He knew I meant it. I may not have been able to follow through on the threat but he knew that I did mean every word of it.

"I'll have your case transferred." He said and then hung up.

It was a bitter sweet victory to say the least. My tough guy act with Spencer Nichols was all bravado and I was in no position to make demands. I decided to take control of what I could and hope for the best with everything else. I found a tax specialist and got my taxes done. I had no idea when I would find steady employment and the refund would come in handy. My next stop was the post office to rent a P.O. Box. There was no telling what Danni would do with my mail once she got her hands on it. She had systematically gone after anyone and anything that would help me survive. I was amazed that I had lasted as long as I did.

Still, my mind drifted to her when I took a break from being pissed off. Love is like a bullet. You can't put it back down the barrel once you've fired it. As bad as it was, I couldn't stop loving her if I wanted to. I contacted the Rental office of the Apartment complex in Mira Mesa and informed them that I lost my job and they said that they would refund my security deposit as soon as possible

I drove toward the court house the morning of January 30th for my Restraining order hearing. I found the public parking lot and paid $10.00 to park the car. I winced in pain every time I had to hand over what little money I had left. I placed my keys and wallet in the plastic tray and walked through the metal detector at the entrance of the court house. The Sheriffs deputies who manned the security check point were more concerned with being intimidating than offering assistance to a tax paying citizen, so I stared at the docket that was pinned to a pegboard on the wall until I found my name under court room 4A.

I have an aversion to court rooms to this day. They carry with them the sense of impending doom as freedom is revoked and fines are levied.

People entered the court room one by one. Some looked somber and some apprehensive. Danni walked through the door next and took a seat on the opposite side of the room. All things considered, she was a sight for sore eyes in her grey pant suit and black silk blouse. She looked around the room in a subtle manner searching for me but looked past me twice.

I looked a lot different since my stay in the county jail. My smile had been replaced by a scowl and I wasn't the best dressed man in town. I stared at her, undressing her with my eyes. I was used to having sex with her on a regular basis and I was way over due. Her eyes met mine just as I was about to remove her bra and she studied my face for some hope of reconciliation.

She stood up and walked my way.

She said "Hi" and took a seat beside me as if we were meeting for the first time.

"How have you been?" Danni asked.

"Me, oh I've been jailed, homeless and unemployed. How have you been?" I asked.

Tears began to form in the corners of her eyes. "Cole, I…" and then the Deputy began calling names.

"Salinas, Westlake? Is that you two?" the Deputy asked.

I told him that we were and he checked his clipboard and told us to separate.

Danni returned to the other side of the court room just as the judge entered.

The judge called the cases on the docket until she got to ours.

"Danni Salinas vs. Cole Westlake."

We both stood and approached the bench.

"Ms. Salinas, you took out this restraining order on January 21st. Do you need this peace order to remain in effect?" the judge asked.

"No, I don't want it. I never did." Danni said as she looked at the carpeted floor.

"Very well. There is still a Stay Away order in effect and I would encourage you both to obey it. Sometimes things get out of hand in relationships and I understand that but violating this order will land Mr. Westlake back in jail. I would like to recommend some counseling so that you both can work through the issues that have brought you here today. The Restraining order is no longer valid. Have a nice day." The judge said.

The bailiff ushered Danni out of the court room and I followed. I saw Danni waiting for me outside the courtroom as I exited. I made a right turn and proceeded down the corridor toward the exit.

"Cole..Cole... Cole, I'm sorry! Talk to me please." Danni pleaded.

"I can't Danni. I've got a Stay Away order against me remember? I shouldn't even be speaking to you." I said.

"Cole I need you. The baby needs you. I need you to come back home. I'm sorry. I want to work this out." Danni said.

I wanted to go home with her but there was too much at stake. I couldn't risk her calling the police again.

"This is beyond us now. The county is involved and I can't go back home." I said.

"I won't tell them Cole. I'll protect you. Just come home." Danni said.

"You'll protect me? How...how are you going to protect me from the police and the District Attorney?" I asked.

I picked up my pace and continued toward the parking lot down the street.

"What about us? What about the baby? Danni asked.

"I don't know Danni. I don't know what's going to happen now. I've got a trial next month. I could be going to jail for a year." I said.

"I'll tell them that you didn't do it." Danni said.

I left her in tears as I drove away. I was too hurt to feel anything other than anger.

My phone began to ring by the time I made it to the traffic light.

"What?" I said as I answered the phone.

"Hey fucker! My cousin wants you to stop by the club on Friday night. He wants to take a look at you." Quick said.

"Really?"

"Yeah, he needs to see if you look scary or not. I told him that all black guys look scary to me." Quick said.

"Give me the address fool."

Quick gave me the address of the club and I made a call to the San Diego Police.

They called back an hour later and told me to meet an officer at the apartment at 6:00PM that evening. I parked next to the police cruiser that was in the circle in front of the complex and met the officer in front of the apartment.

"I called you about getting my things." I said.

"I understand your situation but let's just get your things and leave as soon as possible. I would appreciate it if you didn't say too much to her while inside. We don't want an altercation." The officer said.

He knocked on the door and Danni opened it shyly. I walked in without looking at her or saying a word and entered the bedroom.

My closet was empty. I checked the shelf above and looked inside once more. My shoes, shirts, slacks, boots, leather and suede jackets were gone. My blood pressure began to rise as I ran over to the dresser. There were a few pairs of socks and boxer shorts left as well as two white tank tops.

"Where is my stuff Danni?" I asked.

"I didn't touch anything Cole. It's all the way you left it." Danni said.

"Are you fucking crazy? I want my shit right now! Who in the fuck do you think you are?" I shouted.

"Hey! Don't say another word to her. I'm not here to supervise an argument. Just get your belongings and go." The officer said.

"That's the point. There are no belongings. You know what…fuck this shit! All of my stuff is gone. She's playing some kind of game. I had a closet full of clothes. Everything is gone. My uniforms, my photo albums, my CD collection, The piggy bank I've had since I was two years old. Everything is gone." I said.

"Mr. Westlake, I need you to leave now." The officer said.

"Is this legal? I asked as I walked out of the door.

"Do you have proof of what you had and it's value? Do you have receipts?" the officer asked.

"Who in the hell keeps receipts for every piece of clothing they buy? For everything they own? For their entire life? I don't have a receipt for my photo album!" I said.

"I'm sorry but I don't have any proof that you had anymore than is here now." The officer said.

"So she can destroy my life and that's fine but me raising my voice is against the law? Is that what you're telling me?" I said.

The officer was beginning to get nervous and I could feel the adrenaline pumping through my veins.

"Fuck both of you!" I said.

I floored the accelerator and left a twenty foot long trail of burned rubber behind me. I wondered what Danni was doing. First she put me in jail and then she takes everything I owned and acted as if she didn't know anything about it. It was official. I hated the bitch. She's destroyed my entire life and had given me an arrest record. That's just what every young black man needs to live a successful life. Consider me a statistic.

I entered the access code into the keypad and the gate to the public storage facility slowly opened. I fumbled with the lock in the dark until it popped opened. I lifted the rolling door and saw that the unit was completely empty. No furniture, no boxes, nothing but dust and a picture of me and Danni that was left on the floor for me to find.

I got a room at the Motel 6 and a 12 pack of beer from the liquor store around the corner. My eye was twitching again and I figured that it would stop if I got it drunk. I filled the bathroom sink up with ice from the ice machine in the hallway and placed the beers in it.

The room didn't have a refrigerator and I needed to be creative. I popped the top and chugged the first beer and then sipped the second. I couldn't keep staying in hotel rooms. My money wouldn't last that long. I was afraid to sleep in my car. Who knows what would happen in the middle of the night. At least Quick found a job for me as a bouncer but that wasn't much money and I had bills to pay.

I called Mike but got his voice mail instead. I left him a message telling him that I was OK and what Danni did. I gave him my new cell phone number and asked him to call me when he could.

The loneliness was unrelenting so I called Quick.

"Hey, what's up?" I asked.

"Hey Fucker. You ok?"

"No man. Danni gave away all my stuff while I was in jail. She wiped me out. I don't have anything. Not a stitch." I said.

"Of course she threw your stuff away. That's what they do when they get mad. Then they apologize. That's how they get you back. You're new at this aren't you?" Quick said.

"I guess. I just didn't expect it that's all. I didn't think she would take it this far." I said.

"Hell hath no fury like a scorned woman. You're lucky that's all that she did. My best friend's wife stabbed him for trying to leave her crazy ass." Quick said.

"Why is she doing this? I didn't do anything to her." I said.

"Yes you did. You destroyed her fantasy when you told her the truth, when you said that you would leave her. That's why she's trying to hurt you. She opened up and made her self vulnerable to you. She took a chance on you and you rejected her. She'll make you pay for that. If she can't have you then no one will. She'll destroy you before she allows you to be happy with someone else. That's how it is." Quick said.

"She was impossible to live with. I thought that leaving was the right thing to do. I was trying to be responsible." I said.

"Responsible? Are you kidding? Cole, this woman is eleven years older than you are. Did you ever ask yourself why she wanted to be with such a young guy? She's a lot smarter than you. She used you to get what she wanted. She couldn't manipulate a man her age but she could control you through guilt and tears. She played you homes. Face it." Quick said.

I sat there silently on the verge of tears. I had been so naive. I had been so stupid. I actually loved her but she used me from the start. Danni never loved me. She just didn't want to move to San Diego alone. I was her free therapist, body guard and fuck buddy.
She isolated me from everyone that I knew. She kept me from meeting people and having friends so that no one could catch on to her plan. She made it so that she was all I had. She tossed me aside like yesterday's newspaper when she realized that I would no longer play along. She used me just like Mac used Blake. She was treacherous and now I understood. Now I understood what treachery was and my world would never be the same.

"Hello? Hey Fucker. Are you there?" Quick asked.

"Yeah, I'm here." I whispered.

"Look, you'll be ok. Think about the future. Think about what things will be like once the trial is over and this is just a bad memory." Quick said.

"It's just that I don't have a lot of money saved and I'm unemployed." I said.

"Yeah but my cousin will hire you, and that's something for right now. Think positive. Be optimistic homes." Quick said.

"Yeah, I'm trying. It's just that I'm out here alone and I don't know what's going to happen next." I said.

You need some money, that's what you need. I know this guy that brings coke across the border. He's got a stack of paper at his place. They say he keeps it in a big tool box. Let's go get it." Quick said.

"You mean rob him?"

"Fuck yeah!" Quick said.

"Are you paying attention? I'll go back to jail if I get into any more trouble. I don't need that shit."

"What's he gonna do? Call the police and say "Hey, I'm a drug dealer and this big black guy and his Mexican side kick just robbed me for my drug money?" come on fucker. Wise up a little. This is the perfect crime. The victim can't call the police and he doesn't trust anyone so he's on his own. It's that easy." Quick said.

"If it's that easy then why haven't you done it yet?" I asked.

"Because I don't know how to do that stuff. I'm a jerk off not a thief. You're a Marine. You could plan it all out. Just like in the movies." Quick said.

I considered Quick's proposal and told him that I would think about it. I ended the call and opened my fourth beer.

I woke up the next morning at 9:48 AM with a hang over and the ringing cell phone didn't help any. I over slept, which wasn't at all like me.

"Hello Mr. Westlake, my name is Wallid Mohamed. I'm taking over your case from Spencer Nichols. I need you to arrive 30 minutes early on February 12th. I would like to ask you a few questions regarding the character and history of Ms. Salinas. Please be prepared to discuss anything we can use against her." Wallid said.

I agreed, ended the phone call and laid there in the bed.

"So it's come to this, me against her in a court of law." I thought.

I checked out of the hotel at 11:00am and drove to the mall. I needed to buy some clothing. Between the court case and trying to find a new job, I would need something to wear other than jeans and a t-shirt. I went back to Miller's Outpost and found a pair of black slacks and a shirt that fit nicely. One of the girls who worked in the store was eying me but I ignored her.

"That shirt will look nice on you. You have good taste." She said.

I thanked her and walked away. She was obviously flirting with me but I wasn't interested. I didn't need anymore trouble. I bought several outfits and some dress shoes and headed back to Shelter Island. I called Mike once more but was greeted by his voice mail again.

I pulled the blanket and pillow that I bought out of the shopping bag and made myself comfortable as the last bit of the sun sank below the horizon. I parked far enough away from the other cars to get some privacy but under a street light to provide a modicum of safety. I hoped that it would be enough. I lay there trying to relax enough to sleep but every sound caused me to become alarmed. Car doors slamming shut, car stereo's pumping loud music as they drove by. The rattle of chains as boats were secured to trailers for the evening. I turned on the radio and found an AM talk show. The sound of another voice gave me some comfort and I didn't feel so alone anymore.

I woke up at about 2:35AM and needed to take a leak. The chill of the night time air cut through me as I walked over to the rest room. The door of the rest room was propped open by a large trash can presumably as a deterrent to violent crime. I checked the corners of the room before I crossed the threshold of the door.

One of the fluorescent lights was out and half of the room was dark. It was the perfect place for a mugging. I heard a sound at the door just as I unzipped my pants and began to urinate.

"Perfect timing. I guess I'm going to piss all over this mother fucker while I beat the shit out of him." I thought.

I zipped up and stayed close to the wall as I silently crept toward the door. I didn't want to fight anyone but it was 2:30 in the morning and I wasn't taking any chances. I approached the door and quickly glanced around the corner. I jumped through the door way and continued running backward and discovered the culprit. The plastic liner in the trash can rattled each time the wind blew.

That Friday night I drove to the Bay Breeze night club to meet Quick's cousin.

"Hey Fucker!" I said to Quick catching him off guard.

He came running down the steps and shook my hand.

"Hey homes. You look Clean. I thought your girl threw away your shit." Quick said.

"She did. This is new." I said.

I was dressed in a pair of black slacks, pleated and cuffed along with a black button up shirt with the sleeves rolled up to the middle of my fore arms.

"Hey, you look like one of the crew. Let's go." Quick said.

We walked up the stairs and past the door man.

"It's cool; he's here to meet Mando." Quick said.

The door man waved us in and we rounded a few corners and then traveled down a narrow hallway. It was early but the club was full of gorgeous women. San Diego's finest. Quick knocked on the door at the end of the hallway and it opened.

"Hey fucker, come one in. Is this the guy?" Mando asked.

"Yeah, this is the guy. Armando, this is Cole." Quick said.

"Good to meet you." I said.

"Like wise. How tall are you?" Mando asked.

"6'4".

"You got any experience?" Mando asked.

"Marine Corps."

"Can you start tonight?"

I stood by the main bar of the club and fiddled with the earpiece to the radio that Mando gave me. It didn't fit very well but I hoped that I would get use to it. The job paid a meager $10.00 an hour and I would be working Friday and Saturday nights. Just two six hour shifts. The rules were simple. No drinking, pay attention to the other bouncers, be courteous but don't take shit off of anyone and most importantly keep the ladies to a minimum. Mando just fired a guy for doing more flirting than working.

Quick was elated at the prospect of my working for his cousin.

"This is gonna be the greatest. I come here all the time. We'll get all the ladies. You're one of the family now. We'll just tell people that you're half Mexican. OK?" Quick said.

"Do you mind? I'm trying to look tough." I said.

"Tough? For what? They don't fight here." Quick said.

"No?"

"No homes. You can't meet the ladies if you're fighting and tearing shit up. That's not sexy!" Quick said.

"Damn! And I was ready to vent a little frustration."

"Just relax and enjoy the sights. This place is the one of the best clubs in town. I thought you knew that." Quick said.

"I've been busy. I didn't have time for clubs."

"Busy? With what, being a bitch?" Quick asked.

"I'll beat you to death and leave your body behind the bar to rot. Is that what you want?" I said.

"No dude. I'm just kidding. You gotta calm down. You're scaring the patron's homes." Quick said.

"To hell with them."

"What do you mean to hell with the patrons? I love the patrons. Each one of them is so beautiful. Black, White, Latinas, Asians. I bet Heaven is just like this but with clouds and Angles and shit. " Quick said. "What do you think?"

"I think I've got bills to pay. I think this job pays $120.00 a week. I think that won't make a dent in my car, insurance and phone bills.

"Damn, is it that bad?" Quick asked.

"It's bad enough. I could be in jail for a year if things don't work out. I thought three days were bad enough."

"Have faith ese." Quick said.

"I have faith that things are fucked until I un-fuck them. Look I really appreciate you hooking me up with this gig. I'm just worried you know." I said.

"A man is as he thinketh." That's what the bible says. You gotta think positive." Quick said.

"I thinketh that I need some money. What about that thing?" I asked.

"What thing?" Quick said.

"The thing with the guy that we were going to go see." I said.

"What in the hell are you talking about homes?" Quick asked.

"The guy that does that thing across the border that we were going to visit."

Quick's confusion was only matched by my frustration.

"Dude, I'm lost here. Help me out." Quick asked.

"The fucking drug dealer who brings the cocaine across the border and cuts it and then sells it and we were gonna rob him for his money and he couldn't call the cops because he's a god damned drug dealer. THAT THING!" I said.

"Oooh, Toons. Why didn't you just say that in the first place?" Quick said. "Let's go by there on Sunday night. We can sneak through the back yard and spy on him."

I spent the next two days working in the club doing what bouncers do. I asked a woman to stop lifting her dress up and flashing her crotch at a guy before his girlfriend kicked her ass. I walked a drunken patron out of the door and put him in a cab. It's pretty much a rule of thumb that it's hard to meet a woman and take her home if you get drunk before she does. I also broke up a shouting match between two guys that started when one of them accidentally stepped on the other's shoe. I learned many years ago to never step on a black man's shoe. The shoes tend to be the most expensive part of an ensemble and scuffing one of them can only end badly for you.

They argued for 40 minutes and called each other every name in the book but never threw a punch. They were dressed too nice to fight. Besides the women in the club were gorgeous and neither one of them wanted to bleed all over their shirt in front of them.

I picked Quick up at his aunt's house at 9:30 PM on Sunday night and we headed for the city of Chula Vista.

"It's good that it's dark and no one can see you. It's just that black guys don't come through here that much." Quick said.

"Don't worry. I won't beat the hell out of you because I'm not offended." I said.

Quick guided me to Toons' house and we circled the block once or twice as I memorized every detail.

"The house is lit up like a Christmas tree." I said.

"Well, we ain't robbing him tonight are we?" Quick asked.

"No. I'm just getting the lay of the land." I answered.

"Then what's the problem?" Quick asked.

"No problem at all. I'm just making observations. This is how I work. I thought you wanted a pro on this job." I said.

"Yeah, yeah, I do." Quick said.

"Then relax and let me work." I said.

Every Marine Corps mission requires a five paragraph order. They teach you that in boot camp. **SMEAC** (Pronounced smeeack), stands for **S**ituation, **M**ission, **E**xecution, **A**dministration and logistics, and **C**ommand and Signal.

Situation: Danni had me locked up for a crime that I didn't commit and I lost my job and now I was broke and I need some money real bad. Toons has the money, and I'd do anything to get it.

Mission: Toons, a local drug dealer has a stack of drug money that Quick and I will misappropriate and donate to the "I need some money real bad" foundation.

Execution: Quick and I will approach the house under cover of darkness by utilizing the available cover and concealment while maintaining a low profile. Quick will gain access to the house through the proper application of "Street Skillz." We will conduct a thorough search of the premises until the money is located. We will then take the money and get away in my car at high rate of speed.

Admin, Logistics: I'm not really sure.

Command and signal: I'm in charge and I ain't leaving without the money. A strict noise discipline will be applied and communication will be through hand signals, facial expressions and the occasional middle finger.

During our surveillance of the house we noticed that there were thick bushes in the back yard that would cover our approach. There was also a guard dog in the back yard. A Pit Bull no less. Entering from the front was not possible given the lack of foliage and multiple street lights. We would launch our assault early in the morning. According to

Quick, Toons made his run across the border sometime during the week. We would have to check every night until we got lucky.

I dropped Quick off at his aunt's house and returned to Shelter Island for the night. I reviewed my plan to rob Toons and wondered if I could actually go through with it.

I would need the money sooner or later and it was only fair. Toons was a drug dealer who had broken the law a hundred times. He had probably destroyed countless lives. Quick and I could get in and out before anyone noticed. It wasn't wrong. It was justice. Besides, I had a freebie coming. I had lost everything so who could blame me for doing this?

I thought of the child Danni carried and wondered what it would think of me doing something like this. I always said that I would be a good example to my children. Then I remembered that I was homeless and unemployed with a pending trial for domestic violence.

"Fuck it. Better to be a paid criminal than a broke one." I thought.

SEVEN

Despite being an aspiring cat burglar, I hadn't given up hope of living a moral and legal life one day. I had a job interview that Tuesday morning. I saw the ad for a Customer Service Supervisor in the news paper. It wasn't what I wanted but anything was better than sitting at Shelter Island wishing for things to change.

I walked in the office, introduced myself to the receptionist, filled out the application and waited patiently. I looked like hell and I knew it. I woke up in the car and showered at the gym only two hours earlier. I was desperate and I looked like it.

"So Cole, your resume indicates that you have a logistics background. Do you have any experience in customer service?"

I proceeded to lie my ass off and I was doing pretty well until the inevitable question was asked.

"So tell me, why did you leave your previous position?"

And that was it. It was over. I went with the lie that I had to leave due to a personal emergency and traveled back home to Washington D.C. for an extended period of time but we both knew that I was lying. I returned to Shelter Island and changed back into my jeans and t-shirt in my car. They would never call me and I knew it.

I had a second interview on Thursday but the result was the same. One call to Dave at Tacwar Systems and I was dead in the water. Being a bouncer was only enough money for food and gas. Robbing Toons was the best I could do at the time. I gave Quick a call and told him about my job search.

"Let's give it one more try tonight." Quick said.

I agreed and told him that I would pick him up from his Aunt's house at midnight.

I approached Quick's Aunt's house and saw him running down the street from someone. I drove past a bare foot Mexican man in his boxer shorts who was swearing at Quick in Spanish. I lowered the passenger side window as I rode parallel with Quick and asked him what was going on.

"I stole my cousin's pills and he's pissed off. Let me in." Quick said.

"Are we still on for tonight?"

"Yeah, let me in fucker!" Quick said.

I unlocked the door and Quick jumped in. I floored the gas petal just as Quick's nemesis was about to kick my rear bumper. I watched him tumble and fall over in my rear view mirror as we sped away.

Quick's shirt was torn and he was covered in grass stains.

"What happened to you?" I asked.

"I had to get the Vicodin from my cousin. I tried to sneak them out of his room but he caught me. He chased me out of my Tia's house and tackled me in the front yard. We fought over the bottle and the pills spilled all over the drive way. I grabbed two of them and started running down the street. That's when you pulled up." Quick said.

"Well you can buy him four bottles when this is over now let's get this money." I said.

Quick and I drove by Toons' house that night at about 1:30 AM to take one final look and then parked a block away.

"You got the ski masks?" I asked.

"Yeah. Right here." Quick said.

"Why do they call him Toons anyway?" I asked.

"Because he's a goofy lookin' fucker. He looks like a cartoon." Quick said.

"Does anyone around here go by their given name?" I asked rhetorically.

"Looks empty to me. What do you think?" I said.

"His truck isn't there and all of the lights are out. Feels right to me." Quick said.

"Let's go." I said.

We crept to the fence at the back yard and lay prone by the bushes. The pit bull was laying on the ground near the dog house in the back yard. Quick pulled out two rolls of salami and filled each one with a Vicodin. He threw them over the fence and they landed close to the pit bull. The dog jumped up and ran over to them. He cautiously sniffed each roll of salami and then ate them. I checked my watch and gave the drug 15 minutes to work.

The pit bull soon began stumbling around and moaning. He toppled over and didn't move.

"Five minutes early. Not bad." I said.

Quick and I put on the ski masks, hopped over the fence and made our way toward the house.

"How can we be sure that the dog's asleep?" Quick asked.

I kicked the dog in the side as we ran by and got no reaction.

"He looks asleep to me." I said.

We approached the back door and crouched down to avoid detection.

"Do your thing." I said as I kept a look out for trouble.

Quick pulled out his lock picking kit and started to work on the door.

"Come on. Come on fucker." Quick said.

"I thought you knew what you were doing." I said.

"I do. It's just been a while." Quick said.

The pit bull started to moan again and stood up shaking its head.

"What was that?" Quick asked as he fidgeted with the lock.

"Nothing. Just pop the lock." I said.

"Was that the dog?" Quick asked.

"Yeah, I think so." I said.

"Fuck this. I ain't gettin' bit in the ass." Quick said as he stood up to run away. I caught Quick by the arm and pushed him back to the ground. The dog caught sight of us and ran our way. He was still high and wobbled from side to side as he trotted toward us.

"Oh, shit! Oh shit!" Quick said as he tried to get up again but I kept him in place.

The dog was almost on top of us and leapt in to the air with his mouth wide open. He was still groggy and slower than he would have been if he hadn't been getting high on the job.

I caught the dog by the collar in mid air and slammed him head first into the wall of the house.

"Ok, he's really asleep now." I said.

"You're loco homes."

"Relax. You pick the lock and I'll walk the dog." I said as I threw the unconscious hound into the bushes.

We stealthily entered the house and closed the door behind us. I Pulled out my Maglight and turned it on while placing my hand over the lens to reduce the amount of light that was visible. The house appeared to be empty as we scoured the first floor for the money. Our search didn't turn up the tool box so we walked up the stairs to the second floor when we heard the sound of someone getting out of bed and heading toward us.

I Pushed Quick backwards to the first floor and we rushed around the corner looking for a place to hide. The only place I could think of was the closet near the living room.

I closed the door until there was barely a crack to see through. The foot steps came down the stairs and headed into the kitchen. I could hear someone open the refrigerator and then head toward our location. An elderly woman walked past the closet with a plate in her hand and sat down on the couch. She turned on the TV and raised the volume until the sound filled every corner of the house.

I looked at Quick furiously and I could make out the sight of him shrugging his shoulders in the darkness. I found Quick's ear and whispered in it.

"I'm gonna tie her ass up and go find the money." I said.

"You can't do that to his Abuelita homes. Just wait 'till she falls asleep." Quick said.

"How do you know she won't stay up until morning?" I asked.

"My Tia does the same thing all the time. She'll be asleep soon. Look at the bright side. She's watching Univision. That's my favorite channel fucker." Quick said.

An hour and a half passed and Toons' grand mother was still awake and still watching Univision. Quick tapped my shoulder.

"I gotta take a piss." Quick whispered.

"Hold it." I whispered back.

"I have been."

"Then tie a knot in it." I said.

"I gotta go! I gotta go now!"

I looked down and found a pair of work boots and gloves on the floor of the closet. I placed a glove in the bottom of each boot and handed them to Quick.

"Piss in these." I whispered.

Quick's facial expression begged for another option but there wasn't one.

"Piss in these or go ask her where the bathroom is." I said.

"Ok fucker. I'll do it. Turn your head pecker checker." Quick said.

"And don't get any on me or you won't have to worry about Toons or his granny." I said.

Quick began to urinate into the boots and I turned my head to peak through the space between the door and the door frame.

"Piss softer. You're making too much noise. Have you been eating asparagus?" I said. The sound of someone snoring caught my attention and I peaked around the door and saw Toons' grandmother asleep on the couch.

"Come on. She's asleep." I said.

We tip toed out of the closet and Quick carefully put the boots down without spilling urine all over the floor. We made it to the foot of the stairs when a bright pair of head lights illuminated the house through the windows of the living room.

Low Fuel

"He's home. He's home!" Quick whispered.

I ran over to the window and saw a young man who could only be Toons getting out of a lowered pick-up truck and walking for the front door.

Quick and I immediately ran for the back door. Quick slipped on a rug and slid across the floor until he hit the wall beside the back door. I lifted him back to his feet and dragged him out of the house.

We closed the door behind us, jumped the fence and ran down the street to my car.

"Damn!" that was close." Quick said.

"We should have jumped him." I said.

"No. That fool is trigger happy. He's always carrying a pistol." Quick said.

"Then I should've tied her up." I said.

"Are you crazy? "Look ese, this wasn't supposed to be that type of thing. I'm not that kind of guy. We were just supposed to get the money not hurt anyone. You're getting out of control lately." Quick said.

"You're not the one who's sleeping in their car. I can't believe this shit. I need that money." I said.

The low fuel light broke into the conversation to inform me that my get away plan had just hit a snag.

"Fuck! Do you have another Vicodin?" I asked.

"No. Why? You're not going back are you?" Quick asked.

"No. I just need one." I said.

I walked in to the court room that my Discovery Hearing was being held in and took a seat in the back of the room. I sat there for a few minutes not knowing what to do when I heard some one call my name.

"Hello, Cole? I'm Wallid Mohamed. Let's talk outside for a minute."

I followed Wallid into the hallway and joined him near a column.

"I've reviewed the tape of Ms. Salinas' call to 911. She sounds pissed off but not in fear for her life or well being." Wallid said.

"Yeah, she was plenty pissed off that day." I said.

"I think I can file a motion to have the charges dropped if we can prove that she was angry and not in fear for her life. I need you to tell me anything and everything that you can think of to discredit her." Wallid said.

"Well, Danni's been in therapy lately and she was prescribed Somaxa but stopped taking it abruptly. I've heard that doing that can make people a little crazy." I said.

"Yes, it is true that an abrupt change in anti-depressant dosage can lead to suicidal and violent behavior. What else?" Wallid asked.

"That's about it." I said.

"There must be more than that. Your future is on the line here. You need to give me a little more to work with." Wallid said.

"Look. Danni's told me quite a few personal things and I will take them with me to my grave. Those things are intimate and should remain between us. I won't violate the trust that we had when we were together. That's the difference between me and her." I said.

"I respect that. I'll see what I can do." Wallid said.

The hearing only lasted 10 minutes. I thanked Wallid for his help and he told me to stay out of trouble and to stay away from Danni since the Stay Away order was still in effect. I exited the court house and breathed a sigh of relief.

I heard a familiar voice calling my name when I reached the bottom of the steps.

"Danni. What are you doing here?" I asked.

"I need to talk to you Cole. Please." Danni said.

"I can't Danni."

"Cole. We have a baby coming. You need to talk to me." Danni said.

"You should have thought about that before you called the police. I'm not allowed to speak to you Danni. They'll put me back in jail."

"You said that you loved me and now you're afraid of them. Some Marine. You're not so tough anymore are you? You're acting like a little bitch!" Danni said.

"It takes one to know one." I yelled back.

"Fuck you! I'll take this baby and leave. I'll run away and you'll never find us." Danni said.

I ignored her and broke into a light jog. Not running just jogging. I didn't want to look like a complete and total bitch after being called one. Danni chased after me shouting my name as passersby stared at us.

I got in to my car and sped out of the parking lot. I stopped at a red light at the next intersection and caught my breath.

"Would Danni really take the baby away? She was just mad and trying to get a reaction out of me. She wouldn't keep my child from me." I thought.

The sight of Danni's car speeding toward me in my rear view mirror caught my attention. Time seemed to flow slowly and I could see the expression on her face. She was irate and it looked as if she was going to ram me.

I didn't want to learn another valuable lesson the hard way and ran the red light with Danni right behind me in hot pursuit. I had a lot more horse power at my disposal but it wouldn't help much in city traffic. Danni was honking her horn and giving me the finger as she changed lanes and dodged the other cars on the road.

I weaved in and out of traffic and ran two more red lights. There was too much traffic and Danni would catch up to me soon. I could loose her if I could just make it to the freeway. A moving van to my right changed lanes and pulled in front of me and then slowed down to make a left turn.

Danni quickly caught up and attempted to ram the side of my car. I pumped my brakes and Danni flew by almost hitting the van in front of me. I changed lanes and drove past Danni on her right side. We locked eyes for a moment. She had the look of a mad woman. She was drunk with rage and totally out of control.

I could see the on ramp to the free way but Danni was right behind me. I floored the accelerator as the light at the intersection turned red. I whipped through the cars and escaped onto the on ramp. I heard a loud crunch and caught sight of Danni crashing into the side of one of the cars at the stop light.

Several weeks passed uneventfully but my situation was getting worse. I managed to pay my car note and phone bill but I was behind on my car insurance. I couldn't find a job in San Diego and I couldn't leave the state until my trial. What little bit I had left was going fast. I was afraid of what would become of me if I did make it through this. I was changing, becoming more savage. I was beginning to develop a "Me against the world" mentality and it threatened to take over my entire attitude toward life.

Quick told me that I needed faith, faith in God.

"Come to church with me and my Tia." Quick said.

"You go to church?" I asked.

"Yeah I go to church. I'm a Christian, fucker. It's good for you and it makes you feel better about things." Quick said.

"Really?"

"Hell yeah, the pastor says that God will bring your blessings to the middle of the road. That you don't have to go all the way, that it won't have to be that hard and all he asks is that you have a little faith." Quick said.

"Faith. Really? That's all?" I asked.

"God said that all you need is enough faith to fill a mustard seed and he'll do the rest.

Have you ever seen a mustard seed fucker?" Quick asked.

"No. I didn't even know mustard came out of seeds." I said.

"Well, they're fucking tiny. You gotta be a sad son of a bitch if you can't fill up one of those with some faith." Quick said.

"I guess so."

"So you'll come to church with me?" Quick asked.

"What could it hurt?"

The Morning Glory Church held service in the gymnasium of the La Mesa Elementary School. It was one of those non-denominational churches that are so en vogue these days. Non-denominational is about the same as non-committal. Make up your mind is all that I'm saying. Be a Baptist, Catholic, Lutheran, Mormon or Jehovah's Witness but pick something and commit to it. I mean it's God for Christ sake.

I met Quick, his cousin and his Aunt at the front of the school.

"Hey Fu....Cole! Welcome. This is my cousin Luis and my Tia Marta." Quick said.

"You look familiar. Have we met before?" Luis asked as we shook hands.

"Only in passing." I answered.

Tia Marta just gave me a dirty look and walked toward the door of the school.

"Not very friendly for a Christian." I said.

"Hey, I told you about the guy that stole her purse didn't I?" Quick said.

"Thirty years ago. I wasn't even born yet. How about I buy her a new purse? Will she forgive me and my race then?" I asked.

We entered the double doors of the gym and were greeted by an usher and given the program for the day's service.

"A gym? They hold service in a gym? I'm leaving." I said.

"You live in your car fool. Where are you going…to the parking lot?' Quick said.

I followed Quick and his family around the perimeter of the folding chairs that had been set-up on top of the basketball court. We walked under one of the basket ball hoops and I was half tempted to ball up the program and dunk it.

We took a seat together and I watched the many different types of people entering the gym. I locked my eyes on an extremely attractive young woman and even got a smile out of her until Quick started cock blocking.

"Pastor Tony, this is my friend Cole." Quick said.

I looked up to see a very large, burley man of about 6'6" tall. Pastor Tony was a middle aged man with a grin that would make the Cheshire cat jealous.

"Well hello, welcome to Morning Glory." Pastor Tony said.

Pastor Tony shook my hand in the same fashion that a Monkey wrench grips a pipe.

"How long have you known Hilario?" Pastor Tony asked.

"About two months." I said.

"Well, you're in good hands. Hilario is a mighty man of God and we're proud to call him our brother here at Morning Glory." Pastor Tony said.

Quick grinned at me and I considered telling Pastor Tony all about his mighty man of God but decided against it.

"Please excuse me. I must get ready for the service. It was a pleasure to meet you Cole. We'll catch up later." the pastor said and then took his smile to the front of the room.

"He's awesome ain't he? I've learned a lot from him." Quick said.

"Oh, so he's the one who taught you to pick locks and piss in people's work boots?" I asked.

"Your weapons formed against me will not prosper." Quick said.

"Neither will the criminal justice system, right." I said.

The band began to sing about the coming of the Lord and how his return would save the world. Pastor Tony gave a rousing sermon about the necessity of leaving behind people from your old life before God can bless you and take you to the next level.

"Those people are children of God but they are also anchors and they will keep you from reaching the glory and blessing that the Lord has prepared for you. The Lord will tear you from them in order to lead you to your blessings if you won't do it yourself. God is a good God and he has a special blessing tailor made for each of us. Not even Satan can prevent the glory of God's plans. You can't carry the dead weight of a sinner with you on your path to prosperity. You will serve them better as an example of God's promise to the righteous and faithful. Let them follow in your foot steps so that we can all join the Lord and his Father together in Heaven." Pastor Tony said.

"Maybe that's what this is all about. Had God planned all of this in order to get me away from Danni? Perhaps he knew that I wouldn't choose to leave her so he tore me away from her and enlisted the aid of the San Diego County Police Department to get the job done.

Then why did I meet her in the first place?" I wondered.

Pastor Tony made his way around the gymnasium greeting his flock after the service was concluded.

"How did I do Marta?" Pastor Tony asked as he took her hand.

"Wonderful Pastor." I feel full of the spirit." Tia Marta said.

"I didn't know she could speak." I told Quick.

"Shut up fucker. Pastor is speaking." Quick whispered.

"Well I hope you'll make this a habit Cole." Pastor Tony said.

"I'm considering it." I said.

"You should. Cole's in a bad situation Pastor. He needs the Lord's blessing. " Quick said.

"Now, let's not air the man's dirty laundry Hilario. Do you want to talk about it Cole?" Pastor Tony asked.

"Yeah sure." I said.

Pastor Tony led me to a corner of the gym away from the congregation and I told him of my plight.

"No matter what has happened or will happen, know that God had his hand on you. A man can't have a testimony without a test. God is making you into the man he needs you to be. He has great plans for you." Pastor Tony said.

"Well, how about a place to live?" I asked.

"You won't have to settle for anything. God's abundance is beyond settling. Let's pray together." Pastor Tony said.

Pastor Tony led me in a prayer for healing, abundance, safety, prosperity and some more good stuff. He gave me his phone number and promised to help me find a job and a place to live.

"Call me if you need me." Pastor Tony said.

I said good bye to Quick and his family and left.

I realized that I hadn't told Wayne what had happened. I had been too embarrassed.

"You need to get the hell out of there." Wayne said.

"I can't. I got a trial date and besides Danni is pregnant." I said.

"Danni is crazy. She'll put your ass back in jail the first chance she gets. If she can do something like that once then she'll do it again." Wayne said.

"I can't leave my child." I said.

"Shit, you won't have to. She's going to run away with the baby, remember." Wayne said.

"You need help. You need to come back home. You can stay with me until you get back on your feet. I'll come out there and get you if I need to." Wayne said.

Low Fuel

"No, I don't want you to do that. You have a family and I don't want you leaving them because I fucked things up." I said.

"You didn't fuck up brotha. It happens to the best of us. Just make sure you don't let it beat you. You can't do this on your own. No man can." Wayne said.

I thanked Wayne for the offer. There was a time when I couldn't wait to get to San Diego and now I couldn't wait to leave. But there were two things holding me back. One was my trial and the other was my lack of money. Driving across the continental United States would take a few bucks and I was flat broke. I called Pastor Tony on the morning of February 23rd and we prayed together, asking God for his blessing.

"A mustard seed. We'll see." I thought.

I met Wallid Mohamed in front of the court room.

"Good news. I meant to call you but I was busy. The City Attorney reviewed the 911 tape and thought that Ms. Salinas sounded more angry than terrified. He decided to conduct an investigation and spoke to her on the phone. She admitted that she lied. She admitted that she started the fight and that you only defended yourself. That's enough for me to file a motion that they drop all charges." Wallid said.

"Holy shit! Are you serious?" I said.

"Yes. Just take a seat in the court room. You won't have to do anything except sign some paper work." Wallid said.

Wallid entered the motion and the judge concurred. I shook Wallid's hand and thanked him for his help. I was sure that things would have been different if I had gone to trial with Spencer Nichols representing me.

I left the court house and bought a celebratory steak and cheese sub and French fries from Gus's sub shop and returned to my favorite parking space at Shelter Island to eat it. I called Pastor Tony and told him what happened.

"God is working his plan in your life he said. Congratulations. You have a strong testimony to share. Praise God!"

I told Pastor Tony of my plans to head back to the east coast and he told me that he had a colleague in Washington D.C.

"He's a soldier of the Lord. You be sure to reach out to him when you arrive. He'll take good care of you." Pastor Tony said.

I worked that night at the club and took up my post by the main bar. It was a busy night full of people. Don Loco, a local rapper was having an album release party there that night. Mando said that the club needed the money and the manager hoped that this promotion would bring in a good sized crowd. The new clientele was a lot younger and rougher than usual patrons and I had the feeling that I'd earn my pay that night.

Several gang members entered the club and started to glare at the rest of the patrons. Some of the regulars began to leave and one stopped to talk to me on the way out.

"Whose idea was this?" she asked.

"The manager thought that bringing a younger crowd in would be good for business." I said.

"Those guys are in a gang or something. This is such a nice place and now you guys are going to ruin it just to make a quick buck. Tell the manager that this isn't the only club in town." She said.

Don Loco arrived with the usual entourage that seems ubiquitous in the rap game. He was escorted to the VIP section of the club and sipped champagne and smoked cigars.

He was introduced to the crowd an hour later and he performed his latest singles "Duckin' bullets" and "Slob a Knob" from his new album "Doin' Ya Dirty." The crowd went wild and a commotion broke out in the middle of the dance floor soon after that. Three of the gang bangers were beating on one man. He tried to fight them off but they were like a pack of hyenas on a wounded gazelle. He wouldn't last long.

"Move!" I shouted at the panicked patrons as I ran toward the action.

I grabbed the first gang banger with in reach and flung him across the room until he slid into the wall. Mando put one in a bear hug but found another on his back. I placed my hands around his throat and pulled him from Mando's back. He tried to hit me but I quickly slammed him to the ground and stomped his chest. More gang bangers joined the fight and were met by the club's security staff.

I carried one out of the club and to the top of the stairs. He broke loose from my grip and spun around to hit me. I lightly tapped his chest and waved goodbye as he tumbled ass over head down the stairs.

"I'll kill your black ass. I'll fucking shoot you." he shouted as his buddies helped him up.

I looked over to see Mando standing beside me.

"This isn't what we had in mind." Mando said.

Seven police cruisers arrived and the party was officially over. It was a failure for everyone involved with the exception of Don Loco. Every rapper needs an incident to sell a record and he got his that night.

Someone fired nine rounds into the front of the club that night after we closed. It made the news and we all knew who was responsible. Mando called me and said that the Mayor's office threatened to close the place down if it happened again.

"I have to let you go for a while. Those guys threatened to kill you and I think they might try to catch you in the parking lot after we close. It'll just be for a little while. I'll call you once things calm down. It's just too hot right now." Mando said.

I tried my luck at a couple of temp agencies and interviewed for some light industrial work in a warehouse. I got a couple of one day assignments at $10.00 an hour but it was even less money after taxes.

Things had gone from bad to fucked. I had $120.00 to my name and that wouldn't last long. They say it takes money to make money, so I decided to make a little investment in a money making venture.

I went to the hardware store and purchased a 10 pound sledge hammer, a roll of duct tape, zip ties, trash bags, a pair of gloves, a four way lug wrench and a 2 ton floor jack. I headed back to Chula Vista on a mission and failure was not an option.

I approached the back of Toons' house at 2:30 am on foot and watched carefully. The lights were out. Everyone was either asleep or had left the house. Quick and I had already checked the first floor which left the second as the only place the money could be hidden. I just had to rush the stairs as soon as I entered.

There was no sign of the dog which was a good thing. He didn't want to fuck with me again anyway. I lowered my ski mask and hopped over the fence. I kneeled near the back door and scanned the area behind me. I stood up right and assumed a proper stance once I was sure that the coast was clear. I swung the sledge hammer at the lock and the door flew open. I closed the door behind me and rushed up the stairs.

Toons exited the master bedroom with a pistol in his hand just as I reached the top of the stairs. He was still half asleep. I swung the sledge hammer as hard as I could and it took a chunk out of the ceiling on its arc toward Toons' chest. The crack of his sternum breaking was slightly audible over the sound of the hammer's impact. He hit the ground like a ton of bricks. I stood above him and kicked the pistol away from his hand. He yelped in agony as I placed a foot on his chest.

I picked up the pistol and tucked it into my waist band. It was a .45 caliber Glock 21. The man had good taste. I zipped tied his hands behind his back and checked the rest of the bedrooms. I found his grandmother fast asleep in her bed and decided that she could sleep through a robbery if she slept through the sound of me breaking through the door and caving in Toons' chest.

I put the glock against his forehead and asked him where the money was. Toons wasn't as stupid as he looked and he told me exactly where to find it.

"Stay quiet or you'll stay quiet." I said as I got the money out of the tool box and stuffed it into the trash bag that was in my pocket. I resumed my search of the house for what ever else I could find. I transcended being a victim and was now a vulture scavenging through his possessions for whatever would help me survive.

In the bottom of the master bedroom closet I found a duffle bag that contained a sawed off Remington 870 pump action 12 gauge shot gun, boxes of ammunition as well as extra magazines for the Glock 21. I threw the bag over my shoulder and continued my search. "Just what the doctor ordered." I thought as I picked up the Rolex that was on his dresser and put it on my wrist. "I needed a new watch anyway."

I rifled through the cedar box on the dresser and found a gold chain and cross. I placed it around my neck and kissed it. I needed all of the help that I could get.

"Don't get greedy." I thought. "That's what causes most crooks to get caught."

I picked up a pair of cuticle scissors that were also on the dresser and walked back out of the bed room and stood above Toons. His eyes studied me in panicked excitement.

"I hit you pretty hard. How's your breathing." I asked as I pointed the Glock at him once again.

"I can breathe but it's hard." Toons said.

It was my first time really looking at him. He did look like a cartoon. Like a cartoon of a young scared kid.

"Look, I need this money. I'm sorry it had to be like this. I won't ever come back. I promise. I just need the money. I'm taking the guns too. They'll only get you in to trouble. I'd go straight if I were you or the next guy to break down your door might just kill you or arrest you. Think about it." I said as I dropped the scissors on the floor beside him.

"Count to 100 and then cut yourself loose. I will kill you if you try to get slick with me." I said.

I counted the money twice while sitting on the bed of my room at the Motel 6. All of that for $900.00. Well, at least I didn't have to split it with Quick. I called Wayne later that day and told him that I would be leaving for D.C. soon. I called Quick and Pastor Tony to tell them the news. Pastor Tony told me to look up Pastor Stephen Reynolds when I got to D.C. Stephen Reynolds was the pastor of the Morning Glory church in D.C. He and Tony met when they played football in college. It was Tony who led Steven to God and saved him from a life of debauchery. Pastor Tony promised to call Steven and tell him to expect my arrival.

Quick on the other hand was much more emotional.

"Damn fucker! You're breaking up the team. You can't have the Cisco Kid without Pancho." Quick said.

"I approve of the analogy as long as I get to be Cisco." I said.

"I'm serious. Why can't you stay here? Mando will hire you back when things cool off.

You're just throwing in the towel. That's not cool homes." Quick said.

"I have no where to live. I've lost everything I own and Danni's still here. I need a fresh start. I need to get a way from here." I said.

It took another 40 minutes to convince him that I was right. Quick said that he understood and wished me well. I didn't tell him about Toons or the money. It was better that he didn't know. I promised him that I would keep in touch but no one ever means that when they say it.

I used part of the money to buy a new spare tire and then headed to Gus's sub shop and ordered a roast beef sub and fries. I took my dinner from the cashier and walked out the door and ran smack dab into Danni.

"Hi." Danni said.

I didn't respond. Danni wore a melancholy expression on her face but she was still gorgeous. Crazy or not, I missed her. I missed my home. I missed our life before the chaos.

"I've been looking for you. I've been checking all over. Where are you staying?" Danni asked.

I pointed to my car as I looked into her eyes.

"I'm sorry Cole. I know I can't take it back but I am very sorry for everything. I was crazy. I was out of control. I don't know what got into me." Danni said as her eyes filled with tears.

"Cole…I lost the baby. I miscarried. I ruined everything." Danni said.

My fury faded away and was replaced by sorrow. Part of me was relieved but part of me died inside. I didn't want a child to be born into this mess but I wanted the baby none the less.

"How?" I asked.

"When I ran into that car. I was so stupid Cole. I killed our baby. I'm sorry." Danni said.

I hugged her as the guilt smashed into me like a run away freight train. None of this would have happened if I would have just stopped to talk to her. I could have prevented all of it. I held her close to me as we stood there in the parking lot. The scent of her perfume caused a flash back that took me all the way back to the Village Pub. I wanted it all back like it used to be. I wanted us back. But there had been too much pain, too much anger, too much betrayal. It was all just too much.

"I'm leaving town tomorrow." I said.

"Where are you going?" Danni asked.

"Back to D.C. My friend Wayne said that I could stay with him for a while."

"God, Cole. No. You can't go. Please!" Danni said.

"I can't stay. I have nothing. I can't even get a job."

Several customers gawked at us as they entered and exited the restaurant. "Look, I've got a hotel room close by. Do you want to go talk?" I said.

Danni and I entered the room and she sat on the edge of the bed. I sat down beside her and she placed her head on my shoulder just as she used to.

"That's a nice watch. Is that a Rolex?" Danni asked as she lifted my arm to take a closer look.

"No, no, it's just a knock off. I saw it one night and decided to pick it up." I said.

"Oh, well, it looks really nice on you. I think everything looks nice on you." Danni said "Cole, I'm sorry about your clothes and everything. I am so truly sorry. I have to tell you something. That cop told me to press charges against you. Burke, the Police Sergeant. He could have let you go that night but he said that I had to press charges or that he would charge me with filing a false police report. He started coming to the apartment to check on me and then he asked me out to dinner. He was stalking me. He kept calling me at night until I told him that I would report him to Internal Affairs if he didn't stop." Danni said.

"My life was ruined because you had a temper tantrum and this guy was horny. I would have died for you and you betrayed me." I said.

"I have to tell you something and I don't know how to say it." Danni said as her voice trembled with fear and anxiety.

"Just tell me. I don't see how things could get any worse. Just say it, whatever it is." I said.

"Cole, I didn't want you to leave me. I wanted you to need me so that you could see that I needed you too… I…I poisoned you." Danni said.

"What?"

"I wanted you to get sick so you couldn't leave me. I wanted to take care of you so you would love me again. I put bug spray in your food. It was just a little and you're a lot bigger than a bug. I just thought it would make you sick but it didn't even work." Danni said.

"You could have killed me." I said.

I was exhausted, emotionally, physically and mentally. I kicked off my boots and lay back on the bed. A minute or two past and Danni joined me.

"God, I'm crazy." Danni said.

"Yeah, you're pretty fucked up." I said.

Danni was crazy and I was crazy to still love her. I kissed away one of her tears. Her lips met mine and we kissed. Danni hugged me tight and then pulled my shirt off. She kissed my chest and I pulled her head back by her hair so that I could bite her neck. I pulled her jeans off and we both gave into the passion of the moment. We were together again and we both forgot about everything that had happened. All of the hurt, anger and betrayal were gone temporarily. I held her close to me all night and dreamed of a different time when the world was beautiful and our future was bright.

I woke up early the next day and carried my bags to the car. I tucked the duffle bag into the trunk and piled the other bags on top of it. I checked out at the front desk and returned to the hotel room. I stood there watching Danni as she slept. I wanted to wake her and tell her good bye but I didn't want to risk a tearful farewell. I wanted her to tell me something that would make me stay but I knew nothing could change my mind.

Danni looked like an angel as she slept. I watched over her for a few minutes and tried to remember only the good times.

The time on my new Rolex was 7:13 AM.

I leaned down and kissed her cheek.

I closed the door behind me and tugged on it to make sure that it was locked. I wiped away my tears and got into my car. I revved the engine and burned out all of the way from the parking lot into the street. I glanced at the bay and continued north on Interstate 5. I thought about the first time I saw the city and how happy I was then.

Things had changed and there was no looking back. I had lost too much, too fast and it had taken its toll on me. I moved to San Diego to start a new life and that's exactly what happened.

EIGHT

I made the trip in less than three days the first time I drove across the country. It was just me and my Jeep Wrangler back then. The cold desert wind whipped through the space between the vinyl top and the metal frame. Bits of sand peppered the side of my face with each gust of wind. It took forever to remove all of the sand from both the car and myself after I made it to Twenty-nine Palms. I swore that I would never buy another convertible as I vacuumed the miniature desert from the creases and seams of the back seat. It was hardly the rocket that I was driving this time. I would be there in a flash barring incident.

Leaving D.C. was difficult then just as it was difficult leaving San Diego this time. My friend Jay invited me to his company Christmas party four years earlier. The idea of free food and free booze was my idea of heaven. Jay introduced me to his boss as soon as we walked through the door, but I was more concerned with meeting the woman of my dreams. Well... at the time I mean.

Her name was Latoya and she was the kind of woman who caused every head turn in her direction when she entered a room. She used to be a catalog model and it was evident in the way she walked. She could've given Naomi Campbell a run for her money and she commanded erection...I mean attention with each step.

I saw her ordering a drink from the open bar and my heart actually stopped beating for a second.

Yeah I know, what else is new?

Latoya was absolutely captivating and I had to be with her. I haven't learned yet I guess. Maybe I never will. Jay noticed my infatuation as did everyone else and pulled me in her direction. He made the introduction and I took it from there. Latoya was overjoyed when I asked her to dance and that's the way we spent the rest of the evening. We exchanged phone numbers and said good bye when the party ended at about 2:00 that morning.

She asked if we could get together the following evening but I had to drive back to the west coast that day. There'd be hell to pay if I didn't return to MCAGCC on time. I spent Christmas Eve and Christmas day on the road becoming more heart sick with each passing mile. I felt as if I had been touched by an Angel and I wanted her back.

We wrote letters back and forth every week and ran up our phone bills until the service was disconnected. I flew back to visit her a couple of times until she told me that she was pregnant.

Latoya had been cheating on her boyfriend Craig with me. I was stunned when I realized that I was just her boy toy. There was a time when I wanted to marry her. It's common for young people to feel lonely after initially joining the military. You find yourself on the other side of the world with a rifle in you hands wishing that you had someone to care about you on a personal level. You wish to be more than a weapon system. You long to return to the waiting arms of that special someone but there is no one. There are only your comrades in arms.

So many young Soldiers, Marines, Sailors and Airmen get married within their first year of service. The exigency for companionship is undeniable. Haste on the other hand can be disastrous. Needy people aren't really cut out for marriage. The desperation and insecurity has a way of spoiling the romance. It's only a matter of time until someone has an affair and it's all down hill from there. Couples like McMahon and Blake are not uncommon, and the end result is always the same. Nothing can stop it. Not the lies or the deception. What has been done in the dark will always come to the light.

It had taken four hours to get to the High Desert from San Diego. Choya bush, boulder, coyote and tumble weed all over again. Passing by MCAGCC actually brought a sense of relief. It felt familiar and safe. I was right back where I started from. I considered driving on base to say hi but decided against it. The embarrassment of answering the questions, "How is San Diego?" and "What are you doing these days?" was unacceptable.

The loneliness of the desert became undeniable after I passed through the city of Needles. There were no towns, no people, just the two-lane interstate. At least ten minutes passed before encountering a car traveling in the opposite direction and I wondered if I'd ever make it to Washington D.C.

I crossed the border into Arizona and the desert sand transitioned from tan to a light shade of red. A sign on the side of the road said that the next service station was 90 miles away. I thought it wise to maintain at least a half tank of gas until I got out of the desert. The little mom and pop service stations in that part of the state had a tendency to close early for the day. I didn't want to spend the evening on the side of the road waiting for help to arrive.

I pressed the scan button on the radio and it flipped through every channel in the FM spectrum several times before it stopped on a hip hop station. The signal was weak and there was no telling how much longer it would last. The lyrics of the song were barely audible over the crackle and hiss of the fading signal, but I could still make them out.

It was the typical rap song replete with references to exotic cars, chromed out rims, champagne, selling drugs, night clubs and last but by no means least, phat asses.

The rapper introduced himself and his record label and finally the producer who collaborated with him to bring this work of art to life. He then said "Ugh" and "yeah" a couple of times and started rapping.

"Pimpin' is an art, Pimpin' is the game, Pimpin' for the paper and I aint got no shame."
"24 inch rims, rhymes like hymns, my heater go pow, her ass like wow."
"Pimpin' is an art, Pimpin' is the game, Pimpin' for the paper and I aint got no shame."
"Bust a dope flow, love the mic like a ho, jack you for your shit and then it's time to go."
"Pimpin' is an art, Pimpin' is the game, Pimpin' for the paper and I aint got no shame."

There wasn't much else to it. Just those lyrics, and the two notes that accompanied them. The signal faded not long after that and I considered myself lucky.

The song wasn't totally with out merit. It caused me to think of Dante. "Would he be alright? Would he get it together?" I thought.

I wondered the same about Danni. She used me, but it was then that I realized that I used her as well. Every man in Danni's life had mistreated her. She took revenge against them through me. I was an easy target and Danni knew that I wouldn't strike back at her. In turn, I used her to prove to myself that I was better than Darrell.

Danni hit me but I was a success as long as I didn't knock the shit out of her. That gave me comfort as strange as it sounds. It had been a symbiotic sickness. Imagine that, two sick people from opposite ends of the country managed to find each other in a small bar in Palm Springs. Was it fate or fortune?

The terrain never changed no matter how far or fast I drove. It was just more of the same with the exception of the occasional burned out Methamphetamine lab that sat off in the distance. The desert was vast and difficult for the police to search. The shoddily built wooden shacks even blended in with the desert when viewed from the air. It was the perfect place to cook up some product.

The chemicals were highly flammable and the desert was littered with the remains of many an illegal business venture. There wasn't much of an economy in that region unless you owned a gas station and overcharged travelers for gas, food and water. Meth was quick money and it caught on like wild fire, literally.

The sun retired below the horizon which signaled that the day's driving was about to come to an end. I learned a long time ago to never drive long distance in the dark. Too much can go wrong in the middle of nowhere like falling asleep and waking up to the sound of your car rolling into a ditch.

I passed a road sign that indicated that I could find food, fuel and lodging in the next town. I pulled into the gas station twenty miles later. I filled up the tank and bought two bottles of water. I got a room for the night at the hotel and left my car in the parking lot. I walked over to the Red Clay Grill and was seated by the hostess. I stared at the poorly arranged menu and then looked away to rest my eyes. Every item listed looked the same and I couldn't make up my mind.

"Hi. I'm Tiffany and I'll be your server." The waitress said.

"You look more like a waitress than a server to me." I said.

"Yeah, I'm that too." Tiffany said with a giggle.

She was a cute girl with brown hair. She was about 5'4" with a hot little body and one to many earrings. I would have noticed that immediately if I weren't so busy being mad at the world.

"Our specials tonight are a Chicken Marsalis served with Jasmine rice and mixed vegetables and an open face turkey sandwich with mashed potatoes and gravy. The soup of the day is a crab bisque." Tiffany said.

"I've been on the road for a long time and my mind stopped working about 80 miles ago. Just give me the turkey sandwich and an MGD."

"No problem!" Tiffany said in a chipper tone of voice and walked off.

There were eleven other people in the restaurant that night. Many of them looked like they were traveling including a family of four that was seated in a booth on the other side of the room. The parents appeared to be in their early thirties and their four year old son climbed under the table as the father tried to restrain him. The mother was oblivious to the struggle that ensued under the table and focused her attention on the infant she held in her arms. The baby was adorable and I instantly thought of the child Danni and I would have had.

Thoughts of regret began to seep into my mind. The four year old let out an ear splitting scream as he bumped his head against the metal frame of the table.

The regret was replaced by irritation. It's a good thing the beer arrived in the nick of time.

"Here you go." Tiffany said.

"You're a life saver. However can I thank you?" I asked.

"Just remember that when you leave my tip." Tiffany said as she walked away.

She had a nice ass and that was enough to bring me back to the land of the living and sexually active.

I chugged the beer and placed the empty bottle back on the table.

"Thirsty?" Tiffany asked as she returned with my dinner.

"Yeah, can I get another?"

"It's your bill. You can have what ever you want." Tiffany said.

I raised an eyebrow as visions of her nude body posed in various positions filled my head.

"On the menu." Tiffany corrected.

"Oh."

"Where are you headed?" Tiffany asked.

"Washington D.C."

"Really?" I've always wanted to go there and see the Monument and the Capitol building and the White House. I can tell that you're not from around here. Where are you from?" Tiffany asked.

"I left San Diego this morning."

"Oh, I love San Diego. It's so beautiful there. I went there as a kid. My parents took me to Sea World. Why would you leave San Diego?" Tiffany said.

"It's a long story."

"Trouble, huh? Well, I won't pry. It's ok. Can I get you anything else?" Tiffany asked.

"Beer." I stated plainly.

"Oh, yeah. Let me get that for you." Tiffany said as she ran off.

The couple with the baby and four year old paid their bill and left. I was happy to see them go and take my guilt trip with them.

Tiffany returned with the second bottle of Miller Genuine Draft and I was eager to resume the conversation.

"What about you? Were you born here?" I asked Tiffany as I sipped my beer much slower this time.

"I was born in Las Vegas. My parents got divorced and my mother moved my brother and me back here. She was born and raised here. She ran off to Vegas to start a new life." Tiffany said.

"Let me guess, she found more than her fair share of trouble." I said.

"You must be a mind reader." Tiffany said.

"No, I just know how the story ends." I said.

It was close to closing time and Tiffany and I continued to talk. I was seated at one of the three occupied tables in the place. The other waitress could handle the other two. I would make it up to Tiffany when it came time to leave the tip.

Talking to Tiffany was refreshing. She wasn't angry like Danni. She was sweet and I found myself smiling during the conversation. There's something about the comfort a woman provides that a man just can't do without no matter how much he lies to himself about it.

"When do you leave?" Tiffany asked.

"In the morning. I was planning on leaving in the morning." I said as I considered staying in town for another day or two.

"That's too bad. I really like talking to you. I get off in a little bit. Do you want to do something?" Tiffany said.

"Yeah, that's sounds good. Everything in this town closes early though. What is there to do around here at this time of night?" I said.

"We'll think of something." Tiffany said.

I paid the check and left her a nice tip. I waited patiently outside in the chilly air until Tiffany came out with a six pack of MGD that she swiped from the storage room in the back of the restaurant.

Tiffany said that she lived with her mother so we headed to my hotel room. She took a seat in the middle of the bed with her legs crossed. We talked and drank and laughed and drank some more. Tiffany told me of her dream of leaving the small town for another life in the big city. She wanted to be a singer.

I asked her to sing for me but she was shy. I begged her and she finally gave in. It was worth the effort. Tiffany had a voice like an angel and I considered asking her to go to D.C. with me. We turned on the TV and watched a movie. I laid down on the bed and she joined me placing her head on my shoulder. Her hair smelled like strawberries. She wrapped her leg around mine and caressed my chest.

I put my arm around her and she snuggled closer to me. We were watching TV but we weren't really watching TV. I felt her lips brush gently against my neck. I turned toward her and kissed her softly. The

Low Fuel

sexual tension rushed out of the room just as the air rushes out of the cabin of a jet liner after an explosive decompression.

Tiffany slid her leg all the way over to straddle me and she began to rock back and forth. I sat up and kissed her as I grabbed her waist and pushed her down against me. She moaned as I helped her off with her shirt. Her body was perfect. I placed her on the bed and tugged at her jeans.

It was never my intention to have sex with her but things happen when you're drunk and horny. Besides, I didn't want to be rude. We both lay there in the bed sweaty and out of breath when it was over. I slowly fell asleep with her there beside me and for a moment I thought I was with Danni.

Being a light sleeper is a skill. It requires sleeping deeply enough to get a good night's rest, but lightly enough to detect danger or anything strange all the way from dream land. I can thank Darrell for motivating me to develop the skill. It served me well while in the Marines, and it would save my ass that night.

I felt Tiffany slowly rise out of bed. I could hear her quietly walk across the carpeted floor of the hotel room. I assumed that she was headed to the rest room, but I never heard the fan cut on which happened whenever the light switch was turned on. I opened my eyes in hopes of getting a peek at her perfect naked body in motion.

There was no such luck, she was gone. I jumped up out of bed and saw my jeans on the floor near the door. I left them beside the bed when I pulled them off.

"Oh shit!"

I tumbled out of bed and picked up my jeans. My wallet was gone and with it the money I needed to get back to D.C. I opened the door and caught sight of Tiffany sprinting across the parking lot. She had a head start but it wasn't by much. I threw on my jeans, boots and shirt and darted outside. I skipped three steps at a time as I ran down the hotel stairs to the first floor. I stayed in the shadows as I approached the open parking lot. I saw a beat up Dodge Neon pull out of the parking lot and head down the road. I raced back across the parking lot and leapt into my car. I was sure to keep my distance and followed her with my lights off.

It was 3:00 AM and the road was pitch black with the exception of Tiffany's tail lights. I tracked her until she turned onto a side street and parked in front of a small house. I watched her run inside from a distance. I got the shotgun, ski mask, gloves and zip ties out of the trunk. There was no telling how many people were inside and I needed a force multiplier.

I stealthily made my way to the house, praying to God that no one saw me. It would be hard to explain what I was doing outside of this white woman's house with a sawed off shotgun in my hand.

I tried to peek into one of the windows on the side of the house but the curtains were drawn shut. I would need to bust my way in. I turned to retrieve the sledge hammer from the car. I neared the front of the house when the front door opened. I recoiled back against the wall when I heard a man's voice say "I'll be back soon."

He closed the door behind him and turned to find the muzzle of my shotgun jammed under his chin.

"You speak and you die. Blink twice if you understand me." I said.

He blinked twice.

"Is Tiffany in there?" I asked.

He blinked twice again.

"Open the door." I whispered.

He unlocked the door and we walked inside. I kicked the door shut behind me and slammed his head against the wall knocking off three framed pictures in the process. He fell to the floor and I charged forward through the house with the shotgun in the "Ready" position.

"Sean? Did you forget something?" Tiffany asked as she came around the corner only to find the muzzle of the shotgun pressed into her right eye.

I grabbed her by her hair and walked her back to Sean who was still writhing in pain.

"Where's my fucking money"? I asked.

Tiffany tried to speak but the shotgun caused her to stammer.

"Stop stuttering and get my fucking money or I'm gonna redecorate this place in a blown out brains motif." I said.

"Here." Sean said as he pulled a wad of cash from his pocket.

"That ain't all of it. Where's the rest?" I asked.

"In the bedroom." Tiffany said.

I picked up the money and zip tied Sean's hands behind his back and kicked him in the face to reinforce the idea that trying me would be a bad idea. I walked Tiffany to the bedroom and saw a crib in the corner of the room with a baby in it.

"Your baby?" I asked.

"Yes. Please don't hurt him." Tiffany pleaded.

"Don't be ridiculous. I came here to fuck you up not the baby." I said.

The baby never cried or moved. He just stared at me with a peaceful look on his face.

There was a strange burnt smell in the air. It wasn't strong but it was the remnant of a regular activity. Tiffany gave me the rest of the money and I counted it all to be sure.

"$815.00. Yeah, that's it." I thought.

I relaxed as soon as the money hit the bottom of my pocket.

"What in the hell is going on here? Who is Sean to you?" I asked.

"He's my son's father." Tiffany said.

"You stole the money for him?" I asked.

"Sean needed it for Meth and we're broke right now. He gets so sick and violent when he doesn't have it. I'm sorry." Tiffany said as her tears fell.

"Yeah, everybody's sorry. I'm sorry that I keep running into dumb bitches with issues." I said as I pointed the shotgun at her again.

"Please don't hurt me. I'm sorry." Tiffany said.

"Don't worry. It'll happen too fast to hurt." I said.

Tiffany's eyes grew even wider and she began to stutter as she begged me not to leave her son motherless.

"You didn't think that I would find you did you?" I asked.

"I didn't think about it. You fell asleep and I took the money. I thought that you wouldn't miss it. You're from San Diego and you're traveling. I thought you had plenty of money." Tiffany said.

"What about the sex? Was that part of the plan?" I asked.

"I wanted to be with you. I really did. I liked you but I needed the money too." Tiffany said.

I told Tiffany to turn around and zip tied her hands behind her back. Her baby continued to watch me. I may be crazy but his facial expression led me to believe that he approved of what I was doing. Maybe someone should've kicked Sean's ass years ago.

I pushed Tiffany down on the bed and removed the batteries from their cell phones.

"Has he ever hit you?" I asked.

"Yes" Tiffany whimpered.

"A lot?" I asked.

"Yes." Again with a whimper.

"That's a damned shame. Let me see what I can do about that." I said as I walked out of the room. "There are few things worse than a woman beater." I said to Sean as I stood above him.

"I didn't hit her. I just…" Sean said before I cut him off.

"Yes you did. You hit her. You're a weak addict and you beat the mother of your child when you run out of Meth. Do you have a job?" I said.

"Not right now." Sean said.

"Does she do this a lot? Bringing you money to get high I mean?" I asked.

"Yeah, sometimes" Sean said.

Sean started to cry and looked at the floor.

"Look at me. I want you to understand that you are the reason why I'm here. You are the reason that she stole from me. You are the reason that she had sex with me. She's starved for a real man and not an addict. And then you have the nerve to hit her. You're a parasite but that's your business. Let me ask you, have you ever had your ass kicked really bad? Have you ever been beaten like you beat her?" I asked.

"No." Sean said between the tears.

"Well, let's see if we can't change your perspective on the whole thing." I said.

Sean's eyes grew as large as dinner plates. He knew what was coming and I was more than happy to bring it. I duct taped his mouth shut and kicked him until I was sure that at least two of his ribs were broken. Sean lay there trembling when I was done and I couldn't have cared less.

I walked back to the bed room and the baby was smiling from ear to ear. I couldn't believe it.

"I'm leaving now. I trust you can cut yourself loose." I said.

"Yes." Tiffany said.

"You were very lucky tonight. Anyone else would have slaughtered all of you. You're as sick as he is. It takes a sick man to beat a woman and it takes a sick woman to stay with him. You need to get some professional help. No good can ever come from this. I'd take my child and leave him if I were you." I said.

I stepped over Sean on my way to the front door. He gave a low moan and scooted away toward the wall.

"You're lucky I forgot my sledge hammer." I said as I closed the door behind me.

I headed back to the hotel, gathered my things and checked out. It was 4:45 am by the time I got back on the road. I was tired and I needed more sleep. I considered pulling over and taking a quick nap but I knew better than to press my luck any farther.

Low Fuel

I continued to look in my rear view mirror for the next two hours. I'd be back in jail in a heart beat if I got pulled over by the Arizona State Troopers.

I crossed the Border into New Mexico several hours later and the color of the sand changed to a dull shade of orange. The sun rose to illuminate the lonely desert road that appeared to stretch on forever. I stopped at a service station with a sign that read "Last gas for the next 100 miles". I didn't know if the claim was true but I decided that I couldn't risk it. I slowly climbed out of the car and gave my whole body a stretch. I was sore from sitting in the driver's seat for hours on end.

I noticed an elderly Hopi Indian man sweeping up the area around the pumps. I paid the attendant and began to fill up the tank. The old man came closer and looked at me as if he knew me.

"Where are you headed Lone Wolf?" he asked.

"You talking to me?" I asked.

"Yes Lone Wolf. You are on a long journey?" he said.

I looked at him curiously and answered his question.

"I'm headed to Washington D.C."

"That is a very long journey. Be at peace Lone Wolf. It's not what you think." he said.

"What? What is that supposed to mean?"

"He says that it is not what you think Lone Wolf." The Hopi said again.

"Why do you keep calling me that?"

"He calls you that. Not me." he said.

"Who is he?"

"Your spirit guide." He answered.

"I'm Catholic. I don't have a spirit guide. I have Jesus. See!" I said as I pointed to the gold cross that hung around my neck.

"You have both and your spirit guide calls you Lone Wolf." he said.

"Really? And what does he call you... Old Crow?" I asked.

"No, he calls me Randy." The old Hopi said.

"You know what? I want you to have a nice day." I said as I put the hose back on the pump and screwed the gas cap back into place. I drove off as Randy waved goodbye.

"Damned drunk!" I thought.

I traveled another ninety miles and couldn't keep my eyes open any longer. I drifted off to sleep and awoke in time to find myself in the oncoming lane of traffic. I stopped at the next truck stop that I encountered to get some "shut eye". It was only a two hour nap but it did a world of good. I crossed into Texas and passed through Amarillo.

I reached Oklahoma and drove for another two hours before I could see that there were dark clouds up ahead. The storm was about twelve miles away and I'd be driving right through the heart of it. Gauging the weather was easy in the big open country of the mid west. It was a skill that I learned in Twenty-nine palms and I was good at it.

I came upon a car on the opposite side of the interstate. There was a man standing behind the car and the trunk was open. There was a woman and two children inside and they looked equally distraught. Part of me thought that I should keep going. I had run into enough trouble dealing with people, but I saw those kids inside and I was parked on the shoulder of the road before I even realized what I had done.

"Having car trouble?" I yelled from across the opposite side of the road.

"I got a flat but I ain't got no jack." The man said.

"Hold on. I'll bring mine." I said.

I pulled the floor jack and four way lug wrench from the trunk of my car and ran across the road. We were in the middle of nowhere and there were no other cars traveling in either direction.

"You gotta spare?" I asked.

"Sure do. We just bought this car from my cousin and the son of a bitch didn't come with a jack. I didn't even think to check. We're trying to get back to Tinker Air Force Base. I'm trying to out run this storm before it hits. It looks like its got twisters in it." He said.

I removed the last lug nut and looked over my shoulder. The storm looked like the handy work of the Devil and it appeared to gain speed at the sight of us parked on the side of the road. It would be on top of us in another five minutes.

"Give me the spare." I yelled above the howl of the rising wind as the first rain drop hit my fore head.

I slapped the spare tire on in record time and told him that he could beat the storm if he got moving.

"You're a life saver. How can we repay you?" he asked.

"Are you Air Force?" I asked.

"Yeah, I'm a Tech Sergeant stationed at Tinker." He answered.

"Then you already have. Now go!" I shouted as the wind began to wail even louder.

The wind got stronger with each second and the clouds made the afternoon sky look like night.

"You're not still going that way are you?" he asked as he climbed into the driver seat of his car.

"I'm going home." I said.

"Thank you!!" The woman said as they sped off in the opposite direction of the impending torrent.

Any sane man would have gone the other way. I had nothing at all and nothing to loose.

"D.C. or bust." I shouted as I crossed the road and climbed into my car.

I fired up the engine and the Flow Master exhaust pipes gave that familiar roar that I loved so much.

The sound was enough to inspire any coward to find a little confidence. The rain fell in buckets. I turned on the wipers and gave the storm clouds a final evaluation.

"Fuck You!" I said and hit the gas.

The back end of the car fish tailed a bit as the wheels struggled to find traction on the shoulder of the road. I figured that I could blaze a trail through the rain and come out on the other side none the worse for wear. I set the wipers at there fastest speed and continued down Interstate 40 like a bat out of hell.

I turned on the radio and pressed the scan button. It stopped on a station that was broadcasting a tornado warning. There were several tornado sightings in the surrounding counties. I got her up to 90 mph before I got the impression that I was driving faster than I could see through the rain. I held the speedometer at 90 mph until I saw the funnel cloud forming off to my left hand side.

I ducked instinctively as a corrugated metal door flew across the road only thirty feet ahead of me. I decided to take advantage of all 525 horses at my disposal and took it up to 120 mph.

"I'm ready to leave this world but I'll be damned if I do it without kicking and screaming first." I thought.

The interstate became my personal drag strip. It was peaceful and even beautiful for a moment. Just me and my car against the best that Mother Nature could hurl at me. There wasn't another car on the road which was a good thing. Visibility under those conditions was about forty feet and I was all over the road. I exited the storm five minutes later and emerged into the bright Oklahoma sun.

My fingers were sore from gripping the steering wheel so tight. I eased up of off the accelerator just in time to see the Oklahoma State Trooper pass on the opposite side of the road.

The Trooper made a U turn and closed the gap between us. He activated the cruiser's lights and pulled me over. I remained absolutely still. Cops in D.C. and California were a little trigger happy and I wasn't too sure about Oklahoma.

The Trooper exited his cruiser and approached my car on the driver's side which gave me reason to relax. Cops in D.C. exit the vehicle with their hand on the grip of their pistol and approach from the passenger side just in case they need to dump nine or ten rounds into the car.

"Hi there, I need your license and registration." The Trooper said.

I dug them out slowly and handed them to him.

"You know, you were driving really fast a minute ago." The Trooper said.

"Well, yeah. I mean I was caught in that storm and there were tornados and stuff and I've never seen anything like that before. I was scared as hell. I just thought that I would be better off the faster I could get out of there." I said.

"Ok. Just sit tight." The Trooper said as he returned to his cruiser to run my license.

I sat as still as possible doing my best to look like a calm law abiding citizen who hadn't conducted a home invasion with an illegal fire arm the previous night.

The Trooper returned a short time later and gave me my license and registration back.

"You're really lucky. That storm has done a lot of damage." The Trooper said.

"Yeah. I was thinking the same thing." I said feeling a little optimistic.

He removed his sun glasses and looked me and the car over.

"We have a big problem with drug traffickers on this Interstate and we have been doing a lot to apprehend the culprits. Do you mind if I search your vehicle?" The Trooper asked.

"Well, no. I was just headed to Washington D.C. for a wedding and I'm running a bit late with the tornados and all. How long will it take?" I asked.

"It won't take long. I'll just check under the seats and the trunk. Go ahead and step out of the vehicle for me." The Trooper said.

I opened the door and placed my left foot on the ground when he received a call on his radio. There was a lot of damage down the road from the Tornado and he was being called that way.

"I gotta go. Do me a favor and slow down." The Trooper said.

"No problem." I responded, hoping that he hadn't noticed the beads of sweat that were beginning to form on my forehead.

I counted my blessings as the Trooper sped off with his lights flashing and siren blaring. The image of the cruiser became smaller and smaller and finally disappeared into the fog and haze that the storm left in its wake. I restrained my lead foot and was rewarded with a change of scenery as I entered Arkansas. I had finally found the grass and tress that I was in search of and I could no longer see for miles in every direction. It had been so long since I had seen anything other than sand. Driving through the deserts of the South Western United States can be awe inspiring and daunting all at the same time. It just never ends until it does.

I stopped for the night in Knoxville, Tennessee and made it a point to avoid the local bar and grill. The drive through of the nearest Krystal's was good enough. I woke up at 6 am, ate breakfast at the Waffle House and was back on the road by 6:50 am.

I pulled into Norfolk, Virginia at 9:38 pm that evening and followed the road signs that told of a hotel at the next exit. The Norfolk Motor Lodge sat back far from the road and looked more than slightly anachronistic.

"Who calls a hotel a motor lodge anymore?" I wondered.

The place looked like it had been there since the fifties and that was entirely possible. I thought about finding another hotel but I was far too tired to risk getting lost in a strange town in the middle of the night.

The attendant at the front desk was asleep when I entered the lobby and didn't respond when I attempted to get his attention.

"Excuse me... Hello... Hey yo!" I yelled but to no avail.

I tapped the bell that sat on the counter that had a sign that read "Ring for Service." The attendant snapped to attention and I noticed that he slightly resembled Vincent Price. "This is just great, out of the frying pan and into the haunted house." I thought.

The motor lodge was actually located on a small hill that was a short drive away from the front office. The hill provided a lovely view of the many trees that obscured the view of the Interstate below.

The interior of room #11 hadn't been redecorated in years and looked as if it was indeed built in the 1950's.

"Do I smell moth balls?" I wondered as I entered the room.

There was a long crack in the mirror near the bathroom and there was a piece missing from the lower left corner. The sheets and comforter looked clean but I wasn't too sure about the carpet. I decided to keep my shoes on and skipped the shower. I placed my bag down on the table that was in the corner of the room near the front door and made my way toward the broken mirror. I turned the knobs of the faucet and washed my face in the sink until I was sure that the day's grit and grime were gone. I looked at my face in the fractured mirror. I hadn't shaved since I left San Diego and I looked very different with a beard. It needed a trim but I decided to keep it.

My body breathed a sigh of relief as I lay down. The bed must have been made in the fifties also. The springs squeaked anytime I shifted my weight. I loved the sound of squeaking bed springs but not under these circumstances. I turned off the lamp that sat on the night stand and the room turned a gorgeous shade of dark. There wasn't even a street light outside the window to provide a warm friendly glow.

The wind picked up and a branch from an over grown tree began to scratch against the roof of the room.

"Yeah, this place is haunted. Well, if you gotta die somewhere, this place is as good as any." I thought.

I couldn't sleep and I stared at the ceiling doing my best to figure out how I had come to be in such a place.

"Fuck! I can't believe that I threw my career away for this." I said aloud.

I had proven Lieutenant Colonel Lassiter right. I couldn't make it in the civilian world and I had driven across the country to God knows what. At least I was somebody when I was in the Corps. I was Sergeant Westlake, the stud, the man and everyone new my name.

"Now I'm nobody, just a jackass whose claim to fame is out running a God damned Tornado." I thought.

The alarm clock that sat on the night stand was an old wind up model and I couldn't figure it out to save my life. I set the alarm on my cell phone and slept as still as possible.

I left at 6:23 am the next morning and made the final push north. Three hours later I was stuck in rush hour traffic on Route 66. I called Wayne and told him how close I was. He gave me directions to his garage in Oxon Hill, Maryland and I wrote them down while holding the phone against my head with my left shoulder and steering with my knees.

Oxon Hill is the type of city that always makes the evening news but for all of the wrong reasons. The body count there rivals Saigon during the Tet Offensive and the County Police have a shoot first, ask questions later approach to law enforcement.

"The rent is cheap here and it's all I can afford." Wayne said when I asked him why he put his shop in a high crime area.

I reminded him that you get what you pay for and then asked if the place came with a complimentary flak jacket.

Cutting through rush hour traffic was an arduous task to say the least. I didn't remember it being so bad when I left to go to Parris

Island. The D.C. area had always been the site of major construction projects and housing developments, but the entire endeavor had increased exponentially since the last time I was in town.

I drove past Alexandria, Virginia on I-495 and didn't recognize any of it. I knew the city intimately since I used to work there, but everything was different now. Tall cranes filled the skyline as they hoisted steel beams to waiting construction workers on the roofs of unfinished buildings.

The sky which was obstructed from view by high rise condominiums and office buildings became visible once again as I crossed over the Potomac River on the Woodrow Wilson bridge. The river didn't look as polluted as I remembered it but I wouldn't be fishing there any time soon. Three eyed perch aren't as appetizing as you may think.

The exit for Oxon Hill led me to the heart of the city and it seemed that there were more cops there than anywhere else in the county. I found the garage after a couple miles and parked my car in a space near the front door of the waiting area. I walked toward one of the open bays and saw a familiar face working on a late model Volvo.

"Cole! Oh shit! You made it. How was the trip?" Wayne asked as we shook hands and hugged.

"Man, you wouldn't believe it in a million years." I said.

"What did you do now?" Wayne asked.

"I think I'm a trouble magnet." I said.

"Let me show you the place." Wayne said.

He gave me the quick tour of the place and then took me back into the office. He pulled a beer out of the fridge and handed it to me. I thanked him and chugged it as I always did at which time he handed me a second.

"You know me so well. I'm glad to finally be here. I can't wait to take a shower and get a good night's sleep." I said.

Wayne was smiling but I knew him well enough to know when something was bothering him.

"Hey, is that Donny?" I asked as I picked up the framed picture of Wayne's son that sat on the desk.

"Yeah, he's getting big isn't he?" Wayne said.

"He sure is. He was a baby the last time I saw him. Now he's a little dude. I bet he's getting into everything and asking a million questions." I said.

"You know it. That's my little buddy. I take him every where with me." Wayne said.

"You're a blessed man. You have a beautiful family." I said while putting the picture back on the desk.

Wayne was speechless for a second and then spoke.

"Look, I need to tell you something. My marriage hasn't been going well at all. Eva and I have been arguing every night and she told me that she wanted a divorce last week. I tried to talk her out of it but she won't listen to reason. She went and got a lawyer and everything. She wants me to move out of our house. She doesn't want you to stay there either but don't worry. You can stay here in the garage."

NINE

I sat there alone in the waiting room of the garage with the wall mounted television turned on to keep me company. I never looked at it... not once. The volume was set at a low setting but it was the familiar electro magnetic hum that made the strange surroundings feel a little more like home. It was a trick that I learned as a kid. My brother and I would come home to an empty house which in and of itself was not a bad thing. It's just that the world seemed so big and frightening to a little kid.

It was as if we were on pins and needles waiting for something awful to break the silence. We were always waiting for something awful to break the silence. The television was the only thing the reduced the fear. It's funny but we kept the volume low then also. There was something about that hum that provided comfort in the face of uncertainty. I was scared then and I was scared now and there was still so much uncertainty.

The tears fell slowly one by one and I sat there with my head in my hands just as I did as a child. Old habits die hard I guess. The emotions of the past few months finally caught up with me. I had done my best to evade them but that never works for long. Sooner or later you have to deal with it all or all of it will deal with you.

To end up living in a garage after driving across the entire continental U.S. was heartbreaking to say the least. I had been on the run for so long and it all led up to that moment. It was a hollow victory and I was ashamed of the things that I had done to survive, but part of me knew that it was only the beginning. Salvation was replaced with calamity and hope was fading fast.

Wayne told me that it would all work out as he closed the garage for the day.

"It's just temporary. Eva will come around. I just need you to stay here for a couple nights until she calms down. I'll clean up the basement for you. It'll all work out. Don't worry."

Wayne tried to convince me but I knew better. Things have a tendency of getting a hell of a lot worse before they even think about getting better. The garage opened at 8:00 AM the following morning and I had until then to get a good night's rest.

I needed a job and soon. I found myself wishing that Toons was a better drug dealer, either that or that I was better at armed robbery.

I purchased an air mattress from the local Target but had to wait for the pump to finish charging before I could inflate it. Swearing at it didn't speed up the process and I decided that actually watching the television would help pass the time.

The only silver lining to the dark cloud that was my life was that Wayne had a customer named Curt. Curt was the manager of the Milan Night Club on U Street in Washington D.C.

"I can talk to Curt about getting you a job working security at his club. That would be a start." Wayne said.

The pump finished charging and I used it to inflate the air mattress. I stood there thinking of how much it looked like a lone life raft adrift in an endless sea of floor tiles. I positioned it so that I could see the TV clearly. My ass sank and hit the floor when I laid down on it. I tried laying on my side but that was even worse.

I spent the rest of the night shaped like the letter "U". Every move I made resulted in the same sound that a balloon makes when twisted into various shapes. I attempted to remain absolutely still but the sound returned each time I took a breath which was quite often.

The rest room provided a place to wash up the next morning and I put all of my effort in to looking as if I hadn't slept on the floor of a garage. I left the garage at 7:00 AM before Wayne arrived to open up for the day. The entire area had changed so much over the past few years but I managed to find a few familiar spots.

The Pawn Daddy pawn shop was still where it had always been and so were the panhandlers who begged each passer by for spare change. They were uncommonly silent as I walked by and didn't ask for a single dime. Perhaps they knew that I was one of them. I walked through the door and was greeted by the sound of a chime that announced my presence. The attendant was on his cell phone and wasn't too concerned about me being there.

That's the nature of the business. No one walks into a pawn shop unless they're desperate to pawn something or too broke to buy something in a real store. Either way, he knew that I needed him a hell of a lot more then he needed me. I took a look at the shop as he peaked over his shoulder, never once halting the conversation to even inform me that he would be with me in a minute. It was the typical pawn shop and I felt embarrassed that I even knew that.

The walls and shelves were laden with tools, fire arms, musical instruments and jewelry. It was a monument to broken dreams and shattered lives, and the owner fed on them just as a vampire would feed on the blood of the innocent. Disaster and despair where the harbingers of profit. What was Hell to most of us was Heaven to the pawn shop owner. It was hard to see the whole enterprise as anything other than immoral. I needed the money too badly to object. Besides, it wasn't my first time.

The attendant finished his phone call and asked how he could help me in a tone of voice that indicated both boredom and annoyance. I guess even the blood of the innocent becomes run of the mill over time.

"I have a watch that I want to sell you." I said.

"Let me see." he said as I removed the gold Rolex from my wrist and handed it over.

He examined the watch and then examined me. I imagined that he needed to determine exactly how desperate I was before he made an offer. I stared him down in order to throw him off. He took his gaze off of me and studied the watch even more carefully.

"This is nice. This is really nice. Where'd you get it?" he asked.

"My uncle left it to me in his will." I said.

It was the kind of lie you didn't bother to sell. It was just enough to remind him that he should mind his own business. Besides, it didn't matter if he believed me or not. I could tell that he wanted it and that was all that mattered.

"Did he leave you anything else?" he asked.

"I'll be sure and bring it to you first if he does." I said.

I didn't want to live a life of crime but who knew what the future would bring. I needed all of the resources that I could get and a crooked pawn shop owner was just what the doctor ordered.

"$700.00 more bucks, not bad." I thought as I placed the cash in my wallet.

That would buy some time but not much. The Rolex was worth a hell of a lot more but beggars can't be choosers. It was stolen anyway and this was one of the few pawn shops in town that would let you get away with selling hot jewelry. I was approached by two panhandlers as I walked out of the door but I didn't stop to chat. I had money to spend and I wasn't feeling very charitable.

Mr. Woods of the local Veterans Administration employment office answered the phone and I introduced myself. I told him that I was new in town and that I needed help finding a job. Mr. Woods made an appointment for me to come in the following day and said that he would take care of me. I spent the rest of the morning making wrong turns and getting lost.

I drove by places from my past in an effort to rediscover the parts of myself that I had lost during the past few months. It was like going back to the factory for original parts to rebuild a damaged car.

I washed my clothes at the Bouncing Bubbles Laundromat in the city of Morning Side near Andrews Air Force Base and located the Bally Total Fitness in Alexandria, Virginia. I worked out, took a shower and changed into some clean clothes.

I returned to the garage later that afternoon and found Wayne examining the exhaust system of a beat up '69 Stingray.

"Yeah, it's all rusted out. You need a new manifold and mufflers." Wayne said but not to me.

"What do you have here?" I asked as I took a look at the under carriage of the car pretending to recognize what it was that I was staring at.

"Hey boy. This here is Manny's Stingray. It's gonna be bad ass when he gets it put back together." Wayne said.

"Who's Manny?" I asked just as a slim white man in his late 50's walked away from the tool box with a socket wrench in his hand.

Manny looked just like Same Elliott would if he were only 5'9", rail thin and smoked the majority of his meals.

"Manny, this is Cole." Wayne said.

Manny and I shook hands and he asked me if I was the one from California.

"Yeah, that's me." I said.

"Why in the hell would you trade San Diego for Oxon Hill?" Manny asked.

"I sun burn easily." I said.

"His woman did him dirty and they kicked him out of town." Wayne said.

"So much for privacy." I said.

"Oh well, enough said. My wife left me thirty years ago and I haven't looked back since. She did me a big favor and didn't even realize it. I'm happier on my own. I don't have to answer to anyone. It's just me and my dog." Manny said and then coughed violently.

It was the kind of cough that indicated a serious problem with one's respiratory system. Manny composed himself, re-inflated his lungs and continued.

"Son, you need to understand that your average woman is nothing but trouble. They make plenty of demands but don't offer anything in exchange. Most of them can't cook, won't clean and only worry about giving orders and going shopping. Don't marry one 'cause then they'll just gain thirty pounds, chop off all of their hair and stop having sex with you. Hell, most of them won't even nurture their own children. They just sit them in front of a TV and let Sponge Bob do the parenting. I don't know this woman you had but if she did wrong by you, then leaving her was the best thing that could have ever happened to you." Manny said.

"It doesn't feel that way." I said.

"Trust me boy, the more time you spend with the wrong woman, the less time you get to spend with the right woman." Manny said.

"Listen to him, Manny knows." Wayne said. "My wife is giving me grief now. I got half a mind to get me a muscle car too and leave her."

"That's right. I don't love shit but my dog, this Corvette, and some good weed." Manny said and then doubled over in another coughing fit.

The coughing continued and became more than a little uncomfortable to watch. I would have told him that he may want to consider cutting back on the weed and focus more on the car, but I didn't know him that well. Manny finally cleared the phlegm from his throat and stood upright once again.

"So what about finding your soul mate, falling in love, marriage, the white picket fence and the 2.5 children?" I asked.

"Love? Soul mate? Kids? Ha! You been reading romance novels or something?" Manny said.

"Ain't no such thing as a soul mate. That's some movie bullshit." Wayne said.

"So why did you do it?" I asked.

"Love ain't nothin' but two people feeling sorry for each other and then thinking that the other one is gonna save them from their bad choices. That's why my wife married me. She needed saving and now look at me. She wants to leave and take everything with her, even my son." Wayne said.

"A man is to be a rolling stone. That's the way God made it. You are to be fruitful and multiply. That's even in the good book. You can't do that if you're laying up under some brawd. This whole thing about settling down and having babies was all a woman's idea. They've brain washed all of us into thinking that it's the right thing to do. I never knew a man who was happy with that life not when he could drive a fast car or go fishing. I'll be good and God damned if I have to ask permission to do what I want to do." Manny said as he suppressed the next coughing fit.

My entire comprehension of reality was in jeopardy. Were they right? Had I been misled all this time?" I thought.

"Did you call your mother yet?" Wayne asked.

"What?" I asked having been ripped away from contemplating my next move.

"Your mother, did you call her yet?" Wayne asked again.

"No. I don't know where she is. She was in rehab the last time I talked to her but that was years ago."

"What about your brother?" Wayne asked.

"No one has seen him in three years. He was strung out real bad the last I heard." I said.

"What about Lucky and Mingo and the old crew…or Serena? She was fine as hell. Call Serena. She'll take care of you." Wayne said.

"Serena got married a year ago and Mingo and Lucky are nothing but trouble. You remember how they used to be. I can't deal with any of them right now. They would just drag me down even farther. I can't risk it. I need to find a job and a place to live. What about that guy at the night club? Did you talk to him yet?" I said.

"Damn my mind is bad. I almost forgot. Curt wants you to stop by tomorrow night." Wayne said.

"What kind of job is that?" Manny asked.

"Big boy is going to be a bouncer down at Milan Night Club." Wayne said.

"Damn that! That ain't no kind of job to have. Earning table scraps for getting punched in the side of the head. I knew a guy who got shot in the back once for breaking up a fight in a bar." Manny said.

"I've done it before. It'll be ok for a while." I said.

"It's different here. These niggas are terrible. You'll have to kill one of them. I'll get you a job with me. I'm a carpenter. Can you work with your hands son?" Manny said.

"I can do anything." I said.

"I'll get you a job as a carpenter's assistant. A man needs a trade. They can never take that from you." Manny said.

"But that job don't pay shit. This man needs some money." Wayne said.

I've got an appointment with the VA tomorrow. They'll help me find something. I'll do that by day and work in the the club at night. I'll be back on my feet in a few months." I said.

It sounded like the thing to say but we all knew that it wouldn't be that easy. It never was.

Wayne lowered Manny's Stingray and he drove away but not before promising to have the fastest hot rod on the streets when he got the new exhaust installed. Wayne closed the shop and retired to his office to balance the books. I sat in the waiting room watching TV until he walked in and threw a beer in my direction. I caught it and chugged it before he opened his.

"So you think the VA can help you find a job tomorrow?" Wayne said.

"Yeah. I have a government clearance. They'll find me a job quick in D.C. The whole city is full of government agencies and military contractors. It won't be a problem." I said.

"That's good." Wayne said.

Wayne was getting at something but I couldn't tell what exactly. I decided to try a different approach.

"Thanks for letting me stay here. I really appreciate it. I would have probably been locked up again if I stayed in San Diego. I won't be in your way for long." I said.

"It's no problem brotha. You got what I got as long as I got it." Wayne said.

"Are you worried about Eva ripping you off in Divorce Court?" I asked.

"No. The garage really hasn't been doing well at all and I'm behind in my rent. I had to let a guy go two months ago and I'm trying to do everything by myself. I put everything into this and now it's all falling apart. My marriage, the shop, everything. I give the fuck up!" Wayne said.

I felt guilty. Wayne had his own problems and I threw myself right on top of them.

"I'm sorry. I didn't know. I won't be here too long." I said.

"Like I said brotha, you got what I got for as long as I got it." Wayne said.

"How do you know Manny?" I asked in order to change the subject.

"Manny came in to the garage I worked in about three years ago with his pick up truck and we've been friends ever since. That was about a year after you left for the Corps." Wayne said.

"He's got a real bad cough. Has he been to a doctor lately?" I asked.

"Manny smokes weed every day, twice a day. He's an old hippie. He couldn't breathe pure air if you paid him. He's been like that since the sixties. It's just catching up to him that's all." Wayne said.

"Was he serious about all that stuff he said about women and marriage?" I asked.

"I don't know…maybe. Manny talks all that tough guy shit but he just moved a woman into his house. He used to work with her a couple of years ago. Manny always wanted her but she was married. Her husband left her a few months ago and she needed a place to stay so he took her in." Wayne said.

"So she's his woman now?" I asked.

"No! She's playing him. She's been there for a month and they haven't even had sex. She sits in his house rent free, eating his food and smoking his weed and she hasn't even had the common decency of giving him some pussy." Wayne said.

"So then what's the truth?" I asked.

"The truth is that I've never known a man who was happy without a woman, and I've never known a man who was all that happy with one. It's just the way it is. Damned if you do, damned if you don't" Wayne said.

"Can't live with 'em, can't fuck without 'em." I said.

"Exactly." Wayne said.

The VA employment office was about as helpful as a swift kick in the balls. I spent half of my time there filling out paper work, and the other half flipping through telephone book sized binders that were full of so called job vacancies. My head began to ache and my vision went blurry as I flipped through page after page. The letters on each page seemed to rearrange themselves to say "You're shit out of luck jackass."

It's amazing how very little the Veteran's Administration actually does to support this country's veterans. A man signs his life away to serve his country, leaves his home and loved ones behind. Ends up in some asshole part of the world ducking bullets, and then spends the rest of his life chasing after the fabled "Veteran's benefits."

Serving your country is like shooting dice in a burning building. You try to get the money and then get out without dying of smoke inhalation or third degree burns. God help you if you lost an arm or leg or worse. You were on your own with an honorable discharge and a pat on the back as a consolation prize if you're lucky. This country asks its service men for so many sacrifices and offers none in return. Most third world shit holes revere their veterans while the United States is eager to forget those who have made it free. It's hard not to feel like a sucker sometimes.

I had enough of the job search and figured that drinking a couple of beers would be a more efficient waste of my time. Mr. Woods asked me how my job search had gone as I reached for the door knob. I paused for a second and decided to tell him the honest truth.

"I can't find a God damned thing it in that big ass book. Only a lunatic would jam all of that shit together in a binder and expect a sane man to find anything other than a migraine. I'm going to the garage... I mean home." I said.

"Hold on young fella. Don't be discouraged. Give me a copy of your resume." Mr. Woods said.

"I gave it to you an hour and a half ago when I first walked in here." I said.

"Oh, that's right. They say the mind is the first to go. Here it is. I'm going to forward it to a company I know. They always come through for me. You'll see." Mr. Woods said.

"Why didn't we just do that in the first place?" I asked.

Mr. Woods was speechless but I wasn't. I chose to hold my tongue before I burned one of the few bridges that I had left in the world. He made the call and arranged an interview for me with a government contractor called Maestro.

I thanked Mr. Woods and headed over to the Maestro office. Once again, I was confronted by the omnipresent code of conduct and I treated it with the same reverence that I always did. Lynette Parker interviewed me and said that she would find work for me even if it was just temporary. I thanked her for her time and drove into to D.C. to meet Curt at Milan Night Club.

Washington D.C. had changed just as much as the rest of the region. I fought my way through all of the traffic and avoided the red light cameras. They say the streets in D.C. where modeled after those in France but I think a crack head had a hand in it. D.C. is the type of city that requires you to make three right turns rather than just one left. All of the one way streets and circles are surely the result of crack head logic. I was born and raised in the city and I still got lost in it. Everyone did no matter how much they lied about it. I spent 27 minutes making right turns until I could get my bearings. I spent 20 more minutes in traffic until I arrived at the club.

I pulled into the parking lot that was on the same street as the club and paid the attendant $8.00.

"What a rip off. Why go to college and become a Noble Laureate when you can just own a parking lot in a major metropolitan city? You'll be a millionaire in 2 years." I thought.

I walked past the long line of patrons waiting to enter the club for happy hour and approached the door man. He was a pretty boy type and I instantly disliked him. He made it a point to flirt with every woman entering the club… even the ugly ones. He was having entirely too much fun on the job and I was slightly jealous.

I told him that I was there to see Curt and he called him on the radio.

"He'll be out in a minute." The door man said.

Curt arrived minutes later to conduct the impromptu interview.

He asked me a few questions and then looked me up and down. I knew the game and I wore all black in order to look the part. It worked and not only did he offer me the job but he asked me if I could work that night.

The job paid a lousy $10.00 an hour. The clubs owner also owned the parking lot, and I would be given a discount and only have to pay $5.00 to park. And that concluded the perks and fringe benefits of the position.

Curt and I descended down the stairs and into the basement where the business office was located. Curt handed me a radio, an earpiece and gave me a brief orientation.

"Now we got a few rules around here. One, you don't leave your post unless there's a fight or you're told to do so. Two, no drinking on the job…ever. I had to fire a guy last month for passing out drunk in the DJ booth. Three, keep the ladies to a minimum. Fourth and the most important, don't hit anyone. We don't need a lawsuit and neither do you." Curt said.

"But I'm free to use harsh language and the occasional choke hold?" I asked.

"That's fine by me, just don't hit anyone." Curt said.

The 10 cent tour was next and I watched the clientele closely. Young urban professionals I think they call them. That's a politically correct code word for educated black folks in their twenties and thirties who go to work everyday and don't commit violent crimes. There was also the occasional thug dispersed through out them. Thug is a politically incorrect term for black folks in there twenties and thirties who don't go to work everyday and do commit violent crimes.

Curt pointed out the location of each bar and stairwell and introduced me to my fellow bouncers.

There was Robby who was posted near the DJ booth at the front of the dance floor. He was a burly guy with a silly demeanor. Robby was there for the women and nothing else.   Nothing made him happier than taking a young woman up on stage and dancing with her. The women loved it because they were getting the attention they so desperately desired, and Robby loved it because he got to rub up against a different woman every night and on the rare occasion, go home with them. Curt constantly admonished him for it but it was all part of the game. Robby wasn't going any where any time soon.

Del was in his early forties. He was jaded and not impressed by anything or anyone. He sat watch over the pool table on the second floor. That was the sight of most of the fights since the patrons had a tendency to gamble on the out come of each game. There were a lot of pool cues that were often used as weapons of opportunity. Del wasn't doing anything for anyone unless they could do something for him first. He called it reciprocity, everyone else called it selfish. Del had been there almost as long as Haymaker.

Haymaker was a fifty two year old man and a local legend. No one knew his real name but he got his nick name in the obvious fashion. By knocking men unconscious with a single punch to the chin. He was from the old school and so were his fists. Haymaker was the type of man they just don't make anymore. He was tough as iron and no one fucked with him. It just wasn't worth it.

Haymaker was of average height and build but what he lacked in size, he made up for in experience and tenacity. His beard was steel grey and his jaw was square. He had a smile that could light up a room and a laugh that was thunderous, but he was all business. One look from him could get the point across without a word being said. All of the male patrons shook his hand when they saw him as if his masculinity might rub off on them. More than the occasional young lady would drop her date's hand and say hi with a hug and a kiss on Haymaker's cheek. He was a class act and I found myself wondering what he was doing in a place like this especially at his age.

Gerald reminded me of Shemar Moore but more hostile. I gave him the nick name G.Q. because he should have been a model or an actor. I mean the guy was that good looking. Every woman in the club knew it and so did his girl friend. She came through whenever she could in an effort to keep him faithful. It had worked so far so I couldn't blame her.

Melvin was the youngest of the bunch. He was a slender college student who worked in the club for extra money. Curt used him as a part time host and part time bouncer. The girls loved him and he made it a point to love each one of them back. Melvin didn't have G.Q.'s problem and he made Milan Night Club his personal playground.

Will was the most professional of them all. He did his job and made time to flirt whenever things were slow. Curt told me to hang out with Will to learn the ropes.

We stood at a post that was across from the main bar and instantly hit it off. Will was originally from Raleigh, North Carolina and had been drafted by the Redskins right out of Howard University but was cut in training camp. Things went down hill from there and he ended up in the club to make ends meet. His girlfriend was understandably disappointed at the loss of a million dollar contract and never let him forget it. I understood all too well but I didn't spill my guts. I just told him that I was new in town and that I took the first job that I could get.

Curt told me to head downstairs a few hours later and shadow G.Q. We stood there watching the women walk by and G.Q. was more than happy to provide the play by play coverage.

"Damn she's got a fat ass and look at them titty balls!!!" G.Q. said.

"Be easy. Here comes your girl." I said.

"Hey baby. This is my man Cole. He just started tonight." G.Q. said.

We shook hands and she whispered something in G.Q.'s ear and then said good bye and that it was a pleasure to have met me. She was beautiful and extremely lady like. Milan wasn't her type of venue. She was only there to safe guard her investment. She had put too much time into G.Q. to let him ruin everything with a one night bang out.

If G.Q. wanted to stray then he would. People are who and what they are when you meet them, and they always will be. All of the kicking and screaming in the world won't change them. You should catch on to that before you start planning the rest of your life with them.   God knows I learned that lesson the hard way.

"You're a lucky man." I said.

"Lynn's the best but I don't know man. She keeps pressing me." G.Q. said.

"Pressing you for what?" I asked.

"Man, she wants what they all want. She wants a baby and to be married and all of that shit." G.Q. said.

"Well, she is marriage material. I could tell that after meeting her. I wouldn't want to lose her. Are you guys compatible?" I said.

"Yeah. My relationship with Lynn is perfect, but I already have two kids and I'm paying child support out the ass. That's why I'm working in this bitch twice a week. They pay cash under the table and my ex's lawyer can't go after it. I'd be broke if it wasn't for this place. They increase the child support every time I get a raise. My ex's hobby is taking me back to court every year and a half. It don't take that much

Low Fuel

money to provide for two kids. I'm paying the note on her new car and she took her boyfriend to Jamaica on my dime. I have a good job. I'm a network engineer but I can't even afford to live anymore. I love my kids but God damn! Sometimes I wish I didn't have kids at all. Who in the fuck can afford this shit?" G.Q. said.

G.Q. wasn't the type of man to tell a complete stranger his personal business but stress and desperation cause a person to behave out of character at times.

"Lynn deserves to be a wife and mother but I can't risk it. What if she did the same thing to me? I wouldn't have shit. I'd be better off dead. Part of me wants to tell her to go find someone else but I love her and shit. I don't know." G.Q. said.

He stood there staring at the floor until the sound of thunder began to roll.

The crowd fled the dance floor like they were running from a three alarm fire. G.Q. and I ran toward the ruckus as Curt' voice called "Code Red: Dance floor!" over the radio. We fought to part the crowd as we ran toward the action.

"Move! Move god damn it!" I yelled as loud as I could until we reached the now vacant dance floor.

It was an all out brawl. There was no rhyme, no reason, it just was. That's the problem with being a bouncer in a large club with more than one floor. It's anybodies guess as to what in the hell is going on by the time you get to the fight. The only solution was to grab everyone and sort things out on the street.

"Don't hit anyone!" I said over and over in my head as I closed distance with the pugilists.

The Marine Corps taught me to break necks and destroy the enemy and now I was doing my best to overcome the reflex training that had been burned into my mind. I counted seven men trading blows as well as Will and Haymaker approaching from the opposite side of the dance floor when I made contact with the first guy. I'm a lot smarter than I look and I knew that approaching him from behind was the best course of action. I hit him like a freight train and locked in a Full Nelson. I sunk my arms down into a tight lock. He was helpless as I twisted him to the side of my body to keep him off balance. I ran him out through the front door as I saw Haymaker knock the first guy out. He put another down before I reached the stairs.

Curt was standing outside the club on the side walk waiting for us.

"Bring that motherfucker over here. Gimme your I.D." Curt said.

Curt collected drivers licenses and made copies of them. He told them never to come back or they'd get more of the same.

"We run this shit! Fuck with us and find out!" Curt yelled at the top of his lungs.

The rest of the night was uneventful and eventually the bartenders announced "last call."

The lights were flicked off and on and we pushed everyone out the door. Reality reasserted itself and every guy who was still in the club gave a last ditch effort to try to get a phone number from the women who were still there. We pushed the last of the patrons out and locked the door behind them.

We conducted a sweep of the entire club to ensure that we were clear. This was the time that we were most vulnerable. Our guard was down and the bartenders began to count their money. We took a seat and waited for Curt to speak to us. He always spoke to the bouncers after a major scuffle.

"Well son. I'm glad to see that you came to play." Haymaker said to me.

"Don't tell me you had doubts." I said.

"Most guys come here for the pussy. Some want to be hard. I don't know who's a coward until the punches start flying. We need more guys ready to put in some work around here." Haymaker said as he gave Robby a dirty look.

"What man? I was there with ya'll." Robby said.

"You were late like you always are. This man was first in. I saw him. He didn't hesitate." Haymaker said.

"I'm just not fast as ya'll." Robby countered.

"Shut up!" Haymaker said and gave a look that punctuated the sentiment.

It was enough to quiet the entire room as the bartenders looked up from tallying their stacks of cash.

"Where are you from son?" Haymaker asked.

"Born and raised right here in D.C." I said.

"No, you aren't from here. You have an accent." Haymaker said.

"I've just lived all over." I said.

"The service?" Haymaker asked.

"Yeah."

"I figured as much. You just don't seem the type for this sort of thing." Haymaker said.

"It's funny but I was thinking the same thing about you. You've got too much class for a joint like this. You've got too much class for a name like Haymaker. No offense." I said.

"I used to be a knuckle head way back when. I went to prison for manslaughter when I was 19. I did a 15 year bid. I had an auto detailing business for a while but this is the only steady work that I can get. My real name is Ronald but don't ever call me that." Haymaker said.

"Yes sir." I said.

"Welcome aboard." Haymaker said and then walked away.

"Damn! How'd you do that?" Will asked. "You got his whole life story and his name. Nobody knows his name. Nobody knows nothing about him. He just knocks mother fuckers out."

"People love me... It's a gift." I said.

Curt spoke to us about the brawl and commended us for not being overly aggressive.

"We can't loose our liquor license. Not under any circumstances. I'll put you out of business before you put me out of business." Curt said.

Curt cut us loose at 3 am and I sped back to the garage as fast as I could. I got three hours sleep before Wayne opened up for the day. I deflated the air mattress and drove the car around the corner where I parked and finished sleeping.

I awoke two and a half hours later to the sound of someone ringing a bell in my ear.
I groped for the phone and answered it just before the call went to my voice mail. It was Lynnette Parker and she wanted to know if I was available for a temporary assignment at the Department of Treasury on Monday morning. I told her that I was and thanked her for the opportunity. I worked Friday and Saturday night at the club and almost made it through the weekend unscathed, until one guy stepped on another guy's shoe and all Hell broke loose.

I arrived at the Department of Treasury 20 minutes early that Monday morning. I was checked in by the officers of the Federal Protective Services and walked through the metal detectors. My point of contact met me and escorted me to the third floor. I would be filling in for the secretary for the Director of Foreign aid for Latin America and the Caribbean. I didn't know the first thing about being a secretary but I needed the money and a normal routine. I sat at the desk answering phone calls and taking messages when I heard a friendly voice say hello.

"Are you with Maestro too?" the voice asked.

I looked up to see a beautiful young woman standing beside my desk.

"Yeah…yes, I'm with them. Just here for a couple of days." I said.

"Yeah, me too. The work is easy and they pay pretty well. I just got out of the Air Force so I'm doing this until I find a full time job." She said.

I introduced myself and she told me that her name was Nyssa. Nyssa had been assigned to the Department of Treasury the previous week and decided to teach me the ropes. Nyssa helped me out a lot and I was grateful since I really didn't know what I was doing. We talked when ever we could and I was eager to get to work each day so that I could see her again. Nyssa was the only person in my life that I could really talk to. She had a level head on her shoulders and the fact that she was cute didn't hurt either.

Soon the inevitable question was asked during lunch.

"Why did you leave San Diego to come back here?" Nyssa asked.

I didn't know what to do. I wanted to lie to her but I wanted to tell her the truth also. I wanted someone to care. I wanted someone to tell me that I didn't deserve the things that had happened to me because I just wasn't sure anymore. Danni may have been crazy but I picked her. Maybe the whole thing was my fault. Maybe I should have left her sooner. Maybe I should have been more supportive of her. Maybe I should've never moved to San Diego with her in the first place. Maybe I should've stayed in the Marine Corps. I was lost in the whole thing and I felt worse the more I thought about it.

"Oh my God! That's horrible. She did that? You didn't try to get her back." Nyssa said.

"Well no, I mean what was I going to do? It was all of them against me. I was just trying to survive." I said.

"You're too nice. I would've gotten even with that bitch. Where did you meet her?" Nyssa asked.

"In Palm Springs." I said.

"Palm Springs? Is she white?" Nyssa asked.

"No, she's Mexican." I said.

"Same thing. Well you learned the hard way. You should've stayed with the sistas." Nyssa said.

"I was with the sistas. I mean I still am. I mean… I just met her and I liked her. I didn't go out of my way to be with her. It just happened." I said.

"Yeah right. You look like the type. Ya'll brothas start doing well and then get ahead of your selves and cross over. Then you get in trouble

and want to come back home. I've seen it happen before. We'll always be here waiting for our Kings to come back to their Queens.
She was wrong but you need to stay home is all I'm saying. And then you were in an all white neighborhood too. You know better. You're lucky you made it out alive." Nyssa said.

She changed the subject and told me that her daughter's father was a dead beat, and that he didn't even bother to show up to the girl's birthday party the previous weekend.

I kept my mouth shut until our lunch break was over and decided to call Pastor Stephen Reynolds when I got back to my desk. His secretary took down my contact information and made a note that I knew Pastor Tony in San Diego.

A lot of good the referral did. I had an appointment to meet with Pastor Reynolds in two weeks and I found that a bit troubling.

"Why would I need an appointment to speak to the pastor of a church? What kind of operation were they running?" I wondered.

The temporary worked dried up two weeks later. The night club was my only source of income which wasn't much to speak of. Lynette Parker assured me that she would find another assignment for me and I prayed that she could keep her promise.

A new bouncer arrived to work at the club one Friday night. The turnover rate for bouncers was high at Milan which was not unusual for a night club in a large city. Bouncers were either quitting or being fired on a monthly basis. The latest addition to the security staff was named Reggie. Curt put him with me since I was a veteran by that point.

"Semper Fi Brother!" Reggie shouted above the loud music.

"You a Marine?" I asked.

"Yeah brother. Curt told me that you were a jarhead so I asked him to put me with you." Reggie said.

Reggie and I compared notes and traded old sea stories. It was the same thing that happened each and every time someone claimed to be a Marine. It was important to gain proof that they were what they claimed to be. Each answer brought on another question until we were both satisfied that the other was the genuine article. I couldn't tell much about him since he was being elusive. I could however tell that he was not afraid to fight, and that was a good quality in anyone, Marine or not.

Reggie became more comfortable and let down his guard. He told me that he was from Philadelphia and that his day job was working at Metrofinacial as a loan officer. Reggie was a braggart and he liked to shoot his mouth off but then again most Marines do.

The never ending stream of beautiful women continued, and Reggie deemed one of them worthy of pursuit. He followed her toward the dance floor and I didn't see him for the rest of the night. I don't know how it happened but I know that he got her name, number and closed the deal.

My appointment with Pastor Stephen Reynolds came around and I drove to his church in Largo, Maryland. It was huge and had more in common with a castle in the Scottish highlands than a church. I spoke to the receptionist and she escorted me back to a conference room that looked as if it came right out of corporate America. I sat there at the end of the table looking out the window at a bird that landed on a tree branch. The bird stood there maintaining its balance and darting its head back and forth as birds do. It pecked at the branch stretched out its wings, and then flew out of view.

I wished that I could trade places with it. I'd fly to Miami for the winter and stare at tits and thongs all day. That would beat the piss out of begging some stranger for help in un-fucking my life. I hadn't been to church in years, and I felt like a hypocrite for what I was about to say. It was at this moment that I had a revelation.

Pride is counter productive. I was always told to take pride in this and that but that was bad advice. Pride is akin to ego and both are a waste of time. A wise man asks for help as soon as he needs it. A fool holds on to pride and refuses to ask for help, until things get so bad that they are almost irreparable. As hard as it was I decided to swallow my pride and beg. It would be difficult but the past few months weren't exactly a cake walk either.

"If I could get through them then I could get through this." I thought.

Pastor Reynolds made his appearance and brought a friend along. He looked sharp in his tailored suit, cuff links and hand made Italian shoes. He shook my hand and introduced me to Deacon Frye. The Deacon was a junior version of the pastor and I figured that he was still in training. Perhaps he would graduate in a few months to go start his own church. It was tax free money and a better franchise than a McDonald's.

"So you were a member of Pastor Tony's church in San Diego?" Pastor Reynolds asked.

I told him that I had just attended a service or two but that Pastor Tony prayed with me about my situation.

"So are you looking to join a church family?" Pastor Reynolds asked.

"Well my chief priority is finding full time employment. I'm kind of in survival mode right now. "I said.

"Well, a church family is very important. It provides the base of faith and through faith in the Lord all things are possible. You could accomplish great things in the name of the Lord." Pastor Reynolds said.

"Well yeah, I agree with that. I just need to get myself back on track. Pastor Tony told me that you may be able to help me out with that." I said.

"Of course, of course we can brotha but it sounds to me that you are young in your faith and we need to get you strong in the word. The word of God is the sustenance that fuels the righteous man. You won't make much progress without it. I know that you're homeless and there may be times when you haven't eaten, but I'm more interested in feeding your soul with the word than I am with feeding your body. You said that you are doing some temporary work right now." Pastor Reynolds said.

"Yes, it's enough for gas and food but not much else." I said.

"No, no that's fine brotha because tithes are important in a church family like ours. It's important that you give tithes because it opens God's blessings for you and it comes back ten fold." Pastor Reynolds said.

I zoned out at that point and watched his mouth move as I tried to figure out what to do next. It was more than apparent that this wasn't going the way I thought it would which shouldn't have surprised me. Pastor Reynolds and Deacon Frye took turns hitting me with the hard sell. Every dollar counted in an enterprise such as theirs.

Pastor Reynolds walked me out of the church when our meeting ended and shook my hand one last time. He asked me to come to his church service that Sunday. He told me that he would pray over me in front of the entire congregation after the building fund offering, which followed the love fund offering, which followed the Sunday worship offering, which came after the Fellowship offering and the praise offering. Pastor Reynolds and Deacon Frye got into a brand new Mercedes Benz and drove off to God knows were.

As a child I was told to find a church if I ever needed help. I was told that the church doors were always open to those who needed help, but that wasn't the case here. The whole thing had been a huge disappointment. Since when did you need to become a member of a church to receive the word of God? Since when were churches in the business of exploiting their congregations for the Pastors new car fund? The whole thing felt more like a Ponzi scheme than a church?

Pride reared its ugly head yet again. I thought about it for a minute and realized that beggars couldn't be choosers. I decided to attend the church service that Sunday and hoped for the best.

I followed the throng of parishioners through the tall doors of the church. The ceiling was at least forty feet tall and resembled the Sistine chapel. The altar was ornate and covered in what appeared to be gold. As a matter of fact, there was gold every where. Gold candle stick holders, gold stanchions, gold ropes, gold planters and gold door knobs. The organist played a hymn and the choir was humming along. I caught sight of Deacon Frye as he took a young woman by the hand. She lit up brighter than a spot light and thrust her chest slightly forward to accentuate her cleavage which was showcased in a low cut blouse.

If I didn't know better I would have thought that I was back in the night club. She giggled and Deacon Frye gripped her hand even tighter. He whispered in her ear and she was visibly excited. This reached a fever pitch and I wondered how far it would go until he looked around prior to going in for the kill and saw me. A smile took over his face. He gave a quick look for the Pastor and then came my way.

"Brother Cole, How are you?" Deacon Frye asked.

I told him that I was fine and he gave me instructions regarding the service.

"I'm glad you came. I'll tell Pastor Reynolds. Now he'll say that we have a guest who is in need of the Lords anointing, and that's when I'll call you forward. Just come up to the altar and Pastor Reynolds will take it from there. The ushers will take you back to your seat after that. OK?" Deacon Frye said.

"OK."

The choir started singing again and the Deacon excused himself and trotted toward the altar. The entire congregation was in motion and swaying from side to side. The Pastor made his grand entrance and the congregation erupted. He shook hands with various members of the church on his way to the altar but always stopped to hug the ladies.

The choir finished singing and Pastor Reynolds started to speak. Every eye was on him. Every man wished they could be him, and every woman wished she could be with him. He had them eating from the palm of his hand. He introduced the praise dancers and they danced to the choir's song. The Pastor complimented them when they were done and said that he looked forward to personally helping these young ladies in developing a personal relationship with the Lord. The young girls melted at the prospect, and their mothers became jealous at the idea that the Pastor's attention would be diverted from them for even a moment.

Pastor Reynolds gave a sermon on the need to give to the kingdom of God with out hesitation and that it would release God's favor unto the church. Deacon Frye helped an old woman to her feet and escorted her to stand before the Pastor. She said that she was signing over her 401K to the church so that the Pastor could ensure that the church continued to grow and do God's will. The crowd cheered and waved their hands in the air. A gentleman to my left began to speak in tongues and jumped up and down.

The ushers passed out collection plates to encourage the congregation to follow her example and they did just that. I passed the plate along to the woman on right when it reached me and was tapped on the shoulder by one of the ushers.

"Excuse me, we're asking for your tithes now." The usher said.

"Yeah, I know. I'm between jobs right now and I don't have any money to spare." I said.

The usher looked at me disdainfully and moved on to the next row. "How many of you out there have ever been in a crisis?" The Pastor asked. "How many of you have ever been alone. How many of you have ever been in need?" he continued. He was brilliant and he played the congregation like an orchestra. They yelled and screamed that they all had been down on their luck at some time in their lives and that the Pastor must have been told this by God himself.

"There is a young brother here today who is in need of a miracle. There is a young brother here today who is in need of salvation. This brother has been wronged. This brother has been hurt. He has been forgotten, but we are going to bring the anointing of the Lord to him this morning and his testimony will be an example for all to see. Come on up here Cole. We are going to pray for you my brother." Pastor Reynolds said.

I slowly stood up, shy and embarrassed but was prodded on by the congregation. The Pastor welcomed me at the top of the stairs. He told the audience of my arrest and that everything I owned was stolen. He told them that I was homeless and living in a garage and that I was also unemployed. I was mortified to be standing in front of hundreds of people and having my dirty laundry hung out to dry. The Pastor prayed for me and waved his hands over my head while the choir sang softly in the back ground.

Pastor Reynolds asked God to rain blessings down upon me as he smacked me in the fore head repeatedly. The congregation hollered with each blow and several women passed out at the thought of God working through the Pastor. An usher walked me off stage when the Pastor was done and I was replaced by another hard luck case who had waited patiently to be smacked in the head as well.

"That was powerful brotha. I feel so full of the spirit right now." The usher said as he walked me back to my seat and handed me another collection plate.

"I thought you already took up the collection." I said.

"That was the building fund collection. This is for the love offering." The usher said.

"What's a love offering?" I asked.

The usher looked at me as if I were from Mars and then informed me that the "Love Offering" was an offering that was given to the Pastor because the congregation loved him and wanted him to be well taken care of.

"What about the Sunday worship collection? Do you do that one too?" I asked.

"Yes we do. That will be in another fifteen minutes." The usher said.

"Wow! You guys take up a lot of collections." I said.

"It's important to pay your tithes. Paying tithes opens up God's blessings for you." The usher said.

"So God won't bless me unless I pay him first?" I asked.

"Paying tithes shows God that you are not selfish and that you are willing to sacrifice on his behalf." The usher said.

"God made me. Doesn't he already know that I'm not selfish?" I said.

The usher looked at me bewildered and then tried a different approach.

"Do we have a copy of your current W-2 on file?" the usher asked.

"No."

"Well, make sure we get one. It's important that you give ten percent of your income to the Kingdom of God. The Pastor is insistent that everyone surrender their tithes each Sunday." The usher said.

"So that's how he got the Mercedes?" I asked.

The Usher snatched the collection plate from me in disgust and passed it on. Each parishioner placed an envelope into it and continued to pass it along. There must have been over a thousand dollars in that one collection plate. It was a complete racket and I was on the wrong side of it. I had been used by the Pastor to fulfill his rock star prophecy.

I wanted to grab the microphone from the Pastor and tell the congregation that it was all a scam, but I would have caused a riot and been trampled to death. It wouldn't have done any good any way.

They were in a trance and they were his to do with as he pleased. It goes all the way back to slavery. Black slaves were told to go to church and praise the Lord, and that it didn't matter what happened to them in this life because they would get their reward in the after life. They were expected to pick cotton all day obediently because God would make it up to them in heaven. The modern day black preacher has just picked up were the white slave master left off. He's keeping blacks in a slave mentality and making just as much money off of the backs of his congregation.

My grand mother always told me to trust my first instinct when she was alive. "Something bad always happens when you ignore that little voice that goes off in the back of your head." She said.

She was right. Deep down inside, I knew that this would be a waste of time during my meeting with Pastor Stephen and Deacon Frye.

I skipped the rest of the service and chose to solve my problems myself. I tried to pawn the gold cross that I borrowed from Toons but it ended up sticking to Pawn Daddy's magnet.

"Sorry dude. Gold don't magnetize. This is just some costume jewelry that your uncle left you. You'd be better off taking it to the scrap yard down the street." The attendant said

My car note was due and this wasn't good news at all. I needed more money or something would have to go. Either the car note or the auto insurance. Talk about being between a rock and a hard place.

"Damn! Look at her. I can see her lunch." Reggie said as a barely dressed woman walked by.

They were all barley dressed. They liked the attention but not that much attention. They were quick to swat at the men who grabbed at them as they walked by. The whole thing made very little sense. The women dressed like they were trying to catch a man's attention but didn't want to be bothered. The men stood along the wall trying to look tough and reached out at women as they passed by. Women sat in groups and carried on their conversations and quickly shooed away any man brave enough to approach in the hopes of introducing himself. There were men who sat down sipping their drinks and watching the televisions that were mounted in the walls. The entire club was full of people who seemed to want nothing to do with one another.

"Why do you think they come here?" I asked Reggie.

"They come here for me. The word about me is getting around. Reggie said.

"I mean the guys too. It's like they're just here. They don't really interact with each other. I mean some of them are dancing, but the rest are just hanging out watching TV. Couldn't they just do this at home?" I asked.

"Who cares? You should be more concerned with getting laid than worrying about why people do the dumb shit they do. Look at all of these bitches. This shit is like being a kid in a candy store. So many flavors and so much time. I feel like a lottery winner every time I come to work. I can't believe they actually pay me to be here. I'm going to retire from here. Go find a one night stand. It's OK, I won't tell. How about her, She's fine or maybe her. That one keeps looking at you." Reggie said as he pointed to a tall, statuesque woman near the main bar sipping an Apple Martini. I did a double take and walked toward her.

"Yeah, that's my man. Go ahead and tap that ass." Reggie said as I stepped away.

I couldn't tell from across the room but the closer I got, the more sure I was that it was Latoya I was walking toward. It had been a few years but she was still beautiful. She had lost a little weight but she was gorgeous none the less.

I promised myself that I would break ties with her and let go of the past but the sight of her reminded me of the time before all of this, and I wanted that back. Latoya seemed to be looking for someone.

"Who?" I wondered.

It couldn't hurt to ask. It couldn't hurt to say hello. It couldn't hurt to go back to her place and bang her into a coma for old time sake.

Latoya turned to face me as I closed the distance between us.

"Still beautiful after all this time." I said.

It had only been a few years but it sounded like something cool to say.

"Cole! Oh my God." Latoya said as she reached to hug me.

She held on to me as if I were a laundry bag full of $100 dollar bills. I did the same and all of the hurt from the past faded away. I forgave her without even thinking about it. Consider it unconditional lust. It just felt good to be held. It felt good to be the recipient of affection from a woman. I didn't realize how much I missed that. I hadn't realized how important it was.

We didn't say a word. Latoya and I were in our own little world while the club passed by until Curt broke the silence.

"Code Red: First Floor! Code Red!"

I begged Latoya to wait there for me and ran toward the stairs. I fell in behind Haymaker and Will as we leapt down the stairs for the first floor. Reggie was too busy securing his latest sexual conquest to be bothered with doing his job. He pulled the earpiece from his ear so that he could focus on the task at hand.

We hit the floor and rounded the corner in time to see G.Q. and Melvin struggling to remove three men from the club. They were big. All over 6'8".

"I hate basketball players!" I thought.

Robby stood between the melee and a young lady who was bleeding from her face.

G.Q. and Melvin fought to hold things together until one of the assailants threw Melvin to the floor and started hitting G.Q. That's when Haymaker put him down. Will and I grabbed the last two and put them out the front door. We tossed them down the stairs for good measure and because there was a crowd watching. We always liked to send a clear message that we weren't to be fucked with. We grabbed them at the bottom of the stairs and held them for Curt.

Curt told us that one of the three asked the young woman for her phone number several times and then hit her in the face with his beer bottle after she refused. She had a 1 inch cut on her face and was on her way to the emergency room.

"Where are the cops?" I asked.

Curt chuckled and walked back up the stairs.

"I missed the joke. What's so fucking funny?" I said.

"They don't call the police. Too many police reports and the Board of Alcohol Beverage Control will take their liquor license. They're out of business if that happens. Just watch your back and don't worry about the patrons. It's us against them." G.Q. said.

I walked back up the stairs to continue my reunion with Latoya after the dust settled. I found her walking away from the dance floor. She was definitely looking for someone. Latoya was scanning the room from left to right when her eyes met mine again.

We stood there as two bashful kids would at a junior high school dance.

"You look good." I said.

"You already said that." Latoya said with a giggle.

"It's still true." I said.

"Are you back for good?" Latoya asked.

"As good as it gets." I said.

We hugged again and she told me that she was sorry. I told her that it was all water under the bridge and that she shouldn't worry about it.

Latoya gave me a look that was worth a thousand words. It was the type of look that said I'm sorry, I've missed you terribly, I wished that I had been with you all of this time and most importantly, I want you to take me home and make love to me.

"Yeah!! That's what I'm talking about." Reggie yelled as he walked by with a young woman in tow.

"We need some privacy." I said.

My aunt is out of town and my daughter is at her friends tonight. Can you come home with me after you get off?" Latoya said.

"I'll come home with you and then get off." I thought.

Time couldn't pass by fast enough. I checked my watch and then checked to see where Latoya had gotten to. I hadn't had sex in a while but this was more than just physical. I had genuine feelings for Latoya at one time and I felt that being with her again would be just like old times.

I drove Latoya back to the two bedroom apartment that she shared with her daughter Latonya, her Aunt Bernice, her aunt's boyfriend Teddy, as well as her niece. They were all out that night. I followed her up the stairs and she glanced over her shoulder to see if I was still there. Latoya opened the door of the apartment and gave a cursory look around as if she were afraid that her aunt had come home early.

I took a seat on the old beat up couch in the living room as she headed toward the kitchen.

"Can I get you something to drink?" Latoya asked as she grabbed a bottle of water from the refrigerator.

"No, I'll just sip some of yours." I said.

Latoya sat down on the couch and then scooted closer to me. Her leg was touching mine and I couldn't help but notice that her dress had ridden up and most of her thighs were showing. I wanted to be between them in the worst way.

We stared into each others eyes for a moment until Latoya put her head on my shoulder and said that she missed me. I hugged her and told her that I had missed her too.

"Are you really back for good?" Latoya asked again.

"I don't know. I don't know anything right now."

"What's wrong sweetie?" Latoya asked.

"Nothing's really wrong. It's just that…"

"Tell me what's wrong. I can tell something is really bothering you. You can't fool me." Latoya said with a smile.

Low Fuel

I told her everything, everything except the part about visiting Toons and my pit stop in Arizona. What she didn't know wouldn't hurt her and I didn't want to make her an accessory.

"I'm sorry sweetie. God, I'm so sorry." Latoya said.

"It's not your fault."

"Yes it is. It is my fault. I was so stupid. I knew you were the one for me but I wouldn't let go of my ex. I was afraid to take a chance. I should have run to you and let go of the past. You were so good to me. I know I hurt you and I'm so sorry. I could have kept you safe. I could have protected you but I let you down." Latoya said as she started to cry.

"It's ok baby. I'm fine." I said.

"No you aren't. I can see the hurt in your eyes." Latoya said and buried her head in my chest.

I held her closer and gently kissed her forehead. Latoya looked up at me and I kissed her. Latoya's eyes begged me to take her. I kissed her again and she told me that she wanted me so bad.

It's amazing how the right words can boost a man's self esteem. I was myself again. I picked her up and carried her across the floor and then remembered that I had no idea where I was going.

"Which room is yours?" I asked as I stood there looking at the two bedrooms.

"This one." Latoya said as she pointed to the room on the left. I carried her through the door and threw her onto the bed. I parted her legs and pushed myself against her as we kissed. Latoya grabbed at my shirt and I helped her pull it off.

"Wait." She said.

"What baby? Tell me." I said as I gently bit her neck. Latoya moaned and I tried not to laugh.

I was all too familiar with this routine. It's the game some women played to get the sex they wanted and still feel virtuous in the morning. Latoya would tell me to wait and stop a couple of times but beg me to continue if I actually did. Then I would nibble on her ear lobe and she would be like putty in my arms. We'd then have sex and it would all be my fault.

She would wake up in the morning and still feel like a good girl. It's how Latoya rationalized not feeling like a whore after her many sexual encounters. It was a hell of an act coming from a woman who cheated on her boy friend with me, but it didn't matter. I was horny and she wanted me. Playing her game was a means to an end.

I caressed her breasts through her dress and then pulled it off over her head. Latoya helped me unbuttoned my pants. I had her thong half way off when she grabbed my arm.

"Wait, wait hold on!" Latoya said but I was in fifth gear and stopping was the last thing on my mind.

"Wait for what? I got a rubber. It's cool." I said.

"No, wait. Stop." Latoya said.

A tear slid down her cheek and I got the same feeling that you get when you stop just short of running into the back of a car after you hit your brakes at the last minute.

"What 'Toya? What is it?" I asked.

"I can't." Latoya said as she sat up on the edge of the bed and wept. "I can't. I'm sorry. I keep messing everything up. I always mess everything up. I missed you so much Cole and I wanted you to come find me and take me away from all of this but I can't do this. I couldn't live with myself if something happened to you." Latoya said.

"Nothing's going to happen to me baby." I said.

"Cole, I'm sorry. I can't. I'm HIV positive."

TEN

The world stopped spinning and I felt weightless and disoriented. It was the closest that I had ever come to an out of body experience. I sat there on the edge of the bed, half disappointed that she said no to fucking me, and half in shock that she was HIV positive.

"Did she say HIV?" I asked myself.

There was no way around it. Latoya said it and I realized that my nightmare paled in comparison to hers. Each letter hit me like a blow from a sledge hammer and part of me thought that it was karma. Latoya sobbed uncontrollably as if she were hearing the news for the very first time herself. I placed my arms around her and brought her close to me. I promised her that everything would be alright. It was the type of promise that closely resembled a lie. It was the type of promise that you couldn't keep but wished that you could. It was the type of promise that you made to make your self feel better because acknowledging that you were powerless was too much to deal with.

We didn't say a single word. We were both at the end of our emotional ropes and didn't have the strength to speak. We just lay there that way all night. It took Latoya half an hour to stop crying and she fell asleep soon after.

Latoya's snoring roused me back to consciousness that morning. Her head was on my chest and I couldn't recall how we got there. The fog slowly lifted and I remembered watching her die a little more inside as she told me her deepest, darkest secret. I had just dodged a speeding bullet. What if Latoya hadn't been so honest? What if she didn't tell me? I was grateful that Latoya stopped me when she did because it was my every intention to fuck her brains out just like I used to.

The sun broke through the blinds at 6:00 am. I watched over Latoya just as I watched over Danni. They were very different yet very similar. They were both gorgeous and both had that slightly self destructive, out of control quality to them. I wondered why I was attracted to that. Honestly, they weren't the only two women I've known who were like that. They were broken on the inside and I hoped that I wouldn't end up the same way.

Latoya's eyelids slowly parted and she was astonished to see me there with her.

"I thought I dreamed you." Latoya said and gave a big smile that almost erased the heart ache of the previous night.

"No, you're stuck with me and the bad news is that I'm hungry, and you know how I get when I'm hungry." I said.

"Oh my God! I better get you a raw steak to chew on." Latoya said.

I laughed and told her that a few scrambled eggs would do the trick.

"Are you ok? Your eye is twitching." Latoya said.

"It does that sometimes." I said.

"I'm sorry Cole. For everything, especially for letting you down." Latoya said.

I wanted to tell her that she hadn't, but the fact was that she did let me down. Latoya had let herself down and her daughter and her family and her friends.

"What happened 'Toya? Who did this to you?" I asked.

Latoya took a deep breath and then told me of the past year and a half of her life. She had become fed up with Craig's lack of concern for their daughter. He wasn't paying child support and he only made an appearance when it was convenient for him. The disappointment of life had become too much so she lost her self in non-stop parties. She found solace in a few random dicks and managed to still feel like a lady in the morning. Latoya met Damon, dick number eight after a few months.

Damon was the kind of man Latoya always wanted to be with. He was tall, handsome and had a great job. He even drove a BMW and he didn't live on the other side of the country. Damon said all of the right things and took Latoya out to eat in the type of restaurants that she had never been to. He was fun and nice, and it almost made up for Craig and his bullshit.

Latoya thought of what a relationship with Damon would be like, but even she knew that he was just an escape and nothing more. Latoya had never even been to his home. They always got a hotel room and Damon tried to make it seem as if he wanted to treat her to a romantic, luxurious get away.

A night in a hotel room was far better than one in a two bedroom apartment with four other people, so she went for it hook line and sinker. It was time away from responsibility. It was time away from life. It was a fantasy and Latoya dedicated herself to it. She fought to stifle that little voice in the back of her head that tried to warn her. Damon was better than Latoya was used to, so who was she to demand more of him even if she deserved it?

Latoya had no idea if Damon was married, or if he even had kids and it was better that way. Latoya could always feign ignorance if he had a wife and she came looking for her. Latoya didn't really know what Damon did for a living. Sometimes he wore a nice suit so she imagined that he was a big time executive or something. Damon was a mystery to her and that's what her friends called him, "The mystery man". He picked her up at work one day and a co worker warned Latoya about him.

"He's not real. He's not being completely honest. He's just not right." She said.

Latoya ignored that warning just as she ignored her first instinct. Latoya was happiest with Damon, whether riding in his car or in the bed. Sex was a diversion from reality, but reality was the only one being completely honest.

The entire affair lasted only two months. Damon disappeared without a goodbye and without a trace. Latoya called his number but it was out of service. Damon dealt with her on his terms, when and where he wanted to. Latoya had not a shred of evidence to prove that he even existed in the first place. Only a few of her friends had seen him. He was gone just as soon as he came.

Latoya started feeling tired and run down six or seven months later. She went to the hospital emergency room with a bad case of pneumonia. They made the diagnosis after some blood work. Latoya was HIV positive and reality was back and in full force. She cried, she kicked and she screamed, and that little voice could be heard telling her "I fucking told you so!" over the din of her panic.

Latoya had been looking for Damon ever since. A year had passed and she had not one single lead to go on. She went to every place she thought he would be. Latoya told the police, but she had no information to provide other than a description.

It was a fore gone conclusion that Latoya wasn't the first, and that she wouldn't be the last. The only thing that could stop him would be criminal prosecution or a bullet. The burden of the man hunt brought even more stress, and sent her to the emergency room on more than one occasion. Stress is bad for a healthy T-cell count and Latoya walked a delicate balance of dedication to revenge and to health. Both were necessary and there could be no future without achieving either as far as she was concerned.

"I just need to find him and ask him why. I need closure." Latoya said.

There's no such thing as closure. Closure is something women invented so that they could have one more conversation with a man who did them wrong long after the relationship is over.

"Closure is not letting go." I said.

It was getting late. I took Latoya to breakfast. I didn't have that much money but I thought that getting out of the apartment would do her a world a good. I took her back home and headed to the garage. There was a familiar Stingray parked out front and I wondered what pearls of wisdom Manny would have to share that day. I sure as hell needed to hear them.

I walked into the waiting room of the garage and saw Wayne and Manny whooping it up, but something was different this time. Manny's demeanor was subdued and I soon saw why.

She was standing to his right and injected more into a man's conversation than any woman should. She was a tall and slender woman in her late forties who had the body of a hot busty 29 year old. Her face on the other hand looked every bit of a hard lived 48 years.

Several of her teeth were missing which was visible when she opened her mouth as wide as possible to laugh as loud as possible. Every fourth word was an expletive, and she was unaware of the resemblance each one of her opinions bore to an asshole. She was no lady, and I knew that she must be Manny's new platonic room mate Donna. All of this I gathered within 20 seconds.

Manny introduced me to Donna and we shook hands. She gave a closed mouth smile striving to look as attractive as possible, and I had half a mind to tell her to knock it off. Donna looked more like a ghoul than a living being and the words "Meth Head" came to mind.

"Getting in kinda late ain't ya?" Wayne said.

"Kinda late. It's noon. You must have gotten lucky." Manny said.

"That's a matter of opinion." I said.

The trio got back to the business at hand. Manny came into a couple grand from some side carpentry work he did, and Wayne was telling him what kind of upgrades he could make to the Stingray with the money. Donna was quick to jump in and insist that a trip to Vegas would be a nice get away for him.

"Manny, you work so hard. You need a vacation. Las Vegas is nice this time of year. You should see the Luxor. It's incredible at night. They shoot this beam of light all of the way to the sky from the top of the pyramid and these lights run down the corners. It's amazing! You know what…I've been to Vegas half a dozen times. I should go with you and show you around. It's a rough town if you go to the wrong spots. I think you'd really like it." Donna said.

She made the recommendation and inserted herself right in the middle of it. I was impressed. Wayne was quiet and I looked on in anticipation for her next move. It was like a dysfunctional game of chess.

"Well, I'll have to think about it. I mean I need to get the car fixed up and the house needs some repairs." Manny said but it was a futile effort.

Donna had him by the throat and he would collapse at any minute.

"I just think that a hard working man should get away from it all every now and again. Working too hard will put you in an early grave. There, I've said it. I'll shut up now." Donna said.

Manny was looking at his feet and Wayne was flipping through the Corvette after market parts catalog trying not to laugh.

"We'll see." Manny said meekly.

Manny was almost done. It wouldn't take Donna much longer to deliver the final blow.

"I just think that you should stop and smell the roses every now and again. That's all." Donna said.

It was obvious to all of us that Manny was going to Las Vegas. It was just a matter of time. Manny and Donna said good bye ten minutes later and left. Wayne and I laughed as they drove off.

"He's about done." Wayne said.

"Yeah, I noticed. She's got her claws deep into him." I said.

"Las Vegas, can you imagine him out there with all of those slot machines and the noise." Wayne said.

"Why don't you tell him that she's a gold digger?" I asked.

"You know better. You can't tell a man the truth about a woman that he's in love with. He'll fight you or worse." Wayne said.

"I guess so." I said.

"So where have you been all night and morning?" Wayne asked.

"It's a long story." I said and then proceeded to tell it. The funny thing is that it really didn't take that long to tell.

"What!!! God Damn you're lucky. She could've gotten you boy. You'd be sittin' here all shriveled up and dying. Then I would have to put you out of the garage. I can't have no Aids up in here." Wayne said.

"It's not Aids, it's HIV and you don't get it like that." I said.

"Don't matter to me. My luck is bad enough and Aids is the last thing I need. What're you going to do?" Wayne said.

"About what?"

"About her. She wants you back. You can bet on that." Wayne said.

My cell phone rang at that exact moment and my sigh told Wayne that he was right.

"Hey 'Toya. How are you feeling?" I asked.

"I'm fine. I just wanted to thank you for last night. You've always been there for me when I've needed you. You're a sweetheart and I wanted to tell you that I'm so glad that you are back. I know that things are hard right now, but trouble doesn't last always. Besides you're my special friend and I'm here for you. Things are going to be fine. You'll see." Latoya said.

I thanked her and told her that I would call her that night. I ended the call and offered Wayne a tissue to wipe away his tears.

Lynette Parker called me and asked me to report back to the Department of the Treasury that Monday. Nyssa was happy to see me and asked me how I had been. I told her about Latoya and the bad news she gave me.

"You need to be careful with her." Nyssa said.

"I am. I didn't have sex with her. We just slept in the same bed. We kept our clothes on."

"That's not what I meant fool. You have to be careful with her because she's very emotional, especially now that you're back in town. You're a good dude and she messed things up in the past. I bet she thinks this is her second chance with you. You didn't run from her the night she broke the news to you. She thinks you love her so much that you still want her to be your girlfriend or wife instead of the booty call that you thought you were getting." Nyssa said.

"She wants you back but not because it will work. She wants you back because she's desperate and she thinks you really love her and you'll be dumb enough to be her man especially since no one else will. You need to run but I know that you won't." Nyssa said.

"Why do you say that?" I asked.

"Because women in peril are your weakness, and she knows that. It probably has something to do with your mother. I hardly even know you and I know that much. I'll bet my next pay check that you won't run from her so please be careful with her emotions. Let her down easy and set some boundaries. You can't be her man because you are in no position to take care of anyone, and you can't risk contracting HIV. Just be her friend and leave if she pushes for more. Now you've been warned. Don't blame anyone but yourself if you mess this up." Nyssa said.

Nyssa walked off and left me sitting there deep in thought.

Nyssa was right, but the funny thing is that I knew it before she even said it. Nyssa just confirmed it all for me.

"Did you beat it up?" Reggie asked.

"Beat who up?" I asked.

"The bitch you left with last week. Did you punish that ass? Reggie asked.

I lied and told him that I did. I didn't have the strength to endure the laughter that would ensue after I told him the truth.

"How is the temp work going?" Reggie asked.

"Not bad. I mean it's easy and it pays ok." I said.

"That's good. These days you've got to have your hands into a lot of things. It's all about multiple streams of income brother. Look, I have a mission for us." Reggie said.

"A mission, with a five paragraph order and everything?" I asked.

"Yeah. Look, I got this opportunity and I need someone I can trust." Reggie said.

"What is it?" I asked skeptically.

"I met this guy Charles. He owns his own mortgage company. Charles is a small fry but he's got potential. He needs help generating business and that's where we come in. I get calls about refinancing mortgages all the time at work. I'll pass the customers on to you and you can interview them. All you have to do is forward their information to Charles and he'll do the rest. We'll close the deals and then split the money. Now that's hot for a part time hustle and don't tell me that you don't have the time." Reggie said.

"That doesn't exactly sound legal." I said.

"You ain't no angel you broke motherfucker. Stop frontin'. You've done some dirt in your time. I can see it in your eyes. You need this money as bad as I want it so stop fucking around and let's run this shit. Marines need to improvise, adapt and overcome, so adapt your ass to the idea of getting this money." Reggie said.

"Why would anyone go through Charles instead of a big, reputable company like Metrofinancial?" I asked.

"The fact of the matter is that 65% of the people calling into Metrofi don't have the Fico score to qualify for a loan. I'll work my magic and pull some strings and get them qualified for more than they ever thought they could get. They'll be so grateful that they won't ask any questions. They'll be too busy thanking God to realize that we're ripping them off." Reggie said.

"I'll think about it." I said.

"Well hurry up. This is a sure thing. We could be real-estate moguls in a few years and your over here bullshittin'. You deserve it." Reggie said.

"What do you know about it?" I asked.

"It's written all over your face. Something's eating at you. Something big. You need a way to make things better and that's what I'm offering. Listen Devil Dog, sometimes you have to do things you don't want to do to get what you need. You could fix everything in a couple of weeks, or you could do it in a couple of years. I need someone I can count on and what's better than another Marine. That's all I'm saying" Reggie said.

"I'll let you know." I said as I walked away toward the pool table.

My phone started to vibrate not more than half way to the pool table. It was Latoya. I wondered what was she doing up at 11:00PM and thought it wise to answer her call. "You're up late." I said.

"I couldn't sleep. I was worried about you and wanted to check up on you." Latoya said.

"What, I'm sorry. The music is so loud in this place, I can barely hear you." I said.

"I just wanted to check on you. I was worried about you." Latoya shouted.

"I'm good. I'm ok." I lied.

"No you're not. What's wrong?" Latoya shouted again.

I could hear the genuine concern in her voice even above the cacophony of the clubs patrons.

"I'm good 'Toya. I'm just a little tired."

Latoya had enough to worry about and I didn't want to add my troubles to hers. It might've thrown her into a seizure or something.

"Ok. You can tell me later but you can't fool me. I know you remember." Latoya said.

I acquiesced and she asked me if I could drive her to a doctor's appointment the next day. I didn't have anything else to do other than feeling sorry for myself so I agreed. Besides, she offered to take me to lunch, and I'm a sucker for free food.

I took up a post a few feet from Del and leaned against the half wall that separated the pool table from the rest of the club.

I was busy staring off into space and contemplating the mysteries of life when Del crashed my exclusive pity party.

"Who pissed in your oatmeal this morning?" Del asked.

"What? No, it's nothing. I'm just thinking about something." I said.

"See, that's the problem. It ain't gonna do you no good. Worrying and stressing about shit you can't control will put you in a Psyche ward." Del said.

"Then how do you fix it all?" I asked.

"You don't and nobody can. You just live and what happens is what happens. You'll miss it all if you sit around worrying about shit." Del said.

"Miss what?" I asked.

"Life nigga! You're sitting here mad at the world and you're in the middle of a gold mine. There's so much opportunity right in front of you but you can't see it. You got the wrong out look on life. You ain't perfect and you weren't meant to be. You live, you love, you hate, you hurt people and you help people, and then you die. That's all it is. Just make sure that you got more checks in the good column than in the bad column when you meet Saint Peter and you'll be ok. There's joy in each moment, and even a selfish bastard like me knows that much. The only person you can count on to help you find it is you. It's everyone else's job to take it from you and make you miserable. Now do me a favor and go tell that silly mother fucker to get off the stairs. I gotta watch the pool table. A nigga stole the damn cue ball last time I left my post. I can't have that shit happen again or I gotta hear Curt's mouth. Why would a nigga take the damn cue ball? That's the type of bullshit that....." and Del's voice faded out against the booming bass of the music as I reached the top of the stairs.

I never liked to walk up on a patron without checking them out first. Their hands, feet, demeanor and all the rest of it. I didn't want to run up on a former Golden Gloves Champion. That's not my idea of an average night on the job.

I was in luck. He was Joe average and I could see that he had a friend with him who was a couple of steps beneath him as I got closer. His gaze was fixed on something or someone off in the distance.

I followed his line of sight and found the object of his affection. It was a young woman in her mid twenties, about 5'7", black and cute. She had a nice body and she was alone. She wore a sexy pair of pumps, an open blouse and a short skirt. Her legs were long and toned and her breast bounced with each step she took.

He had good taste but he didn't look her type. Her attention was all over the place and he was the last place it would stop.

"Hi Lisa." He said as she reached the top of the stairs and took the first step.

"Hi." Lisa said as she continued down the stairs.

"You look really nice. It's good to see you again." He spurted, as he struggled to say something charming before she got out of ear shot.

"Again?" Lisa asked.

"Yeah, we met here a couple weeks ago. My name's Derek." He said.

"Hi Derek." Lisa said as she looked over his shoulder to scan the crowd and then continued down the stairs.

Utter disappointment took over his face as Lisa reached the bottom of the stairs, rounded the corner and disappeared from view.

"Well, you tried." His friend said as if that would make up for the night of wild passionate sex that he just missed out on.

"How we doing fellas?" I asked.

"Just chillin." Derek said.

"That's good, that's real good now do me a favor. Chill somewhere other than on the stairs. The Fire Marshall will shut us down if we let people block the steps. It's a violation of the Fire Code." I said.

"Ok, no problem. I was just waiting to talk to that girl." Derek said.

"Yeah I saw that but you went about it all wrong." I said.

"What do you mean I did it all wrong?" Derek asked with the tone of a man who was slightly insulted. That was a good sign. Derek knew enough to get upset. That meant that he wasn't a total pussy, just a little misled. Informing him of the error of his ways wouldn't be a complete waste of time.

"Well for starters. She was here looking for someone else. A woman like that isn't loose so trying to talk to her was a waste of time. Second, you're a nice guy and this isn't your type of crowd." I said.

"Yeah, but you saw her. This isn't her type of crowd either." Derek said in a feeble attempt to defend himself.

"That's true but she's here looking for someone, someone other than you. I'd try Starbucks or Borders if I were you. That's your type of crowd." I said.

"You know what…you're right. I don't even like this place that much. Coming here was Terrance's idea." Derek said as he looked in the direction of his friend.

"What? This place is hot. Look at these women." Terrance said.

"It's not his type of crowd either." I said and they both started laughing.

"I'm Derek. He said.

"Yeah, I caught your name just before she walked away." I said.

"My name's Terrance Johnson-Moore." Derek's friend said and then extended his hand.

"All that huh? Please tell me your last name isn't Moore also." I said to Derek.

"No man. My father's last name is Moore. Johnson is my mother's maiden name." Terrance said.

"No wonder she walked away from you. Look at who you hang out with." I said to Derek.

"What?" Terrence asked.

"Moore is your father's name, Johnson is your mother's maiden name, your finger nails look like they've been manicured and clear coated within the last week and let me guess, you sit on the toilet when you take a piss." I said.

Terrance's mouth was agape and he was in shock, more so at my apparent clairvoyant abilities and less so because he was offended.

"Your mother wore the pants in your family didn't she?" I asked.

"No, no. She's a business woman. I mean she's very successful. She...She" Terrance stuttered.

"She's bossy, selfish, controlling and argumentative. It's one thing to hyphenate her name but to hyphenate her son's name is egregious. She probably named you too. I bet she took away one of the few joys a man has in life when it comes to having a family.
Naming your first born son and giving your daughter away at her wedding is all a man gets. That's it. I guess she figured that your old man was good enough to marry and take care of her and her children, but taking his last name was just asking too much but what do I know, my mother's a drug addict." I said as I walked off.

"Do I walk funny or something?"

I turned around to see Will looking as if he had lost a winning lottery ticket.

"Believe it or not, I never really noticed." I said.

"Damn!!!" Will shouted.

"What's wrong big fella?" I asked.

"Man, I was downstairs standing my posts and this guy was talking to me for like an hour and a half. He said he was in town on business and wanted to know where he could hear some jazz and where a good restaurant was. So I told him. Then he said he had to go so I was like bye nigga. But he asked me how he could get in contact with me. I thought I missed something so I asked him what he was into. I guess part of me was hoping that he was a sports agent and that he could get me a try out with the Ravens or the Eagles or something. So he says "No, I just want to talk." So then I was confused so I said "about what?" and he said "You know..." and that's when I got it. This mother fucker was trying to get with me…a fucking dude man. I told him to leave or I'd fuck him up and he was apologizing and saying he didn't know and no harm no foul and shit. So tell me do I walk funny or something. Do I look like one of them? Come on Cole, tell me." Will pleaded.

"No, you're all man. That's just life in the big city. There's a con artist every twenty feet and no one is being honest. Everyone's concerned with what you can do for them and getting what they want at any cost. Be careful and don't trust anyone from this point on." I said.

"It's not like that in Raleigh. People have a sense of common decency. Damn, that was the last thing I needed. My girl just left me. I'm behind on my rent. They're talking about evicting me. I need a real job, not this bullshit. Things can't get any worse." Will said.

"It can always get worse and sometimes it does." I said.

"Man, I lost a million dollar contract with the Redskins and I was going to propose to my girl. I lost it all." Will said.

"You never had the contract and any woman that leaves a man just because he hit a snag in life isn't a woman worth keeping. You haven't lost everything. I'd trade places with you in a second." I said.

"Yeah right" Will said.

I spent the next twenty minutes telling Will exactly what I meant.

"Things are going to work out for the best. You're going to be fine because I'm going to be fine and if a jackass like me can make it, then you're a shoe in." I said as I slapped him on the back and walked away.

I stared at my watch repeatedly which of course caused the hands to move even slower. My time keeping was interrupted by Reggie when he stopped by to ask me if I thought about his offer.

"I'm still working on that one." I said.

I noticed someone approaching from my right after Reggie left and looked up to see a gorgeous young woman walking my way with a smile on her face and half empty glass of merlot in her left hand.

"There you are. I wanted to find you and thank you for sticking up for me that night." She said as she gave me a hug.

I had no clue as to who she was or what I had done, until I noticed a small scar on the bridge of her nose.

"Oh. You're the girl that they hit with the bottle. What are you doing back here?" I said.

"I'm not afraid of those assholes. I refuse to let them intimidate me." She said and then lost her balance.

I caught her and pulled her close to me to steady her. Her breasts were mashed against my chest and my crotch was pressed against hers. My hands were in the small of her back. I looked into her eyes for a moment and then released her while holding on to her right hand.

"Oops. Thank you." She said.

"You look really nice tonight." I said.

I couldn't help it, flirting is an involuntary reflex for me. She thanked me and kissed my cheek and then giggled.

"My name is Keisha." She said.

Keisha had the most beautiful hazel eyes and I got lost in them for a moment.

"I'm Cole."

"Thank you for saving me Cole." Keisha said.

Keisha spent the rest of the night either hanging all over me or sitting down beside me. We talked, well she did all of the talking and I listened. It was hard because she really wasn't saying shit. I just kind of nodded and said "really?" or "oh yeah?" as I peaked down her blouse to look at her melon sized tits. It's amazing how a hot chick can bore you to death by talking too much. It's also amazing how you can tolerate being bored to death by a hot chick.

"I want you to take me home." Keisha said.

I was no longer bored but I did have a problem. I didn't have a home.

"I just moved out here from San Diego and I'm staying with a friend and his wife. Let's go to your place." I said.

"I live with my mother and step father. We can't go back there. Come on. I need you right now." Keisha said.

"I know a place." I said.

I fumbled with the keys as Keisha grabbed my ass and unzipped my fly.

"Hurry, hurry." Keisha said as I opened the door of the garage and ran in to enter the code to deactivate the security alarm. The last thing I needed was the police kicking down the door while I was in mid stroke. Keisha removed my belt and unbuttoned my pants. My pants hit the floor as I reached under her skirt and squeezed her ass. Keisha jumped up and wrapped her legs around my waist and told me that she wanted me to fuck her.

I shuffled across the floor with my pants still around my ankles kissing her all the while and sat her on top of Wayne's desk. Keisha put her legs straight up in the air and took off her thong. I stroked her with my fingers. She moaned in ecstasy as I tore at the condom wrapper.

I banged her on Wayne's desk, the waiting room chairs, in mid air and finally on the air mattress. We lay there trying to figure out what to do and say next when it was over which is what usually happens after freaky sex with a perfect stranger.

"Oh my God! I needed you so bad. I can't believe this. It's my first time." Keisha said.

"You're a virgin?" I asked.

"No boy! It's my first time in a garage." Keisha said.

I took Keisha back to the club the next morning so that she could get her car. She slept the entire way.

"Another satisfied customer." I thought as I waved good bye to her when she drove away.

I showered at the gym. Bought a sausage biscuit at the local deli and picked up Latoya later that morning. She was grinning from ear to ear and squeezed my arm.

"Ouch." I said sarcastically.

"I'm sorry. I'm just excited to see you." Latoya said.

"So where are we going?" I asked.

"To the clinic, I have to have my blood work done. I need to stay on top of my health or ...well you know." Latoya said.

"Yeah, I got ya." I said.

"I really appreciate you coming with me Cole. Getting my test results can be stressful sometimes. Remember the time you flew all the way back here for Memorial Day weekend that time?" Latoya said.

"Yeah, I could've gotten in big trouble for that one. We weren't to go more than three hundred miles from base and I went 3000." I said.

"I was angry when I found out what you did, but it made me feel special." Latoya said.

"You were special...I mean you know, you are special." I said.

"Oh, turn left here." Latoya said as we pulled into the parking lot of the clinic. I took a seat in the waiting room and shuffled through the pile of magazines on the table for a minute and a half before I found one that didn't cater to expecting mothers.

I flipped through the first few pages when I heard the nurse ask Latoya if her husband wanted to come back with her.

"No, he'd rather wait there" Latoya said.

Latoya emerged fifteen minutes later with a glum look.

"Ready?" she asked.

"Bad news?" I asked as we drove out of the parking lot.

"My T-cell count is low and that's not good. The doctor says that I'm stressed out and that has a detrimental effect." Latoya said.

"Well being HIV positive is stressful, right?" I asked.

"Yeah but it's not just that. I've been looking for Damon and my home life isn't good either. My mother wants me to move back to North Carolina but I would feel like I failed if I went back home." Latoya said.

"Failed at what?" I asked.

"I came up here to start a new life and I got the exact opposite. My mom gets on my nerves but I do miss her. I don't know what to do anymore. I feel so lost." Latoya said.

"I think you're blessed to have a mother who cares about you. I think you should consider moving back home." I said.

"How's your mom?" Latoya asked.

"I don't know and I don't think I want to." I said.

Latoya and I stopped at Antonio's Pizzeria for lunch and she treated me to a couple of slices of pizza. She was happy to be out. She was happy to not have to worry about anything for a while. We picked her daughter Latonya up from the day care center and made a pit stop to pick up her asthma medication from the pharmacy. I had never met Latonya but her mother told her all about me. Latonya asked me if I was going to stay or if I had to go away again.

I didn't really know how to answer her. The truth of the matter was that I hadn't thought about it until that moment. Things hadn't gone so well since my return to D.C. and I wasn't opposed to the idea of moving. Wayne was the only friend that I had in the area but he had his hands full.

"Hello, I'm home." Latoya said as we entered the small two bedroom apartment.

"Who's that?"

"Aunt Bernice, this is Cole. Don't you remember?" Latoya asked.

"Honestly girl, it's hard to keep up with you and all of these friends of yours. You need to pick one and settle down for a month or two." Aunt Bernice said and then lit the cigarette that dangled between her lips.

"Leave that girl alone before you give her a complex or something." Teddy said.

"She'd be lucky if that's all she gets." Aunt Bernice said.

"Don't mind her. She's just like that before that time of the month. I think you two make a cute couple." Teddy said.

Latoya was smiling again and the rest of her body smiled with her. My mind began to think of ways to excuse myself and make a run for it.

The entire apartment reeked of cigarettes and I would smell like that for the rest of the day unless I could get to the gym to shower before it closed.

Latonya's wheezing broke me out of my train of thought.

"Here baby, use your inhaler." Latoya said as she helped her daughter administer a dose. Latoya's wheezing quickly faded and I wondered how in the hell anyone could expect a child with asthma to do anything other than wheeze in an apartment full of cigarette smoke.

"So are you two back together?" Teddy asked.

"Teddy! You're embarrassing me." Latoya snapped.

"I don't mean no harm but inquiring minds want to know." Teddy said as he opened a 24 oz can of Olde English 800 and propped his feet up on the coffee table.

"You need to be more concerned with getting a job then worrying about who she brings home." Aunt Bernice said.

"I'm gonna get me a job. Don't you worry about me." Teddy said.

"You say that same shit everyday Teddy and I don't see no damn job yet. Keep playing with me, hear?" Aunt Bernice said.

"You know you love me baby." Teddy said as he kissed her on her cheek.

"I'd love you more if you had a job." Aunt Bernice said.

Aunt Bernice's daughter came home a while later and spoke as loud as she could on the telephone. The place was entirely too small for so many people, and I totally understood why Latoya fell for Damon in the first place. I found myself wishing that he would come whisk me away too.

I stayed for another 10 minutes which seemed like 10 hours. Latoya apologized to me for her aunt and Teddy.

"Teddy thinks that I should be married by now." Latoya said.

I got the feeling that Teddy wanted Latoya out of the way so that he had more room to lay on the couch and live off of Bernice. Teddy was one of those guys. The type that was content to spend the rest of his life living off of a woman or a series of women. The type that wanted nothing more than a couple bucks for a cold beer, and a pack of cigarettes out of life.

I couldn't feel sorry for Bernice since she picked Teddy out of the billions of men in the world. Bernice wanted it that way since Teddy was too pathetic to leave until she told him to go, at which time she would beg him to come back and entice him with a beer and a pack of Menthol Cools. Talk about low self esteem. Bernice was as sad as

Teddy was, and Latoya and her daughter were caught up in the middle of the whole thing.

It wasn't exactly the best example for Latonya. Someone needed to do something soon or Latonya would be living there with her daughter in ten years time.

"Remember what I said about being blessed to have a mother who cares about you?" I asked Latoya as she walked me to my car.

"Yes. Why?" Latoya said.

"I would start making plans to move back home to North Carolina if I were you. You can't make anything work in a situation like this. Latonya can't even breathe in there. I'm sorry to be so blunt but it's the truth. The two of you need to be with family that loves you. That's what you really need." I said.

"What about you? You just came back into my life. I don't want to leave now." Latoya asked.

"I'll be fine. Besides, you need to do what's in the best interest of your child." I said.

Latoya told me that she would think about it as we hugged goodbye.

Wayne was sitting at his desk with a slender Chinese man in his early thirties standing beside him. He wore a white t-shirt with a few stains on it, a denim jacket, khaki cargo pants and a pair of dirty white Nikes. His external appearance was that of an average man but he was another animal entirely. He was smooth and bold and looked like trouble.

I could tell by the way the cigarette dangled from his lips as he spoke with a thick Chinese accent and slapped one hand with the other to drive his point home. Wayne didn't allow anyone to smoke in his office yet this guy got away with it. He was short but he was a bad little fucker. All of this I gathered in the first few seconds of looking at him.

"Hey. How ya been?" Wayne asked as I entered the garage.

"I'm good." I said.

"This is Tommy. Tommy, this is my friend Cole from California." Wayne said.

I asked Tommy how he was doing and he steadied the cigarette in his mouth and shook my hand.

"How you know Wayne?" Tommy asked as if to verify my credentials in someway. Apparently, the subject matter of their conversation was for members only. I told him the story of how we met years ago and Tommy seemed to approve.

"Damn! You big. What you do for work?" Tommy asked.

Wayne interrupted before I could answer and told Tommy that I was between jobs but that I did temporary work for the federal government.

"You could do a lot of damage. Big guys are good, real good." Tommy said and then dug in his pocket and produced a business card.

"You need a job. I need a big guy. Call me when you get a chance." Tommy said and handed me his card.

Tommy's Chinese American Restaurant
Oxon Hill, Md.
Tommy Chang
President/ Owner
(301) 555-1166

Tommy said goodbye to Wayne and left. Wayne never took his eyes off of Tommy as he walked through the door and seemed relieved when the head lights of his car turned the corner.

"Trouble?" I asked.

"Trouble should be Tommy's middle name." Wayne said.

"He looks like a handful." I said.

"That's an understatement. Tommy is the son of a Triad gangster all the way from Hong Kong. His father was into everything from drugs and weapons to sex slaves. He got busted 13 years ago and Tommy took the charge for him and did 7 years in a federal penitentiary. Tommy's been back for two years and he's on the fucking war path. It's like he's trying to earn a reputation or something." Wayne said.

"So he's a gangster like his old man?" I asked.

"Tommy is the Devil. Well…he's the son of the Devil. Don't get involved with him or you'll regret it. Trust me, you will regret it." Wayne said.

"How do you come to know an official Chinese Triad gangster like him?" I asked.

"The same way I know everyone. He came into the shop I worked at and needed his BMW worked on." Wayne said.

"A Beamer? Well, he's driving an 8 year old Honda Accord now." I said.

"Tommy's hot these days. I think he's still under Federal surveillance. He dresses like a bum and drives that beat up car but he's the real deal. Don't doubt that. Tommy's heavy and much more dangerous than he was when I first met him. He stops in here every now and again to say hi. Tommy was an ok kid when I first met him but now…now he's Tommy." Wayne said then sighed, said "fuck!" and put his head in his hands.

I asked him if everything was ok aside from Tommy.

"No, I'm all out of beer and I'm shit out of luck." Wayne said.

Wayne looked at the floor for a moment and then looked up.

"The bank told me I have 30 days to vacate the garage. Business hasn't been good at all and I'm behind on my loan payments. I tried to reason with them but it's over. I got to have someone help me liquidate all of this stuff. I may be able to sell the tools and keep my head above water for a while. I'm sorry. Maybe you can find some where to stay before then.

Eva's being a bitch and I don't know how much longer I'll be living in our house when she finds out about this. I'm sorry man." Wayne said.

"So you think Tommy can help you with all of this?" I asked.

"No, Tommy's just a friend. He stopped by to get an oil change." Wayne said.

I hated being lied to especially by a friend but I didn't push the issue.

Thirty days wasn't a lot of time. I felt like I was tied to a set of railroad tracks while a freight train sped my way.

Latoya could tell that there was something wrong and demanded to know. I told her about Wayne losing the garage and her reaction was to be expected. She asked me to move in with her.

"Aunt Bernice said it's ok. Please Cole." Latoya pleaded.

"I'll be fine 'Toya, trust me. Besides the floor may collapse if you add a sixth person to that two bedroom apartment." I said.

My last night in the garage felt bitter sweet. I actually wished that I could stay there. It had a refrigerator, bathroom, sink, running water and a television. My car had none of those amenities and that's where I would be living until I could come up with a plan B.

Keisha called me the night before.

"I need you to fuck me garage style." She said.

Keisha was a freak and I couldn't say no. I didn't know how to tell her that it would be for the last time. My final performance was amazing for which she gave me a standing ovation and a hickey on my neck to show her appreciation.

I lied to Wayne and told him that I would be staying with a friend. I didn't want him to worry about me when he had so much to deal with. The parking lot of the Kenilworth Shopping Plaza was the site of my first night out of the garage. I backed the car up into a parking space near the edge of the parking lot. There were plenty of trees there that would conceal my presence. I tried to get comfortable but I didn't have much success.

I barely slept that night. I took a piss in the tree line at about 1:30 AM. I told myself that I was in the field just like in the Marines. The situation didn't seem so bad after that but it still sucked. I took a shower at the gym the following morning and wondered how long it would take them to notice that I was late in paying my membership fee for the month.

"Damn! You look like hell. Don't you know that stress will kill you? I can make it all better. Just give me a chance." Reggie said.

"Shouldn't you be off looking for your next fuck friend?" I asked.

Reggie would be relentless if he knew that I had spent the past three nights in my car. My phone started to vibrate. It was Keisha. She was at the door with two of her friends and she needed me to get them in. One of the few perks of knowing a bouncer is being able to get into the club for free. Keisha introduced me to her two friends who were just as gorgeous as she was.

Keisha wrapped her leg around mine as she hugged me and then pressed her body close to mine.

"I'm going to show you how much I appreciate you later." Keisha said and then gave me a deep tongue kiss.

Keisha and her friends sauntered through the club and headed for the dance floor.

"Damn! They are phat as hell." Melvin said. "You've got to hook me up."

"Yeah, no problem, take your pick and let me know. I said as I headed back up the stairs to the second floor.

I reached the top of the stairs and passed the area with the pool table when a nicely dressed young woman approached me.

"That video is disrespectful. Can you talk to someone about it because I don't think it's appropriate." She said.

I focused my attention to one of the many wall mounted televisions that were dispersed through out the night club. The image of a woman wearing a red thong was prominently featured along with the words "The Dirty South's Best Booties". She was shaking her ass while men threw money at her. A few seconds passed and she was replaced by a new woman who appeared wearing a neon green thong and doing a split.

"You mean that video?" I asked.

Low Fuel

"Yes. This isn't a strip club. How can you show something like that?" she asked.

"How is that video any different from that?" I asked as I pointed to a women on the dance floor who was bent over and grabbing her ankles while a man behind her grinded on her ass.

The young woman stood there flustered and couldn't formulate a response.

"Every night women come in her to be fondled by strange man. They dance to degrading music that refers to them as bitches and ho's. They dress as scantily as possible and love to be gawked at. This whole fucking place is disrespectful and you're worried about a God damned video. Lady, I don't have time for dumb shit. You need to leave because you are obviously in the wrong place." I said.

I stepped away from her and continued on my way but it wasn't long before I was confronted by yet another idiot.

"Hey Devil Dog. Watch those guys over there." Reggie said as he nodded his head in the direction of six men near the main bar.

They were overly aggressive and pushing their way through the crowd, spilling drinks and stepping on toes.

"Yeah, I see what you mean. We should head that way." I said.

I started walking in their direction when I noticed that Reggie had a woman pressed up against the wall and was speaking into her ear.

"Why am I surprised?" I wondered.

I carefully moved through the crowd to get a better look at six thugs when someone bumped into me.

"Watch yourself nigga." He said.

I turned to face him and locked eyes with Pastor Reynolds and Deacon Frye who were with two women who obviously weren't their wives. The two of them were dressed in those 15 button double breasted suite jackets with the baggy slacks and matching gators. The Pastor's suit was fire engine red while the Deacon wore canary yellow.

"This suit cost more than you make in a month..." Pastor Reynolds said and then caught himself when he finally recognized who he was talking to.

"The word of God fuels the righteous man, isn't that what you said?" I said.

"Code Red dance floor" Robby screamed into the mic."

I told Pastor Reynolds that I would send him straight to the emergency room if I ever saw him in the club again and then moved in the direction of the dance floor.

I could see the six miscreants pounding the hell out of a lone victim who was doing his best to throw the occasional punch and protect himself simultaneously. He didn't stand a chance. They wouldn't stop until someone made them stop and that's where Haymaker came in. He hit the first one with his name sake and put him to sleep. He turned to face the second but slipped on the wet dance floor as he threw a punch. Haymaker fell to the ground and grabbed his right knee. Will picked up the slack by grabbing Haymaker's intended victim and slammed him to the ground. Melvin arrived to the fray at the same time but caught a straight jab to the face at which time his nose exploded in a shower of blood.

I was fifteen feet away from contacting the enemy when one of them sensed impending doom and hurled a champagne bottle in my direction. The bottle was moving too fast and I was too close to avoid it. I tucked my chin down and prepared myself for the impact.

The bottle skipped off my fore head and shattered against the wall to my right. I became enraged at the thought of being permanently scarred by this asshole and ran toward him even faster. Horror gripped him when he saw that I hadn't been slowed one bit by his last ditch effort to save himself. He turned to run but it was too late. I kicked him in his ass and he slid across the beer drenched dance floor.

I snatched him up by his arm and opened the door to the rear stair well. I grabbed him by the belt and shirt collar and made him the recipient of the "Throwing your ass down the mother fucking stairs award."

He yelped as he tumbled and skipped his way down each step and landed in a pile against the door at the bottom of the stairs. I jumped down the last five steps and landed with one foot one his chest and the other on the floor. I pushed open the exit door and dragged him into the alley. I was oblivious to the world around me as I entered into a savage fugue. There was no blood but my head was throbbing from being struck by the bottle.

I dropped him into a large puddle of piss and sewer water and kicked him in the face. He rolled over and tried to crawl away but his knee was injured during his trip down the stairs and he didn't make much progress. I stalked him slowly and thought that the fool should've just laid there and let me get it over with. I twisted his shirt into my fist and punched him in his face repeatedly. He begged me to stop right before he lost consciousness. His body went limp but I held him up with my left hand while I gave him the "Fist across the chin award" with my right.

The bright light being pointed in my face was more upsetting than surprising.

"Who would interrupt this prestigious award ceremony?" I wondered.

I turned my head and saw two police officers exiting their patrol car and pointing their pistols at me.

ELEVEN

The silhouette of the officers was barely identifiable through the intensity of the cruiser's spot light. They trained the light on my eyes just as they were taught in the Police Academy.

"At least they got that part right. Let's see if they stick to the rest of the play book." I thought.

"Let him go." One of the officers said. "Turn around and place your hands on the back of your head."

They'd be telling me to walk backward toward the sound of their voices next.

I wasn't that far from the back of the club and I could dart through the alley for U Street when the time was right. Odds are that they would chase me before they shot me in the back. I wasn't going back to jail. That was unacceptable. I had nothing to loose and thought that it maybe be better if it all ended there that way.

Their mouths were moving but I couldn't hear anything. My eye was twitching again and it was all that I could concentrate on. I wondered why it wouldn't stop and how much longer it would continue. The officers stepped from behind the open doors of their cruiser and advanced in my direction. They both wore full beards and one in particular needed a trim.

The senior officer had a head full of dread locks and his partner's hair was braided with black beads at the ends. They both wore Nikes with there police uniforms and were closing the distance with me.

It was settled then, it would end there. Visions of Parris Island flashed before my eyes and I searched my training for something that would be of assistance.

"The mission of the Marine Corps rifle squad is to locate, close with and destroy the enemy through fire and maneuver or repel the enemy's assault through fire and close combat. Yeah, some of that should work." I thought.

I just needed them to get a little closer. I raised my hands to chest level to feign my surrender.

"Cole! Cole! Hey fellas. He's one of my guys." Curt said to the officers as he ran toward me.

"He's not responding to our verbal commands." One of the officers said as he looked at me over the sights of his service pistol.

Curt slowly took me by the fore arms and lowered my hands. He looked me in the eyes.

"They'll smoke your ass or you'll do something that you'll spend a lot of time in prison for. Relax and I'll make this work out." Curt said.

A wise man once said that a word to the wise is sufficient. Curt was adept at diffusing a hostile situation except for when he was the cause of it. He knew what to say and those few words brought me back to the land of the sane and rational.

"We just had a big brawl on the dance floor. Six mother fuckers just jumped one guy 'cause his cousin wouldn't give her number to them. They hit Cole in the head with a champagne bottle and he lost it but he's ok now. Ain't that right Cole?" Curt said.

I agreed and gingerly surveyed the lump on my forehead with the finger tips of my right hand.

"Is everyone ok?" one cop asked.

"Melvin looks like he's got a broken nose. Haymaker fell and broke his leg or something. I told him to stop wearing those leather soled shoes a long time ago. They slip too easy." Curt said.

"That's too bad but I need to know why your man didn't stop when we told him to. That's how mother fuckers get killed. I'm a family man Curt. I don't need that shit on my conscious. You need to come across big this time." The officer said.

"I was just trying to do my job when this guy hit me with a bottle. Then you guys show up and you have corn rows and beards and Nikes and shit. I'm from California; I've never seen a cop with all that hair before. I thought you two were with him or something." I said.

Cops in DC were allowed to have long hair, beards and wore sneakers with their uniforms. They were more concerned with looking cool than being professional peace officers. It was hard to tell the thugs from the police at times.

The officer thought about it for a second and then said that he would have to run our records. I told him that I had been arrested for assault but that the charges had been dropped after an official investigation by the City attorney of San Diego County.

My punching bag on the other hand wasn't so lucky. He had an outstanding felony warrant for attempted manslaughter on his son's mother. He was wanted by the U.S. Marshalls and they hadn't had much luck with catching up to him.

"Is there a reward for his capture?" I asked.

"Yeah but I don't think you want to press your luck unless you're going to try to collect it from a jail cell." The officer said.

"Let's go." Curt said as he pushed me toward the alley.

"I'll see you tomorrow Curt. We'll square up then." The officer said as he got into his cruiser and drove off with his prisoner.

"Are you crazy? I understand beating the hell out of that guy but trying to fight the cops. That shit is crazy. Are you going to be a liability? I've been happy with you till now." Curt said.

"I'm good. I just got jacked up from everything. I'm cool." I said.

Curt and I made our way to the front of the club and pushed our way through the crowd that stopped to watch the fracas. The EMT's wheeled Haymaker passed us on a gurney. Curt ran to his side and spoke with him for a moment. Del, Will and I stared at him from the side walk. We saw a bit of our own mortality in him. If this could happen to a man like Haymaker then it could happen to any of us. Haymaker was a fulltime bouncer which meant that he had no medical insurance. Being injured meant that he was out of work and being out of work meant that he was shit out of luck.

"How's Melvin doing?" Will asked Del.

"They broke his nose. Robby took him to the Emergency room." Del said

"What was this shit about in the first place?" I asked.

Dell explained that the six aggressors approached a young man and his female cousin.

"They asked her for her number and she said no. They kept harassing her so her cousin stepped in. They all jumped him like a bunch of bitches. They probably would have tried to rape her right there if we didn't break it up."

I spotted the victim of the beating standing on the sidewalk. His cousin held a wad of paper towels up to his eye brow which was still bleeding.

"You need to call the police and press charges." I said.

"I thought you guys called them." He said as he peered at me with his one good eye.

"They won't. They won't do anything that could put their liquor license in jeopardy. You need to document that this even took place. This shit could happen again to someone else." I said.

He stood there processing what I said when his cousin spoke up.

"He's right Marques. I'll call them." She said.

"Good. You do that." I said.

I turned to walk away and saw Curt glaring at me from across the street.

"What'd you tell him?" Curt asked.

"It's a free country Curt. I can have a conversation if I want to." I said.

"Are you fucking crazy?" Curt asked.

"Yeah and so are you. So are Del and Robby and G.Q, and anybody else who let's a pack of wild animals get away with hurting good, decent people just to stay in business. " I said.

"Cole, I swear to God…I'll fucking fire your ass if I see a cop take a report from them." Curt said just as a police cruiser stopped in front of the club with its lights on.

"We really need to talk Curt." The officer said.

It was the same cop from the alley.

I drove to the Kenilworth Shopping Plaza. It was 12:30 am. I felt as though I did the right thing but Curt didn't see it that way. He fired me right there on the side walk. I threw my radio and ear piece at him and he promised to kick my ass if he ever saw me again. I backed the car up close to the trees as I had done for the past three nights. The Low Fuel light came on and illuminated the interior of the car in an orange glow before I could turn the engine off. I couldn't win for losing. I laid my seat back and bundled up in my blanket and pillow.

I spent another day in my car before I realized that no one was coming to my rescue. There was no call about any temporary work. No call from Curt apologizing and asking me to come back to the club which was a good thing. There was nothing to go back to. There was nothing other than ten measly dollars an hour and the occasional champagne bottle to the head.

Reggie called me three times that day but I didn't answer the phone. I wasn't in the mood. Keisha called and asked me what happened that night after the huge fight. She wanted us to take her two friends back to the garage to party. They had never had sex in a garage either. Keisha was less than pleased when I told her what happened.

"You got fired? How do I get into the club now Cole? What are my friends going to say?" Keisha asked.

"Did I mention that I got hit in the head with a champagne bottle?" I asked.

Keisha and I argued for a while until she hung up. I didn't know it at the time but she and Will became very close soon after I was fired. Keisha continued to get into Milan Night Club for free, and Will enjoyed the occasional ménage trios. They married a year later and divorced nine months after that. It had something to do with infidelity so the story went. I guess the old saying is true, "you can't make a ho into a house wife but you can still bang her in the waiting room of a garage."

I knew that Latoya would know that something was wrong when she called me so I told her before she could ask.

"Can I take you to dinner? Just a steak and cheese or something I'm afraid." Latoya said. I accepted the invite and picked her up at 4:30PM.

"I'm worried about you." Latoya said.

"That's my line isn't it?" I said.

"You're a God send Cole. That's why I love you." Latoya said.
I was caught off guard.

"Yes! I said it. I love you. You're a good man no matter what has happened, no matter what you did to that guy in the alley. I just want you to know that I appreciate you and I thank God for a second chance to have you in my life for however long it lasts." Latoya said.
I thanked her and finished my sandwich. It was everything I wanted to hear but under the wrong circumstances.

"Why couldn't she have said it three years ago? Why couldn't Keisha have said it three hours ago?" I thought.

Latoya kept giving me that look for the rest of the ride to her place. It was the look of love and I felt guilty. I knew this would happen and I knew that it could only end poorly. I knew that it could only end with hurt feelings and four letter words. It was inevitable and it was only a matter of time.

"Latonya's going to be excited to see you. She really likes you." Latoya said.

"I like her too. She's a sweetheart, just like her mother." I said.

I parked in a space in front of Latoya's apartment building and she reached over to give me a hug. I had been physical with Keisha but it felt different when Latoya touched me. She actually cared about me and I could let my guard down when I was with her. Latoya squeezed me tight and it felt as if she may never let me go…until she noticed the hickey that Keisha left on my neck.

"What in the fuck? Who did that? I didn't do that shit so what's up? You must've lost your God damned mind if you think you can have some other bitch sucking on you and then come kick it with me. I don't play that shit." Latoya said.

Latoya slammed the door shut after that and gave me the finger as she walked into the apartment building.

Reggie called 15 minutes later as I drove down the street licking my wounds.

"Hey Devil Dog. I'm glad you stopped screening your calls. Haymaker tore his ACL when he fell during that fight. He won't be working in the club for the next couple of months. Everyone is asking about you. Will even asked Curt to give you your job back but he's still pissed off at you. So how's the temp work going?" Reggie said.

"You're an asshole. Did you know that?" I said.

"Look Marine. You need to prevail. Anyone can survive but few of us can live again. I can show you the way but you need to cooperate." Reggie said.

"I have more important things to worry about." I said.

"Like what, living in a garage? Yeah, that's right. Will told me your whole life story. You need to be careful about who you spill your guts to." Reggie said.

I shouldn't have been surprised but I was.

"Look, I just rented a room in a row house in North East D.C. It's only $500.00 a month. Just give me half and we can be room mates. Than we can run this deal and get this paper." Reggie said.

Living in my car was getting old but I found myself wondering if I could trust Reggie. Calling him shady would have been an understatement but then again he was a Marine, and Marines take care of each other. I had $347.00 to my name and would need to make wise decisions.

A good night's sleep always helped me with big decisions. It was 10:30 PM before I got comfortable enough to fall asleep. It was 11:45 PM when I awoke to a bright light shinning in my eyes. It came in through the driver's side window and I put my hands up instinctively.

A thief would have already shot me or been beating me about the head with a pipe. I knew who this was which is why I reacted the way I did.

I slowly sat up right, keeping my hands in view the entire time. I opened the door slightly and the officer pulled it the rest of the way. He scrutinized the interior of the vehicle looking for drugs or other illegal offenses. I knew that he already ran my tags while I was asleep. He spoke only when he was sure that I was mostly harmless.

"You haven't been drinking have you?" the officer asked.

"No, I'm just camping out." I answered.

"This isn't a good place to stay. The convenience store over there got robbed last week." the officer said.

A word to the wise was indeed sufficient. I thanked the officer for his largesse and obeyed every traffic law on the books as I drove away.

I thought of Reggie and his offer. My first instinct was in overdrive but I was tired and I needed a shower and a safe place to sleep.

Reggie was forty minutes late when he finally arrived. He carefully parked his Nissan Pathfinder in front of the house and activated the alarm as he walked my way. He loved his SUV and spared no expense on the stereo and speakers. He washed and waxed it every weekend and polished the chrome rims until they were immaculate. I got the feeling that it was the only thing in the whole world that he really cared about.

"Sorry brother. I had to make a run and got caught up. Let me show you the place." Reggie said.

It was the typical Washington D.C. row house. The outside looked to be a hundred years old and the inside looked seventy. There were paint buckets, rollers, brushes and a couple of plastic tarps on the floor of the living room.

"Is the land lord redecorating?" I asked.

"Yeah brother, this place is going to look brand new in a couple of months. You'll see." Reggie said.

Reggie led me up the stairs to the bed room on the right. The room was large enough to share and there was a bathroom across the hall.

"I could do worse than this." I thought.

I had as a matter of fact and moving in was a "no brainer."

I gave Reggie the money and he helped me get my stuff out of the trunk of my car.

"Hello gentlemen. You must be new to the neighborhood."

We turned to see a tall and slender man standing behind us. He wore thick glasses and he was in desperate need of a haircut. He looked like a reformed drug addict who still savored the occasional crack rock.

"Yeah, we're new in town. What are you selling?" Reggie asked.

The man appeared confounded for a moment and then resumed his sales pitch.

"I have a 32" television with a remote and it's only forty bucks." He said.

"Does it work?" I asked.

"Of course it does." he said and took offense as if he were a legitimate salesman.

Reggie and I lugged the television up the stairs and sat it down in the bedroom. It was an antique, with knobs and a wood grain exterior. We plugged it in, crossed our fingers and held our breath as the picture slowly came into focus.

"Hot Damn!" I shouted.

It was just what the room needed. I hadn't watched television in days and I was elated to see anything.

"Yeah brother!! Now look, here's Charles' number and here are the questionnaires. I'm going to call you with their names and tell you what they're looking for. You just need to call them, ask them the questions here and fax the completed sheets to Charles. He'll start the paper work and then I'll need your help closing the loans but I'll teach you all of that later. Now…" and that's when we were startled by a slight pop that came from the television.

The screen went black and the sound faded out as well. We looked at each other for a second and then ran for the door. We searched for that crack head for two hours but he was long gone. He was already high and passed out on the floor of the local crack house by that point.

The television was working again by the time we got back to the house but only for another 20 minutes. That's when it decided to take another break and went dark again. Reggie got a couple of beers from the refrigerator in the kitchen and handed me a second beer after I chugged the first. We decided that getting buzzed would buffer the disappointment of being sold a lazy TV and got back to trading old sea stories.

"Did you ever get deployed to the Gulf" Reggie asked.

"No. Uncle Sam put me in the middle of the Mojave dessert and forgot all about me." I said.

"You didn't miss anything except using camels to test fire weapons. I damn near cut one in half with my M-259 once." Reggie said.

"You mean M-249, there's no such thing as an M-259." I said.

"Yeah, that's what I meant. I better stop drinking. This shit has my mind twisted." Reggie said.

"Your mind was twisted before that beer you shit bird. What kind of Marine doesn't know his T.O. weapon?" I said.

Reggie gave a lame excuse and quickly changed the subject to the last chick he met at the club. He was nervous for the first time since I met him and I would have noticed if I hadn't been drinking faster than I was thinking.

Lynette Parker called and offered me a two day temporary assignment that I happily accepted. I needed the fax machine to send the questionnaires to Charles. Reggie called just as he said he would and I counted the money I had yet to make.

"Now look brother, call Tamara Hodges. She's looking to refinance the loan on her house." Reggie whispered in order to avoid detection by his boss. Reggie would be fired on the spot if she knew that he was diverting potential customers toward his get rich quick scheme.

I conducted the interview while speaking under my breath. I thanked Mrs. Hodges for her time and ran over to the fax machine to send the questionnaire to Charles. I felt someone approaching from behind as I waited for the confirmation sheet to finish printing.

"What are you up to?" Nyssa asked.

"Nothing."

"Yeah, sure. Come with me to lunch." Nyssa said.

I accepted the invitation and thanked God that I had enough money to cover the expense.

"How have you been?" Nyssa asked.

I told her that I was ok but her feminine intuition was in full effect and she knew better. Nyssa asked me about working at Milan Night Club and how Latoya was doing. I was evasive but she had a way of getting the truth out of me.

"Well, I told you so." Nyssa said.

"Well it doesn't matter, Latoya's pissed off. I've never heard her curse like that before. She got ghetto as hell." I said.

"You sound disappointed." Nyssa said.

"It's just that I can't get anything right these days. I keep getting fired from jobs and by women a like."

"You did the right thing...sort of. They should have called the police. The average person wouldn't have gotten involved. I give you a lot of credit for that but you aren't done with Latoya yet. She's going to call you when she needs you most. Just make sure you make the right decision this time." Nyssa said.

A week passed since my lunch date with Nyssa. Lynette Parker hadn't contacted me about any work assignments but I was happier to stay home and conduct phone interviews. Reggie and I had 16 loans to close out of 42 previous inquiries. I waited with the anticipation of a seven year old the night before Christmas at the payday that was to come.

I flipped through several furniture catalogs and looked for a stylish living room suit for my new apartment. I finally decided on a tan leather couch and love seat and circled them with my pen.

"They'll look nice." I thought as I closed my eyes and imagined myself sitting in them.

Reggie came home that night exhausted from a hard day of ripping people off.

"We've been doing pretty good. How much do you think we'll make once all of these deals are closed?" I said.

"We'll be sitting pretty brother. I don't have all of the figures yet. I'll call Charles tomorrow and compare notes. We've got to keep him honest. I need you to go to the Kinkos in College Park tomorrow while I'm at work and pick up the newly printed loan papers. I don't' have any money on me right now. They shouldn't be that much. I'll hit the ATM and pay you back tomorrow night. Then I can show you how to close a loan. We'll have to wrap things up quick once Charles is done with everything. We don't want these suckers to get away. I hate catch and release fishing." Reggie said.

I got up early the next morning and traveled to the Kinkos in College Park. The attendant at the front desk said that they had no record of Reggie's order. I called Reggie and left him a message on his cell phone. I went back to the house that day ready to work but my phone didn't ring at all. I waited a few hours before taking a nap. Making money was hard work and I needed a break.

I was awoken by a man who pushed open the door of the bedroom and asked me who in the hell I was.

"I'm Cole. I'm renting this room with Reggie." I said.

"Renting a room? I'm paying you people to renovate my house not to sleep on the job. Where in the hell is Reggie? He cashed my check and hasn't even painted the living room." He said.

"Reggie's at work." I said while clearing the sleep from my eyes.

"Work? Renovating my house is his work. Fuck it! I'm calling the police! He said as he pulled his cell phone from his pocket.
I jumped up from my air mattress and ran to get my things from the closet. He grabbed my shoulder and told me to wait for the police to arrive. My duffle bag with the two stolen guns inside was in the closet and I decided that leaving was in my best interest. I shoved him back and snatched my clothes from the hangers. He charged toward me and tried to wrestle me to the ground but my right cross knocked him out cold.

He fell with his hands still extended in front of him and I prayed to God that I hadn't killed him. I checked to see of he was still breathing and he was. I left him lying where he was and raced to remove the few things that I had from the room and put them in the trunk of my car. I ran back into the house to grab Reggie's things rather than let the Police seize them as evidence. I opened the closet that he kept his clothes in and it was empty. All of his clothes were gone. Everything was gone except for a book that sat on the top shelf. I pulled it down and read the cover.

Jarhead
A Marine's Chronicle of the Gulf War and Other battles
By Anthony Swafford

I looked everywhere for Reggie. I called his cell phone but there was no answer. He quit working at the night club and the trail went cold after that. Reggie had the money and had probably left town. He found his sucker and was on to the next one. I was ashamed of my stupidity and vowed to take my revenge upon Reggie if I ever saw him again.

Wayne told me that he had been busy minimizing his loses by liquidating his assets in the garage when we talked on the phone that evening. He asked how I was doing and I told him that I was still renting the room with Reggie.

"That's good. You're doing better than Manny." Wayne said.

I asked him what happened and he told me that Manny and Donna took the trip to Las Vegas. Manny hated it, Donna loved it. The noise and lights gave Manny a migraine and he couldn't find a connection for some good weed to take the head ache away. Donna on the other gambled uncontrollably. She disappeared on the second day there and lost all of her money within a three hour period. Donna spent another twelve hours in a Las Vegas Police Department drunk tank. Now she needed to stay with Manny even longer.

My cell phone beeped several times during my conversation with Wayne, indicating that I was receiving another call. I checked the display and saw that it was Latoya. I told Wayne that I would call him later and took her call.

I thought Latoya would apologize or ask me how I was doing but she called with a crisis of her own. Aunt Bernice gave Teddy hell for staying out all night and he beat her ass right there in front of Latoya and her daughter.

"I'm scared Cole." Latoya said.

"You need to move back to North Carolina. It could be you next time." I said.

Latoya cried for a while and then said that she would give her two weeks notice to her boss the following day.

"Don't tell anyone or Bernice may try to stop you. She doesn't want to go without the extra money each month. Just start packing and reserve the U-haul truck and I'll do the rest." I told her.

"I don't really have the money Cole. What am I going to do?" Latoya asked.

I told her that I would take care of everything.

"How are you going to get the money?" Latoya asked.

"Just start packing."

I met Tommy Chen in China Town at a parking lot on G Street. He was happy to see me.

"This will be good. You'll see. We make a lot of money together." Tommy said.

I followed him a block down the street and into a building with a sign in Chinese. We walked down a few stairs an entered a restaurant that sat beneath street level. I was the only non-Chinese in the place but it didn't matter since I was with Tommy. The patrons watched us as we entered but not because of me. Tommy was a big deal and the patrons alternated between trying to look at him and avoiding eye contact.

They whispered to one another and the sound built to a fever pitch until Tommy turned his attention toward them. They were silent after that.

We took a seat at a table large enough for eight people. Tommy lit a cigarette and let a plume of silky gray smoke out of his nostrils.

"I thought you couldn't smoke in restaurants in D.C." I said.

"This not D.C., this China Town." Tommy said.

He smiled, took a long drag from his cigarette and then clapped his hands twice. A waitress hurried over and bowed her head.

"I get you real Chinese dinner, Not that shit Americans eat. No sweet and sour. No chicken wing. Can't sell real Chinese food to niggas. They won't eat it. They only eat Mambo sauce." Tommy said.

He spoke sternly to the waitress in Chinese and she wrote the order down as if her life depended on it. She ran off and returned with two Chinese beers as quickly as she left. I took a sip and savored the taste of the alcohol. It had been a long time since I had a beer.

The food arrived a short time later and it was more than apparent that they rushed it especially for Tommy. It was a large Peking duck with rice and fresh vegetables. I hadn't had much to eat that day. I treasured each bite and it took me some time to realize that Tommy was speaking to me.

"It's ok here. Not many speak English good. I need help with some collection. Chinese don't trust bank. They borrow money from each other for loan. I give loan to some men. They don't' pay back quick enough. I get tired of waiting. They keep money at home. Some keep in safe, some under bed. I need you to scare them. Then they pay me." Tommy said.

I looked up from my plate and asked who was first.

"Tang Lee Leung. He owe me a lot. He young and like night clubs. He wear nice clothes and jewelry. I want you to get him when he come home. Tell him to pay his debt. He'll know what it mean. Then take his SUV and bring to me." Tommy said.

"Why me? Why not another Chinese?" I asked.

Tommy thought for a moment. I could tell that he was trying to decide what to disclose and what to keep to himself.

"You know I do time in federal jail. No Chinese will deal with me. I'm hot. Too much trouble to deal with me. I need to be smart and get other help. It's ok. It's safe cause they don't know who you are. Chinese don't work with Blacks so you safe. They don't connect us. I give you $200 a job. Tommy said.

"$300.00" I countered with a mouth full of food.

"$250. Times are hard." Tommy said.

"Deal."

Tommy gave me Tang's address, description and a bit of advice.

"No gun. More time if you get caught with gun." Tommy said.

Tommy continued to talk but I was deep in thought. I had reached a fork in the road. The next move would set the pace for the rest of my life.

I have a philosophy about life that I call "The Law of the Point of no Return." I had done a lot of wrong lately but I liked to think that it was justified. I needed the money but doing this for Tommy meant that I was crossing a definite line in the sand. The Marines call it the Line of Departure. Cross that line on the map and you were on your way to war. There was no turning back.

The human mind can rationalize anything into being the right thing to do, even murder. It's like the first time a child swears. It's a big deal but it means less and less each subsequent time until you become unconscious of it. The same is true of stealing, pre-marital sex, taking a life and this.

"So, do we have a deal?" Tommy asked.

It was a chilly night but my ski mask kept my face warm. The ground was hard and unforgiving. I lay there in the bushes with the aluminum siding of the house pressed against my right shoulder. There wasn't that much space but I made it work.

"Improvise, adapt and over come." I thought.

This mission was important for Latoya and Latonya. I told myself that I was doing it for them so that I could live with myself. I caught the bus to Tang's neighborhood. I crawled on my stomach through Tang's back yard and stopped in the front of his house. I spent another 86 minutes waiting there in the prone position.

It was the classic definition of discipline. I didn't move an inch in order to avoid detection by the neighbors. Two bright headlights swept over the top of the bushes and fixed themselves on the garage door a few seconds before it opened. Tang pulled onto the drive way in a brand new Lexus RX Hybrid. Tommy was right. Tang was doing well for himself. Tang parked his SUV in the garage and the door slowly lowered. I scurried toward the drive way and rolled under the garage door before it shut.

I hunkered down behind the vehicle and waited for Tang to exit it. The driver side door opened and I watched his first foot hit the ground and then his second. I was quick and resolute. I slammed him into the wall of the garage and left a large dent in the dry wall. A properly placed choke hold made my point for me but I thought I would add to it just to be sure.

"You owe some money don't you Tang?"

He didn't speak, he just gurgled. I loosened my grip a little.

"I'm sorry. I'll pay it. I have it. I'll pay him. I swear." Tang said.

"That's good news and for that I'll let you live but this visit will cost you." I said in a voice slightly reminiscent of Michael Keaton in the first Batman movie.

I stomped on his ribs a couple of times until I felt two of them give way.

"I'm getting too good at this." I thought.

I zip tied his hands behind his back and dragged him into the kitchen.

"Count to 200 and then use the scissors on the counter to cut yourself loose." I said.

I took his car keys and a six pack of beer from the fridge and left.

Tommy was happy to hear that things went well. I met him behind his restaurant and gave him the keys to the Lexus. Tommy passed them to a young Chinese man who drove the SUV away.

"Where's he going with the truck?" I asked.

"Chao Li take truck to Philadelphia. Truck get chopped up. He drive car. You get money. Everybody have job." Tommy said.

Tommy counted out $250.00 and gave it to me.

"I give you call with next job." Tommy said and closed the back door to the restaurant behind him.

I stood there in the alley for while and thought it best to leave before I got robbed. It wasn't the best neighborhood after all.

Latoya was ready to make her escape a week later. She left the apartment as if she were going to go to work that morning but came back home after Bernice left and Teddy went to see his other girl friend. Latoya packed up her belongings and I helped her place them in the U-haul truck. I drove the truck and Latoya followed me in my car. I begged her to be careful.

"She's fast and she'll get away from you if you're not careful. Please be careful, this car is all I have left." I said.

Latoya said that she understood and adhered to the speed limit.

We picked Latonya up from the day care center. Latoya hadn't told her about the move because she didn't want her to slip and tell Bernice. Bernice could be vindictive and would have done anything to stop Latoya from leaving. Latonya protested and cried as she asked if her friends could come along.

The drive to Rocky Mount North Carolina wasn't as long as the trip across the country but it was long enough especially through rush hour traffic. It took hours to get out of D.C. and past Richmond, Virginia. The open road awaited us once we did. I kept a close eye on Latoya once we were able to pick up speed. It was only a four hour drive but that was a lot of time for something to go wrong. It was a lot of time for Latoya to fall asleep and wrap my Trans Am around a tree or guard rail.

We pulled into Rocky Mount at 10:17PM. I helped Latoya out of the car and carried Latonya who was fast asleep. Latoya's mother came stumbling out of the house when we were half way up the walk way. They hugged and cried tears of relief. They were finally together after years of begging. They could be a family again. They could put aside all of the petty differences from the past and get down to the business of loving and caring for each other.

Latoya's mother looked me up and down as if to compare the real me to the description her daughter had given her.

"Not what you expected?" I thought.

"Momma, this is Cole. Cole, this is my mother Laverne." Latoya said. Laverne stared at me again and then hugged me as well.

I spread my arms as far as they would go until I touched Latoya's back. It had been months since I last slept in a bed. I was warm and undressed. Sleeping fully dressed in the driver's seat of a car is so cumbersome and constricting. I was free if only for 7 or 8 hours.

I reached out for Latoya and she scooted back for me still asleep. The whole thing was involuntary. It was what we did four years ago when we were together. It's what I did with Danni and it was what Latoya did with Craig and Brian and Marcus and Anthony and Todd and Antoine and Damon.

We woke up that way. Latoya rolled over and smiled that critically acclaimed smile of hers. I was surprised to see her. I dreamed of Danni all night long. I grinded on Danni all night long. I wanted Danni all night long. Latoya's mother was a church going woman but she allowed us to sleep in the same bed that night. Having her daughter back was more important than anything else in the world. She could be pious later.

The smell of bacon, home fries and scrambled eggs filled every nook and cranny of the house. The smell wafted under the door and into my nostrils as I showered. We ate breakfast together, watched TV together and then had lunch together. It was a relief to be among people who weren't trying to screw me over or smash a bottle over my head.

Latoya's extended family members arrived later for the welcome home party. Aunts, Uncles, Cousins, nieces and nephews all asking the same question. I was getting tired of introducing myself and explaining how I knew her. Latoya saw my discomfort and came to the rescue. She took me by the hand and walked me off to the side of the house.

"Sit down sweetie." Latoya said as she pointed at a large tree stump.

I sat down and she took up residence on my lap. She placed her arm around me and hugged me.

"You feel good." Latoya said.

"Oh yeah?"

"YES!" Latoya said.

She giggled and then continued.

"Isn't it beautiful here? I forgot how much I missed it. I wish you could stay."

"Really, for how long?" I asked.

"As long as you want." Latoya said.

I was conspicuously quiet.

"I'm sorry for talking to you that way, about the hickey. It's none of my business. I just got jealous. I screwed up and to see that some other woman had a chance with you really got to me. You could have had some common decency and worn a turtle neck but I was wrong. You've always been there for me, even when I didn't deserve you. I just want you to know that I'm here if you ever need me. You name it and you've got it." Latoya said.

The party lasted well into the early morning and I over indulged in a pint of Corn liquor.

"Rocket fuel, I drank rocket fuel and lived to talk about it." I thought as I awoke the next morning with Latoya resting on top of me. My head was still foggy but I knew one thing. I had to leave as soon and as courteously as possible. Latoya opened her eyes and gave me that look. That look that says I love you and I need you and don't ever leave me or it would break my heart and I would spend the rest of my life in therapy.

"Better to leave now and let it hurt a little than to leave later and rip her heart out of her chest." I thought.

Sunday morning's breakfast was more sumptuous than the previous days. I considered it a farewell meal. The three of them walked me out of the house and onto the porch.

"Thank you dear. You're a special young man and God will bless you." Laverne said.

Latonya jumped into my arms and wouldn't let go.

"When are you coming back?" Latonya asked.

"Soon as I can." I lied.

Laverne pulled Latonya away and they returned inside the house. Latoya walked me to the car.

"Momma really likes you. You can always come here whenever you need to." Latoya said.

I hugged her and thanked her for the offer.

The ride back up I-95 North was peaceful. The rhythm of the road was like a lullaby and my mind was worry free for the time being. My phone rang six miles past Richmond.

It was Tommy. He needed me for an urgent job. I told him that I was tired and that I was on the road but he was insistent.

"This is important. I need to get this bastard tonight. He coming home with a bag. I need that bag. I give you $300.00 this time." Tommy said.

I agreed and made it back to D.C. by 2:00 PM. I checked my P.O. Box at the post office and pulled out a single envelope. The name Danni Salinas was featured prominently at the upper left hand corner as well as a change of address sticker in the center of the envelope.

Tommy was waiting for me in the parking lot of the post office when I came out. I placed Danni's letter on the passenger seat of my car and walked across the lot toward Tommy. He gave me the info and told me how important this was. Dennis Fong would be coming home with a bag of money from a deal with another Chinese business man. He was selling a Chinese restaurant.

"Getting rid of the competition?" I asked Tommy.

"Just get me the bag." Tommy said.

I took a nap in the car for a few hours. I needed to catch up on my sleep so that I was sharp for the mission that night. I woke up to watch the sun finishing setting and its golden rays dance off of the surfaces of my surroundings. I had taken up my position six hours later in the bushes that ran parallel to the drive way of Dennis Fong's house. It took an hour to low crawl all of the way from the woods in the back yard to that spot. The next door neighbor came out to smoke a cigarette and have a phone conversation a short while later. I remained motionless until he flicked his cigarette into the grass and went back inside.

Dennis' Cadillac pulled into the drive way and he got out of the car carrying a leather satchel. I took him by the throat so that he couldn't make a sound and pushed him to the ground near the front wheel of his car.

"Give me the bag and you won't get killed." I said.

Dennis resisted at first but gave up when I squeezed his throat even harder. I took the bag from him and stood up to leave when I heard someone yelp just like Bruce Lee did in Enter the Dragon when he kicked the shit out of Bolo Yueng.

I turned around to see two Chinese men in mid air with their feet pointing in my direction. I dodged the first kick but wasn't so lucky with the second. I hit the ground in a tumble and sprung up just in time to get punched in the face. The two of them were much too fast and I found myself trying to block kicks that found their mark a split second earlier. I struggled to keep one between me and the other but it was hopeless.

They started jumping over top of each other while doing spin kicks until I was knocked to the ground again. One grabbed the bag but couldn't wrestle it from me. I took advantage of the situation since he had both hands on the bag and slammed his face into the left front quarter panel of the Cadillac. I had one down but the second kicked me in the side of the head and threw a flurry of punches too fast to counter. I swung back but missed and had my legs swept from beneath me. I fell to the ground and saw the silhouette of a man in the air above me.

I rolled out of the way until I bumped into the second guy who stomped me until his friend caught up to the both of us. It felt like they kicked me for hours as I covered up to protect myself. I got lucky and caught one of them by the foot. He only weighed 148 pounds and made a perfect bat. I swung him into his friend and then tossed him across the lawn. I lost my balance after that and fell against the driver's side door of the Cadillac.

I was out of breath and having trouble seeing out of my right eye.

"Where did these fuckers come from?" I wondered until I saw the Honda Civic parked on the street with both doors still open. "They must have pulled up while I choked Fong."

I made it to my feet in time to get kicked over the trunk of the Cadillac and into the bushes on the other side of the drive way. I laid there panting. I considered playing dead but I knew that they would kill me before they let me go.

I could hear them speaking Chinese as they helped Fong to his feet. He didn't sound too pleased with their failure to ensure his safety. My car and shotgun were too far away to be of any help but I did have a back up plan. They hurried in my direction and one of them was dumb enough to come into the bushes looking for me.

That's when I hit him in the left collar bone with the sledge hammer and knocked him flat on his ass. I struck the second man in his hip after he leapt into the air. He landed on the trunk of the Cadillac and cracked the windshield with the back of his head.

Fong started to run. I was in too much pain to chase after him. I chose a wiser course of action and threw the sledge hammer at him. The hammer hit him squarely in the back and he tumbled to the ground.

"My back, help me! My back!" Fong said.

I picked up the satchel and the sledge hammer.

"Have mercy!" Fong pleaded.

"Sorry, I'm all out of mercy but I've got plenty of pain left if you want some more." I said.

"You Devil!" Fong shouted.

"No. I'm not the Devil, I just work for him. You should've just given me the fucking bag asshole." I said as I limped my way across the back yard and through the woods.

I was too tired to meet Tommy that night. My back was sore and my right eye was swollen. That wouldn't have been so bad but my eye started twitching which caused it to hurt even more. I got my pillow and blanket from the back seat. There was no way to lay that didn't

Low Fuel

hurt my entire body. My phone rang repeatedly with Tommy's calls but I sent him a text message saying that I would give him the bag at 11:00am that same day.

I awoke and checked myself out in the rear view mirror that morning as I was in the habit of doing each day. I looked almost as bad as I felt. I rolled over on my side and Danni's letter caught my eye. I had been busy getting my ass kicked and forgot all about it. I ripped it open and my tax return check fell out along with a note.

"Dear Cole,

I held on to your tax check for a couple of months hoping that you would call looking for it. I needed to hear your voice but I realize that you probably need the money a lot more. I miss you very much and I'm sorry for the pain that I have caused you. I betrayed you and I know that nothing I can say will ever change that. I lost control and gave into my anger. I made you pay for the wrong that other men had done to me. You were the best thing that ever happened to me and I didn't always appreciate you but I would give anything to have you back. I've found God and have been attending church services and bible study regularly. My faith is strong and I am a very different person now. I wish that you could see me. I think that you would be very proud of me. I wish I knew how you were doing. I wish I knew if you were safe or happy. I wish you would come back home.

I wish we could serve God together. I can make it up to you. I can love you the way I should have. I thank God for you each day and I pray that you can forgive me for all of this. Please know that you can call on me for anything, anything at all. It's the least that I can do. I hope that one day you can find it in your heart to forgive me.

¡Te Quiero Mucho Papi!

Danni

I could hear her voice as I read the letter. I felt nostalgic until Manny's words came back into my head. "I don't know this woman you had but if she did wrong by you then leaving her was the best thing that could have ever happened to you."

I picked up the tax refund check and it was only for $240.00. I neatly folded the letter up and placed it back into the envelope.

Getting your ass kicked has a tendency of changing your outlook on life. It made me want to carry a pistol which is what I did on my way to meet Tommy. I put a fully loaded magazine in each one of my back pockets. I checked a third magazine to ensure that it was fully loaded with 13 rounds of 230 grain full metal jacket .45 ACP cartridges and slapped it in the magazine well of the Glock 21. I yanked the slide back and let it slam forward, seating the first round into the chamber.

I put on my sun glasses and made the ride to Oxon Hill.
Tommy stood beside his car in the parking lot in front of his restaurant. He flicked the ashes from his cigarette and placed it back on the edge if his lips. The lot was almost full of cars so I parked a few spaces away from him.

"You had me worried when I get your text. How did it go?" Tommy asked.
I held the satchel up in one hand and lowered my shades with the other.

"Oh shit! What happen?" Tommy asked.

"You didn't tell me that Fong had bodyguards." I said as I handed him the bag.

"Fong is powerful man. He has many men but he normally travel alone." Tommy said as he placed the bag into the trunk of his car.

"Well, I put two of them into the emergency room." I said.

Tommy slipped me the $300.00 and I tucked it into my pocket.

"I got another job for you." Tommy said.

"I'm on vacation for a while. I'll let you now when I'm ready to go again." I said.

Tommy looked disappointed. He tried to find something to say that would change my mind but he was interrupted by the sound of an engine revving. Next was the sound of tires squealing in a turn and finally the sound of gun fire. A black BMW X-5 careened around the corner and two men leaned out of the rear windows. One was armed with an UZI and the other with an AK-47.

The rounds whizzed over head and ripped through the surrounding cars. Auto glass shattered and showered me as I dove to the ground for cover. Bits of asphalt exploded as the bullets struck the ground and ricochet over top of me. I lay flat on the ground and watched the wheels of the BMW come to a stop on the street across from the parking lot.

This was no drive by. They were getting out of the car. This was an assassination and they weren't taking any chances. They wanted us dead or one of us in particular. I saw a foot hit the ground as the first shooter exited the car. I had to make my move at that moment. It was the only time that they were vulnerable. It was the only time to take them by surprise.

I stood up in a perfect isosceles stance, just like on the pistol range back on MCAGCC. "Smooth is fast. Smooth is fast. Apply the fundamentals of marksmanship and you'll always hit your target. Breathe control, sight alignment, sight picture. Smooth is fast." Top Strummer always said.

The target was blurry and my sights were clear and focused. I pulled the trigger and let loose with a series of double taps. Bang, bang. Bang, bang. Bang, bang. I crouched down and moved to my left after firing six rounds. The first gunman jumped back into the X-5 and the second leaned over him to point the AK-47 out of the window and return fire. I got off two more rounds when the car to my right began to look more like a two ton piece of Swiss cheese than an automobile. I hit the ground again and fired at them from under the chassis of the vehicle in front of me. The slide of my pistol locked to the rear indicating that it was empty. Thirteen rounds go by fast when you're having fun.

I pulled out a spare magazine from my left rear pocket, slapped it into the magazine well of the pistol, and pressed the slide release bringing the weapon back into battery. They had superior fire power but I had better cover. They figured out that things weren't going the way they planned when I dumped another nine rounds into the BMW.

They peeled out and sped away as their rear windshield exploded. I rolled over and tucked the glock into my waste band. The side walk was empty. Everyone ran to hide when the shooting started. Tommy was lying on the ground in a growing pool of blood, still puffing his cigarette. He held on to a wound in the side of his torso and looked up at me.

"Shit! Shit! They got me. How they know it me. How they know?" Tommy said over and over again.

My ears were ringing from gun fire and his voice was muffled.

"Shut up and relax." I said as I elevated his feet and placed them on the near by curb.

I took his shirt and folded it up to use as a pressure bandage on his wound.

"You do this before for shot people?" Tommy asked.

"Only in training." I said.

I reached for my cell phone to call for an ambulance but was stopped by Tommy.

"NO! No call. They know you here with me. They arrest you. You need to go." Tommy said.

"I can't leave you here shot and bleeding in the Goddamned street." I said.

It's ok. I hold shirt tight till police come. I be ok. You need to go. Leave town. It's ok. Get away. Go now!" Tommy said.

The carnage behind me shrank in my rear view mirror as I sped away. I felt guilty for leaving Tommy there like that but he was right. They would arrest me if I stayed and it would be for a lot longer than three days this time. I needed a place to hide until things cooled off but where?

TWELVE

The drive to Louisville, Kentucky from Washington D.C. takes about 11 hours on a good day. It took me 13. I left D.C. as soon as I could after the shoot out. I set the cruise control at 60 mph and kept a look out for the State Police. I spent all night driving through the mountains of northern Maryland and West Virginia. Wayne was from Louisville and still had family in the area.

"I called my Aunt Cassie. She said that it was ok for you to stay with her. I didn't tell her anything but we need to think of something to tell her. She wouldn't understand this shit. I told you not to fuck with Tommy. I told you he was the Devil." Wayne said.

"I needed the money." was the only defense that I could muster.

I met Wayne's Aunt Cassie and her daughter Charlene seven years earlier. They came to visit Wayne and Charlene took notice of me immediately. She began to flirt but I wouldn't cross that line. Charlene was Wayne's cousin and they were like brother and sister. I couldn't do that to him no matter how much I wanted to. Odds were that Charlene would hate my guts in six months time anyway and I'd have to explain what happened to Wayne. I felt as though I made the right decision at the time, but I wondered what my life would have been like with Charlene given the results of my relationship with Danni.

I stopped at a do it your self car wash in Charleston, West Virginia. It had been months since I washed my car and it showed. I scrubbed the grime and dirt off of the chrome rims and sprayed Armor All on the dashboard until it was shiny and dust free. Maybe I was attempting to wash away the events of the previous day but it didn't work, and the memory of the fire fight came rushing into my mind again and again.

I remembered looking at the whites of their eyes as I pointed my weapon at them. The flash from the muzzle of my pistol bloomed and blocked them from view with each round I fired. I saw each shell casing being ejected from their weapons as they fired at me and Tommy. I recall each hole I put in the back of the BMW X-5 as they drove off.

I felt numb as if I hadn't been hit by the full effects of the previous day's events. I was afraid that the police would catch up to me. I was afraid that I killed an innocent person who happened to be walking down the street. There was a part of me that was even afraid for Tommy.

"Would they put him back in prison? The Devil wouldn't have told me to go as he lay on the ground bleeding. The Devil wouldn't have put my safety before his own." I thought.

I returned to Interstate 70 and Kentucky's blue grass fields stretched out before me. I had never been to Louisville and I only knew that they threw one hell of a party during the Kentucky Derby. It had to be a slower pace of life.

"What trouble could I run in to out here?" I wondered.

I'd find a job and lay low for a few months. I could return to D.C. once things cooled off and then make some real money and a life for myself.

I arrived in Louisville at 8:00AM. Aunt Cassie was at work so I would need to wait for her to get off. I found the Jefferson Mall and parked on the perimeter of its parking lot. I slept for five hours straight and didn't wake up once. I had zero sleep between waking up to meet Tommy and driving to Kentucky. It was a miracle that I didn't fall asleep and run off of the road. It was a miracle that I didn't get hit by any bullets.

I knocked on the door and the butterflies in the pit of my stomach began to flap their wings at a vigorous pace. Aunt Cassie answered the door and rushed to hug me.

"Welcome Cole! Come on in." she said.

Aunt Cassie was still preparing dinner and told me to have a seat in the living room.

"Wayne told me that you fell on some hard times and needed a place to stay. He told me that Eva didn't want you staying with them. It's better that you come up here. I never liked that girl anyway. Charlene is on her way over. She'll be happy to see you." Aunt Cassie yelled from the kitchen.

I washed up in the bathroom and tried to look like a normal person instead of an accused woman beating, county jail inmate, home invasion conducting, banging a chick in a garage, damn near getting arrested by the police in an alley, mortgage re-finance scamming, Chinese mob loan shark enforcing, shoot out in the parking lot of a shopping plaza having degenerate.

Charlene arrived thirty minutes later and gave me a friendly church hug. I watched her walk across the room until she took a seat at the kitchen table. Time had been kind to her and she looked better now than she did when I first met her. I had to remind myself to take my eyes off of her.

"Where's Marcus baby?" Aunt Cassie asked.

"He had to work late." Charlene said as she shot Aunt Cassie a look.

"That's too bad. I thought it would be good for Cole to meet him. It would be nice for the boys to be friends." Aunt Cassie said.

"Maybe next time." Charlene said as she brushed my leg with the side of her foot.

Aunt Cassie blessed the table and we ate dinner. I volunteered to do the dishes but Aunt Cassie wouldn't hear of it.

"No baby. You sit down and catch up with Charlene. I'll take care of the dishes."

Charlene took me by the hand and led me to the living room. She sat closely beside me and her foot brushed my leg again. Charlene asked me how I had been over the past few years and I lied to her of course. Charlene had a predilection for bad boys and I couldn't run the risk of turning her on even more than I already had.

"The Marines…so you must be tough?" Charlene asked.

"Not really. I just liked the uniform." I said.

Charlene laughed, told me that I was far too modest and placed her hand on my thigh.

I would have been excited under normal circumstances. A woman like Charlene giving me some play was always a good thing unless she was your best friend's cousin. I wanted to jump her bones but I couldn't. We talked for a few hours until Charlene had to leave. Aunt Cassie walked her to the door and Charlene said that she would stop by later to check on me.

"Bring Marcus with you when you do baby." Aunt Cassie said.

Aunt Cassie and I called Wayne later that evening and told him that I made it to Louisville in one piece.

"You're in good hands out there. It'll be hard for you to get into trouble in Louisville." Wayne said.

I felt the same way about San Diego once.

"Have you heard anything about Tommy?" I whispered.

"Hell no! I ain't going any where near him." Wayne said.

Aunt Cassie walked me down into the basement of the house and showed me were I would be staying. It was a finished basement with a bed and dresser in the corner. There was a bathroom with a shower also.

"Here you go baby. You can make yourself at home. Here's my phone number at work. Call me if you need anything." Aunt Cassie said.

I thanked her and told her that I would check out the local temporary agencies the next day. I was sure that I could find some work since there were so many warehouses in the area. I also gave her some money for the rent.

"I don't have much but I wanted you to have this." I said.

Aunt Cassie told me that it wasn't necessary but I insisted.

I started working in a sheet metal shop that made metal panels for industrial air conditioner units a few days later. The work was simple. Slide pieces of sheet metal into large pneumatically driven machines that chomped and bent them into preprogrammed shapes.

The noise was deafening and the shop suffered at the hands of the elements. It was a big open metal structure with two sets of large, sliding doors at either side. The wind whipped through from end to end and the ceiling leaked sometimes when it rained. The pay was meager and the machines were dangerous. Each sheet metal press had a hand guard in place but one moment of complacency would result in a mangled arm. Aunt Cassie was a dream come true. She welcomed me into her home and I helped her cook dinner in the evenings.

Aunt Cassie was a church going woman and I took comfort in her good nature. She always had something positive to say and words of encouragement to offer. She spent a lot of time at bible study or at a shelter for battered women. Aunt Cassie was like the mother I always wanted and I was happiest when I was with her. It didn't take long for me to open up parts of myself that had been closed for years. Aunt Cassie seemed to enjoy my company as well.

"It's good to have a man around the house. Helps me sleep better." Aunt Cassie said.

Charlene stopped by several times and had dinner with us. Charlene's foot always found my leg and her eyes always found mine. It was the type of look that made me feel uncomfortable as well as horny.

Aunt Cassie went up stairs to rest her eyes after dinner and I almost begged her not to leave me alone with Charlene. Charlene brushed her body against mine as we cleared the table. She backed into me again as I approached her to put the dishes in the sink. Charlene felt every bit of me and took pleasure in it. She placed her hands on the sink behind her and pushed her chest in my direction. I was preoccupied with staring at her breasts and didn't realize that she was smiling at me until she started speaking.

"You've grown up to be quite a man."

I thanked her and tried to move past her to put the dishes in the sink but she shifted to her left to block me.

Low Fuel

"There's a place in town that I want to show you. You should meet me there for happy hour after work tomorrow." Charlene said.

"Will you be bringing Marcus?" I asked.

Charlene took the dishes from my hands and leaned toward my ear and whispered "No".

"Then when do I get to meet him?" I asked.

"Ask my mother." Charlene said.

"I'll be sure to do that." I said.

"You're afraid of me aren't you?" Charlene asked.

"I'm afraid of a few things in this life but trust me, you are not one of them."

"You're afraid my mother will find out?" Charlene asked

"That would be unfortunate but not really."

"Then why can't we do this?" Charlene asked.

"Wayne is my best friend and you're his favorite cousin. I can't cross that line."

Charlene gave me a curious look and then changed tactics.

"I know that you want me." Charlene said.

"What gave me away, the drool or the hard on?" I asked.

"Both. Tell you what, keep the drool and just give me the hard on." Charlene said with a giggle.

"Are you normally this forward in your mother's kitchen?"

"Only when I see something I want." Charlene said.

"Charlene look, you're beautiful and sexy and fun and classy but you already have a man." I said.

"I want a new man." Charlene said.

"I can't."

Charlene kissed me on the lips gently and then said "You will." and walked off.

I watched her switching her ass on the way out of the door.

"So much for staying out of trouble." I thought.

"Where you from?" a voice asked.

I turned to see a young white man of about 19 years standing behind me. I didn't notice him approaching. The sound of nine sheet metal presses going at the same time was more than enough to cover his foot steps. It was an innocuous question but I was still paranoid about the shoot out.

"Every where." I said.

"Well, you sure as hell ain't from here. Ever been to Chicago? Now that's a city. Chicago and Memphis, they really know how to party." He said.

"Chicago yes, Memphis no. Ever been to Grant Park?" I asked.

"Where in the Hell is that?" he asked.

"Chicago." I stated plainly.

"Oh, well I ain't never been but I seen it on TV. Looks good to me and the women are fine as hell. My name's Lamar." He said.

"A white guy named Lamar? What kind of town is this?" I wondered.

"I'm Cole."

"Good to meet you." Lamar said with an outstretched hand.

We shook hands and Lamar asked me how long I planned to stay in Louisville.

"I'm not sure. I'm just passing through but things could change you know." I said.

"You're lucky. I've never been out of Kentucky. I went as far as Paducah a couple of times. I got cousins out there. Haven't been back in years though." Lamar said.

"That's a horrible story. Be sure to give it a happy ending the next time you tell it." I said.

Lamar looked at me confused until he figured out what sarcasm was and decided that he could laugh.

"I'm at press # 6 over there. I better get back. I'll talk to you later." Lamar said.

"Yippie!" I said with even more sarcasm.

Lamar and I talked during the lunch break and the conversation was pretty much a question and answer period. I didn't mind too much. It made me feel like I wasn't such a complete fuck up.

I headed straight back to Aunt Cassie's house after work and found a note for me in the kitchen. She would be at the women's shelter after work and wouldn't be home until about 10 PM. Aunt Cassie also said that there was left over fried chicken, potato salad and collard greens in the refrigerator for dinner and that I should help myself. I ate dinner and headed down to the basement to take a shower. It was a blessing to be able to take a shower whenever I wanted to. I found joy in being able to piss in a toilet instead of the tree line beside a shopping plaza parking lot.

I stepped out of the shower and walked out of the bathroom while drying off my shoulders. I looked up and saw Charlene sitting on the side of the bed wearing a blouse that was opened to the third button, a skirt and heels. She sat there smiling with her legs crossed.

"I would ask if you've ever heard of privacy but I am in your mother's house." I said.

"I missed you and I wanted to see you. I had no idea that I would see this much of you."

Charlene said as she stood up and walked my way.

I was trapped, cornered with no where to run. Charlene came closer and my right eye twitched a bit and then stopped.

Charlene placed her hands on my chest and slid them down to the small of my back.

"Are you sure that you aren't afraid of me?" Charlene asked.

"Positive." I said.

Charlene slowly pulled the towel away from me and dropped it to the carpeted floor.

"And now? Charlene asked.

"Charlene, we really shouldn't do this. You're making this whole thing really hard." I said.

"Yeah, I can tell." Charlene said as she smacked me on my ass.

I lifted her skirt, grabbed a cheek in each hand and kissed her deeply. Charlene wrapped her arms around me and kissed me back. I picked her up and threw her on top of the bed. I reached for her ankles and yanked her back to me bringing the comforter with her. I pulled off her pumps and then her thong. I pushed her legs apart as far as they would go and gave her what she had been asking me for. Charlene was a screamer and I put her in every position I knew.

Charlene woke up two hours later and pulled my arm on top of her until we were spooning. She spent the night with me in the basement and I prayed that the smell of sex hadn't risen up to Aunt Cassie's bed room.

I couldn't slip into my normal trance at work the following day. Not even the cadence of the sheet metal presses slamming could take me away. Charlene danced through my mind, naked, with me on top of her, with me behind her and with her on top of me. Charlene had a gorgeous body. Her long legs, thin waist and phat tits were right out of an adolescent wet dream. Charlene was a Goddess and she wanted me. She wanted me beyond just the physical. I knew that look. The look Charlene gave me before she succumbed to the Post Coital Coma. Charlene had feelings for me, and maybe ever since we first met.

There were however, a few red flags to take note of. Charlene was forward and she was cheating on her boyfriend but she preoccupied my mind in a way no one had. Not even Danni. I loved Danni with all of my heart and I didn't love Charlene... yet. But Danni never gave me reason to double check myself. She didn't give me reason to make sure that I said something cool, or reason to make sure that I wore the perfect outfit or that my hair looked good. The truth was the truth. Charlene was just as much trouble as I was. I wanted her even though I tried not to.

"Lunch, lunch!" the supervisor called out.

You would think that they would get a bell or a public address system but that's the way they did it. The supervisor walked out to the middle of the floor three times a day and shouted either "Break" or "Lunch." And that was Louisville, Kentucky. It was like going thirty years back in time. The entire city was an anachronism. While some of the suburbs were modern, all of the buildings in town were old and the demeanor of the people matched.

They were friendly and all of them spoke to say "Good Morning" or "Hello".
It wasn't uncommon to pass several buildings that were built in the 1930's but had wireless internet access. Or to pass a 70 year old man in overalls and a mouth full of chewing tobacco who was talking on a Blue Tooth head set. It was the best of both worlds, slow enough to not be overwhelming, but still with the latest technology.

I sat down at a table beside Lamar as I had grown accustomed to doing for the past week. He was head strong and impetuous in the way that young men can be, but a lot of great men start out that way. Lamar could be anything in life if pointed in the right direction. He reminded me of myself a little, if I was shorter, country and liked to line dance.

"How's tricks, Trick?" I asked.

"Takes one to know one?" Lamar answered.

"You need to have gotten laid last night to know about me. What do you have for lunch, fried possum? I said.

"Fried possum beats the hell out of chitterlings and watermelon." Lamar said and then pulled out a small flask and poured a portion of its contents into his bottle of soda.

"What do you have there? I asked.

"The finest hand made Kentucky straight Whiskey ever made. This here is Maker's Mark Bourbon." Lamar said.

I commandeered the flask from him and sampled it.

"Wow! Ok. That's not bad but do you really need to do that on the job?" I asked.

"I had a rough night and I need to mellow out." Lamar said.

"Getting inebriated around large powerful machines that can punch holes through sheet metal is a better way to loose an arm than mellowing out." I said.

"My grandmother drinks a lot and she's hard to get along with. You wouldn't understand." Lamar said.

"I understand addicts just fine. What I don't understand is why you think being irresponsible and getting tipsy at work is going to improve things." I said.

Lamar was dumbfounded and I finished making my point before he said something else stupid.

"I like a drink just like anyone else, but self destructive behavior never helped anyone improve their situation. You're on course to be just like your grand mother in a few years. Where's the rest of your family?" I asked.

"I don't know my dad. My mother's an alcoholic. I went to live with my Granny when I was 13. I used to run away a lot but the cops always brought me back. I was in foster care for a while, but they gave me back to my granny after a couple of years." Lamar said.

"What's her problem with you?" I asked.

"She just don't want me around. She likes to party and I guess I'm in the way. She's 52 going on 22. She's got a lot of men friends and stuff." Lamar said.

"Why don't you leave and get your own shit?" I asked.

"Can't make no money around here. Not legally any way. The only young people with places of their own around here are women on welfare and drug dealers." Lamar said.

"You're a man now and a man needs to have his own castle. You can't expect to live under your grandmothers roof and have anything other than trouble. You're a prime candidate for the military. It saved my life." I said.

"I can't be a Marine like you. Y'all are crazy." Lamar said.

"You don't know what you can be until you grow a pair and try. We both know what will happen if you stay here. Besides, you don't have to join the Corps. You can go Army or Air Force." I said.

"What about the Navy?" Lamar asked.

"What about them?" I said.

"I don't know about that. I'm not trying to take orders and get shot at." Lamar said.

"What in the fuck makes you so special? Good men have been taking orders and getting shot at for hundreds of years. Besides, you're taking orders here. Sometimes you have to do what you don't want to do to get what you need. You can enjoy your life later." I said.

"Cole, this is Marcus." Aunt Cassie said. I shook his hand and said hello. I searched his face for a sign that he knew about what happened between me and Charlene. The coast was clear so I became my usual charming self.

"Marcus, show Cole where the broken fence is. I'm going to finish dinner." Aunt Cassie said.

I helped Marcus get the tools and lumber out of his pick up truck and followed him to the back yard and the broken picket fence.

"What happened to the fence?" I asked.

"A bad thunderstorm came through last month and a tree limb broke off and fell on it. It's a good thing Miss Cassie wasn't out here working in the yard. It could have been her." Marcus said.

"You have a lot of tools here. Are you a carpenter?" I said.

"No, I'm an independent contractor. I used to work construction but I decided to go on my own a couple of years ago." Marcus said.

"How's it going?" I asked.

"Well, it's feast or famine. It's not a steady check like before, but I wouldn't go back to punching a clock. There's something about being in charge of your own life that makes a man feel good." Marcus said.

Marcus and I worked together to repair the fence and I grew to like him. We could have been best friends if I hadn't fucked his girlfriend.

We had the fence fixed and painted three hours later. We came back into the house to wash up for dinner. I left the bathroom after washing my hands and heard Charlene's voice.

"Marcus…hey." Charlene said.

"Hey baby." Marcus said as he gave her a hug and a kiss on the cheek. Charlene looked at me over Marcus' shoulder and I looked away.

"What are you doing here?" Charlene asked.

"Your momma asked me to come by so me and Cole could fix that broken fence." Marcus said.

"Well damn, are you dating me or her? You need to let me know next time. Go and get the bags out of my car." Charlene said.

Marcus ran off to get Charlene's bags and she followed him with her eyes until he was gone.

We groped each other and kissed passionately until we heard Aunt Cassie walking our way across the kitchen floor. Charlene stepped back and straightened out her clothes and fixed her smudged lip stick with her finger tips. She pointed at my lips and I turned to wipe the lipstick from them moments before Aunt Cassie came around the corner.

"Charlene, set the table for me baby." Aunt Cassie said.

"Yes ma'am." Charlene said and walked toward the kitchen to get the silverware.

We all took our seats at the round kitchen table. The seating order was Cassie, me, Charlene and then Marcus. Aunt Cassie said the grace and we served our selves. Aunt Cassie was an incredible cook, and I found myself thinking that I could get use to living that way. Charlene asked her mother how she got the pot roast so tender and rubbed her foot against my leg as if to tell me that I was still on her mind.

"Marcus, get me some butter for the rolls." Charlene said.

Marcus jumped up without hesitation and Charlene used the opportunity to mouth the words "I missed you." to me while his back was turned.

Marcus was a "Yes" man and he did anything Charlene wanted.

"I can't find it. Where is it Miss Cassie?" Marcus asked.

"Let me show you baby." Aunt Cassie said as she walked over to the refrigerator.

"I missed you more." I mouthed back to Charlene.

We locked eyes and had a moment alone together. It was brief but it was quality time. I wanted to take her right there. The attraction was deeper than physical. She was intriguing. I could see us being together, me, Charlene and Aunt Cassie. The only problem was Marcus, but he would probably thank me for taking Charlene off of his hands. I got the feeling that Marcus was no longer happy with their relationship either. I guess the sex made him a glutton for punishment. I know that was my excuse.

"How are the ladies at the shelter doing mom?" Charlene asked.

"Everyday is a struggle for them, but they find the courage to make it one day at a time, one small victory at a time. The road to success is about small victories not one big one. We can't win everyday, but faith will manage if we hold on and believe that we can achieve our goals." Aunt Cassie said.

"Amen." Marcus said.

"Mica made me so proud the other day. She's been clean and sober for 3 months and she's serious about getting her life back together. She's cut ties with her daughters father and her old friends. I went with her to visit her daughter and I know that she'll get custody of her again soon." Aunt Cassie said.

"You're an Angel Miss Cassie." Marcus said.

"No baby. We just need to be willing to help those who need it. The Devil wins if good folks don't try to make a difference in their own way." Aunt Cassie said.

Marcus and I retired to the living room to watch the Kentucky Wildcats game while Aunt Cassie showed Charlene her photos of the ladies at the shelter.

I opened up my bottle of Maker's Mark and poured Marcus a drink and then made one for myself.

"You've got to love a Southern woman." I said.

"A Southern Woman is why I can't loose these 15 pounds." Marcus said as he slapped his belly.

"That may be true, but you have to admire a woman who takes pride in her culinary skills and her ability to feed and nurture her family. They don't make them like Aunt Cassie anymore." I said.

"That's true. Charlene can cook like her mother but she's bossy. She's not sweet like Miss Cassie." Marcus said.

"Yeah I noticed." I said. "What does she want?"

"I don't really know. Charlene's really critical of me sometimes and for no reason. It seems like there's no pleasing her at times and not only during that time of the month." Marcus said.

I felt his pain, and for the first time I felt guiltier about what I had done than I was scared about getting caught doing it. Marcus was a good man who was sure of who and what he was. He was easy going and hard working. He was dependable and loyal but he was passive, and that was Charlene's problem. She wanted him to be more aggressive. Charlene wanted Marcus to tell her to shut the hell up and sit the fuck down when she got out of line, and that would never happen. Marcus wasn't that type of guy no matter how much Charlene wanted him to be. Marcus loved Charlene and did whatever she said, which pissed her off even more. Charlene was the type of woman who needed a man who could handle her. She couldn't feel safe and secure with anything less. She couldn't relinquish control and submit to anything less.

Charlene criticized Marcus and became even more belligerent in an attempted to provoke him into stepping up and being more of a "Man". She argued with him to force him to stop everything he was doing and put her in her place. Charlene needed someone who could be a blessing one minute and a bastard the next.

Charlene called me the next morning while I was at work, and asked me to meet her for happy hour after work at The Fast Track Bar in Bardstown.

"I need to talk to you about something." Charlene said.

"Charlene, how are we going to talk in a crowded noisy bar during happy hour? Meet me at the park instead. It's quiet. It's picturesque. It's private. We'll talk there." I said.

Charlene agreed and I turned my attention back to my sheet metal press.

I saw Lamar walking through the door at the end of the shop. He was late and the supervisor jumped in his ass because of it.

"Rough night?" I asked as he walked past my press.

"I just overslept. My grandmother and her boyfriend were partying and getting high. They didn't stop until late. I couldn't get to sleep until 1am. I can't stand this shit anymore. I wish things where different." Lamar said.

"Well, it's like they say, Want in one hand, shit in the other and see which fills up first." I said.

"It's not funny. This is my life." Lamar said.

"It's simple Lamar, shit or get off of the pot." I said.

I sat on the park bench and watched Charlene get out of her car and walk my way. She was perfection in motion. My mind raced with what if's and should'ves. I stood up as she approached and brought her close to me. I kissed her and told her that I was happy to see her. She told me that she missed me all day. We stood there for five minutes just looking into each other's eyes not really saying much, just being near each other... just being close. It was exciting. It was dangerous.

Charlene and I took a walk along the bike path that bordered the pond. I threw rocks at the ducks and she told me to stop.

"Wait, hold on. Just let me hit that fat one. I can take it home and your mother can cook it for dinner." I said as Charlene reached to take the rock form me.

"Give me the rock Cole. Please." Charlene said.

"Have you ever had Peking Duck?" I asked.

"No Cole. I haven't had Peking Duck. Now can you just give me the rock and not kill any ducks?" Charlene said.

"Beg me and I'll think about it." I said.

"You're mean." Charlene said.

"Look whose talking." I said.

"I'm not mean to you." Charlene said.

"No, you're sweet to me." I said.

I gave her the rock and she kissed me and took my hand. We sat on a bench and looked out at the sun as it set.

"How do you feel about me Cole?" Charlene asked.

"There are times when I can't think about anything other than you. Then there are times when I feel as though I shouldn't even be here, and then there are times that I feel bad for Marcus." I said.

Charlene squeezed my hand and looked out over the pond.

"I want us to be together. I've wanted that since we first met." Charlene said.

"What about Marcus? Why are you with him if you don't really care about him?" I asked.

"I do care about him. I just don't love him." Charlene said.

"Then why are you with him?" I asked.

Charlene gave me a look and I gave her one of my own.

"Charlene, I need to know. He's a good man. I feel guilty about this whole thing. I feel guilty about a lot of things lately." I said.

"Marcus is a good man. He's always there for me and I don't want for anything when I'm with him, but it's not enough. I need a man like you. I want a man like you." Charlene said.

"You mean a man who's down on his luck and lives in your mother's basement? I'm no one to hedge your bets on Charlene." I said.

"I want you Cole and I know you want me. I'll stop seeing Marcus. I already have actually. I don't make him happy and we both know that. I've just settled for him. I feel guilty because I know it's wrong to do. I knew that I was leading him on and that I was keeping him from someone who could really love him, but I didn't want to be alone either. I deserve to be taken care of." Charlene said. "Aunt Cassie really likes you and so do I. We could be a family."

"I'm trouble Charlene. I always have been." I said.

"I can get this right and so can you. We can be happy. We can be in love. You don't have to be alone anymore baby." Charlene said as she held my face in her hands.

I kissed her and we didn't say another word. We just watched the sun set below the trees and waited for a new day.

Charlene and I had only seen each other a few times over the course of the next two weeks. She had been distant and used work as an excuse. She also hadn't parted ways with Marcus yet. Charlene said that she was waiting for the right time.

"Happy birthday!" Aunt Cassie and Charlene yelled as I walked into the kitchen after work. Stress can cause you to loose track of the basic things in life. It was my own birthday and I had forgotten all about it. I was twenty seven years old going on forty seven.

I looked at Charlene for a second, made a wish and blew out the candles on the cake.

"I have a special gift for you." Charlene whispered into my ear.

"Where is it?" I asked.

The answer was her place and that's where we went after we said goodnight to Aunt Cassie.

"I like your style. You have a good taste." I said as we entered Charlene's apartment.

"Make yourself comfortable." Charlene said as she walked out of the living room.

"We just got here. Where are you going?" I asked.

"You'll see." Charlene said.

I sat down on the couch and Charlene returned five minutes later wearing black stilettos with a bustier, thong and garter belt with the hose to match. Charlene straddled me and said that she could make me very happy if I gave her a chance.

"Prove it." I said and she did.

We started on the couch, rolled on to the floor, made a quick stop in the kitchen to get the whipped cream and finished in a puddle of sweat in her bed. It was undeniable. Charlene was irresistible and I needed to be with her. She tenderly placed a hickey on my chest and looked deeply into my eyes.

Charlene's gaze was intense and I felt uncomfortable after a while. I asked her to tell me what she was looking at in an attempt to break the silence, but she placed her index finger against my lips and told me not to ruin the moment. Charlene was reckless when it came to matters of the heart, and she wouldn't let anything stand between her and what she wanted.

"I'm your woman, ok." Charlene said.

"You're mine?" I asked.

"Yes!"

"All mine?" I asked again.

"Yes! I'm your woman and I'm going to make you very happy." Charlene said.

"You already have." I said.

The problem with having great sex on a week night is that you run the risk of over sleeping, and that's exactly what happened. The clock read 2:36am and I went into a panic attack when I woke up.

"Oh Shit! God damn it! Shit!"

Charlene was jolted from her sleep and asked me what happened.

"It's 2:30 in the morning. I over slept." I said.

"So, you don't have to be to work until seven. Right?" Charlene said.

"I never went home last night. What's your mother going to say when I come in at 3 o'clock in the morning? She's going to know what we did." I said.

"Cole, she's not going to know that we had sex on every flat surface in my apartment. Relax. She goes to sleep early. She won't know if you came home at 10:30, 11:30 or 4:30." Charlene said.

Charlene had a point. Aunt Cassie had been so busy with her day job and volunteering at the women's shelter that she was undoubtedly sound asleep. I got dressed and kissed Charlene goodbye on my way out her door. I drove home and thought of exactly how I would sneak into the house without Aunt Cassie noticing. I turned the key and slowly opened the door. I crept in and closed it behind me. I took off my boots so that I could tip toe across the hard wood floor as quietly as possible. I got as far as the door to the basement steps when I heard Aunt Cassie call my name.

"Cole, what are you doing?" Aunt Cassie asked.

"Me, I was just sneaking back in the house." I said.

"Well, nice try but I've been waiting on you. I knew that this would happen sooner or later. I saw the way Charlene looked at you seven years ago when you two first met. I saw the way you two hugged today. We need to have a talk." Aunt Cassie said.

I took a seat at the kitchen table and Aunt Cassie sat down directly across from me.

"You two don't have to hide anymore. I already know that you two want to be together, and I know that you're trying to figure out how to break the news to Marcus." Aunt Cassie said.

"How do you know all of that?" I asked.

"Boy, I've raised two children and I work in a shelter for battered women. I've seen it all. It's ok Cole. I approve. You have my blessing. Just be gentle with Marcus. He's a good man and he doesn't deserve to be hurt. But I think he knows it's coming. Marcus knows that he should have left Charlene a long time ago but he couldn't. Charlene takes after her grandmother may she rest in peace. She's a handful, but it looks like she's finally found a man who's time enough for her." Aunt Cassie said.

Aunt Cassie and I spoke for another hour and she made me feel at ease about the entire affair.

We became one happy family over the course of the next few weeks but Charlene hadn't ended things with Marcus and I was tired of waiting. I told Charlene about my conversation with her mother but she showed no signs of progress.

"Did you change your mind about me? Is my novelty wearing off?" I asked.

"No baby. I just need some more time." Charlene said.

I reminded her that she had wasted a lot of time and then demanded an explanation. I didn't get one.

Square bits of sheet metal shot from the chute on the side of the sheet metal press. Each tiny piece fell to the floor with a clink. Each clink added to the rhythmical pounding that placed me in a trance until the vibration coming from my left hip caught my attention. Charlene was calling my cell phone and I wondered what she wanted. I allowed the call to go to voice mail and decided that she could wait but Charlene called back two more times.

"What?" I said as I answered the phone.

I hadn't heard from Charlene in two days and now she blows up my phone in the middle of the work day. Charlene was a fire cracker but I was a fire hose. I was ready to lay into her when I heard the sound of her crying.

"Cole, Cole! My mother was attacked. I need you." Charlene said.

I set another land speed record back to the house. The hair on the back of my neck stood up when I saw a police cruiser parked in front of Aunt Cassie's house. I considered coming back later, but thoughts of Aunt Cassie being injured gave me reason to fight my fear of being arrested for the many crimes that I had committed. I was half way up the drive way when the officer emerged from the front door.

I picked up my pace to rush past him.

"Hey." I said as I jogged past him.

The officer nodded and I thought that I was in the clear until he called out to me.

"Excuse me sir. Is that your Trans Am?" the officer asked.

"Yeah." I said shyly waiting for him to draw his pistol and tell me to lay prone on the ground.

"It's a beauty. That's the 5.6 liter engine right?" the officer asked.

I told him that she had a 6.0 liter crate motor and he told me that he wanted a sports car but that his wife forbade it. He told me to have a nice day and I started breathing again soon there after.

Charlene was in the living room holding an icepack to her mothers face. I walked toward Charlene to console her when Marcus emerged from the kitchen with a cup of tea for Aunt Cassie. I knelt down beside Aunt Cassie hoping that Marcus hadn't noticed my transition.

"What happened?" I asked.

"Some bastard hit my mother!" Charlene said.

Marcus gave Aunt Cassie the tea and put his arm around Charlene. She placed her head on Marcus' shoulder and he tenderly kissed her fore head. Aunt Cassie sipped the tea and thanked Marcus.

"Mint tea always calms my nerves. Thank you Marcus." Aunt Cassie said.

"Who did this to you?" I asked as I transferred my anger from Charlene toward seeking revenge.

Aunt Cassie told us about Mica, the young woman who she was helping at the shelter.

"The father of her child used to beat her and sells drugs. His name is Pernell. The two of them were driving to Memphis last year when they got pulled over by the police. The cops found the marijuana and pills that Pernell tried to hide under the seat. He had prior convictions so he convinced Mica into taking the charge since it would be her first offense.

Child Protective Services took Mica's daughter from her and she spent 3 months in jail.

Mica went back to Pernell when she got out on parole but he just beat her again. That's when Mica came to the shelter. She's been working so hard to get her daughter back and now Pernell wants to ruin all of her hard work." Aunt Cassie said.

Aunt Cassie had gone with Mica to visit her daughter when Pernell showed up with his crew. They were a mini mafia and they held the whole community hostage in the midst of their criminal enterprise. Pernell tried to take Mica with him but Aunt Cassie intervened. That's when Pernell struck her and abducted Mica. Aunt Cassie hadn't seen her since and there was no telling what Pernell had done to her.

"I'm scared for Mica. Someone needs to do something." Aunt Cassie said.

"The police will find her." Charlene said.

"They don't care about that girl or anything else that happens in the projects. They won't even go into that part of town. That's how those boys get away with doing what they do. There's no one willing to stop them. Mica could be dead by now." Aunt Cassie said.

Aunt Cassie stood up to put her empty tea cup in the sink and I followed her into the kitchen leaving Marcus and Charlene in the living room.

"I'm going to go down there and find her myself Cole." Aunt Cassie said.

"And then what?" I asked.

"Then I'll bring her home."

"Those boys will kill you Cassie." I said.

"I'd go to Hell and back to save that girl."

"You won't have to. I'll go." I said.

Aunt Cassie's eyes welled up with tears and she thanked me profusely.

"There's just one condition, you can't tell anyone about this. Things may get messy and you're the only one around her that I trust. I just need you to take me down there tonight and show me around. I'll take it from there. We can go after Charlene and Marcus leave." I said.

I needed to steady my nerves so I poured myself a drink. I took a sip and sat at the kitchen table. I could hear the three of them talking in the living room. I could just walk away but Aunt Cassie wouldn't. She would get herself killed or maimed trying to rescue Mica. Aunt Cassie had been good to me, better than I deserved and I owed her.

I stared off into space thinking, pondering and contemplating various ways to resolve the situation when a familiar figure entered my field of vision. Charlene took a seat across the table from me and gave me a half hearted smile.

"I've missed you." Charlene whispered.

"You missed him too." I said and then took another sip.

"I'm going to let him down easy. It's just taking a little time." Charlene whispered.

"I haven't heard from you in two days, and something tells me that it would've been another two days if your mother hadn't been assaulted. But it's ok. I'm a lot smarter than I look. I understand completely. Your feelings for Marcus run deeper than you would like to admit. I don't blame you for following your heart. You just didn't handle things well with me. But you got one thing right. You called me today." I said.

"What are you going to do?" Charlene asked.

"About you or what happened to your mother?" I asked.

"Both." Charlene said softly.

"I'm going to do what needs to be done. Don't worry. It'll all work out for the best and everyone will get what's coming to them." I said.

Charlene and Marcus left at 10:00 PM. Aunt Cassie and I departed an hour after that.

We traveled down the street past the shelter and I took notes as Aunt Cassie told me about Pernell and the spots he frequented. We drove through the neighborhood and took notice of a group of people standing by a couple cars in the parking lot of an apartment complex. I could make out a plume of smoke being exhaled by a large man with dread locks, and a joint being passed to a young woman on his right. There were several beer bottles resting on the roof of a Chevy Caprice and one asshole in particular who was rapping along with the song being blasted from the stereo.

"That's him, the one in the tan jacket! That's Pernell!" Aunt Cassie said.

"Who's the big guy with the dreads?" I asked.

"They call him Junior." Aunt Cassie said.

"Let me guess, this is the average week night for these guys." I said.

"They're awful. All they do is get high, sell drugs and terrorize the community." Aunt Cassie said.

"Good." I said.

"How is this a good thing?" Aunt Cassie asked.

"Because now I know where to find them." I said.

"What about Mica? How are you going to find her?" Aunt Cassie asked.

"Don't worry. I'll introduce myself to Pernell and he'll give her to me." I said.

"Just like that?" Aunt Cassie asked.

"Just like that." I said.

I went to work the following day and quit. They should have seen it coming; it was only a temp job after all. I wanted to say goodbye to Lamar and give him some last minute advice but he didn't come to work that day. I poured myself a drink after work and took a nap. I left the house at 10:00 PM and scoured the neighborhood near the Women's Shelter until I found Pernell's car parked in front of a liquor store. Pernell and Junior were in the middle of the usual week night party with the usual suspects.

"This will be easy. I'll be in and out and he'll be too high to put up a fight." I thought.

The party ended two hours later. Pernell pushed one of the women into his Chevy Caprice and drove off while the others went their own way. I followed Pernell at a distance and watched as he swerved all over the road until he reached the parking lot of the apartment complex. I parked my car a block away and snuck through the woods with my ski mask on and my shotgun in the ready position until I reached the edge of the parking lot. I surveyed the area from the tree line and spotted Pernell alone in the driver's seat of his car. I saw no sign of the woman he was with until I noticed her head bobbing up and down in his lap.

Low Fuel

I tapped the muzzle of the shotgun against the driver's side window of his car.

"Show me your hands." I said as I pointed the shotgun at his face.

His eyes darted toward the glove compartment.

"Easy now. You ain't that fast. Now show me your hands." I said.

He obeyed my instructions and I opened the door and searched him for weapons. He was clean.

"Where's Mica?" I asked.

"Upstairs in apartment 313." Pernell said.

"Let's take a walk. All of us." I said.

I took Pernell and his date out of the car and into the apartment complex with my 12 gauge in the small of his back. We took the stairs up to the third floor and stopped at apartment # 313.

"Open the door." I said.

Pernell unlocked the door and I told his date to have a seat on the couch that was in the living room. Pernell led me to the bedroom where I found Mica tied to the radiator. Mica's face was bruised and she looked as if Pernell had been using her as a punching bag since her kidnapping.

"I'm getting you out of here." I said as I untied Mica.

Mica was quiet and didn't even look at me. I left Pernells date in the apartment with his weed and a bag of chips. I took Pernell down the stairs with Mica behind me. We got to the second floor when Junior came around the corner of the stairwell. Junior was about to greet Pernell when he saw me with my ski mask on. I pointed my shotgun at Junior before he could go for the .357 Mangum that was holstered on his hip. I moved past Pernell to take Junior's pistol and then shoved him to the floor.

"Don't fucking move!" I said.

I looked up at Pernell and then back down at Junior. I now had too many people to control and I would have to quickly come up with a plan before I lost control of the situation. Mica screamed as Pernell jumped over the hand rail and landed on the stairs below. I grabbed Mica's hand and gave chase. I let her go at the bottom of the stairs and pushed the door open in time to see Pernell getting into his car. Pernell opened the glove compartment and pulled out a 9mm semi-automatic pistol. He drove straight for me firing wildly.

I returned fire with my shotgun and watched his windshield shatter as I sent four rounds in his direction. Pernell swerved and crashed through the trees at the edge of the parking lot. I turned to find Mica but got tackled by Junior as he exited the stairwell. I dropped the shotgun as he collided with me. Junior straddled my chest and I fought to keep him from taking one of the two pistols I had tucked into my waist band.

Junior pounded on me relentlessly.

"Get off him asshole."

I looked up to see Lamar pointing my shotgun at him. Junior climbed off of me and I pistol whipped him with his own gun.

I took my shotgun back from Lamar and told him to take Mica's hand. The three of us ran toward Pernell's wrecked car.

"My car is through the woods there." I said.

"I know. I saw you park it." Lamar said.

"Wait for me there." I said.

Lamar and Mica ran off through the woods and I turned my attention toward Pernell. His car had barreled into the woods and hit a large tree. Pernell was so busy ducking my gun fire that he hit his face on the steering wheel at the time of the impact. I yanked open the door and pulled him on to the ground. Pernells jaw was broken and his face was a bloody mess.

I pointed my shot gun in his face and told him that I would come back to kill him if he ever hurt Mica again.

"Leave town and don't come back." I said.

Pernell lay there groaning as I ran through the woods and caught up to Lamar and Mica.

Mica was in tears and thanked us for saving her.

"What are you doing here?" I asked Lamar.

"I'm getting off the pot." Lamar said.

I asked for clarification and Lamar explained.

"I saw you drive by and followed you. I wanted to tell you that I joined the Marines today. I ship out to Parris Island in two weeks. I saw you run through the woods and I followed you. I didn't know you were going to war." Lamar said.

I was proud of Lamar and wanted to tell him so. I wanted to tell him a lot of things but there wasn't any time.

"You've got a lot of heart Lamar. You're going to make a good Marine." I said.

Lamar thanked me and shook my hand

"I owe you one. Now get out of here. That's an order." I said.

Mica and I saw an ambulance headed in the opposite direction as we made our get away. I dropped her off a block down the street form the women's shelter and drove off into the night.

"It's done. Mica's free. I took her back to the shelter." I told Aunt Cassie.

"Oh my God! Thank you Cole. How did you do it? What about Pernell?"

"I took care of it. It's better that you don't know how." I said.

Aunt Cassie studied my face searching for the man she thought she knew. I don't think she ever really thought about how I would get Mica away from Pernell. Maybe she thought I would just ask nicely but that really wasn't an option. The reality of what she agreed to was now apparent and she didn't know whether to be grateful or horrified. She settled on a combination of the two after a while and hugged me.

"I know it was a hard thing to do. Thank you Cole." Aunt Cassie said.

She was a sweet woman but she was wrong. It wasn't hard to do at all. I was proud of what I did to Pernell and I wanted to do it again.

"I'm leaving tomorrow." I said.

Aunt Cassie tried to convince me to stay but it was like talking to a brick wall. I strayed further beyond the "Point of No Return" than I intended. I feared that I would only bring her more trouble.

I slept late the next day and woke up to a large farewell breakfast prepared by Aunt Cassie. She served my plate and sat down at the table with me. We talked about everything other than my leaving and the events of the previous night. Aunt Cassie stared at me on occasion and quickly looked away when I noticed.

I said goodbye to Aunt Cassie and placed my bags in the trunk of my car along with my new .357 Magnum. Charlene pulled up just as I opened the driver's side door of my car.

"Cole...don't go." Charlene said.

"I can't stay here any longer." I said

"You've gotten in the habit of running. You have to put down roots someday." Charlene said.

"You're right but it won't be here and it won't be now." I said.

"I need you Cole." Charlene said.

"And Marcus too? You know I don't like to share." I said.

"I just need more time Cole. I'll tell him and then…"

"And then we can be together until you realize that you're not over him. Keep it. I don't need it." I said.

"You love me Cole, I know you do." Charlene said.

I didn't respond.

"What about us? What about my mother? She loves you. I love you. You can't run from that." Charlene said.

"I'm not running Charlene. I'm just getting off the pot."

THIRTEEN

"Two more hours to the Kentucky - West Virginia border and then what?" I asked myself.

After all of my effort, I had only traded California for Kentucky, Danni for Charlene and a jail cell for my car. There's an old saying that is oh so true, "No matter where you go, there you are."

Things would be the same no matter where I went unless I took the bull by the horns and made some big money. Reggie was a bastard but even a broken clock is correct twice a day.

"Sometimes you have to do things you don't want to do to get what you need."

I needed a city with some action. I needed a city with a lot of cash changing hands. I needed a city big enough to get lost in.

"Maybe I'll go to Miami." I thought.

My phone rang and I checked the display before answering. It was Wayne and he was excited about something.

"Where are you headed?" Wayne asked.

"How did you know I left?" I asked.

"Aunt Cassie told me this morning. I asked her why but she said to ask you. So where are you headed and what did you do this time?" Wayne asked.

"I'm going to Miami and I'll tell you why I left later." I said.

"Well, I got a good thing going if you need some money for the trip down there." Wayne said.

"Really?"

"Yep. You could make a lot of money real quick if you hurry. This is going to play out soon so come on. Hell, I might even ride down to Miami with you when this is done." Wayne said.

"What could it hurt to make a quick pit stop? I had to pass through Washington D.C. on the way to Miami any way. Besides, I did need the money and I did have plenty of time. I'd be in Miami with a new outlook on life within a week or two if I played my cards right." I thought.

"This is it, alright. Ain't no more after this. Anymore than this and you'll get busted. This shit is a numbers game. The further you push your luck, the better the chance that you'll get caught. Adonis said.

LaJohn walked into the living room with a stack of checks and handed them to Adonis who in turn counted out six of them and gave them to Wayne.

"Where are you going with this batch?" Adonis asked.

"I'm going to the check casher in Temple Hills and then to District Heights." Wayne said.

"No nigga! You've been there before. I told you that you can't go back to the same place more than once. Take this shit out to Morning Side, alright." Adonis said.

LaJohn laughed to himself as he turned to leave the living room.

"Alright." Wayne said.

I looked on, quietly studying the dynamic between the two. Wayne must have been pretty desperate to let a punk like Adonis talk to him that way.

Adonis was a mid level con artist/pretty boy who loved himself more than his six illegitimate children that he had by five different women. He really didn't do his name sake justice, but you couldn't convince him otherwise. Adonis had a scar in the middle of his forehead and another one on his right cheek. His nose was too big for his face and his chin was pointed. He wore a mustache but it was scraggly and needed a trim. His eyes were too far apart and his eye brows had been arched. He even licked his lips one too many times a minute just like L.L. Cool J does.

Adonis was a genius so the story went. He graduated from high school two years early and went to Cornell on a full ride but dropped out because the curriculum didn't hold his attention. The art of the con was what his heart truly desired and he dedicated himself to becoming one of the best. Adonis perfected novice scams at an early age to buy candy, then clothes and his first car. He quickly moved up to identity theft, grand larceny and fraud.

Adonis wouldn't know an honest days work if it stood between him and a mirror.

His latest baby's mama and sixth child lived with him and so did LaJohn. LaJohn was his personal assistant/flunkey, and it was his job to carry the pistol, keep Adonis' schedule, and take the fall if it came to that. LaJohn was the type of guy who didn't know what to do with himself, and it was Adonis' pleasure to keep him busy with an assortment of illegal activities.

Wayne had been running with Adonis for a couple weeks and made a few grand. With any luck, I could do the same. The scam was easy. Adonis would go out to bars and night clubs during happy hour to do some recruiting. He was looking for single women with jobs that were exploitable. Bank tellers, secretaries, accountants, or loan officers for example.

Adonis' latest recruit was a forty two year old single mother of three who worked in the payroll department for Advanced Auto. They started seeing each other and of course had sex. Adonis made the sales pitch and she went for it. She provided a stack of blank checks and the templates for employee IDs. Adonis gave the checks to a couple knuckle heads and created IDs for each one of them in his home "laboratory". They took them to liquor stores and check cashers throughout the area. Adonis took twenty percent from each check that was cashed. He knew how many checks he gave out and he knew how much money was coming back to him. Adonis would give her a cut of the money which she was grateful to receive, since the father of her three children hadn't sent her a child support check in four years.

It was a win-win scenario for Adonis. He gave her a fake name and she didn't know anything about him. She just wanted the money and the companionship. Adonis would be long gone by the time the feds caught up to her.

Wayne was one of Adonis' knuckle heads but I was a day late and a dollar short.

"My boy here is trying to be down too. He's cool. I've known him for a long time." Wayne said.

"Naw nigga. This shit is done. Run these and that's it. I'm working on something else. I might be able to use him for that. We'll talk about it when you bring my money back." Adonis said.

Wayne looked at me apologetically but it wasn't necessary. I'd be knocking Adonis' door off of the hinges with a sledge hammer in one hand and a shotgun in the other if he didn't want to cut me in.

Wayne and I climbed into his pick up truck and drove away from Adonis' house. It was only 4:40pm but it would be dark before we got back to Adonis' place.

"Is my car going to be safe here?" I asked.

"Shit, Adonis works for Kwesi. Kwesi runs shit around here. Ain't nobody gonna steal nothing near Adonis. Adonis is heavy." Wayne said.

"Adonis is a wannabe no matter who he works for, but I'll deal with him if you can get this money tonight." I said.

"Don't worry. I've made $3,500 in the past two weeks. I'll get a "G" tonight." Wayne said.

"I leave town for a few months and you turn criminal?" I asked.

"I'm not a criminal. This is just a temporary fix. I still owe the bank for the loan on the garage. I got bills and Eva's still bitching about me losing my business. I just need some breathing room. I gotta do what I gotta do." Wayne said.

Charlene called my cell phone a few minutes later. I checked the display and ignored her call.

"Trouble?" Wayne asked.

"More than you know." I said. "Where are we going first?"

"This old Korean guy has this liquor store in Forestville. I cashed a check there last week." Wayne said.

I reminded Wayne that most people got paid on a biweekly basis and that returning so soon may arouse suspicion.

"Fuck that! I get paid weekly." Wayne said and then stomped on the gas pedal.

We pulled into the parking lot of a small liquor store and Wayne put on his disguise. It was a ball cap. That's it... just a ball cap. He fiddled with it until he was satisfied that his true identity was obscured and exited the truck. I wished him good luck and watched him walk into the liquor store. I continued to watch the door as if I could tell what was happening inside.

Wayne emerged seven minutes later with a big smile on his face and a hand full of cash.

"See. I told you. It's that easy. I just made $650.00 that quick. You just got to have the balls to pull it off." Wayne said as he started the truck.

Wayne drove us to a check cashier in District Heights and parked in the lot.

"Hold up. Didn't' Adonis tell you not to come back here?" I asked.

"Adonis is paranoid. I'm getting this mother fucking money." Wayne said.

"We can find another check cashier. They're a hundred of them around here." I said.

"Just wait here. Shit! You're worse than Eva with all that nagging." Wayne said.

Wayne adjusted his disguise once again and entered the check cashier. The attendant stood behind bullet resistant glass and the place was empty. Wayne smiled and then presented his check and bogus identification to the attendant. The attendant examined the check and ID and then took them to the back of the room.

Several minutes too many passed and Wayne came to the realization that something had gone wrong. He tapped on the bullet proof glass of the booth and the attendant returned.

"Damn brotha! What's taking so long? The check ain't that big." Wayne said.

"We have the Check a Check system here and your check has an alert on it. Advanced Auto put a hold on that check number. I have to call the police when that happens. They told me to keep the check. You can talk to them when they get here." The attendant said.

The blood in Wayne's veins went cold and then froze solid. Plan A had proven to be an abject failure and it was time for plan B. Wayne stood there speechless until he figured out a suitable course of action.

"Damn. OK brotha. Let me go tell my ride that I'll be a while. I'll be right back. I'm coming right back. I just have to tell my ride." Wayne said.

Wayne exited the check cashier calmly and then broke into a full sprint once he cleared the door.

Wayne used to run track in high school and told stories of how fast and smooth he was to anyone that would listen. He won several trophies and even led his school to the state championships two years in a row but that was 20 years ago. Time has a way of changing things and so did the extra thirty pounds Wayne was carrying.

Wayne ran out of breath half way to the truck and thought about stopping to rest but decided that that would be the second worst decision of the day.

I saw him running toward the truck and reached for the key that was still in the ignition. I started the engine and pushed the driver's side door open. Wayne stumbled five steps later, fell to the ground, rolled over twice, climbed back to his feet and continued running. He wasn't dressed for the occasion at all and his steel toed work boots sounded more like a Clydesdale in a clumsy gallop than a man running for his life. Wayne fell into the driver's seat and slammed the door shut. He struggled with the seat belt for exactly 12 seconds before realizing that leaving the scene of the crime was far more important than obeying the national seat belt law.

The wheels of the pick up squealed and we shot out of the parking lot. Wayne gripped the steering wheel tightly and zigzagged through traffic until he reached the on ramp of the Beltway.

"Problem?" I asked.

Wayne tried to speak but then held up his index finger as caught his breath. I gathered through deductive reasoning that something had gone terribly wrong and that we were headed back to Adonis' place for plan C.

"Where's the ID?" Adonis asked.

"He kept it. He kept the check too." Wayne said.

"That's evidence! Why didn't you get it back?" Adonis asked.

"He was behind bullet proof glass. What was I supposed to do, throw rocks?" Wayne said.

Adonis jumped to his feet and threw a note book across the room that would have hit LaJohn had he not ducked in time. The lamp behind him wasn't as fortunate and exploded into a hundred pieces.

Wayne stood up and I thought that they would come to blows but Adonis caught himself.

"Ok… ok. These things happen. This is what they call an occupational hazard. At least they didn't catch you. You've never been arrested so you're not in the system. This will blow over but you're hot and I can't use you anymore." Adonis said.

Wayne protested but was cut off.

"Look, I ain't going to prison for nobody. You made your money nigga now get."

Wayne stomped off toward the door. I sat there still looking at Adonis. Adonis turned to face me and asked me what I wanted.

"You said that you could use me for something else. You need talent and I need the money. So, tell me all about it." I said.

Wayne asked me if I was leaving with him and I told him that I would catch up to him later. Adonis and I had to work a few things out. Wayne slammed the door shut and went back to his happy home. Adonis and I got down to business.

"I like your style. You're calm and polished like a pro, but I can tell that you'll tear some shit up if you have to. Where're you from?" Adonis asked.

"I've rested my head in a lot of places." I said.

"Ok, ok. A man of mystery. That's even better. I don't like people knowing my business either. That's a smart choice. Most of the guys I deal with are ghetto or convicts or both. They can't even talk and they look like criminals. That's why I can't really pull off any of the big jobs I've been planning. But you…you speak well and you could put on a suite and tie and pass for a banker, or you could rock some jeans and a hoodie and jack a motherfucker for his shit. You got versatility and that's what I need. I have this plan that I've had in mind for three years now, but I didn't have anyone to help me with the finer points. You're the right man for the job. I'll get you paid. Hell, this is just the tip of the ice berg. I have some associates that are making big money." Adonis said.

I told Adonis to put the cart back behind the horse and relax.

"I'm leaving town in a few weeks but maybe I'll stick around a little longer if this works out." I said.

"You'll change your mind when the money starts rolling in." Adonis said.

I craned my neck to peek over Adonis' shoulder and focused my attention on LaJohn who was cleaning up the pieces of the broken lamp.

"We need to speak privately." I said.

"LJ…get that shit later. We need to talk. Go on!" Adonis shouted.

I waited for LaJohn to leave the room before I told Adonis that I didn't want to meet anyone else with whom he was associated, and that I would only work through him. Adonis agreed and handed me a sheet of paper with the name Alan Thornton written on it along with a social security number. The words "Atlas Movers" were also written across the bottom of the page.

"So what do I do with this?" I asked

Adonis gave a sly grin and explained the plan to me. His lady friend at Advanced Auto had reached the end of her usefulness. It was time for a new scam. Adonis needed to create a front company in order to make his own checks. There was however, a bit of setup that needed to happen first and that would be my responsibility.

The job was dangerous but danger was my middle name. I would have to take the information that Adonis had given me to the court house in Rockville, Maryland and impersonate Alan Thornton. I would then apply for a business license for Atlas Movers. I wouldn't get very far if I couldn't pull it off. There was a Sheriff's Department office in the court house as well as a small jail.

Adonis would give the business license to his associates who would use it to open a bank account for Atlas Movers. I'd take the account information to a print shop of my choosing after that to have checks printed with security features and watermarks so that they could pass as legitimate. Adonis would give the checks to his crew and it would take about five days before the bank caught on to the scheme. By that time Adonis and his associates would have the money and there would be no trail to follow. It was a good plan and the best part of it was that I would be paid $2,000 if everything went according to plan. That was a pretty good pay day for a few days work.

I was some what reluctant in trusting Adonis to hold up his end of the bargain after getting ripped off by Reggie, but this was a different situation. The roles were reversed this time. I knew where Adonis lived, I knew where to find his girlfriend and child, but he didn't know anything about me. Adonis fancied himself a gangster but that didn't matter to me. I'd crush his punk ass if he got slick with me and leave the body for LaJohn to bury.

I took a longer shower than usual at the gym that morning. I needed a moment's peace and it was the best that I could do. I could almost imagine that I was taking a shower in my own home if I closed my eyes tight enough. The water blanketed me in a shroud of privacy and kept out the racket of the locker room. Sleep and showers… sleep and showers were all that kept me sane.

I put on a dress shirt and slacks and drove to Rockville. The courthouse was a huge complex and there were at least 10 Sheriffs Deputy's cruisers parked outside of it.

I parked my car in the parking garage down the street and steadied myself. The metal detectors at the entrance of the court house remained silent as I walked through them and I was surprised for some reason. I checked the directory and found the licensing office on the third floor.

The elevator door opened and I was face to face with a Sheriffs Deputy. I exited the elevator car and began to breathe after he passed by me. The hall ways of the court house in Rockville reminded me of the court house in San Diego. I had a flash back but reminded myself that I was a free man this time.

I spotted the licensing office at the end of the hall and approached the counter after I entered it. The gentleman in front of me concluded his business and left.

"Can I help you?" the clerk asked.

I told her that I needed to apply for a business license for my new moving company. She handed me a form to fill out and I completed it at the counter. I committed the name and social security number to memory but it took me a while to fill out the form since I needed to disguise my hand writing.

I returned the application to her and she asked questions that I wasn't quite prepared for.

"How many employees do you have?"

"I have six right now." I said.

It sounded like a good, round number and I hoped that she would go for it. She informed me that I needed to give her my insurance information for Workman's compensation. She was annoyed to hear that I didn't have it yet. I swallowed hard and hoped that I hadn't given myself away.

"You need to bring that information back to me as soon as you get it or you'll be fined severely." She said.

I thanked her for the information and waited as she printed the license. She took the $30.00 for the licensing fee from me and handed over the license. I left the court house just as smoothly as I walked in.

Adonis was happy to get the business license and told me to come back in two days. He'd have the bank account set-up and I could take the account and routing number to a print shop to have the checks made.

I swelled with pride. It was the start of a new career for me. I could do anything if I could walk into the belly of the beast and walk out with a license to print money.

Wayne called later that night and told me that Charlene asked him to check on me. She told him everything, from our romance to me rescuing Mica from Pernell.

"Are you crazy? I send you up there till things cool off and you fuck my cousin and start a war with a drug dealer. Adonis told me what you did. He told me that he didn't need me anymore and that you two were going to take over the city. I told you that this was just a temporary fix. What in the fuck are you doing?" Wayne said.

I tried to defend myself but it was useless.

"I don't need this shit Cole. My life is hard enough without you turning into John God damned Dillinger. Call Charlene and tell her that you're fine. I can't have this shit in my life. I have a wife and child." Wayne shouted and then hung up.

I was in shock and then spent the next few minutes feeling hurt. I thought about it for a while and realized that I couldn't blame Wayne for the way he felt. He lost his business and he was in the middle of losing his family. I shouldn't have gotten involved with Charlene but life is what happens while you're making other plans. I could only hope that time would heal all wounds and that I could make it up to Wayne later.

I found Pronto Printers in the yellow pages after Adonis gave me the business license back along with the bank account information. The owner greeted me with a firm hand shake and I told him that my name was Rickey Washington. He offered me a cup of coffee as he poured a cup for himself. I wasn't a coffee drinker but I thought that accepting it would be polite as well as in keeping with my alias. He seemed more starved for company than he was for my business and engaged me in a conversation about the weather, current events and ultimately, my business.

"I just started my own moving company and I need to have checks printed." I said.

"Well I have a catalog right here." He said as he handed me a large binder with hundreds of pages in it.

I flipped through the binder for a few minutes and finally decided upon a teal colored check with a water mark and several other security features.

I made the order, picked up the checks a week later and delivered them to Adonis.

"So now what?" I asked.

"I'll have the checks ready by tomorrow morning. The crew will run them this week and I'll have your money by Friday evening at the latest. Adonis said.

The week passed by slowly. I called Lynette to see if she had any work but she didn't. The low fuel light reappeared and I cussed at it for doing so. I filled the tank and winced at each dollar that was added to the total. I was running out of money and needed the two grand that Adonis promised me.

Aunt Cassie called and I spoke to her for almost an hour.

"Charlene is worried about you Cole." Aunt Cassie said.

"She needs to worry about Marcus." I said.

"Charlene cares about you a great deal. She's just lost right now. She'll work it out soon. Please don't hate her Cole." Aunt Cassie said.

"I don't hate her. I couldn't if I tried." I said.

"We miss you Cole. Maybe you could come to visit again after a while." Aunt Cassie said.

"Maybe after a while." I said.

We prayed together and she asked God to bless me. I missed her terribly and wished that things were different.

I awoke Friday morning in the parking lot of the shopping center with a smile on my face. Two thousand dollars tax free dollars would mine by the end of the day and it would only be a matter of time until I had a home of my own again. Miami was calling and I couldn't wait to hit the road.

I called Adonis at noon that day and he told me to come by his place at 6:30 pm.

"My crew is still out there working the checks but I'll definitely have your money by then. I want to talk to you about another job I have in mind when you get here." Adonis said.

"Oh yeah, does it pay as well as this one?" I asked.

"Trust me big fella, this one is a guaranteed ten grand. I think you can stay in town for a couple of weeks until we pull this one off." Adonis said.

Suddenly staying in D.C. for a little longer didn't seem so bad anymore. My phone rang as I drove to Adonis' house. Charlene's name illuminated the display of the cell phone and I ignored the call. Charlene continued to call repeatedly until I answered the phone.

"What?" I yelled.

"Cole, are you ok? Wayne says you're out of control and I'm worried about you." Charlene said.

"You need to worry about Marcus and leave me out of it." I said.

We began to quarrel and I pulled over onto the shoulder of the road to give her my undivided attention. I wanted to end the call but she compelled me to argue with her. I finally told Charlene to never call me again and pressed the END button thirty minutes later. The clock on my dash board read 6:47 pm.

I became alarmed the closer I got to Adonis' house. There were several Prince Georges County Police cruisers and black SUVs parked in front of his house. Two swat cops brought LaJohn out of the house in cuffs and placed him in the back of one of the cruisers. I continued driving straight and obeyed the thirty five mile an hour speed limit.

"Did they get Adonis? Did they get my money?" I wondered.

I was broke with only seventy seven dollars and a tank of gas to my name. I continued down the street another eighth of a mile and saw a familiar figure emerge from the woods on the right side of the road.

Adonis waved his arms frantically in hopes of getting my attention. He had a wild desperate look in his eyes and I had half a mind to keep driving but I hoped that he had my money with him. I pulled over and he quickly climbed into the car.

"What in the fuck is going on? I saw the cops and they arrested LaJohn." I said.

"Man, fuck! One of them motherfuckers got caught and told the police everything. I barely got out in time. I told LaJohn to shred everything and leave." Adonis said.

"What about the money? Where's my money?" I asked.

"Ain't got no money nigga. That's what I'm trying to tell you. The cops came before I could get it." Adonis said.

"FUCK!!! I need that money!" I yelled.

"We gotta go. Kwesi is gonna find out about this shit. That motherfucker will kill me. I got some dudes in Camden. They can hide us out for a while. We got to go right now. This shit is grand larceny. They'll put us under the jail for this." Adonis said.

"I ain't going to fucking New Jersey. I'll take your ass to the Greyhound station but fuck Jersey." I yelled.

I felt something poking into my right side and took my eyes off of the road long enough to see that Adonis had a pistol on me.

"We're going to Jersey motherfucker. I can't let you get caught too. Just drive and we'll be cool." Adonis said.

My Glock 21 was under my seat and the rest of my tools were locked in the trunk. They wouldn't have done any good any way. The inside of my car wasn't the ideal place for a shoot out. I needed to get his pistol away from him but how? I kept my eyes on the road and cut them on Adonis every now and again to follow his pistol. He was nervous and sweating.

"Fuck! I can't believe this shit. I can't believe one of them bitches snitched on me. I've been good to them. How did he get caught? This shit is simple." Adonis said.

"It's a numbers game remember? The more times you do it the better your chances are of getting caught." I said.

Adonis told me to shut up and pressed the pistol against my side even harder.

"I should shoot your ass and take your shit." Adonis said.

"You could but I'm willing to bet that your punk ass can't drive stick." I said.

"Fuck you! Gimme your cell phone. They might've tapped my shit." Adonis said.

I gave him my phone and he made a call. I assumed that he called someone in New Jersey and told them about his situation. He spoke to them for two minutes and then ended the call.

"Yeah, that's what's up. I'm good. My folks are waiting for me but I don't know what you're gonna do." Adonis said.

We passed the exit to Columbia, Maryland and continued up I-95 for about an hour and a half.

Adonis played with the stereo and I thought that I could try to take his pistol but he noticed me watching him.

"You should get with the program nigga. We can still get this money but you want to act like a little bitch and quit." Adonis said.

"This may be a good time to give up a life of crime and start all over again." I said.

"Fuck that. I'm not done. I'm still in the game. I'll retire after the big hit." Adonis said.

The Maryland State Trooper in my rear view mirror took my attention away from Adonis and his pistol. The Trooper was in the fast lane and approaching quickly. I thought about telling Adonis to look at the cruiser and then taking the gun while he was distracted, but realized that it would be hard to do without the Trooper seeing the commotion.

"Maybe I can rattle him a little by pointing the Trooper out." I thought.

"Be easy, there's a State Trooper behind us." I said.

Adonis leaned over to see the trooper in the left side mirror and began to sweat profusely.

"It's all good. It's all good. They don't know your car." Adonis said.

"They don't know my car but my tags are dead." I said.

Beads of sweat formed even faster on Adonis' fore head. The trooper slowly caught up and rode parallel with us.

"What's he doing?" Adonis asked.

"He's looking at us." I answered.

"What does he want?" Adonis asked.

"I think he's looking for you." I said.

Adonis took the pistol from my side and slid it between the passenger seat and the door but kept it in his hand.

I looked over at the Trooper who in turn looked at the Marine Corps sticker on my rear window and saluted. I nodded my head and watched him as he pulled off.

We continued north on I-95 and I thought of tactic after tactic to get the gun away from Adonis. I could wait to stop for gas and try him then, but that would only draw attention.

Maybe I could slam on the brakes and grab the pistol after he hit the windshield. The last thing I wanted to do was get to Camden. I had to do something before we crossed the state line. I had to do something soon and without the gun going off and putting a hole in me or my engine.

My fingers became sore from gripping the steering wheel so tightly. Maybe I could throw an elbow to his face and knock him out. That worked for Schwarzenegger in the movie Commando. I was preoccupied with thinking of other action movies to help plan my escape when I heard the sound of someone snoring.

I looked to my right and saw Adonis slumped over, asleep and drooling. He relaxed his grip on the pistol and it slipped from his hand into his lap. I gently took his pistol and turned on to the next off ramp. I pulled over on to the shoulder of a rural two lane road and retrieved the zip ties from the trunk. Adonis woke up just after I opened the passenger side door and slammed him to the ground. It was dark and he looked up at me silhouetted in the moon light.

"Who are you?" Adonis asked still groggy from his nap.

I told him that it wasn't important but that he should roll over on to his chest before I stomped his guts out. Adonis tried to argue but the sight of his own pistol being pointed at him ensured his compliance. I used the zip ties to hog tie him and placed him on the shoulder of the road. I removed the magazine from his pistol and ejected the round from the chamber. I tucked the empty pistol into his waste band but only after I wiped my finger prints from it.

"No, no, no. Don't do this shit. Don't leave me here. Please!" Adonis said. "Don't do this shit man please don't leave me out here in the dark man. Please."

Adonis told me that he had some money and that he would give it to me if I would just drop him off in Camden, New Jersey.

"That's right. You do owe me some money." I said.

I searched his pockets but all he had was the pistol. He ran out of the house so quickly that he forgot his wallet and his money and anything else that would have helped him get away.

"You're broker than I am stupid." I said.

"I got the money hidden at home." Adonis said.

"Too little, too late fuck head. The police have already confiscated it by now. I'd better leave you where you are. I think that's for the best." I said.

Adonis begged me not to leave him again but I told him not to worry.

"You won't be out her long. I'm sure a cop will come by before too long and cut you loose. I just hope that there aren't any bodies on that pistol of yours." I said before driving off.

I laughed all of the way to the on ramp of I-95. It was pretty funny until I realized that I never did get my money.

Being a light sleeper is a skill. It requires sleeping deeply enough to get a good night's rest but lightly enough to prevent your wallet from being stolen. I had mastered the art of sleeping lightly and it saved my ass once again. I dreamed of a time when things where better when I was compelled to wake up. I opened my eyes and saw the roof of my car, then the steering wheel, the dash board and finally a man walking past the front of my car. I reached beneath my seat and pulled out the Glock 21. I sat up slowly and saw the man climbing into a tow truck.

I parked in the parking lot of an Enterprise rent - a - car in Alexandria, Virginia hours earlier and thought that it would make the perfect camp site. I thought my car would blend in among the other rental cars but the fact that I was about to be towed away proved me wrong. His reverse lights snapped on and illuminated the entire area. I raised my seat and then started the car. I put it in gear and sped away just as he lowered the tines and started to back up. The low fuel light came on to reward me for my brilliant escape.

I parked in front of pump number 3 at a Mobil gas station. Flashing blue and red lights grabbed my attention as I climbed out of my car.

The flashing lights belonged to a police cruiser pulling over an unfortunate driver. I watched the officer exit his vehicle and considered driving away, but I thought that he would have his hands full with the large man who jumped out of the car to confront him.

"What? What you pulling me over for?" he asked the officer.

The officer told him to put his hands on the roof of his car and he did so but only after arguing first.

"Do you know why I stopped you?" the officer asked.

"Now how in the fuck am I supposed to know why you do the dumb shit you do?" the man asked in return.

"Give me twenty dollars on pump three." I said as I handed the money over to the cashier.

Unbeknownst to me at the time, the officer smelled the scent of marijuana coming form the man's car. The officer told him to step to the rear of his vehicle and moved to search the interior of the car. The officer saw the driver approaching him from behind and turned to face him. The officer went for his Taser but it was smacked from his hand. The driver was taller, high and out weighed the cop by thirty pounds.

The officer took a few steps back and used his pepper spray but the shifting wind blew half of the stream back into his face. The two of them scuffled there for a few moments coughing and cursing before I walked out of the door. The driver slammed the cop against the driver's side door of his car by the throat. The cop could only try to hold the mans hands so that he couldn't take his pistol from him.

They grunted and strained as the officer's radio handset dangled from its coiled cord.

"Help, help me!" The officer yelled as I passed by on the way to my car.

I stopped and evaluated the peace officers plight and gave a few words of wisdom.

"Fuck you. That's your job. I don't see you trying to help me." I said pointing my finger at him disdainfully. That's what you get for fucking with people."

I left him there. I left them both there.

"May the best man win." I thought.

The parking lot at Landmark Mall in Alexandria, Virginia served as my day time camp site. I watched people enter the mall one by one. I would have given anything to trade places with one of them, even the fat and ugly ones. I would have given anything for a second chance at life. I would have given anything to have stayed home the night that I met Danni, or for a chance to save Latoya, or even for a chance at the money that Reggie and Adonis fucked me out of.

I saw a family of four walk toward the automated, sliding doors of the mall. The father reached down, picked up his daughter and then held his wife's hand as they crossed the threshold of the door. Their son followed closely behind and I saw the daughter kiss her father's cheek just before they disappeared from view.

The tedium of living in a car drove me closer to my breaking point. I started talking to myself to combat the solitude, and even made a game out of watching the people that entered the mall. I tried to imagine who and what they were to one another. Where they were from and what they were buying. Maybe a birthday gift or a new tie for work. Maybe one of those guys walking into the mall had saved up for months to buy an engagement ring for the love of his life. She would cry tears of joy as he got down on one knee and pledged his undying love for her. She would show the ring to all of her friends and they would tell her how lucky she was. Her father would pay for the wedding and they would fly to Acapulco for their Honeymoon. Their first child would be born two years later and they would live happily ever after...until the divorce.

I drove toward my evening camp site tired and weary. Being homeless and shit out of luck is draining. The police officer behind me activated his lights and I pulled over on to the shoulder of the road. He trained his spot light on me and took his sweet time getting out of his cruiser.

Low Fuel

I was too tired to care. My tags were dead, I had no insurance, there were three illegal guns in the trunk of my car, and I was probably wanted by the FBI for my interstate crime spree. I'd be in prison for a very long time if the officer had his way.

"At least I won't be homeless anymore." I thought.

The officer approached the car and asked if I knew why he stopped me. I told him that I had no idea and asked him for a clue.

"Are you aware that your tags and registration are expired?" the officer asked.

"I am." I said.

"Then why are you still driving." The officer asked.

"I lost my job in San Diego almost a year ago and I moved back here to start over again. Things didn't go the way I planned and now I'm homeless. Everything I own is in this car but I'll be sure to renew my registration as soon as I can." I said.

"Is there anything in the car I should be worried about?" the officer asked.

"I wish there was." I said.

"Why is that?" the officer asked.

"Because then I would sell it and renew my registration." I said.

The officer looked at me for a moment and took my drivers license.

He returned several minutes later and handed my driver's license back to me.

"Do you know that I can impound your car and have you arrested?" the officer asked.

"Maybe you should." I said.

The officer looked inside the car and saw the blanket and pillow in the back seat. He examined me for a while and asked me where I was stationed. The question caught me by surprise. I was ready for him to tell me to step out of the car but he didn't. I was sick of running and part of me wanted him to take me in.

"MCAGCC in Twenty-Nine Palms, CA." I said.

"How long have you been out?" he asked.

"About eighteen months." I said.

"Maybe you should go back in." the officer. "My old man was a jarhead. He'd kick my ass if I didn't take care of one of his brothers. Get out of here and fix those tags as soon as you can. Maybe someone can let you stay with them for a while until you get back on your feet." He said.

I thanked him and carefully pulled back into the flow of traffic.

Charlene told me that she was sorry. She begged me to forgive her. I told her that I would think about it. She kissed my lips softly. I grabbed her around her waist and kissed her back passionately. We grabbed and pulled at each others clothes until most of them were scattered around the room. Charlene kissed my chest and I pushed her to the floor. I lifted her skirt to her waist. Charlene bit my neck and was in the middle of leaving a hickey when I pushed myself inside of her. She moaned and clung to me as if she had dreamed of this moment ever since I left Louisville, Kentucky. I bit her lip and then woke up humping the driver's seat of my car.

I looked around but there was no Charlene, just the darkness and the cold. It was bitter cold and the wind buffeted the car with each volley. Each gust seemed to rip through the steel body of the car and then through my clothes. I started the car and turned the heater on.

It had been a month and a half since the day the cop let me go. Christmas and New Year's Day had come and gone and winter was in full effect. I took a couple of temporary assignments from Lynette Parker three weeks earlier but they hardly made a difference.

Wayne wouldn't return my calls and I didn't want to bother Latoya with my troubles. She had enough to worry about.

The DJ on the radio said that it was 5 degrees outside. It was the coldest night on record in the past seven years. I put on every bit of clothing that I owned but it didn't help any. I need a pair of gloves but found that a couple of socks made decent mittens. I tied a t-shirt around my head and pulled the blanket up to my eyes. I couldn't feel my toes anymore and I shivered uncontrollably. I turned the heater up as far as it would go but it just wasn't good enough. I guess no one at Pontiac figured that I would need enough heat to survive a cold winter's night when they designed the Trans Am.

The low fuel light pierced the darkness just to spite me. That was it. I had .63 cents to my name and the car was almost out of gas. I'd be stuck in the parking lot if I left the car running and I'd freeze to death if I cut it off. I shut the engine off and thought warm thoughts. The sun rose the next day and while the temperature increased by only thirty degrees, it was enough to stop the shivering.

The funny thing about not eating for three days is that the pain goes away by the middle of the second day and is replaced by an intense headache. That stops by the third day and is replaced by a loss of equilibrium and blurred vision. I got out of the car and crossed the street to the Home Depot to use the rest room. The world was hazy and unfamiliar. I struggled to maintain my balance as I walked down

Low Fuel

the aisles to the men's room. I braced myself against the wall of the stall and sat down to urinate.

I sat in the car for the rest of the morning, too weak to be horrified by my lot in life. My eye twitched violently and I pressed the palm of my hand against it until it surrendered. I tried to think of a plan to escape my latest peril but I drew a blank each time. I took off the gold cross that I stole from Toons and held it tightly in my hand. I needed a solution. I needed a way out. I placed the .357 Magnum that I took from Junior on the passenger seat and stared at it.

I thought about selling it but then realized that no one reputable would buy it. I considered trying Pawn Daddy but I knew that he would only sell it to a criminal who would use it to rob someone or take a life. I had made so many poor choices lately. It would be better to do nothing than to risk making another.

The wind continued to buffet the car and the world went on without me.

I thought of all that I had done to survive over the past year and found it ironic that it would end that way. It was at that moment that I quit. It was at that moment that I gave up on life and everything that I ever wanted from it. It was at that moment that I decided God had better things to do than be concerned with my well fare.

"I've never asked you for much. Just give me a reason not to." I said aloud.

Precious minutes passed by with no change, no difference and no answer.

"Yeah, just like I thought." I said as a single tear rolled down my left cheek.

I reached for the .357 Magnum as the second tear fell. I held the pistol in my right hand and the gold cross in my left.

I studied the lines and curves of the revolver and then shifted my attention to the gold cross and the likeness of Christ that hung from it. They were just two pieces of metal but there was a fundamental difference. One would end the suffering. The other wouldn't. I dropped the gold cross and lifted the revolver. I cocked the hammer and my cell phone rang.

The phone rang four more times before I answered it.

"Hello Cole, This is Lynette with Maestro. I have a permanent position that I think you would be perfect for if you're interested."

I accepted the position. Lynette gave me the address and told me to be there at 8:00 AM sharp on Monday morning.

I stared at the revolver and then the gold cross. They were just two pieces of metal but there was a fundamental difference. One would end the suffering. The other wouldn't. I put the pistol away and clutched the cross tightly in my right hand. The sun set once again.

I awoke at 8:26 PM. A car made a left turn at the intersection behind me and its headlights crossed over a building that was under construction.

"Copper." I thought.

The electricians working on the building would have a pile of copper wire scraps somewhere inside. I just needed to find it without getting caught.

I waited until midnight to make my move. I parked the car near the back end of the construction lot and saw the security guard asleep in his car. I emptied the contents of my duffle bag into the trunk of my car and slung it across my back. I remembered what Tommy said.

"No gun. It's more time if you get caught with a gun."

I put my ski mask on and grabbed the Maglight from my car. I scaled the fence and took cover behind a trailer. I scanned the area before me and ran toward the incomplete building. The copper would be on the floor that was still under construction. Ironically, the doors of the building were locked shut but the windows hadn't been installed yet. I climbed into the building through an open window frame and was immersed in darkness. The floor creaked with each step I took. I turned on the Maglight and covered part of the lens with my hand to keep the intense light from being seen by anyone outside of the building. I spent 15 minutes on the first floor but found no copper there.

I started up the stairwell toward the second floor. I was weak and my vision was blurry from the hunger. I lost my balance occasionally and steadied myself by grabbing the hand rail. I made a right turn at the top of the stairs and found a make shift plywood door with a master lock on it.

"Bingo!"

I kicked the door open and saw a gang box in front of me. I walked past it and found a pile of one gauge copper wire behind it. It was a bonanza. I was preoccupied with stuffing the copper wire into my duffle bag and didn't hear the foot steps until they reached the top of the stairs. I crept toward the plywood door to see who was coming.

I remained motionless and saw a young man and a girl walk by. He looked to be about 19 years old. She was much younger, maybe 16 or 15. The two of them entered a room down the hallway and closed the door behind them. I heard two male voices speaking to them. The

Low Fuel

young girl told her date that she thought they were going to smoke some weed. He told her that they would and that his two friends were going to join them.

I cautiously moved back toward the pile of copper wire and silently filled up my bag. I exited the room and was half way to the stairwell when I heard the young girl tell someone to stop touching her. A male voice laughed and she screamed until someone covered her mouth.

I moved closer toward the sound of her muffled screams and placed my duffle bag on the floor. I peaked through the space between the door and the frame. There were two young men holding the girl down. One of them had his hand over her mouth. A third climbed on top of her and began to unbuttoned her jeans. It was only a matter of time until they were done with her.

I pushed the door open and hit the first one in the face with the Maglight putting him down hard. The second met the same fate. The third shrieked and ran out of the room. The girl screamed at the sight of the large man in the ski mask that stood before her and scurried to the corner of the room.

"Please don't hurt me." She said.

"Hurt you? I just saved your ass…literally." I said. "How old are you?"

"I'm fifteen." She said as she wiped at her tears.

"Fifteen?!? You ought to be ashamed of yourself." I said.

"I didn't know this would happen." She said.

"What in the fuck did you think would happen? You come to a construction lot in the middle of the night to get high and you're surprised that three guys tried to rape you. You're a fucking idiot. Get out of here before I beat some sense into you." I said as I raised the Maglight above my head.

I kicked her in the ass as she sprinted for the door. She stumbled and ran into the darkness.

I walked out of the door to retrieve my duffle bag and saw the security guard, now awake and rounding the corner. He must have heard the commotion and came to investigate. We looked at each other for a moment and weighed our options. I ran down the hall, grabbed the duffle bag and turned back in the opposite direction. The guard gave chase as I slung the duffle bag across my body. I ran back into the room and jumped through the open second floor window. I would have been home free but the duffle bag got caught in the open window frame.

I hung there by the strap while the Security Guard beat me about the head and shoulders with his flash light. He took a break to call the police on his cell phone. I hopped up and down until I fell from the second floor window into the trash dumpster below. I lay there in the pile of insulation and dry wall for what seemed like an hour.

I climbed out of the dumpster and fell to the ground. I crawled away for a few yards until I found the strength to get to my feet. I pulled with all of my might to scale the fence and fell to the ground on the other side.

I saw flashing lights in my rear view mirror about two blocks behind me. I down shifted into fourth gear and then back into fifth. I turned the head lights off and made a quick right at the next light. I barely missed a pick up truck at the intersection and floored the accelerator.

I needed to get away before more cops joined the chase or a helicopter locked on to me with its Infra Red camera. I made several quick turns and pressed my luck as I raced down an alley. I ran through a red light and made a left turn. The tires squealed and the engine revved as I drifted around the cars that were stopped at the intersection and straightened out the steering wheel. I slammed the gear shift back into fourth and saw a familiar Nissan Pathfinder approaching in the opposite lane.

I watched Reggie watch me as we crossed paths. He peaked over his left shoulder to see if I would change directions and chase after him or continue straight.

Reggie watched me speed away as the traffic light at the intersection turned red and he collided with the first police cruiser that was chasing me. The officer in the second cruiser pushed on his brake pedal as hard as he could and came to the startling realization that ABS brakes did very little to stop a speeding vehicle that was in close proximity to a two car pile up.

The copper in my duffle bag sold for $415.00 at the scrap yard. Needless to say, I filled up my belly and my tank. I reported for my first day on my new job and was greeted by Nyssa. She was happy to see me and I was even happier to see her.

Wayne called to check on me a few days later. Time heals all wounds and this time was no different. He told me that Manny was looking for a roommate. It turned out that Manny came home early from work one day and found Donna in his bed with some guy. She was using his house as a brothel and the proceeds went toward her habit.

Manny threw them both out…naked. Manny only wanted $300.00 bucks a month to rent a room in his house in Annapolis, Maryland.

The place was a dump but it beat the hell out of living in a car. I took my first pay check and moved in. The commute from Annapolis to D.C. was a long one but it was worth it.

I dropped Nyssa off at the Friendship Heights Metro Station after work one day and headed home. Annapolis has its own weather pattern and I watched the sky turn from clear to cloudy to rainy. The sound of the rain hitting the roof of the car put me into sort of a trance. You know, the type that enables you do something and then not remember doing it 10 minutes later. I was in my own little world and my mind began to drift.

That old Hopi in New Mexico was right. It wasn't what I thought at all and maybe most of it wasn't even about me. Maybe it was about the people I found myself surrounded by and the effect we had on one another. Maybe it was about the choices I made both good and bad. Maybe it was about being humbled. Maybe everything happened for a reason, even the disasters.

I was almost home when the low fuel light came on. I changed lanes and pulled into the Mobil gas station that was on the corner of Riva road. I paid the attendant and returned to the car to pump the gas. I stared at the rain as it bounced off the street and thought of my life and what it meant if anything at all. I didn't consider myself a bad person but I knew one thing for sure, sooner or later, I would have to pay for all of the wrong that I had done.

That's just how life is. No one really gets away with anything. I arrived home a short while later. I took the mail form the mail box and quickly ran through the rain to the front door. I went through the bills and advertisements and found a letter addressed to me from Danni Salinas.

Manny had fallen asleep on the couch in the living room while watching television. I turned it off and tip toed by him. I took a seat in my bedroom and opened the letter. Danni told me that she loved me and hoped that I was doing well. She hired a private investigator several months earlier and found her daughter just in time for her twelfth birthday. They were happy to have found each other and they both felt complete for the first time in twelve years. She thanked me for loving her, and said that she hoped that we could see each other again one day. She even had the audacity to spray some of her perfume on the letter.

"Bitch!"

I thought of everything Danni and I lost, and considered all that we gained in exchange.

"Well, at least someone got something they wanted out of life." I thought.

I folded up the letter and placed it on the desk beside me. I opened my bottle of Maker's Mark Kentucky Straight Bourbon Whisky and poured myself a drink. I took a sip, savored the taste and counted my blessings. It had been a long trip. I was exhausted, but I was home and the low fuel light was off.

EPILOGUE

__Quick and Luis approached the back yard as stealthily as possible. "Are you sure about this?" Luis asked.

"Yeah, fucker. Wise up a little. It's the perfect crime. What's this puta going to do, call the police and tell them that we robbed him for his drug money? We'll be in and out fucker, it's that easy." Quick said.

Luis took notice of the Pit Bull that was in the back yard just as Quick said it would be.

"Mira fool, does this shit really work? Getting the dog high I mean. I'm not trying to waste my stuff on a fucking dog homes." Luis said.

"Yeah fucker. Watch this." Quick said as he threw four rolls of Vicodin laced salami over the fence in the Pit Bull's general direction.

The Pit Bull toppled over in a drug induced coma fifteen minutes later and the two made their way toward the back door of the house.

"Make sure that fucker is asleep fucker." Quick said.

Luis cautiously approached the dog and poked him with a stick that he found in the yard.

"Is he out?" Quick asked.

"I think he O.D'ed fool. Poor doggy, how much of that stuff did you give him?" Luis asked.

"Twice as much as last time homes. I ain't getting bit in the ass for nobody. Now look out for 5-0 fucker." Quick said.

The two of them made their way into the house four minutes of lock picking and two minutes of swearing later.

Quick already knew the money wasn't on the first floor so they made their way up the stairs with the intention of scouring the second floor for the tool box full of money.

They took each step carefully in order to make as little noise as possible. Luis even caught Quick by the arm when he lost his balance and started falling backward.

"Watch what you're doing." Luis whispered.

They reached the top of the stairs and Luis was knocked unconscious by a blow from a rolling pin wielded by Toons' Grandmother. She took a swipe at Quick who finally managed to live up to his nick name and turned to run back down the stairs but was confronted by a very angry Pit Bull with a very bad hangover.